SLEEP TIGHT

SLEEP TIGHT

A NOVEL

J. H. MARKERT

CROOKED
LANE

NEW YORK

Published in the United States by Crooked Lane Books, an imprint of The Quick Brown Fox & Company LLC.

Crooked Lane Books and its logo are trademarks of The Quick Brown Fox & Company LLC.

ISBN: 978-1-63910-873-2

Cover design by Heather VenHuizen

Printed in the United States.

Crooked Lane Books
34 West 27th St., 10th Floor
New York, NY 10001

For

Tim Burke
Coach, mentor, loyal reader, and friend,
This one is for you

"My God, My God, save me from the thing I can't see. Save me from the eyes in the darkness. Keep them away from me . . ."

—Prayer, Unknown Author

Before

THE BOY COLORED so hard the black crayon snapped in half in his hand.

This wasn't uncommon with that color.

He remembered the darkness around those eyes was thick, and only the right amount of pressure could reproduce that deep, dark black.

From his seat on the hardwood floor, he pulled another black crayon from the bucket beside him and resumed coloring, furiously, hurriedly—he could hear that Mother was on her way up.

He'd done something bad, and she was mad.

And when she was mad, she got mean. But he couldn't remember what he'd done this time.

"Noah," his mother's shrill voice called from the stairwell outside his closed bedroom door. "Noah Nichols!"

Her footfalls made the steps groan.

Made his heart feel wrong, sick and swollen and thumpy.

He imagined her knee-length cotton skirt, thick like a curtain, swooshing upon each step, her big feet crammed into heavy shoes.

He pressed hard on the picture.

Had to get it dark.

Had to get it right.

Her voice grew closer outside the door. "Noah, I'm coming up. Someone's been a baddy boy!"

He imagined the stairs splintering under her weight, her falling through into a dark, dusty hole, plunging into the basement where all the spiders slept, into the cellar with the snakes and guttersnipes, into the earth with the worms and the roots and the dinosaur bones, and he imagined her dying down there.

Decaying into dust.

Like motes.

He colored, hard, broke another black crayon. He tossed it aside with the others, content that he'd finished the picture in time. Finished it enough.

"Noah!" She was right outside the door.

What had he done?

He blew crayon dust from the picture, scattering the black remnants through the dust motes hovering at the sun-touched window. Black slivers settled on the faded floorboards, blending with the dozens of other colors staining the wood like a paint palette, like he imagined a rainbow might if it suddenly blew apart into billions of minuscule pieces.

The doorknob rattled.

"Noah, unlock this door, right now! Right now!"

He wasn't supposed to lock the door. She had sworn the next time he locked it Father would get out the belt, the one with the globs of hardened glue in each of the holes.

But he didn't remember locking the door.

He looked down at the colored picture in his hands and it scared him.

It was signed in red crayon at the bottom right corner—Dean.

The doorknob shook like it might snap off. "Do you want the ark, Noah? Is that what you want?" He tried not to look at the closet door in the corner of the room, small like a hobbit door, looming as large as a tunnel now.

The words painted carefully above it.

"Don't put me in the ark," he whispered to himself.

He stood, weak-kneed, and shuffled toward the wall, eyeing the expanse of drawings he'd tacked to it, all various versions of the eyes—they numbered in the dozens—after his return from that scary house.

The bedroom door shook, and his mother screamed about flood waters and the ark.

"*NOAH!*"

He grabbed thumbtacks from the Tupperware bowl on the floor and pinned his picture to the wall with the rest of them, hanging there like a giant collage, all signed by names he didn't know.

Missing Teens Found in Twisted Tree

Month Long Hunt Ends in Tragedy

*Y*ESTERDAY AFTERNOON, SHORTLY *after 4 PM, the hunt for two missing teens, Grisham Graham and Jeremy Shakes, both seniors at Twisted Tree High School and stars of the football team, came to a sad and disturbing ending. After an anonymous letter was dropped on the steps of the Twisted Tree Police Department hinting at the location of the missing teens, the bodies of both boys were found buried twenty yards from the abandoned Crawley Mansion, a popular Twisted Tree haunt for teenage dares, a stone's throw from the town's famous twisted trees. Both boys were found with similar head injuries, fatal blows from a blunt instrument, believed to be a hammer. With the first reports of the two boys missing coinciding with the night of Jeff Pritchard's arrest four weeks ago, authorities are now investigating a suspected link between the two incidents, as the Crawley Mansion, the last place the boys were known to have been, is only a mile through the woods to Pritchard's "House of Horrors." Grisham and Jeremy both had promising college careers . . .*

CHAPTER

1

THE PORCH LIGHT was on.

It was ten minutes before nine, and her fourth-grade daughter was still awake—her small silhouette had been at the living room window and disappeared as soon as they'd pulled to a stop at the curb. Four fat raindrops plopped against the windshield, and then a steady drizzle fell.

Tess Claiborne paused before getting out of her partner's idling unmarked sedan.

"You okay?" Danny Gomes drummed the steering wheel with his thumbs, something he knew drove her crazy—not so much that he'd do it, but because he had no rhythm. No sense of tempo. No hint that it was even a particular tune. And for someone like Tess, born constantly needing to get to the bottom of things, his drumming was like fingernails on a chalkboard. But who was she to gripe? Her car had a dead battery she hadn't had time to mess with, and she was grateful for the lift.

She said, "Fine," and looked back at the now vacant window. Truthfully, she wasn't yet ready to face her own daughter, and she didn't like how pathetic that felt. If it hadn't been clear before the breakup with Justin, it was now—the *favorite* parent was the one kicked out and she was left to deal with the confusion.

And with Danny being her husband's best friend, Justin was often the favored spouse there as well. Tess glanced at him.

He stopped drumming.

Rainwater cascaded down the windshield. She straightened her white blouse and fingered the shoulder holster that held her 9 mm. "Turn the wipers on. Please."

He did. The water cleared. "Better?"

She nodded. "I'm talking to a lawyer tomorrow."

"What? Tess, really?"

"Yeah, Danny, *really*. You got a problem with that?"

"No, I mean . . . hell, I don't know. Maybe. Just seems fast, you know? What about counseling? Eliza gave you that number, right?"

"What about minding your own business?"

Danny shifted in his seat to face her. He had corn nut dust on his shirt from earlier, right above his belly, where he liked to wipe his hands after eating anything powdery. "What about your business is ours and ours is yours? We tell each other everything? The Four Horseman and all that shit?"

"We were joking," Tess said, remembering back to the night the four of them had said something along those lines, all of them drunk around the firepit, Justin even saying they should make a blood pact, like they were teenagers, Tess crumbling the wrapper of the Dum-Dum she'd just dunked into her vodka tonic and plopped into her mouth and calling Justin an idiot, because it was just that way between them.

Thick as thieves. The two couples, always together.

And now it was all shit because of her husband.

God damn you, Justin.

She looked away from her partner, back to the house, the vacant window.

She couldn't tell who Danny was more pissed at—Justin for cheating or her for kicking him out. Which she'd had every right to do. Even Danny's wife, Eliza, a social worker who still somehow made time to properly raise their five kids alongside Danny, had admitted to that. Or maybe Danny was pissed off in general because their world had been disrupted.

The silence between the two of them lately had made their job as detectives in the Missoula Police Department more difficult and her partner's habits more annoying, highlighting the fact that Danny was a goofball who often flew by the seat of his pants while she was nonstop serious.

Thunder vibrated in the east, a slow rumble. Tess grew uneasy. Her heartbeat quickened.

A storm was coming.

Danny scratched his thinning brown hair and exhaled like a puffer fish, something he did when he was resigned to something. "You going to be okay tonight?"

Tess nodded. "I'll be fine." Her phobia about storms, a problem since her teenage years, back when she'd gone by Tessa, wasn't his problem.

"What time is the thing, tonight?"

"Midnight. Eastern time."

"Hopefully it'll give your dad some peace."

"Yeah," she said, thinking of the execution that was to take place across the country in a few hours. "Hopefully." She watched the rain, opened the car door. "I'll see you in the morning." She closed the door, dodged Julia's pink bicycle in the middle of the sidewalk, and hurried inside.

Tammy and Lincoln Bellings were neighbors who had become regular babysitters since she'd kicked Justin out two weeks ago. They'd raised four children who were grown and out of the house and relished the time with Julia. Tess entered the kitchen and found Tammy with her hands in the sink, suds to her elbows, Lincoln at the table playing checkers with Julia.

Tess said, "Look who's still awake."

Julia shot her mother an annoyed look, a staple for months now since she turned nine, and more frequent since Justin's departure.

Lincoln moved a checker. "It's my fault. She suckered me into one more game." He moved a checker and collected the pieces he'd jumped. Julia frowned, studying the board like she was wondering how she could have missed that move. Lincoln said, "I charged your car battery."

"You didn't have to do that, but thank you."

"We do for neighbors, Tess." He stood from the table, ruffled Julia's sandy hair, and handed his wife her raincoat.

Tess watched Julia move the pieces off the checkerboard.

Tammy touched Tess's arm, lowered her voice. "Hang in there. And call if you need anything." She lowered her voice. "I'll say a prayer for your father tonight."

"They're at the cabin," said Tess. "Figured they'd need their privacy."

Tess saw her neighbors out and locked the door behind them. When she returned to the kitchen, Julia had readied the checkerboard for another game.

"Not tonight, honey. It's already past your bedtime. It's a school night."

Julia stood abruptly, shoving the checkerboard to the floor, the pieces scattering. "*Daddy* would have let me." She ran from the room.

Tess called after her, but her daughter was already down the hall, slamming her bedroom door.

Thunder rumbled; Tess's heartbeat raced. She pulled a glass from the cabinet, filled it with two fingers of Old Sam on the rocks, and sipped until warmth slowed her heartbeat. She'd have Julia pick up the checkers in the morning, she thought. She sipped bourbon. The caramel note reminded her of Twisted Tree, her childhood home-town in Kentucky, where bourbon was not only a drink, but a lifestyle.

Deciding she didn't want to face an argument in the morning, Tess began picking up the red and black checkers, plucking them piece by piece from the tile floor.

Until thunder sounded again, a fierce clap instead of a rumble.

Tess flinched, then out of annoyance kicked the remaining pieces across the floor and left the kitchen, thinking how she and Eliza always had to be the disciplinarians while their husbands were the playmates. The women loved their children just as much as their husbands, yet it was always Justin and Danny the kids ran to when they returned from work. How Justin, as soon as he'd walked in the door, had dropped his briefcase in the foyer, his symbolic way of leaving his work at the door—something she'd never been able to do—and stood there like a statue with his arms out to either side. He called it the Panda Tree. Julia would come running from whatever room she'd be in and jump at him. Sometimes she'd cling to his chest like she was giving him a hug; sometimes she'd land sideways and cling to him that way. But no matter what angle she'd jump from, she'd cling there like a panda on a tree and there they'd stand stock still, like she was attached by Velcro, until one of them would break character and start laughing.

Tess found herself at Julia's bedroom door, smiling at the memory despite herself. She nudged the door open and saw her daughter on the bed, pretending to sleep, her arm around her new doll she'd named Dolly. Tess went on to her own bedroom, tried to ignore the smell of Justin's cologne she'd sprayed nostalgically that morning. *Pathetically.* Somehow it still lingered, like memories tend to do. She tossed her purse to the floor, kicked off her flats, removed her holster, and locked her gun in the middle dresser drawer. She stripped down to her bra and panties, turned sideways to catch her profile in the vanity mirror. At thirty-three her figure was still athletic, toned. Eliza joked with her about her still having that body, while Eliza, after five kids, had grown somewhat heavier—curvier and more voluptuous, she'd say, adding that Danny, because he was such a good husband, had graciously gained weight right along with her. They'd joke about Tess and Justin still being fit because they only had one child, hinting, like always, that they were well past due for another.

Hinting that one was easy, when it wasn't.

Tess would force a smile, but deep down it hurt every time it was mentioned. Not that she couldn't, but more that she wouldn't, and it was well known among the four of them that Justin had wanted another child now for years.

Tess turned away from the mirror and did what she'd always done whenever the guilt crept in—think back to how difficult it had been with the first. The rigorous delivery. The problems she'd had breastfeeding. The postpartum depression weighing down on her for nearly a year. The sleepless nights. The constant crying of a colicky baby.

Julia had been a difficult infant.

Danny and Eliza seemingly had gone through none of that, with any of their five, or if they had, never admitted to it.

Eliza just seemed to be better at it. At motherhood.

And this had all become more prominent in Tess's mind since she'd forced Justin to leave.

Screaming at him two weeks ago because she couldn't stand to look at him. And now, here she was putting her shoulder-length brown hair into a bun and slipping on one of Justin's T-shirts, because old habits die hard.

She was starting to miss him.

Rain tapped against the roof, spilled over gutters that needed cleaning. Her wedding ring rested on the dresser.

Tomorrow's problem.

Lightning flashed outside the window. More thunder, louder this time. She finished her drink and put it down hard on the dresser, still annoyed at how Julia had stormed out of the kitchen earlier.

But it *was* a school night and she needed to get to sleep.

With Justin not in the house, she wondered if she had what it took to play both roles, good cop and bad.

Her bedroom door creaked open.

Julia stood in the threshold with Dolly in one arm and her frayed pink blanket in the other. "Mommy, does the lightning come first or the thunder?"

Her baby blue eyes reminded her of Justin. Daddy's little girl. *God damn him.*

And now her daughter was inheriting her fears.

At that moment the electricity went out. Tess forced herself to seem calm. "Should I get the candles?"

Julia nodded. "I'll get the paper."

* * *

The walk-in closet perfectly buffered the storm noise.

It was dark except for their candle glow—this was a Justin idea from years ago, using artwork to take their minds off the storm. But it was the first storm where it was just the two of them. Julia tilted her candle, plopping yellow wax on the paper, adding to the shape that had already dried.

Julia stared at it cockeyed. "Kind of looks like a flower." She looked at her mother's paper. A red blob smeared the middle of it. "Is that an elephant?"

"I guess it could be. That does look like a trunk." Tess added two more drops to form a leg, and then another to make the trunk longer.

Sometimes instead of dripping wax they'd draw pictures. Pictures to form words, like charades but drawing, another Justin idea that Julia favored. Tonight they just dripped wax, but on top of the papers was a picture they'd made in the last storm, showing a Christmas tree and a cookie with a plus sign in between. *Christmas cookie.* A very simple word game, but Tess liked the wax better. With the wax she didn't have to think.

Julia leaned forward and tilted one drop of yellow into what could have been the head of Tess's red elephant. "There. Now it can see." She blew her candle out and rested on the floor, her hair fanned out like wild grass over her pillow. She closed her eyes as distant thunder rumbled. "You remember when Danny tried doing the Panda Tree with all five of their kids?"

In the dark, Tess said, "Yeah, I remember."

Then her daughter asked, "When's Daddy coming back home?"

A lump formed in Tess's throat. She'd rather talk about the storm. "I don't know."

Julia left it at that, and Tess was relieved.

A few minutes later, Julia snored softly.

Tess watched her daughter sleep, watched her skinny chest rise and fall with only a hint of sound. It made her heart swell.

She checked her phone; she'd forgotten to take it off vibrate earlier. Justin had sent a text ten minutes ago.

How U holding up? Candles are in the closet. So is the paper. Talk soon?

She didn't respond. She placed the phone face down against the floor and the closet went dark again. It was ten o'clock. She wondered how her parents were doing at the cabin. She could see her father in his recliner listening to the radio, waiting for word that *it* had happened.

Midnight in Kentucky.

The execution.

2

"AN EYE FOR an eye," a woman in an anti-abortion shirt screamed outside the Kentucky State Penitentiary in Eddyville, where low clouds covered the prison grounds like a purple caul. "He deserves to die."

The lines had literally been drawn across the parking lot hours ago, with white paint, and now death penalty protesters shouted across No-Man's Land at the supporters, all of them holding signs as riot police struggled to keep them at bay.

FRY FATHER SILENCE

KILLING IS NEVER RIGHT

ABOLISH CAPITAL PUNISHMENT

The state was minutes away from putting a man to death by electrocution, once the most widely used execution method in the US. In seventeen years, exhausting every appeal known to the courts along the way, Jeff Pritchard—a former parochial school janitor who had for years disguised himself as a priest to his victims, to kill what he considered the outcasts of society—had yet to say a word.

He was not a priest and never had been, but the pictures from his arrest at Twisted Tree, with him wearing the stolen priestly garments, had flashed all over the news and internet and had become so ingrained in the minds of the public that they'd taken it as fact. After it was clear he'd gone silent, completely refusing to talk, the newspaper had dubbed him Father Silence.

News crews from every state crowded the woods around the prison, maneuvering to get as close as they could to the wrought-iron gates. Cameras flashed. Many clutched candles. Various religious sects shouted at one another over the morality of what was about to happen; others were irate over how long it had taken.

"Abolish capital punishment," screamed a suited man.

"Do it for the children!" shouted a woman with her hair in locks.

"Fry Father Silence!"

From every angle it was videoed—by phone, on tripod and iPad, the atmosphere seeming dangerously close to riot.

But inside the prison walls, the execution process moved on.

And all was silent.

*   *   *

The warden followed four prison guards as they escorted Jeff Pritchard to the execution room at the end of No. 3 Cellblock.

So far, all had gone as practiced.

On a humid night in May 1911, an eighteen-year-old boy named James Buckner had made history as the first electric chair victim in Kentucky, and while awaiting death had been baptized, reborn, and spent his last hours reading the Bible.

Jeff Pritchard had participated in none of those customs. He'd denied the chaplain, refused a last meal. Fellow death row inmates whispered goodbyes as he made the long walk. He nodded, but his eyes never wavered from the black door at the end of the hall.

The execution room that housed Old Sparky was sterile and cold, having not been used in over thirty years, the state having transitioned from the electric chair to lethal injection in the late 1990s. But the new governor, Clinton Bullsworth, was an old-school ball-buster who'd campaigned on finally putting Jeff Pritchard in the ground *hot*.

Bullsworth knew that lethal injection had the highest rate of botched executions, and he didn't want to take a chance with Jeff Pritchard. Truth was—and he could be heard saying it in a viral TikTok video—he wanted to see the man sizzle. The electric chair was recommissioned, and Old Sparky was set for a comeback.

Media watched from the adjoining room through shatterproof glass, as the guards helped Pritchard into the chair. After the first strap was fastened, the warden faced the adjoining room. On the other side of the glass sat members of the victims' families. The executioner. Pritchard's lawyer, Barrett Stevens. The sheriff, the prison doctor, the chaplain. The only people who declined the invitation were the detectives who'd caught him nearly two decades ago.

Pritchard avoided eye contact with the families, but nodded at his lawyer, then the governor, who took a step back from the glass inside the viewing area. The guards tightened straps around Pritchard's arms and adjusted electrodes at his calves and wrists. They pulled the thick leather belt across the man's chest and dropped the wired leather mask over his long hair. Only his lips and nose showed through the holes.

The warden nodded and the guards left the room, faster than they'd practiced.

"Jeff Pritchard, can you hear me?"

Pritchard nodded.

"You have been judged by a jury of your peers, sentenced, and condemned to death by electrocution. If you have any last words before the electrocution is carried out, please state them now."

In his years on death row the man in the chair had never given the warden, police, counselors, or reporters a word. He'd turned down psychologists, NBC, ABC, CNN, Fox, and Barbara Walters.

But now his lips moved, and he whispered something the warden couldn't make out—but the guard standing nearby went pale.

The circular clock on the wall read midnight.

The warden signaled the executioner, then joined him in a side room. The first charge of 1,500 volts started with a low whine and a loud snap as current surged into Pritchard's body.

CHAPTER

3

A FTER THE STORM passed, Tess blew out candles, opened the closet door, and lifted Julia from the carpeted floor.

She was almost to the hallway when Julia mumbled. "Sleep in your bed."

Her daughter hadn't posed it as a question, more of a statement. Justin always said children in the bed were the best forms of birth control, but he wasn't here, and Tess didn't feel like sleeping alone either.

She tucked Julia in on Justin's side and watched her slip back into sleep. Tess had told herself earlier in the day that she would not turn the television on tonight. Her father had said the same thing, and he and her mother had escaped to the cabin in Lolo National Forest to get away from the media swarm. It wasn't as bad as the days right after Pritchard's arrest, but three weeks ago the local media had begun to call, requesting interviews and statements, and her father obliged, until Mother put a stop to it and demanded they go out of town.

But Tess doubted that her father, a decorated former detective who had arrested Jeff Pritchard along with his partner, Burt Lobell, was passively sitting by. He was probably awake now, watching CNN.

Just as they'd made a pact *not* to do.

But Betsy always said Tess got her stubbornness honest, from Leland no doubt, and if they wanted to do something they did it. In the kitchen, Tess poured bourbon on the rocks, returned to the bedroom, and turned on the television.

A beautiful woman with a microphone spoke to a well-dressed man at the CNN studio.

"*. . . and finally, the controversy came to an end this morning after midnight when Jeff Pritchard was electrocuted in the state prison in Eddyville, Kentucky. As one of the most mysterious serial killers ever to—*"

She turned the television off and dropped the remote on the bed. Her heart hammered. *Jeff Pritchard. Father Silence.* No matter what he was called, he was dead.

However deep they bury him won't be deep enough.

She considered calling her dad. *Leave him alone. He's fine.* Probably drinking Old Sam just as she was. She sent him a text anyway: **Well, it's over. How are you and Mom doing?**

She hit Send and waited, doubtful he'd text back—he wasn't a fan of texting. She put her nose to the rim of the rocks glass, smelled caramel and vanilla notes that reminded her of home, and downed a healthy gulp of the bourbon to bury any memories trying to resurface.

Buried memories from her teenage years that Justin, a professional psychologist, had too often tried to *unbury* over their ten years of marriage. Hers was a childhood that had been good, up until it wasn't. But she grew tired of his questions. She wasn't his patient. She was his wife. And after a while felt like she wasn't even good at that.

Her phone rang.

She smiled, found her hand shaking slightly as she answered it. "Daddy."

"Tough detective still calling her old man Daddy?"

Tess paused only slightly "He's finally dead."

"As a doornail," he said.

"How do you feel?"

"On the record?"

"Sure."

"Relieved."

"And off?"

"Relieved."

"You could have texted me that much."

"Then I wouldn't have gotten to hear your voice in the middle of the night, sugar."

The quiver in his voice hadn't gone unnoticed. Try as he might, her father wasn't a good actor—he wore his emotions on his sleeve—and the phone did little to mask his unease.

He's hiding something.

"Mom in bed?"

"Drawing a bath. She has her way of relaxing." Ice clinked in a glass as he swallowed. "And I've got mine."

She did likewise and the sip went down smoother than the previous ones.

Now that she'd heard the ice in the glass, she realized her father sounded tipsy. But who could blame him on this night? "Have you heard from anyone?"

A pause. Another sip. "Burt called. Talked briefly. He's hiding too, at least for the night."

Together Burt and her father had led the charge into Pritchard's house on the night of his arrest. He and Burt had talked regularly for several years after her family moved to Montana, but now only on occasion. At least they kept in touch. Tess knew that sometimes talking to his old partner made him sad, and she wished now that she hadn't asked. She had always thought Burt had been hurt when his partner of so many years up and left suddenly, a month or so after Jeff Pritchard's arrest.

Tess had been a young teen, suddenly struggling to maintain friends when it had never been a problem. Her parents said the move was because of the attention they were getting, to get away from the circus, although by the time they moved out west the media swarm had all but stopped. Not completely, but close enough. The reporters were no longer hounding them; her father and Burt weren't on the news nightly. But her family pulled up stakes, moving from a distilling town they'd always loved until so much evil got dug up and fears surfaced.

Tess felt it then as she did now—somehow, they'd moved because of her.

That need to protect.

But from what? What had she done? Those were the memories lost to her—the ones Justin knew were in there hiding—from during that time when Jeff Pritchard was arrested.

I don't need to be fixed, Justin, she'd once screamed at him, not able to admit to herself that her anger was at least partly stemming from the fact that he wasn't wrong.

"River's high tonight," her father said, pulling her back to the present.

The Pattee River snaked behind their cabin in Lolo. Her father liked to sit on the back porch and drink his morning coffee black, and listen to the water flow

"You okay, Daddy?"

A long pause. "Nothing like they'd ever seen before. The execution." He took another drink. "That's what my insiders said. Took three cranks of voltage to send him back to hell."

Tess had a hard time remembering her father before that arrest—only that he had used to smile more—but Mom said what he'd seen in that house changed him for good. He'd started drinking more and sleeping less, and when he did manage to close his eyes, the nightmares would wake him up. That went on for years, waning over time but never going away. Mom said he'd had a nightmare last week.

Tess let her father talk, because he rarely did.

"The governor threw up, and then the warden laid into him. They argued right there in front of everyone. Should have never churned up Old Sparky again." *Another drink.* "And the smell. On the phone, my guy . . . he said he thought he'd never get over the smell."

Ice clinked in an empty glass. Tess felt queasy—this wasn't good for either of them. "How about we talk tomorrow? I'll bring Julia out to the cabin. Maybe a pizza from Tony's."

"I'd like that. So would your mother." He paused. "How's Justin?"

"Justin's Justin." She hoped he wouldn't ask for more because she wasn't prepared to give it. Justin and Leland had always gotten along—Justin got along with everyone—bonding from day one like frat brothers over sports, Leland the father figure Justin never had. Yes, her father had been pissed when he'd heard what Justin had done, but not pissed *enough* for Tess's liking. He'd told her more than once to remember that she wasn't married to the job. That she spent too much time working and not enough with her family. Like her husband's affair was somehow partly *her* fault.

Just when she was about to say goodnight, he said, "It was the best thing for all of us."

At first she thought he was talking about Justin's affair, but realized he'd gone back to earlier. "What was?"

"Us moving out here."

He left it at that. Didn't explain why, and she didn't ask. More fodder for tomorrow when the sun was out and the bourbon bottle was topped.

"Love you, Daddy."

"Love you too, sugar." She was about to hang up when his voice caught her. "Tessa?"

"Yes?"

Nothing. He was wrangling, holding back something. *Stop trying to protect me.* But all he said was, "Goodnight."

She ended the call.

Finished her bourbon.

Didn't sleep all night.

CHAPTER

4

LISA BUCHANON SLEPT with a shotgun next to the bed.

Hoped she wouldn't have to use it, but figured she might.

She'd refused to watch the news in the days building up to the execution of Jeff Pritchard. It all brought about too much anxiety.

And too many in the small town of Twisted Tree already thought she was crazy, living in this house after all that had been found in it seventeen years ago. Would have thought her crazier still, had it not been for the picture the newspapers had posted when she'd bought the place years ago. She was what many considered an attractive woman. In her forties, but still single. What the papers had called southern genteel.

But if Jeff Pritchard was executed at midnight, as was reported through the grapevine, then it surprised her none that the first rock came through her living room window at 12:01. Followed soon by laughter and the sound of some other things that weren't so heavy colliding against the façade of her house.

Her house.

Not his anymore.

Damn kids.

They took off as soon as she opened her front door and fired a shot into the trees, speeding off on their four-wheelers and bikes, and a few of the faster ones on foot, their laughter trailing like gun smoke before dissipating altogether out near the main road.

Her front yard all a mess.

Eggs all over her porch. The walls. The door. One window shattered. The two dogwoods festooned with what looked like dozens of unraveled toilet paper rolls.

She waited for a beat to make sure they wouldn't come back, glad at least that the electrocution was finally over. Wondered if living in the house of a former serial killer would be easier now that the serial killer was dead.

She went inside, locked the door, and called the police.

CHAPTER

5

I NSIDE THE BOWLING Green Monastery of the Poor Clare Colettines, Sister Mary Rose awoke atop her straw mattress when the
Caller knocked on her cell door, summoning each sister to the
12:45 AM hour of Matins.

It was a tradition of the Poor Clares to rise in the middle of the
night, to pray for the world while the sky was dark, a time when so
many sins were committed.

She sat up in silence, but with a loud, heavy heart, as she felt it in
her bones that it had already taken place, and that Jeffrey Pritchard,
the boy she once knew at the Sisters of Mercy orphanage, was dead.

Without delay, she changed her long-sleeved nightgown for her
habit, opened her wooden door, and filed in with the other twenty-
three Poor Clares shuffling barefoot and in contemplative silence
toward their Office Choir inside the chapel.

Where Sister Mary Rose, again, prayed for his soul.

As she'd long since forgiven him.

Before

*F*ROM DETECTIVE LELAND *Patterson's recorded interview with Todd Blackstone (retired veterinarian from Bowling Green, Kentucky)*

> **Blackstone:** *And you're sure it's him? He killed all those people like they say? Including the children?*
>
> **Detective Patterson:** *It's him. It's Jeff Pritchard. Of that we have no doubt.*
>
> **Blackstone:** *Now, don't get me wrong. I don't mind talking. But what does it matter now?*
>
> **Detective Patterson:** *Because, Doc, the investigation, with me at least, doesn't stop with the who. And I won't get any sleep until we can get down to the why.*
>
> **Blackstone (leaning back in his chair):** *Because he won't talk.*
>
> **Detective Patterson:** *He won't talk.*
>
> **Blackstone:** *So that whole Father Silence thing is real?*
>
> **Detective Patterson:** *Aside from him not being a priest, yeah, he's gone silent on us. But I've been told you had an encounter with him when he was a boy? In your clinic?*
>
> **Blackstone (nodding, closes his eyes briefly):** *It was a first. And a last, I'll say that much. Jeff was nine years old. I was doing a check-up on an adorable kitten, a Ragamuffin, if I*

remember correctly. This day became etched in my mind for many reasons, Detective. You sure you don't want something to drink?

Detective Patterson: *No, thank you, I'm fine. Go on.*

Blackstone (sipping from his coffee): *I looked out the window, saw a young boy pulling an old Radio Flyer wagon. Classic red, dusty from the side roads. In it was a dog, obviously wounded. I finished my exam with the cat and met the boy at the door.*

Detective Patterson: *Did you know him?*

Blackstone: *No, not really. We'd never met.*

Detective Patterson: *But you knew who he was?*

Blackstone: *Yes. He was an altar server at church. And I'd seen him walking the back roads around town, pulling groceries in that same Radio Flyer.*

Detective Patterson: *Alone?*

Blackstone: *Yes, which is why I wasn't shocked, at first, that he'd come alone to my clinic. The boy seemed very independent. Parents were pretty hands off.* **(Another sip of coffee.)** *It was a fully grown golden retriever, hit by a car that morning. The poor dog was a bloody mess, trembling inside that wagon, covered by a blanket the boy had put atop him. He had to be put down, and when I told Jeff this he nodded, tears in his eyes. He knew. That's why he brought him, he tells me. To end his suffering.*

Detective Patterson: *Parents?*

Blackstone: *I asked where they were. He tells me, they said it's not our dog. Not their problem. You see, the boy had somehow acquired the dog a year before, and the deal was that he took care of it. So he did the best he could.*

Detective Patterson: *I've done the math. Jeff's old house . . .*

Blackstone: *Not yet burned down at the time.*

Detective Patterson: *But it was four miles from where your clinic used to be.*

Blackstone: *He pulled that dog for four miles, yes. And he held him, lovingly, while I put the poor dog down. Just him, by himself. And then he insisted on wheeling the dead dog back. I offered to cremate him here. Explained that I would take care of it. Everything was free of charge, but he insisted on taking the dog home and burying it himself. But I remember, clear as a bell, that boy when the dog was put down, him petting it, singing softly in his ear.*

Detective Patterson: Do you recall what he was singing?

Blackstone: That children's lullaby. "Good Night, Sleep Tight." What, you know it?

Detective Patterson: He'd sing the same thing to his victims, so yes, I've heard of it.

Blackstone: Damn if that don't turn it all even creepier to me.

Detective Patterson: I'm sorry, Doc, but did you ever see Jeff Pritchard again?

Blackstone: Yes. He came by, six more times over the next four years. Each time, pulling wounded animals in that Radio Flyer. Each time, he'd say, can you save them? All of them near death, castaway mutts he said he'd found. Wanderers. Wounded wanderers, he'd call them.

Detective Patterson: And you'd put them down?

Blackstone: Of course. There's nothing worse than a suffering animal. His words. I agreed, of course.

Detective Patterson: Pardon my bluntness, but didn't you ever think of calling his parents? Or maybe even following him home?

Blackstone: I did. Both. On the phone, his father was standoffish. Claimed the boy just had his eccentricities. His oddities. But they knew what he was doing and left him to it. But that . . . that wasn't enough for me, Detective. So one day I followed him home. Watched from afar as he buried whatever animal it was this time.

Detective Patterson: And?

Blackstone: The boy, beside the house, near the woods that bordered their property, had his own pet cemetery. And there were more than just those six buried animals. You see, he had each little mound marked with a cross made of sticks.

Detective Patterson: Upside-down cross?

Blackstone: No, these seemed upright.

Detective Patterson: How many? Doc?

Blackstone: At least two dozen. **(Looks at me dead on.)** I should have known, Detective.

Detective Patterson: In hindsight, a lot of people should have known a lot of things. But unfortunately, the world doesn't ever run in reverse. And one thing I've learned to be a hard truth is that hindsight never proves useful.

6

JUST LIKE THE past two weeks taking Julia to school, the morning drop-off line was bumper-to-bumper and nearly snaked around the block of the neighborhood-enclosed school, moving like cold molasses. Tess checked her watch, willed the line to move, recalled how on the first day she'd driven her daughter to school instead of Justin, Julia had kept up a running commentary. *Daddy didn't go that way. Daddy cut through that street. Daddy rolls his windows down. Sometimes he blares the music and car dances whenever the line goes slow. The teachers think it's hilarious.*

Of course they do, she'd thought.

Julia, swaddled in a blue raincoat and chewing the last of her Pop-Tart, unlatched her seat belt and opened the door.

"Julia, we're not to the parking lot yet."

She pointed to a cluster of kids walking past the car line. "*They're walking in.*"

Those are walkers, thought Tess, and you're not. And then she sighed. *Pick your battles.* If Justin had offered that nugget of advice once, he'd given it a dozen times. "Go ahead then," she said. "Walk with them. But stay close."

Julia rolled her eyes, then slammed the door before Tess could say goodbye. Her pink book bag bounced on her shoulders as she caught up with the other kids on the sidewalk and turned the corner toward the main entrance. Once Julia was out of sight, Tess pulled the car out of line and turned in the opposite direction.

Somebody honked.

Tess waved.

Ten minutes later she pulled into the police station, and drizzle had started to fall.

She hurried inside the lobby, where Marla Wolfe, their dispatcher, sipped coffee from a lipstick-stained Styrofoam cup and nodded toward Tess's office. "You've got company. He got here about ten minutes ago."

Tess sucked in a deep breath and opened the door to her office. Acted like she had her shit together.

Justin was in the same style white button-down he'd worn when they'd first met in college. Same type of shirt she'd nearly ripped from his chest, buttons and all, three dates in. He sat relaxed in an armchair across from her desk, brown hair wavy but trimmed. Horn-rimmed glasses and a tweed coat. Blue jeans and loafers. The prototype college professor. A young Indiana Jones.

He didn't stand when she entered, but said, "Good morning."

Tess hung up her coat and moved to her desk. "Justin, what are you doing here?"

"I'm a psych consultant for the department. I work here, sort of."

"I mean here. In my office, Justin. What are you doing in my office?"

"Just checking on you, Tess. Last night you got hit by both sides."

"Both sides?"

"The storm? Jeff Pritchard . . . his execution?"

"I survived." Tess let out a deep breath, stared out her office window.

"Nothing resurfaced?" Justin asked.

"No, Justin . . . *Jesus.* Stop. Not today."

"And your parents?"

"They're fine. Talked to Dad last night. We're glad it's over." Tess sat at her desk, and all at once her frustration, her resentment, her anger at Justin surged, hot and strong, and she had to stop herself from lashing out at him, for sitting there, for *existing*, for having done the thing that wrecked their marriage, that caused him to not be there last night of all nights.

She took a long breath, waved her hand. "Just go. Please. We'll talk later." She stared at a dull spot on her desk until the door closed, and then channeled her frustration toward her work. According to Justin, her work and dedication to the job had been part of the prob-lem. *She'd allowed her ambitions of becoming a famous detective like her father to cloud reality. She'd often been a distant wife, a hands-off mother. Too many nights spent at the office and not in their bed.*

Too many nights on the road.

She'd been raised on *CSI*, *Miami Vice*, and *Murder, She Wrote* reruns, but at thirteen, after the family moved out west, thanks to a new friend down the street, her entertainment interests grew darker. *The Silence of the Lambs* novel was like her Bible, the movie *Se7en* her most-watched film. She'd always wanted to follow in her father's footsteps. She'd begged to go to work with him. She'd work imaginary cases beside him in his office while he worked the real ones at his desk, and her drive had only been exacerbated after the move out west, when she'd initially known no one and was often bored. In high school, she took classes in criminology and forensic science. She graduated from the University of Montana and took a job with the Missoula Police Department soon after her father retired from it. Two years into the job she was selected for a four-month investigative training program at the Rocky Mountain Information Network in Arizona. She became a full-fledged homicide detective and had dreams of one day working a case the magnitude of Father Silence.

Be careful what you wish for, her father had told her.

For ten minutes, Tess looked through files on a reopened robbery case in which a bank teller was shot and killed. She and Danny were to wrap it up this afternoon. So where was Danny? They had a meeting in five minutes, and he'd typically arrive early just to chat, or, as he called it, *shoot the shit*. The day had begun to trickle toward normalcy. But her father always told her that in their line of work, normalcy never lasted long. Could blot out the sun in a snap. One minute someone was alive, and the next they weren't.

And that's when we get the call, sugar.

Tess suddenly felt queasy, as if she'd eaten something that unsettled her, but she hadn't eaten all morning.

And then someone knocked on the door. Not Danny, who rarely knocked—it was Marla who stuck her head in.

"Line one, Tess. Says it's urgent."

She picked up the phone, the queasiness turned to dread. "Hello, Detective Tess Claiborne speaking."

"Oops," the voice said.

"What? Who is this?"

"I'm sorry," a man said. "We . . ."

"What?"

And then the voice blurted out, "I did the bad thing."

Tess squeezed the receiver. "What are you talking about? Who are you?"

"They're both dead."

Tess went rigid. "Who is this?"

"I'm the Outcast," he said, not proudly, but more resignedly, sincere. "I'm sorry. Don't bother tracing this. I'm at a cabin in Lolo National Forest. Pattee Canyon Drive. They can both see the darkness now."

"Who?" she screamed, although she already knew.

Mom . . . Dad . . .

"I'm sorry," the voice said again.

The line went dead.

CHAPTER

7

D ANNY WAS FIRST on the scene.
He'd been two miles from Lolo when Tess called, frantic.
Once he'd secured the cabin, he reached out to Eliza and asked her
to call Tess, to try and convince her to stay away, but she wasn't having any of it.

"I'm almost there, Danny. And I'm coming in."

Tess ended the call, parked, and ran toward the cabin forty yards
through the trees. Eliza called again, and she let it go to voice mail.
Members of their team were marking off the perimeter with yellow
tape, others were taking pictures inside and out. Their CSI van was
parked next to a pile of chopped wood and two officers were searching the muddy forest floor with flashlights; an ID technician was
casting a footprint moving away from the porch.

Danny came down the steps with a tape recorder to his mouth.
When he spotted her, he put the recorder in his pocket and embraced her.

Tears welled her eyes. "How bad is it?"

"It's bad, Tess. You shouldn't be here."

She saw into the cabin, the front door propped open. An officer
walked out with a plastic bag in hand. Two more followed a set of
tire tracks around the back of the house. "Their Jeep, Danny," she
said. "They drove it here. It's gone. He must have escaped in it."

"Tess."

"It's an oh-nine Jeep Grand Cherokee, bright red. It had a scratch
on the driver's side door. The license plate is, damn it, I can't remember, it's . . ."

"Tess, we've got it all. We're already out searching for it."

Tess looked. No windows had been broken. "Any suspects? Witnesses?"

"Not yet, but he left fingerprints everywhere. And the murder weapon."

She broke down at the word *murder*. He tried to console her, but she stepped aside, rubbing tears from her cheeks. "I'm going in." Danny gripped her arm, but the hold was tenuous, and she broke free. She sucked in air and opened her eyes wide, readying herself. "He's proud of what he's done, Danny. Leaving evidence. Calling me. The way he spoke on the phone, it was like he knows me."

Danny followed behind her. "Tess, you shouldn't. I'm telling you . . . It's bad."

Tess saw blood as soon as she entered the cabin, and followed the trail to her father, who sat tied to a rocking chair facing the near wall. His head lolled, chin to chest. His pale face didn't look like him. *It's me, sugar. Dear old Daddy.* The eyelids were closed and mucked with stark black paint, two dark circles over the closed mounds of his eyes.

They can see the darkness now.

She swallowed past the tightness in her throat, then saw the death blow on the back right portion of his head—hair clotted with blood and bits of bone. He literally had his brains beaten in. A hammer—presumedly the murder weapon—lay on the floor next to the chair. Chalk outlined the parts of the hardwood floor where they could walk without fear of contaminating the scene. The hammer was marked as well, hair stuck to the head of it.

A newspaper article had been pinned by a kitchen knife, eye-level to the wall in front of her father.

The headline read: FATHER SILENCE EXECUTED!

So this was personal. A revenge killing.

Tess moved along the chalked pathway. Ninhydrin spray showed blue latent fingerprints on the floor around the hammer and on the wall surrounding the article.

Police Chief Anderson Givens emerged from a back room wearing a suit and a tie sagging loose from his collar. "Oh Jesus Christ, Danny." He ran a hand over his short salt-and-pepper hair. "I told you to stop her at the door."

Danny raised his arms as if to say, *How was I supposed to do that?*

"Need an army for that, boss," Tess said.

Givens was a fair man she'd always respected—one of the few at the department to never hit on her—but she figured he knew that on this he would not get her compliance. Minutes after the call, he'd ordered two of his men to keep her at headquarters, but they'd proved easily swayed: She'd threatened to tell Stanley's wife about his affair with one of the drug addicts he'd rescued three months prior and threatened to kick Butch in the balls.

So now here she was in the thick of it.

Givens sighed. "I'm sorry."

She ignored him. A technician coated a swath of the floor with black powder, brushing the wood surface, adhering it to the deposited sweat and oils of the print. Next, she applied the clear lifting tape, smoothed out the air bubbles, and transferred it to the glossy surface of the lift card. The tech carried the mirror-image replica to the kit.

"Perfect print," Tess said.

"We're getting them everywhere," Danny said.

"There was a struggle," Givens added. "We found skin tissue under your father's fingernails, and a few strands of short, dark hair. May have scratched him during a fight."

That's because he's a fighter. He's always been a . . .

She stopped abruptly. Her mother was on the kitchen floor, naked except for the towel twisted around her right knee. Chalk outlined her body. Tess covered her mouth when she saw her mother's face. Her eyes were closed, and like her dad, two round blotches of black paint covered them, staring like two dark wells. There was a swollen red wound on her back right shoulder, consistent with a hammer blow.

Danny pointed. "Two to the head."

"One to slow her down. One to drop her. One to finish her off. Jesus." A banana-shaped smear of blood marked her left thigh. "Tell me she wasn't . . ."

"She wasn't raped, Tess. No sign of it."

Tess spun away. *Somebody put something over her. A blanket, a sheet, a towel, something.* But she didn't say it. Her mother's body was their evidence.

"Bathtub is full of water."

"Must have happened soon after I called last night. She must have heard Dad struggling."

"We'll find the Jeep, Tess." Danny fleetingly touched her arm. "We'll get these prints to the lab as soon as possible."

"We need to find him before he does this again." Her eyes darted around the room. "He's left his mark. Painting over their eyes. He's going to do this again."

"Come on," said Givens. "We need to get you out of here."

She nodded, silently agreed. She glanced to the rocking chair again. A wallet rested on the floor next to a spot of blood. She knelt. "My father's wallet."

"We checked it," said Givens. "His prints are on it as well."

She looked up. "Give me a pair of gloves."

"Tess . . ."

Danny held up a hand, asking their boss for some leeway.

Tess slid thin latex rubber over her unsteady hands, grabbed the forceps from the lab kit. She searched the wallet's money pocket, carefully spreading the leather folds with the forceps. She didn't know how much money he'd had, but from the fact that bills remained and the credit cards were in place, she surmised that no money was taken. Next she flipped through the folds of pictures in the middle of the wallet. He'd insisted on keeping real pictures. Tess had flipped through them weeks ago when she and Julia were poking fun at him, showing him the technology of smartphones. Each picture in his wallet had its own clear plastic sheath. She stopped at the seventh sheath. It was empty. A picture was missing. The eighth, ninth, and tenth sheaths held pictures. She started at the beginning again, her hands shaking so badly it was difficult to keep the wallet still. She got to the seventh sheath again and dropped the wallet.

"No! Oh my God, no. Her picture is missing."

"Who?"

"Julia's." She stood, clutched her head with both hands, mumbling. "School picture. It had her name on the back. Her grade. Her school."

She sprinted for the door.

8

T ESS PULLED TO a skidding halt on the wet pavement, stopping inches from the bike rack beside the main entrance to
St. Thomas More Elementary School.

My parents are dead. She'd thumb-tapped earlier on the run to
Justin before starting her car. *Julia may be in danger. Go to the school.*

She sprinted to the entrance. The door was locked. She banged
on it, saw the buzzer and held it pressed. Finally, the door unlocked.
Officer Stanley ushered her down the hall.

"Principal's office," he said. "First door on the left."

Tess turned the corner into Mrs. Young's office. She'd been there
before, ten months ago with Justin when Principal Tamatha Young
informed them that Julia was head and shoulders academically above
her classmates. School was easy for her and at times Julia acted bored.
Tess had felt proud then; now she was frantic, on the verge of throwing up. She barged in and Mrs. Young looked up from her desk,
distraught.

Justin sat in a chair catty-corner from the desk, face in his hands.

"Where is she?"

Mrs. Young swallowed hard. "She was counted absent on roll call
this morning."

"She hasn't missed a day," Tess said. "She's never missed a day of
school."

The principal looked defeated. "I received the roll call sheets
shortly after school started. I called your house but got no answer.
I tried your cell, but it went to voice mail."

Justin touched his forehead. "I was in a department meeting."

"We weren't alarmed until the police called us. I'm so sorry."

Tess looked up from the floor. "It's not your fault."

Justin turned on Tess, his voice shaky. "Didn't you drop her off?"

"I did."

"Then what happened?"

"I don't know."

"Did you see her enter the building? Tess?"

Tess paused, shook her head. "I dropped her off down the line."

"What?"

Tess raised her voice. "She was with a cluster of other kids."

"Did you see the other kids?" Justin asked, and then said to the principal, "You got a yearbook?"

"We're already pulling them from their classes," Mrs. Young said. "So far most of them didn't even notice Julia walking behind them."

"God damn it," Justin said, burying his face in his hands again.

Someone knocked on the door. Mr. Jenkins, Julia's third grade teacher, entered with a little red-headed girl from the same class. A friend of Julia's. Her name was Maggie, but Tess knew that everyone called her Freckles. Her big brown eyes darted around the office. Mr. Jenkins handed Tess Julia's pink book bag. "Found this in the back of my classroom, leaning against the wall."

Tess broke down crying, clutching the bag to her chest.

Justin clenched his hand into a fist as if to punch the air but brought it to his mouth instead. "When did you find it?"

"Few minutes ago, Mr. Claiborne." Mr. Jenkins put his hand on the small girl's shoulder. "Maggie here said she carried the bag into school for Julia."

Tess knelt before the girl. "Maggie, did you talk to Julia this morning?"

Maggie shook her head. "No."

"Then how did you get her book bag?" Justin asked.

"He asked me to take it."

"Who?" Justin asked while Tess searched through the bag.

"The man with the sunglasses."

Justin knelt next to Tess and clutched Maggie's shoulders. "He asked you to carry the book bag in?"

She nodded, scared. "And put it against the wall. He said he was her uncle."

Tess could tell Justin was fighting to control himself. Neither he nor Tess had siblings. Julia had no uncle, other than Danny, who was close enough to be. Justin closed his eyes, opened them. "Then where did they go?"

"Into the parking lot. Said they'd be right back." Maggie teared up. "Where's Julia?"

While Tess watched their exchange, she rooted through Julia's book bag, found a paper that seemed out of place. "Justin." She held out a handwritten note, and Justin read it.

> *Tess, I have your daughter now. Don't worry,*
> *I'll keep her safe.*
> **The Outcast**

Justin's grip went slack, and the paper slid from his fingers. Tess sobbed next to him. He put a comforting hand on her shoulder, gently squeezed it. "We'll find her."

She walked, as if catatonic, from the office.

In the hallway her pace quickened into a jog, and then a sprint as she burst through the doors and into the sunlit parking lot. She doubled over beside the car and allowed the tears to flow. The church loomed across the parking lot, where she and Justin had married ten years ago.

He has my daughter. My girl.

The realization hit her in a wave of nausea, and she hunkered to the pavement, heaving three times. *Get it together. Get it together.* She felt Justin's hand on her arm, felt his questions coming. She stood, hugged him before he could ask anything. He wiped her face with the pad of his thumbs and they both blinked away tears.

Three police cars squealed into the parking lot, sirens blaring, lights casting blue and red prisms against the brick and stone church façade. They could interview Freckles, but she doubted the little girl could give them much. *The man with the sunglasses.* It was a start. It had been raining this morning. A man wearing sunglasses in the rain would stand out.

"Tess."

She looked up to find Danny hurrying toward them from one of the cars that had just arrived. He nodded toward the church. "Father Beacon just reported his car stolen."

And then they simultaneously saw another vehicle, parked on the far side of the parish property, along the fence line. *Son of a bitch.* They were scouring the city for her father's Jeep and here it was right under their noses.

Abandoned.

Tess pulled her 9 mm, started across the parking lot, and Justin followed.

"Stay back," she told him.

Justin didn't listen. He ran toward the red Jeep Cherokee, knowing that every second wasted was another nail in the coffin.

If it was a trap, then so be it.

I have your daughter. Don't worry, I'll keep her safe.

Tess was right on his heels.

The Jeep was empty.

Justin smacked the glass with his open palm and screamed.

Tess suddenly felt dizzy, outside of herself, a bystander watching the horror unfold, and heard herself shouting to not touch anything and there might be fingerprints and evidence. Her heartbeat was in her ears. Her mind looped back into focus. She looked through the driver's door, then took one sidestep to her right, toward the back seats. There was a Polaroid picture on the middle one. One of those old-school pictures that would slide from the camera and finish developing as you shook it. Justin stood behind her now, looking over her shoulder as she reached into the Jeep to grab it.

To hell with the evidence.

Danny hurried across the parking lot toward them, shouting something about Father Beacon's missing car, but it was all white noise to Tess.

The Polaroid had already ingrained itself in her mind, and Justin saw it with her.

A simple shot taken from the front seat to the back—of not one but two children, Julia and a brown-haired boy of roughly the same age.

And they were both smiling for the camera.

Before

*T*HREE WEEKS HAVE *passed since the arrest of Jeff Pritchard—now known across all channels as Father Silence—and the body count continues to rise. Aside from the four children found poisoned in the basement, the remains of what are believed to be at least fifteen other bodies, all adult males, have been unearthed from beneath the floor of the barn and carport, along with a driver's license identifying one of the victims as Allen Bigsby, a twenty-year-old dishwasher first reported missing from Twisted Tree more than eight months ago.*

Forensics are working around the clock to identify the others, coordinating with missing person reports from in town and from neighboring cities. Because of Pritchard's refusal to speak to anyone, authorities are left to speculate on motive, but one common thread connecting the known victims is that they all seemed to be society's so-called castaways: the troubled, neglected, addicted, and homeless. In his own warped way, Pritchard may have believed he was helping them.

Attempts to gather information from the only known survivor, Noah Nichols, have repeatedly been made, but thus far have been unsuccessful, as the traumatized boy remembers very little from his month-long captivity. But if there is such a thing as a silver lining to tragedy, authorities have found no signs of physical or sexual abuse with the victims. Of course, mental abuse can carry multiple horrors of its own.

CHAPTER

9

THE SMELL OF the spruce trees reminded the Outcast of home.

He told Julia and the boy that the air back home had another smell to it altogether, something special, something unique, called the Angels' Share. They looked at him funny, like most did, but he told them *You just wait and see*, and to give him a minute so he could reflect and say a quick prayer.

Truthfully, he didn't feel right. His head hurt. He assumed it was the tension of the last twelve hours. Twelve hours he'd like to forget. Or maybe it was excitement, but he didn't think so. Excitement implied joy, and he'd gotten no joy from what he'd done back at that cabin—and what he'd witnessed—which was why he'd felt the need to enter the church last night and pray for forgiveness.

Now he hoped to wash his hands of it. Play it smart and not get caught. He'd be back home in no time. At the Playhouse, where life was fun and comfortable.

He kept telling himself he'd done the right thing with the Claiborne girl. Her life was getting ready to be torn in two anyway. Two houses. Two Christmases. Two Thanksgivings. Fights over custody.

Either way, there was no rewind button on this, only forward, and faster forward.

He squeezed the sides of his head to keep his thoughts in order. Sometimes they got muddled. Sometimes he was a kid again and everything was dark.

No suffer the children.

The Outcast shook his head. Heard the latch unlocking, the door creaking open. Sometimes memories came with sounds.

Soon you'll be back home.

That helped settle things.

Until he thought of the hammer he'd left behind at the cabin.

Good thing he always carried two. That one had been bloody after the deed was done and he didn't want to touch it.

Shouldn't matter.

Hard to match prints to someone who didn't exist.

10

As usual, the glass-walled conference room at the police station was like an icebox, but Tess was too numb to notice.

She sat with her elbows on the round mahogany meeting table, staring blankly toward Danny sitting opposite her. Justin sat to her left, eyes rimmed red.

Tess reached to the middle of the table and grabbed the Polaroid photo they'd pulled from her father's Jeep. Julia and the unknown boy, both smiling like they were on a family trip to the zoo. Amber Alerts had been issued for both children. Details, down to the tiny mushroom-shaped birthmark on the underside of Julia's right arm, had been rushed across the lines.

Danny broke the silence. "Tess, you're sure you don't know this other boy?"

"Positive."

"Justin?"

Justin shook his head.

"That means he's not limiting revenge, or whatever this is, to you, Tess." Danny sighed, rubbed his face. "The pictures are all over the news. The National Center has all the information they need."

"We don't know where this other boy was taken from?" Tess asked.

"No, not yet." Danny scribbled notes on a legal pad.

"No lab results yet?" Justin asked.

"Still waiting," Danny said, unable, Tess noticed, to even look at his best friend. "It takes time."

Tess said, "FBI? Behavioral Sciences?"

"I contacted Quantico. We're in the system. If anything similar happens somewhere else, we'll know about it."

Justin lit a cigarette. "We have enough from the cabin to make a profile."

Danny said, "When the fuck did you start smoking again?"

"The day I stopped drinking." He managed to say that without looking at Tess—she knew he'd stopped drinking after the *incident*. His one-time drunken fuck-up with what's-her-face. Justin exhaled smoke. "I think it'll be serial."

Danny waved the smoke away. "We can't jump to conclusions."

"I've studied serial cases." Justin stubbed his cigarette out on the table top, as if the two inhales he'd taken had been enough. "I know how to profile. You know what it takes to kill someone with a hammer? He left his signature at the cabin, painting black over the eyes. Phone calls and notes. Two dead."

"A violent killing spree maybe," Danny said, with a tone of caution, although Tess could tell her partner didn't disagree. "Revenge, more than likely."

"If it's revenge," Justin gritted out, "why my daughter? Why me and Tess? We didn't arrest Jeff Pritchard."

Danny shook his head. "I don't know, buddy."

"Shit—Burt Lobell was my father's partner when they arrested Jeff Pritchard. We need to warn him." Tess looked at Danny. "And he has three grandchildren."

Danny stood, phone to his ear. "I got it." He moved away as he waited for someone to pick up his call. He said over his shoulder to the table, "But it's too early to call him serial. We find more bodies with black over their eyes and we'll go down that road." He peeled off and continued with his call.

Tess watched both men, the tension between them palpable. Friends since childhood, they claimed they'd fought before, but she'd never, in her twelve-plus years of knowing them, witnessed them disagreeing until now.

Danny returned to the table. "The two missing children . . . that's our main focus," he said. "Finding the children. Find . . ." He choked up. "Finding Julia."

Justin clenched his jaw, and when Danny put a hand on his shoulder, Justin let the tears flow, but regrouped quickly.

Danny watched them both. "Word is being sent out now to Twisted Tree, Tess, warning your father's old partner."

"Thank you," Tess said. "Father Silence is behind this. From his grave. Somehow. That's the connection." And then last night's phone call with her father registered. "*Fuck.*"

Both Danny and Justin looked at her.

"Last night," she said. "Dad told me he'd heard that Jeff Pritchard finally spoke at the end, a few last words."

"What did he say?" asked Justin, suddenly more alive in his seat.

Tess shook her head. "I don't know. I didn't want to hear it last night," she said. "I . . . it doesn't matter now. This Outcast, he could be trying to copy."

"Father Silence use a hammer?" Justin asked.

"No."

"He paint their eyes black?"

"No. He didn't, Justin. But we can't ignore the newspaper stuck to the wall, referencing his execution. That was the trigger."

Just then Police Chief Givens walked into the room. He'd already warned Tess she couldn't be on this, it was too personal, but as the parents of one of the children and the daughter of the two murder victims, she needed to be here to answer questions on both. And her viewpoint was clear. *Point taken, but try and distance me at your peril.*

She eyed the chief and went on. "If not revenge, then this was done in his honor. Father Silence, sick as it sounds, had fans. Especially women. They'd send him letters in prison. Love letters, even. All the way up to the end. And we're sitting here waiting while this psycho runs off with my daughter." She glanced at Justin. *Our daughter.* "We don't know where he's going . . . what he's going to do . . ."

Justin scooted his chair over, touched her arm. She allowed it for a moment, but then pulled away. As a teen she'd sneaked into her father's office to look at his investigation on Jeff Pritchard. She'd search papers for bits of information her youthful brain couldn't yet process. Pictures of the bodies dug up from under the barn and carport. *Troubled adults. The unwanted and mentally wounded.* If this man was taking a page from Father Silence's book, Julia was the break from the pattern. Up until those final victims found inside his basement, Jeff Pritchard's previous victims had all been adults. And specifically, males.

Danny said, "So what do we know of Father Silence?"

"Little," said Justin.

Tess composed herself. "He fancied himself a priest."

"He was no priest," Justin said, with venom. "Being a priest was the perfect disguise for him. And for a long time, it worked. But he was no priest."

Tess said, "Pritchard murdered the outcasts of society. Unwanted. Homeless. And the . . ." She paused, as haunts from her own past flashed in the form of white pills and alcohol. "The addicted. He basically put them down."

"Like dogs," Justin said.

"Funny you say that," said Tess. "My father did some digging on Pritchard's childhood, in Bowling Green, Kentucky, where he grew up. Had his own pet cemetery for wounded dogs he'd helped save. Helped put down. He called them wounded warriors."

"Jesus." Danny took notes.

Justin shook his head. "And gradually he moved on to people."

Givens rubbed his face in disgust. "So there was never any evidence of abuse from Jeff Pritchard? No sexual or physical abuse?"

"No," said Tess. "Not that we know of. Just the mental kind."

"And the neglect kind," said Justin. "Those five kids were locked in a basement for a month."

Danny asked, "Why did he keep them alive for that long? We don't think he did that with the other victims. The adults. And why did Silence suddenly switch to children?"

Tess looked at Justin. "From what they found in the basement, Dad thought he schooled them in some way. There was a small classroom with desks. And a chapel. Hence the scars on the victims' arms."

Danny asked, "What scars?"

"He'd branded a small cross on the underside of their forearms. An upside-down cross."

Justin choked mid-sob, stood, and walked away from the table.

"Where you going?"

"I don't know."

The conference room door opened before Justin could leave. Father Beacon, in his black clerical garb, stepped inside the room with nervous eyes and wispy brown hair. "They told me to come on in." He wasted no time. "The man with the sunglasses. I saw him last night."

"When?" Tess asked.

"About nine. He came into the church. Sat in the front pew. I told him it was good timing because I was getting ready to lock the doors. He said he only needed a few minutes to pray, and he'd be on his way."

"Did you get a good look at him?"

"Yes, him and the boy."

"The boy was with him?"

"Yes. I didn't know. I'm sorry. He gave no sign. The boy. He almost seemed . . ."

"He seemed what, Father?"

"He seemed happy." Father Beacon put a hand to his face; he'd gone pale. Tess ushered him toward a seat and the priest continued. "When he was finished, I walked them out the back of the church. Asked them if they were hungry or if they needed shelter. He declined both but seemed grateful for the offer. Outside the rectory, I stopped to get something out of my car."

"The missing Jetta?" asked Danny.

"Yes. And he said, 'Nice car, Father. How's it ride?'"

Tess patted Father Beacon's shoulder, and then she told Danny to get Glen O'Donnell, their sketch artist.

The Outcast would soon have a face.

11

G LEN O'DONNELL, THINNING hair in a noticeable combover, shuffled into the room with a set of pencils in one hand and a sketch pad in the other. His eyes fidgeted behind glasses with lenses nearly as thick as the bottoms of Coke bottles.

He sat between Danny and Father Beacon and compulsively arranged his pencils on the table. Glen had his quirks, but he could conjure faces from other people's minds and draw with uncanny detail, his sketches often more accurate than the composites rendered by computers. Glen pushed his glasses up his rail-like nose, smoothed his combover, and focused on the witness.

Tess scooted her chair away from the table and encouraged Justin to do the same, as Danny and Chief Givens homed in.

Danny leaned toward Father Beacon. "I'm going to ask you some questions, Father. Answer the best you can, as descriptively as you can. Details are important."

Father nodded, cleared his throat.

When Danny got down to business, it was like a second, supremely focused personality emerged. "I'd like you to close your eyes for me, Father. Picture the man first entering the church last night. You're there again. You said the front pew. Can you see him walking up the center aisle?"

"Yes."

"Before getting into the pew, does he genuflect?"

"Yes. He knelt. Then very deliberately motioned the sign of the cross."

"Reverently?"

"Yes, very much so."

He's Catholic, Tess thought. *Devout.*

"Does the boy genuflect?"

"Yes, but only because the man did. He was imitating him." Father Beacon had begun to relax. "He was wearing sunglasses."

"The boy or the man?"

"The man," Father Beacon said. "Thought that strange seeing how it was dark and rainy. Even inside he never took them off. I should have suspected. I'm trying to remember what kind of sunglasses they were, but—"

Glen said, "You're still viewing from afar, Father. Focus on that."

Father nodded, closed his eyes. "He looked around the church like he was nervous. But then soon settled into prayer."

"How?" Danny asked.

"Like anyone, I suppose. Elbows leaning on the seat back. Head bowed."

"And the boy imitated this too?"

"Yes."

"Did the man do anything that could hint if he was right- or left-handed?"

Father Beacon thought on it, but then shook his head. "I'm sorry." And then, "Although in the parking lot—after he asked about the car, he waved. With his right."

"And you never saw him get into a vehicle?"

"No. I reached into the console to get a spare lighter. I'm a smoker. I'm not proud of it. When I closed the car door they were gone."

Tess felt sick to her stomach. "The boy sounded like a completely willing traveler."

"He gave me no suspicion whatsoever."

Beside her, Justin buried his head in his hands. Tess rubbed his back.

Danny glanced at Tess, slid the photograph across the table, and asked Father Beacon to open his eyes. "This the same boy?"

"Yes." He looked over at Justin and Tess. "I'm sorry. I assumed he was the man's son."

"And he very well could be. We've yet to ID him," Danny said. "What happened next? He's finished praying."

"He stands. Thanks me. And then I walk them out the back door."

"Does the boy say anything?"

"No."

"Happy?"

"Content."

"The man. What kind of gait did he have?"

"Excuse me?"

"Walk, steps . . . what kind of movement to his walk?"

"I suppose he walked fast. Hurried. Everything he did was in fast motion, now that I think on it. His steps were large, awkward."

"Limp?"

"No, just . . . strange, I suppose."

Tess wrote on her notepad: *Possibly right-handed. Possible abnormality in gait? Uncoordinated? Long legs?*

"He's standing next to you now," said Danny. "What is he wearing?"

"Checkered flannel button-down. Red and brown. Partly untucked."

Tess wrote: *Disorganized? Messy?*

"With jeans and brown boots. Large feet. Size fourteen if I had to guess."

"Did he ever smile?"

Father shook his head. "No, not that I recall. He was very serious. Reverent . . . until he asked about the car."

"He's standing beside you again, Father. Can you see him clearly now?"

"Yes."

"His race?"

"White."

"How tall?"

"Six three. Six four."

"Weight?"

"Two twenty. Strong, built. Broad shouldered. Big hands, long fingers."

"What about his complexion? Was he tan? Pale?"

"Not tan. But he isn't pale either. Somewhere in between."

He'd slipped into present tense, thought Tess, seeing the events unfold a second time in his mind.

"What shape are his ears?"

"Small. Too small for his face. The left one is crumpled."

"Like a cauliflower ear?" asked Danny.

"I suppose so, yes."

"His hair? Color and style?"

"Short. Black. Combed straight toward his forehead. Like the Romans of antiquity."

"No part?"

"No."

"What about his eyes?"

"Can't tell behind the sunglasses." Father closed his eyes. "I remember now. His sunglasses. They were Ray-Bans. Old ones. The kind that hooked around the ears. The left one didn't fit as snug because of the ear."

"Describe his face."

"His hairline is low. Strong features. Defined jawline. He's not unattractive. Sideburns were trimmed. Ended below the ears."

"Facial hair?"

"Some dark stubble."

"Lips?"

"Full. He has a slight cleft in his chin."

"Nose?"

"Large. Slightly crooked, to the right. Like it had been broken in the past."

"Tattoos, scars?"

"None that I could see."

Glen sketched furiously. Tess scooted closer, watched over his shoulder—he already had the face outlined with hair and was now penciling in details.

"Age?"

"Thirties. Good shape."

"Any nervous twitches, like Glen here?"

"No, but like I said, he was hurried. Hyper almost, at times."

"Teeth?"

"Hardly opened his mouth. He grumbled. Didn't say much. Like he was afraid to. But from what little I saw they were straight enough."

"Jewelry? Necklace? Earrings? Watch?"

"No. Hold on, he's wearing a necklace. His shirt isn't buttoned all the way. I can see it clearly now. The chain has a gold cross. Inch long, hanging from the bottom of a loop."

Tess jumped in. "An upside-down cross?"

"No. A cross as it should be."

Tess scribbled furiously on her notepad to keep up.

Danny's phone pinged. All eyes shot to him as he checked his incoming text. He read it, then put the phone down. "Father, they found your car."

"And the children?"

"It was empty," he said, still reading from his phone. "Abandoned in a ravine behind the college."

"Prime picking for a new ride," said Tess.

Glen blew pencil dust from his sketch pad and held it up for them to see.

Justin stalked out of the room like he might get sick.

Tess stared at the picture in horror, not because she recognized the man, but seeing the suspect suddenly made it more real.

Father Beacon, with tears on his cheeks, closed his eyes, slowly nodding, whispering, "That's him. I'm sorry. That's him . . ."

CHAPTER

12

CHIEF GIVENS ORGANIZED groups to get the Outcast's sketch out across the state, hitting bus stations, train stations, and airports, on the heels of Julia Claiborne's released picture on the news earlier in the day.

Despite Tess's insistence that they report the unknown boy as missing as well, they held off, and the chief reminded her that the Missing Persons Unit was handling the children, and she was Homicide. The FBI had been notified and were sending regional agents from their CARD team, the national Child Abduction Response Deployment unit. They'd already begun mapping the area for any registered sex offenders, the Bureau's technical and forensic resources at their full disposal. As of yet, the boy's picture matched none of those found in the database. For all they knew, he was the man's son, or nephew, which could explain why he'd been smiling in the Polaroid picture left inside the Jeep. But Julia's smile made no sense and would haunt Tess if she let it. She had to stay busy. Had to stay on track to prevent a complete meltdown. Clean fingerprints had been pulled from her father's Jeep and Father Beacon's Jetta. They'd been sent to the labs as matches for those found at the cabin, but so far, no luck on an identification.

So far, on paper the Outcast didn't exist.

Danny had told her to stay put, to go home and rest. Givens warned her away from the crime scene at the cabin, and promised she'd be kept in the loop. She'd nodded as if she agreed—*he was right, it was too personal*—but nothing short of a bullet would keep her from working it in secret.

She left the office while Justin was in the bathroom dry heaving. She ran hot and cold with wanting to be around him. If he hadn't cheated, she never would have kicked him out. *He* would have taken their daughter to school, and he damn well wouldn't have let her get out of the car until they'd reached the parking lot, which is where the man must have been waiting, somewhere between her car and the school's entrance.

She called Givens and told him to interview every parent in the school to see if . . .

He'd cut her off—they were already on it. Nothing on the front entrance's main camera either.

Go home.

So she did.

She poured bourbon and paced the kitchen, glanced at Julia's open bedroom down the hallway, and started crying. She sat at the table but felt guilty even doing that, being idle. She downed the rest of her bourbon in one shot. Paced some more, looked out the windows as a few cars coasted past.

Probably reporters.

Yes, I was a hands-off mother, she could tell them. *I was on the road too often, missed too much, and when I was home I overdid it.* For Julia's first communion she didn't need the extravagant bouncy house Tess had brought in. Julia had fun in it, but the real joy was in how Justin had knelt eye level right there in the church, kissed both cheeks, and told her she was the cutest angel on earth. Julia asked why he was crying, and he'd said because what you're wearing looks like a wedding dress and life just all of a sudden fast-forwarded.

Tess poured another bourbon, sipped it, and then, summoning strength, poured the rest down the sink. She'd dealt with addicts of every sort on the job, and she'd always believed herself above it all, until Justin one night years ago when Julia was a toddler, said she drank too much. That it worried him. And he knew about the pills.

What pills?

You know what pills.

Despite what was portrayed on television shows, firing her weapon had been rare. The one time she'd done so was at the crime scene of a drive-by, where a known gang member had been gunned down on his front lawn while flipping a burger on his grill, and while they were there taking pictures and asking questions of his street friends, the suspects returned for more, opening fire again with semiautomatics. Tess was hit in the upper part of her right thigh. She fired from the ground and blew out the back tire, and the two men inside were now in jail for life. The bullet had gone clean through her thigh and lodged in the first step of the concrete stoop. She later stole the bullet from the evidence room and kept it in a jar atop her dresser, which Justin thought morbid.

She told him it was a reminder.

Of what?

Not to get shot again.

The doc wrote her a script for pain pills, Oxy, and although they did little for the pain, they calmed her at night when she couldn't sleep, made the anger subside, made it not matter as much as the drugs coursed through her bloodstream and somehow soothed the hurts from long ago, from the time in her childhood she'd successfully all but blocked out, memories of why her parents had moved her from Twisted Tree. She'd gone from perfect child to troubled teen seemingly overnight. She'd started sneaking her father's Old Sam bourbon not too long after she'd had her first period to help cope with the nightmares. Just in case he caught on, she'd fill the bourbon bottle with a little water to make it look like it wasn't evaporating. She'd ignore it when he thought that batch of Old Sam was weaker than what he was used to and swore to take it back into town for a good bottle but never did. And the two teens from her school were found murdered in the woods—Grisham Graham and Jeremy Shakes. Before she could even ask why, they were packing for their move out west.

Tess sat with her back against the sink cabinet; didn't even remember slithering down there, refusing the urge she'd beaten years ago. For a year, she'd taken those white oval pills, when in reality she'd only needed them for those first two days, if that. But the doctor had okayed more refills, and once he didn't okay them anymore, she found another that would. And when those avenues dried up, it was easy to dip into confiscated pills from the evidence room. Luckily, Justin caught on before work did, and after three painful weeks of home detox where she pretended to have the flu and then the removal of a gall bladder—which she'd really lost at age eleven—he got her clean.

From the pills.

Because she was an addict.

But she never stopped drinking.

Because that was never an addiction, she'd told herself, finishing off the bourbon in her hands, the one she didn't remember pouring.

13

A FTER A TEXT from Justin, asking her where she'd gone, Tess had responded very simply.

Home.

And she assumed that's where Justin was headed now too. But the longer she stayed cooped up in the house with too many things like blankets and teddy bears and dolls and crayons and puzzles, the quicker she wanted out. There was a dirty knife on the counter from just yesterday, when she'd cut the crust off Julia's grilled cheese, and then into four equal triangles because—she'd learned from Justin, after doing it wrong one day—that was the only way she'd eat it.

Her cell phone buzzed with an incoming call. It was Eliza. Danny had, no doubt, asked his wife to check on her. Not that she wouldn't have anyway—they were as close as sisters. But as much as she loved her best friend, Eliza could be a weather front in her own way, an anxious talker when Tess, at this moment, didn't want to talk to anyone.

She answered in hopes of keeping her friend from storming over. "Hey."

"Oh my God, Tess, I'm so sorry," Eliza said. "I'm coming over."

"No," Tess said, although her words were weak. She needed Eliza now as much as she didn't. "I'm okay."

"You're not," Eliza said. "There's no way you can be after this. Not yet, anyway. Just stay there. I'm getting in my car now."

"Eliza, it's getting late. Just stay there and put your kids to bed."

"Right, Tess, as if that's possible right now. And the sun's just now setting. It's not late. Look, my parents are here. They'll get the kids to bed." Eliza and Danny often said that's what parents were for, to watch the kids, to which she and Justin always agreed with a laugh. Tess surprised herself by letting out a chuckle now, and Eliza said, "There you go. Let that out as much as the tears, Tess. Julia always makes us laugh and cry, so let it out. We'll find her. I'll be there in a minute."

She hung up.

For a moment, Tess felt comforted by this—there was no one better to lean on than Eliza Gomes. She was an excellent social worker, yes, but an even better rock.

Tess paced the kitchen, phone in hand, trying to clear her head of the emotion overriding what would typically be her work mode. Two dead victims. Blunt force trauma to the head. Somebody killed your parents.

This is not your case. This *can't* be your case.

All things she knew Eliza would say to her when she arrived, in what, five minutes?

He spoke . . .

Her father's voice from last night over the phone.

Father Silence had broken his silence. Her father was going to elaborate when they met the next day over pizza, but that visit now would never come.

Tears welled again.

Her parents dead.

Her daughter missing.

She couldn't be a prisoner inside the house. God knew Eliza would have nothing but Tess's best interests at heart, which was why there was no way she'd let her leave once she arrived. So if Tess was going, she needed to go now.

Sorry, Eliza.

Tess grabbed her purse and left by the back door, where she hoped no photographers would see her.

At first she just drove, and then after a few miles realized she was heading toward her parents' house. Her father had kept all his files on Jeff Pritchard in a black briefcase. When she got to their house, she let herself in and searched every room but couldn't find it.

Because he'd probably taken it to the cabin.

That's where she went next.

Her phone rang on the way to Lolo. It was Eliza. She let it go to voice mail. Seconds later, Danny called. This could be about the murders, so she touched the dashboard screen and his voice stormed through.

"Damn it, Tess. I told you to stay put."

"When did our relationship become one where you tell me what to do, Danny?" Her knuckles were bone-white on the steering wheel; she knew she was driving too fast on the wet roads.

"Tess, you know what I mean."

"Where are you?"

"Your house."

"Why are you at my house?"

"Checking on you. Eliza's here, pacing, saying fuck a lot. She's gonna rip you a new one, Tess."

"Well, she knows where the wine is. Tell her to have at it."

Danny sighed, heavily, both resigned and annoyed, she could tell, and then he said, "Justin was here too. He's gone now."

"Where'd he go?"

"I . . . I don't know."

"Then why the hesitation, Danny? Or do you just not want to tell?"

"I'm not his keeper, Tess. He just left. Stormed out. He's torn up just like you are, and now the only people in the house are the two that don't live here. Where are you?"

"Bye, Danny."

She touched End on the screen, then increased her speed toward Lolo. If the Outcast had a connection to Father Silence, it was possible, almost probable, he was not originally from Montana. Her instincts pointed back home. To Kentucky. Possibly even to Twisted Tree, if this was about revenge—most of the people involved with Jeff Pritchard's arrest were still living there.

It was closing in on seven o'clock when Tess arrived at the cabin. The setting sun poked holes through foliage. The crime scene was marked off with yellow tape. A wide-bellied officer stood before the porch, puffing on an e-cig, which he pocketed when Tess approached. He moved nervously, like a man ready to do or say something he didn't really want to.

"Chief Givens said to direct you back to the station, Mrs. Claiborne."

"Five minutes."

"I'm not—"

She put a finger to his lips and shushed him.

He stepped away, raised his hands as if in surrender. "Fine. Sorry. I don't blame you, Detective Claiborne. I'd do the same thing."

"Call me Tess. And I only need a few minutes."

He nodded, hoisted his belt into a thick belly. "Holler if you need anything."

Inside the cabin, the bodies were gone; only the chalk outlines remained, and the dried blood. Evidence tags took the place of the real things—the knife in the wall, the newspaper article on Father Silence, the wallet next to the rocking chair. She passed it all on her way to the back bedroom. Her father's overnight bag still had clothes in it; he was used to living out of a bag. Mother was the opposite; she took her clothes from the suitcase and placed them neatly in drawers as soon as she got wherever she was going.

The suitcase wasn't on the bed, or under.

She stood, hands on hips, surveying the room, the floor, the walls. The furnace kicked on. Air from the floor vent billowed the curtains across the room, revealing a streak of black paint on the window. She pulled the curtains apart and saw two eyes painted in black on the glass, probably the same black paint used to seal her parents' eyes closed.

"Son of a bitch." She tied the curtains back, allowing in what little daylight remained over the river, and backed away. The eyes, no larger than two softballs, crudely painted, stared at her, watched her. She stared right back, stepped aside, and saw where the eyes were pointing. The closet across the room. She opened the double doors, moved her mother's hanging clothes aside, and there it was, Dad's black briefcase resting on a shelf.

The man wants us to find him. There's something he wants us to know.

She carried the briefcase to the bed, popped it open.

On many nights as a child, she'd watched her father at the dining room table with these papers spread out before him, his evidence, theories and interviews, the puzzle of Jeff Pritchard's life sorted into stacks.

Now it was Tess's puzzle.

A folded paper rested atop the mound of files. She unfolded it, knew right away this was what he'd alluded to last night on the phone, and read what her father had written: *He finally spoke. Beware the one that got away. What does it mean?*

Beware the one that got away.

Tess closed her eyes. The one who got away . . .

She heard river water. Her father's voice. Boots on gravel. The weight of a hammer in her hand. She felt weightless as she dropped to the floor.

A car door slammed outside.

She blacked out.

Before

*T*ESS WAS SUPPOSED *to be in bed.*

But she couldn't sleep.

It had been weeks since she'd had a good night's sleep.

Not since . . . that night, and everything that happened.

What all had happened? That's what terrified her the most—she knew it had been horrible, so horrible her parents had pampered her for days, and now weeks, with her favorite foods, her favorite ice cream . . .

All just to get her to talk?

To get her to tell them what was wrong?

To tell them why she'd suddenly gone so distant. Inside herself—her mother's words, as she'd overheard them talking about her nearly every night since . . .

But she had holes in her memory, and the holes seemed to be growing deeper by the day.

It was the phone call that had gotten her out of bed.

Her father had gotten the call he'd been expecting from his friend and partner, Burt Lobell, who, unlike her parents, had gone out of town with his wife for a week to escape it all.

Her father took the call in his den and closed his door, but the door was thin and Tess had good ears, and even though she was supposed to be in bed she was wide awake now.

Now that her father sounded so distraught on the phone, talking to Burt, who apparently had missed everything that had occurred during the day with Noah Nichols.

The boy who'd escaped Father Silence. The only one to survive his captivity in Jeff Pritchard's "House of Horrors." Tess knew something had happened today—someone had been killed—but just not exactly what, or who.

Tess quietly lowered herself to the floor, putting her ear as close as she could to the small spacing between the bottom of the door and the hardwood floor. She hoped she wasn't casting a shadow he'd notice under the door. She hoped her mother wouldn't suddenly awaken and find her here, desperate to learn more about what she had no business learning at her age.

Not to mention what she'd done days before.

"I've seen murders," her father said through the phone to Burt, who was on a beach somewhere in Florida. "I mean we see them every day, right? But he's just a boy, Burt. I mean, Christ, he's just a boy. How could a boy . . . I mean when we carried him out of that house, he looked innocent. He, he . . ."

Tess heard Burt, who'd always had a loud, boisterous voice, say: "Slow down, Leland. We're talking about Noah?"

"Yes, Noah Nichols. The only one we found alive."

"And you're saying he killed his father? This morning?"

"He didn't just kill him, Burt. He used a shard from the broken bottle of Old Sam his old man was drinking. He cut out his eyes. He carved the word Outcast into his father's chest . . ."

14

"Tess."

She felt a hand on her shoulder. A soft voice in her ear. She opened her eyes. Danny helped her to a sitting position, her back against the bed frame. "I passed out."

"Blacked out," a familiar voice said across the room. It was Justin in proactive mode, his collar unbuttoned, sleeves rolled to the elbows, hands on his hips, staring at the painted black eyes on the window. "There's a difference."

Tess made it to her feet, stood between the two men. *What were they both doing here?* She handed Danny her father's handwritten note from the open briefcase on the bed. "Pritchard broke his public silence. Those were his last words."

Justin asked, "What does it say?"

Danny held up a hand while he read, tried to make sense of it. "Beware the one that got away?"

"It wasn't in the papers, or the news," Tess said, slowly regaining her equilibrium, although she could still feel Justin's questioning eyes on her. "Dad had insiders everywhere. He wrote down everything. Always did." She pointed to the window. "The Outcast painted the eyes on that window so we would find it."

"Why would he do that?" Danny asked.

"He wants us to know," Justin said. "It's a game. I'm telling you, he's gonna do this again." He reached out his hand for the note and Danny handed it to him, with reluctance, Tess could tell. "The kid who survived Pritchard? What was his name, Tess?"

"Noah Nichols," she said, still staring at the painted eyes on the window. "He'd be about twenty-six right now. A month after his rescue, Noah killed his own father. Cut out his eyes. Carved the word Outcast into his chest."

"And you're just recalling this now?" Danny asked. "Are these the famous holes in your memory Justin always talked about?"

"Fuck you, Danny," Tess said.

"I'm sorry . . ."

"Fuck both of you."

Justin made a move to touch her arm, but she stepped away. "Tess, we need to—"

"Justin, not now."

Justin exhaled, but let it go.

She'd get to the flashbacks, she owed him that much, but not now. "And I'm not just recalling Noah Nichols," she said to Danny. "It's not like he's some secret. But now there's a connection."

Danny said, "And a suspect."

Justin shook his head. "Noah Nichols is too obvious."

"He was locked up after killing his father," Tess said. "He did time in an asylum. Danny, make the calls. Either way, I'm flying to Kentucky in the morning to find out."

Justin said, "Then I'm going with you."

Danny held up a hand as if to temper the situation. "Look, I understand the urgency, but the two of you aren't—"

"Danny, stop," Justin said. "She's our only child."

Tess could tell Justin regretted his words as soon as he'd said them.

Danny had gone quiet, too—like because he had five kids perhaps one of them was expendable? Danny rubbed his forehead, looked on the verge of retaliating but didn't. "Chief Givens isn't going to allow it."

Tess said, "He can't stop me from going home after a personal tragedy."

Danny shook his head, glanced at Justin brooding across the room, and said to Tess, "The little boy in the second picture has a name now. I heard from the National Center before I got here. Richard Moore, eight years old. An orphan, taken from a residential children's home in Boise, Idaho, two days ago. He must have taken him first, then came here," Danny said to Justin. "You know you really shouldn't be here." Justin ignored him. Danny raised his arms in dismay. "Just thought it needed to be said."

"Noted," Justin said. "Did the children's home report him missing? The kid?"

"Not right away," Danny said. "Richard evidently had a history of running away, but according to them he always came back."

"Orphan," Tess said, thinking out loud. "Outcast child. Poor. Unwanted." *Why Julia? It doesn't fit.* Tess touched her temples as if a headache had just struck, but it was only a realization. "What am I thinking? I can't leave here without knowing where our girl is."

"You're right. We can't. But . . ." Justin paced, held up a finger in thought mode. "Outcast killer. Imitation. Revenge. The motive is a combination of these. Or maybe some debt owed to Father Silence."

"Go on," Danny said.

"Think about his name," Justin said. "His own moniker."

Danny said, "The press gave him the name Father Silence?"

"But he embraced it like a warm blanket," Tess said.

Justin went on: "The hammer wounds killed your parents, Tess, but painting their eyes black . . . *that* is something different. That reflects a psychological need of the perpetrator." Justin suddenly appeared more focused than Tess had seen him since the nightmare started, showing why the department had brought him on as a consultant in past cases. "He's more than likely a psychopath. Psychotic. Obsessive-compulsive. Obsessives normally kill according to a particular style or pattern. They take souvenirs, like eyes, heads, sex organs, whatever. My point is, he left his calling card, his signature on the crime. Repetitive killers almost always do this. They often come from dysfunctional families, seeds of abuse from childhood. You're right, Tess. Too obvious or not, Noah Nichols must be questioned."

"I'll place the calls," Danny said.

Tess noticed the puzzled look on Justin's face. "What is it?"

"Something doesn't fit. These killers, they're normally geniuses at eluding detection."

Danny said, "He seems to be doing just that, Justin."

Justin pointed to the eyes on the window. "He wants us to find him."

"And Noah Nichols may be a wild goose chase," Danny said. "Something to throw us off his trail. He could be playing us like a fiddle."

"He phoned in his own crime," Tess said.

Justin nodded. "He left the murder weapon on the floor. Fingerprints everywhere."

"All evidence we haven't been able to use."

Tess's cell rang; she pulled it from her pocket and answered in a hurry. "Hello."

"Tess."

Her knees nearly buckled; it was him. "Where is she, God dammit?"

"Did . . . did you find the eyes?"

"Yes, I found the eyes."

"Painted on the window?"

"Yes. What do you want? How did you get my number?"

"They're eyes in the darkness, Tess. S-someday you'll understand how bad the d-darkness can hurt."

"Put Julia on the phone," Tess screamed. "I need to hear her voice."

The Outcast breathed heavily, as if contemplating.

Five seconds later Julia's voice said, "Daddy?"

Justin approached but Tess held him at bay. "Julia? Hello! Julia?"

The Outcast returned. "She d-doesn't want to talk to her parents any . . . anymore."

"Put her back on the phone!" Tess screamed, and then forced herself to soften her tone. "I want to talk to my daughter!"

The Outcast said, "She asks, is it because of me that they fight?"

More breathing across the line, and then a click.

"He hung up." Tess turned, found Justin sitting on the floor, his back against the wall, sobbing into his hands. "We lost him." She knelt before Justin, placed a hand gently on his arm.

He looked up, red-eyed, and composed himself with a deep breath and exhale. "He stutters . . ."

"You're right," she said. "He stutters. He didn't do that before."

"He doubts himself." Justin made it to his feet, his sudden emotional episode seemingly over. She wasn't used to seeing him cry, and it unnerved her.

Justin looked at Danny. "He's in over his head."

"Which means he'll make a mistake," Tess said. "And she's alive."

Danny gently took her by the elbow. "Tess, come on. I need to get you home. Eliza's there waiting for you."

"She's alive," Tess said again. She entered the hallway, paused at the bathroom door. "Go on. I've got my own car."

"You just blacked out," Justin said, behind her. "And I can smell the bourbon. You're not driving."

She entered the bathroom and closed the door.

"What are you doing?" Justin asked from the other side of it.

She heard Danny say, "She's going to the bathroom. What's it look like she's doing?"

Tess flipped the light. Bathwater remained in the tub. Her mother's toothpaste and toothbrush rested beside the sink, next to her reading glasses and contact case.

The problem was, Justin knew her too well, and probably had an idea what she was about to do.

"Tess!" Justin again.

"Justin, go home. I'll meet you there." She opened the cabinet above the sink, exposing shelves lined with medicine bottles. She turned the bottles, read the labels, stopping when she found the orange bottle of hydrocodone her father never took after his knee surgery a year ago.

"Don't undo it all," Justin said through the door. He must have heard the creak of the medicine cabinet when she opened it. He had no way of knowing there were pain pills left over in here, and had he known, or thought of it, or thought she'd ever slip back, he would have confiscated them and buried them ten feet underground. "Tess . . ."

"Go home," she insisted.

"What's going on?" she heard Danny say on the other side of the door.

"She has secrets too," Justin said. "Right, Tess? Don't undo it all."

She stared at the bottle of hydrocodone. She'd spotted the bottle of pain pills last year when her father had asked her to go in and grab his blood pressure medication. She'd closed the bathroom door then, too, as she stood for a couple minutes, contemplating, wrangling, getting as far as twisting off the cap and dumping a couple into her hand, before hearing Julia outside playing, at which point she'd cursed herself for being tempted. Because the truth was, she was always on the verge. Always tense. Always wishing she wasn't. Then she had put the pills back into the bottle, grabbed the blood pressure meds for her father, closed the door to the medicine cabinet, and flushed the toilet to complete her deception.

But she'd been stronger then.

She'd had a family.

Now she slid the bottle of pain pills into her pocket, flushed, and opened the bathroom door. She avoided Danny's eyes. "I'm ready now."

"What was that about?"

"Where's Justin?"

"He just left. In a hurry."

"Where?"

"I don't know," Danny said. "Just said he needed to get out of here." He eyed her up and down, like he could see the bottle of pain pills through her pocket. "Do I need to search you for something?"

"Try it, Danny. I dare you."

He didn't.

And instead, followed her out the front door.

15

D ANNY HAD WAITED at the curb for Eliza to usher Tess inside her own home, which had been watched by two media vans previously parked where Danny now was, driving off after he'd chirped his car siren and told them to relocate before he got angry.

He'd texted his wife moments ago, warning her they were on their way from the cabin in Lolo, that Tess had been in no condition to drive, that she probably needed some food. He doubted she'd eaten all day. Eliza, having come out to greet Tess as soon as Danny pulled to a stop outside the house, waved to Danny from the front porch—and then started to close the door before Danny decided a wave wasn't good enough.

Car running, he ran up to the porch and kissed Eliza on the lips. He hugged her, long and hard, before letting her ago, and on the way down the steps she called out, "Got your Kevlar?"

He said he did and patted his chest, feeling the vest beneath his clothes. It's what she said to him every morning before he left for work, and it had started the day after Tess had been shot years ago. Not that Kevlar would have stopped the bullet that had passed through her thigh, but the incident itself had reminded them all that they weren't indestructible, and that just because they had guns to protect themselves didn't mean they couldn't still get shot.

Only then had Danny driven off, a half-assed wave to the two media vans relocating on the other side of the street. They didn't have to move. The street was public property, but they'd no doubt seen the fury in his eyes and probably heard the tension in his voice, tension that for the past several hours still felt stuck inside his throat like he needed badly to throw up.

They'd traced the earlier call from the Outcast to Tess's phone to a Missoula resident named Morgan Sample, a nurse at the hospital who'd only minutes before returned home from a double shift at the NICU.

Tess had wanted to accompany him to Morgan Sample's house, but Danny had told her no chance and was glad now for the solitude his otherwise empty car provided. The weird interaction at the bathroom door inside the cabin earlier had left Danny thinking—no, in fact knowing—Tess was hiding something. Hiding something from her past, yes, which Justin had insinuated to Danny one night when the two of them were sharing beers and talking shit they didn't want their wives to hear, but also hiding something now.

When she'd exited the bathroom back at the cabin, she'd looked guilty, and she'd said nothing in the car, barely looking at him as he covered the ten miles back to their house.

He may have grown up with Justin, friends since parochial school and through high school and college, but he'd worked long enough now with Tess to know that when she went quiet, she felt ashamed about something. And angry, there was that too, but what he saw tonight was guilt and shame and the possible reasons for it were gnawing at him as he drove.

Her kid is missing, Danny.

That's what you saw back there, a mom who'd just lost both parents to a gruesome murder scene and now her daughter was missing. Her *only* daughter, as had been brought up back at the cabin. His and Eliza's goddaughter.

Danny gripped the wheel tight with both hands, so tight he felt he could bend it in his grip. His goddaughter. Tears oozed down his cheeks, and he let them run in cold wet trails off his chin.

The house was only five miles away and he broke traffic laws to get there in a matter of minutes, dialing Justin on the way and going straight to his voice mail.

"Hey, it's Danny. Call me, buddy."

Buddy sounded false coming out of his mouth; he was still pissed at Justin for what he'd done to Tess. Not that now, in hindsight, he wasn't blindsided by it all—there'd been warning signs for months, maybe longer. Justin had been on his phone more, and sometimes secretive about it. He'd seemed distracted when the four of them got together. He and Tess had seemed less handsy, less communicative, less . . . fun. And a month ago during a Friday night cookout and game night, when Danny had conjured up one of those rare moments of outside-the-job seriousness while flipping burgers and asked, *Is everything okay between you and Tess?*, how Justin had so casually said, *Yeah, of course, we're fine, why wouldn't it be*, while avoiding any eye contact whatsoever, Danny had been kicking himself now for days for not fully picking up on it then. That Justin and Tess really were in trouble, and that Justin, who'd *never* been one to cheat on anyone, was flirting dangerously with going down that path.

With *what's-her-name*. None of them would say it.

They all knew her name to be Amy Prescott, a gorgeous first-year professor straight out of her doctorate and unattached and flirty—at least she was the only time Danny had met her at some cookout or another, even flirting with him, which was weird, as even Eliza said he wasn't much to look at anymore.

Justin had always been an attention-seeker, not in an arrogant way, but he'd never shied away from the spotlight, something Tess had for sure given him for much of their marriage, especially early on, when they'd been inseparable, when he and Eliza almost daily told the two of them *to get a room already*. As flashy and exuberant and outgoing as Justin could be, he was still down to earth and surprisingly sentimental. He might have sometimes deep-down craved attention, but even deeper down *needed* affection.

And damn if he hadn't gotten lost one night looking for it, suckered in by that . . . *no, no, can't blame the woman, it takes two to tango.*

Danny squeezed the steering wheel again, turned onto Morgan Sample's street, her ranch house at the end, surrounded by three police cars with their sirens off, lightbars flashing red and blue strobes into the night.

Justin, you dumbass. Where are you?

As he closed in on the house, he glanced at his cell phone on the passenger's seat, wishing like hell Justin would call him back, fearing he'd gone out and done something stupid. He'd already made the mother of all marriage mistakes, he was in a state of shock, and Danny prayed he hadn't driven off to *her*.

The one they wouldn't speak of.

The one Justin promised to never see or talk to again, the one who, even now, according to Justin's colleagues, was already applying for bigger jobs in the private sector because she needed another quick beat on her résumé. The one who, even though Justin had never seemed to have a problem with alcohol, because of the *one-time-and-it-meant-nothing* event, propelled him toward deciding never to drink again.

Hopefully, Danny thought, as he parked next to one of the three police cruisers, that's all he was out doing, drinking, way better than the alternative. Justin had been a social drinker anyway, only with friends, rarely around Julia, and mostly on weekends.

Danny got out of his car, pocketed his phone, and moved quickly toward the house. A female officer held the door open for him and pointed to Morgan Sample, still in her nurse uniform, on a sofa with a blanket wrapped over her shoulders, sipping from a large coffee mug, the steam from it clouding her pale face.

The house wasn't cold, but Morgan sure looked like *she* was.

Cold and shocked and probably still not seeing how close she'd been to losing her life. Or maybe that's what she was seeing now as she blew into her steaming mug, alive.

Danny introduced himself, held out his hand for a shake, and wasn't surprised by how strong her grip was—being a neonatal intensive care nurse brought with it a certain toughness that belied her small size. And as soon as Danny let go of her hand and their eyes connected, she seemed warm, not only to him, but in general. She placed the mug aside and removed the blanket from her shoulders.

"I won't take much of your time, Ms. Sample. I'm sure you're still a little shaken."

"Pissed more than anything," she said. "If I'd known . . ."

"Known what, Ms. Sample?"

"Call me Morgan, please. The two kids that were with him. If I'd known they weren't *with* him, I would have . . . ," she said, pausing, wrestling with her emotions before collecting herself with a long blink and a deep breath. "I would have fought back."

"Morgan, you're a hero for surviving, and talking, right here and now. Okay?" She nodded, wiped her eyes. He handed her a tissue from the box propped on the arm of the sofa. "Now let's start from the beginning. From what I was briefed, you'd just gotten home when he knocked?"

"Yes," she said, with another exhale. "I'd been home for only a couple of minutes. Maybe he'd been waiting. Maybe he was stalking me?"

"I don't think that's what we're dealing with," said Danny. "If he was waiting for you in particular, I don't think he would have spared your life." Especially after what he'd seen done to Tess's parents at the cabin. "Did you let him in?"

She shook her head. "No. He creeped me out from the start. It was dark. It was weird that he had sunglasses on."

"And you've seen our composite sketch of our UNSUB?"

"Yeah, it's the same guy, I'm sure." She reached for her mug again, sipped from it, held it like she needed her hands warmed. "He asked to use my phone."

"And you said?"

"I stammered, a little bit in shock. Maybe I didn't say no right away, although my brain was screaming for me to close the door and lock it and call the police. But I held it open long enough for him to step in. And he was too strong. Too powerful. I tried to scream, but I was so panicked it froze in my throat, and then he had his hand over my mouth. I tried to bite his fingers." She lowered her head, shook it, and when she looked back up at Danny, tears welled in her eyes, and she was biting her lower lip so hard it paled. "His hands smelled like soap. Like he'd recently washed them. It was jarring. Sorry."

Danny gave her a moment. "And then what happened?"

"I thought he was going to kill me with that hammer," she said. "He led me into the kitchen, sat me down at the table, asked me if I had duct tape. I told him where it was. He taped my arms behind the chair so I couldn't move, and then my ankles to the feet of the chair." She chuckled, as if remembering something. "He asked if it was too tight. I mean, really? At that point I thought maybe okay, he's not gonna kill me, you know? Next, he taped my mouth shut. He wasn't rough about it either. I'd hate to say he was gentle, but he was, even with the hammer hanging from his belt. And then he said, *I just need to use your phone, and then I'll be on my way.* Except he stuttered with the word *just.* Took him like four or five times to get it out." She shook her head in dismay. "I nodded toward the counter, next to the fridge, where I have a landline pretty much just for my parents, because they still call it. The police already took it. I'm not worried about it. I'll never use that phone again." She sipped from her mug. "Jesus. Sorry."

"It's okay," Danny said. "And then he made the call?"

She nodded.

The call they'd all heard inside the cabin.

"Were the kids with him initially?"

"No, they must have been inside the car," she said. "It wasn't until he'd taped me to the chair that they came in."

"Both the boy and the girl?"

"Yes. The boy, he was standing at the screen door," she said. "The man saw him standing there. Said *I thought I told you to stay in the car.* He wasn't mad, just a little frustrated. And more worried than anything. And then the boy said he had to use the bathroom. So, get this, he asks me if the kid can use my bathroom. I nodded, yes, of course, but here I am bound to a chair and he's *asking* my permission. So in walks the boy and the girl, who . . ." She broke down, used the tissue Danny had given her a minute ago, and continued. "Who I now know is the missing girl, Julia . . ."

"Claiborne. Julia Claiborne, yes," said Danny, gritting his teeth. "What you tell us now can still save their lives, Morgan."

"That's the thing, they didn't even seem like they were in danger."

"How did they look? Did they even look afraid?"

"I didn't see them. He told them both to wait at the door while he pulled me out of their line of sight. And when he let them in, he ushered them down the hallway to the bathroom, shielding their eyes like it was a game or something." She wiped her eyes with the tissue. "He was careful not to let them see me, because then, of course, they might have freaked out. But he made the call, the one you're talking about, in this room, with the kids. They never knew I was here. At one point, the girl, Julia, she asked whose house this was, and he said . . ." She closed her eyes, opened them. "He said, *some nice lady's house.* She's letting us use her phone. All while I'm tempted to scream behind the tape over my mouth in the next room."

"And why didn't you?"

"He told me he'd put the hammer through my skull if I made a sound," she said, sniffling. "He said, don't make me snap. *Don't make me snap and do the bad thing.*"

"The bad thing?"

"That's what he said."

Just like he'd said over the phone about Tess's parents at the cabin.

"He was so strange, Detective. He was so big. I thought he was going to kill me. Even when he was being nice."

"But you're sure it was a boy and a girl?"

"Yes, I distinctly heard both. I should have screamed anyway."

"And then you'd be dead, Morgan, and he would still have the children, and you wouldn't be giving me this valuable information. You got it? Tell me you understand that or I'm not leaving."

She nodded.

"Good. Now after the call, what happened?"

"The kids seemed agitated. Maybe it was the girl who'd begun to whimper a little. I could hear the yelling over the phone. Her parents, I assume. I could tell the man was getting anxious. So he tried to calm the kids down. Said something about not listening to the devil's voice. And that he hoped he was doing the right thing because the paint was already squeezed from the tube, and he couldn't put it back in." She lowered her head between her knees, like she might get sick.

"Morgan, stay with me. You okay? You need to—"

She sat up again. "I'm fine. Nausea. I don't know what he was talking about, paint out of the tube, or what, maybe what's done can't be undone, but he was good with them. I'll say that much. He was gentle with them."

"And next?"

"He told them to play the statue game. To wait where they were and to not move a muscle. Then he came back into the kitchen. I thought he was gonna kill me right then, but instead he knelt beside my chair. I'm literally about to piss my pants, and he put his lips to my ear and asks for an iPhone charger. A *charger*. I mean, really? I pointed with my head where one was plugged into the wall next to the counter, and he took it. Not before plugging it in, though. He took the kids back out to the car and then came back for his phone and the charger. I mean he comes into my house because his phone died? *Really?*" She started crying again, angrily snatching another tissue from the box.

Danny put his arm around her shoulders and gave her a side hug—she needed it. He released his grip on her before he started in with *his* emotions. He was the professional here. He was also too close to the case, but wasn't about to step aside like he'd demanded of Tess. He handed Morgan his card and asked her to call if anything else came to her or if she just needed to talk.

"Detective Gomes? There's something else."

Danny stopped at the door, turned toward Morgan Sample, who was standing now. "Before he left with the kids," she said. "Julia . . . she asked him where they were going now. He said the playhouse."

"The playhouse?"

"Yeah. Somewhere called the playhouse."

CHAPTER

16

Tess hadn't eaten all day. She hadn't had time, and truthfully felt too nauseous to even try.

Eliza had raided their fridge and pantry and put together a quick meal of pasta and marinara sauce with garlic bread, and insisted Tess try and eat, but not much got past the lump in her throat. She nibbled the bread, managed to get down a few rotini corkscrews, but then gave up.

Eliza didn't fight her on it—she'd barely touched her food either. "Maybe it was the smell I was going after? It smells good in here, right? Like an Italian restaurant?"

"It smells fine," said Tess, staring down the hallway from the kitchen.

Julia's bedroom was visible from her angle at the kitchen table. Dolly leaned against the footboard of the bed, Minnie Mouse on the bedspread. Barbie dolls on the floor next to scattered Legos. Justin didn't like Julia playing with Barbies; he didn't like the body image most of them portrayed. Tess hadn't disagreed but had given in one day when she'd needed a win.

Eliza watched her. She finished her glass of white zinfandel, stood abruptly from the table, walked into the hallway, and closed Julia's door. Tess was taken aback, not knowing how to interpret that.

Eliza sat back down. "She's not a memory, Tess."

Tess looked away. "I know."

"I don't like that look in your eyes. That's a give-up look." Eliza gripped her hand across the table. "Danny's gonna find her, Tess. You hear me? Look at me." Tess did, right into Eliza's brown trusting eyes. "We'll have her back in that room, sleeping and playing. All the kids here making their normal ruckus. Right back to annoying us with their noise like they always do. You can count on that."

Tess nodded, took her hand back, tried another bite of her food, and smiled. "It's good."

"You don't have to eat it." Eliza wasn't a bad cook, it's just that Danny was better, and when he was home, did most of it. Eliza took both of their plates and moved them next to the sink. "You always eat like a bird anyway." She looked over her shoulder toward Tess. "How about you get some rest. Go lie down. I'll clean up."

Tess stood. "I've got work to do."

"Then go work," Eliza said. "Don't just sit there like a zombie. You're at your best when you're getting something done." She waved a hand toward the living room, where she knew Tess liked to work, her papers strewn out on the coffee table in front of the couch. "Shoo, fly." Before Tess made it to the door, Eliza said, "Hey . . ." She caught her gaze again. "My Danny will find her. You got that? She's his goddaughter. He'll bust down walls, Tess. He'll knock down buildings. He'll find her."

Tess forced a smile and left the room, knowing if she didn't the tears would start up again. Eliza's eyes had begun to glaze, and not much got her going more easily than when Eliza cried, not something she typically did. At least not in front of anyone else. Danny called her a robot when it came to those kind of emotions—he was typically the crier in the family—but when Eliza cried, they all felt it. What she saw daily as a social worker almost made their work pale in comparison.

Tess moved to the living room with her glass of wine, hoping, for now, that Eliza wouldn't follow her. When she heard dishes being cleaned in the kitchen, Tess sat on the couch and opened her father's briefcase, taking special care to remove all the papers and files and newspaper clippings and organize them on the coffee table in front of her. In a world of forensics and technology and computers that had largely passed him by, by the time he'd retired from the force, his briefcase was always his stubborn way of clinging to the past. He'd used that briefcase since his first day on the job back in Twisted Tree.

And now it was hers.

She swallowed half of her glass of wine in one gulp, but that did little to calm her shaking hands, that subtle tremor she'd felt coursing through her body like a live wire ever since the Outcast's phone call at the station. She knew what would calm it, knew it to a certainty because she wasn't so far removed from that year of dependency that her mind wasn't right now salivating for the pills inside her pocket. She swallowed the rest of her wine, forced a couple of deep breaths, and willed her mind to focus.

She shifted her legs and accidentally kicked something on the carpet.

On the floor, next to her right foot, was a bracelet made of plastic emojis—little yellow faces laughing and smiling and wide-eyed—that Julia had made from a kit Tess had bought for her while they were at Target together a month ago, giving in to her daughter when Julia had flashed that *please, just this once* smile Justin always fell for. Tess had given in that day because, even though the event between her husband and that other woman hadn't yet occurred, Tess had been sensing for months that it maybe could, and she was distracted by it and overeager in that moment to get on her own daughter's good side because she was sensing things going south. And that Justin wasn't the only parent who could spoil their daughter.

She'd even gotten Julia ice cream that day after leaving the parking lot, and then fixed her favorite meal—chicken tenders and mashed potatoes—like it was her birthday when it wasn't, all because she was tired of being the second option of only two. The least favored parent. All because she was jealous of another woman. Jealous that she knew how much her husband was coveted by another woman. Jealous because she'd had the irrational thought—no, a sudden image that had hit her like a lightning strike right there in the store's checkout lane while staring at a box of breath mints—of that other woman one day flashing that pretty smile at Julia like *she* was her mother. because her real mother was too busy and distracted.

It had been nonsensical. Irrational, perhaps.

But was it really out of the realm of possibility?

Justin was a catch, and, over the years, she'd practically let him go. Not so much thrown him back, but damn close, with the lack of attention she'd shown him.

It was just that that coworker—Tess refused to say her name—had been in too many of his stories from school. Too many of his stories from their after-school drinks. And she didn't like the way Justin unconsciously grinned whenever *her* name came out of his mouth. She didn't like the way that woman looked at him at any of their work get-togethers, how she was younger and childless and unattached and seemingly unburdened by life, while Tess rarely felt *un*affected by the constant weight of it, and sometimes, on bad days, fully buried beneath it.

You have holes, Justin liked to tell her. *In your memory, Tess. You're hiding something. You're hiding pain, Tess, and you won't open up. You never open up to me.*

She couldn't deny that; in fact, she'd done him one better and over the years had begun to not only *not* open up but to shut him out because of it.

And once you started shutting someone out, to close someone out emotionally, the door was much more easily closed completely than reopened.

Focus, Tess. Focus.

She lifted the Julia-made emoji bracelet from the carpet and slid it onto her wrist, and the feeling of it immediately gave her strength, a connection that was more than the slight physical weight of it on her arm, but an embodiment of *she loves you, Tess, and she knows you love her.*

She does.

She does, as Eliza had told her repeatedly upon their embrace earlier in the foyer, when Tess had given way to her tears and told her friend that she and Julia had clashed last night over a game of checkers.

A game of checkers, Eliza, that I wouldn't allow her to play because she needed to go to bed.

Tess put her face in her hands, rubbed her eyes, and exhaled tension. Her cell phone buzzed with an incoming call. She found herself hoping it was Justin—none of them knew where he'd gone after leaving the cabin—but saw it was Danny.

"Any news?" she asked immediately.

"No, sorry. Well, maybe, I don't know. I just left Morgan Sample's house. She's safe. He broke in, tied her up, just to use her phone."

"Julia was with him?"

"Both kids. According to Ms. Sample they didn't even seem scared. It's bizarre, I know, but that's at least some kind of a lifeline to hold onto, Tess. But she said he mentioned taking them somewhere called the Playhouse."

"The Playhouse?"

"I don't know anything more than that. Just thought you needed to know."

"You heard from Justin?"

"No, I haven't," he said, sternly enough for her to drop that line of conversation. "But I heard from Givens. Noah Nichols can no longer be a suspect."

"Why not?"

"He's in a hospital for the criminally insane, in Twisted Tree, Kentucky."

My hometown . . .

"Tess, how are you holding up?"

"How do you think I'm holding up, Danny?"

"I know, stupid question, just thought it needed to be asked. What's Eliza doing?"

"Dishes."

"Give her a kiss for me."

"Will do."

He hung up.

Tess dropped the phone on the couch cushion.

Eliza appeared in the entrance to the living room, leaning against the threshold with her arms folded. "Was that Danny?"

"Yeah, nothing much new." Tess puckered her lips and made an air kiss in Eliza's direction.

"What was that for?"

"That was from Danny."

"Nice," Eliza said. She looked over her shoulder, toward the hallway, toward Julia's closed bedroom door. "You mind if I open up that door again?"

"I'm not the one who closed it."

"Yeah, true," said Eliza, as if contemplating. "I think it's better open." Tess nodded, and Eliza migrated down the hallway, opened Julia's door, and then disappeared into the bathroom next to it, where Tess, a few seconds later, heard crying.

Something about hearing Eliza's tears—and the fact that she felt she needed to have them in private—coupled with the paperwork and evidence and files inside her father's briefcase made Tess so overwhelmed that she felt a panic attack coming.

Just do it, Tess.

That's why you grabbed them from the medicine cabinet.

She pulled the hydrocodone bottle from her pocket for the third time since she'd returned from the cabin, hating how just holding it instantly made her feel better, calmer, that rush of . . . of . . .

Of nothing, Tess. That's what you want. You want to feel nothing. Anything besides the serrated torture ripping through the very core of you.

This time, with Eliza in the bathroom, she opened it and no longer had the courage to resist. After staring at the contents of the full bottle for what seemed like an eternity, she popped one in her mouth and buried the bottle back in her pocket. Sweating now, because shame strikes immediately. It doesn't have to wait to enter the bloodstream because it was already in there lurking.

She thought of Justin all those years ago, holding her hair away from her face and rubbing her back as she hurled into the toilet for days, detoxing twelve months of pain pills, of poison, from her system. An addiction she'd managed to keep from her father, who maybe should have picked up on things, or maybe he did, but out of regret and his own shame at not protecting her enough when she was a girl had turned a blind eye. An addiction she'd managed to keep from her two best friends. She said *I'm sorry* in her head, maybe to her father, maybe to Eliza and Danny, maybe to Justin and Julia, but mostly to herself. She crunched it to get the drug into her system faster and washed the bitter remnants down with the saliva in her mouth.

Just something to take her away for a bit. Take the edge off.

She closed her eyes and took enough deep breaths to calm her heart, and with each beat it slowed; with each tick of the wall clock behind her, the drug seeped more thoroughly into her bloodstream. She opened her eyes, more ready to work now. More ready to face the nightmare. She leaned forward, scanning her father's notes, found an article dating back to 1989, about a sex abuse scandal with the Roman Catholic Church in Newfoundland, Canada. That didn't fit this case; Tess set it aside.

Jeff Pritchard wasn't a priest. He only pretended to be. She reached for notes from the inventory her father had taken from Pritchard's house the day after his arrest.

. . . Behind the stage in the basement was a door leading to a hidden room with no overhead light. After busting the lock on the door, we found a framed reprint of Leonardo da Vinci's Last Supper hanging on one wall, along with a book of da Vinci's artwork on the floor. The other three walls were filled with pencil sketches, mural paintings, expertly done. The inside of the door had hundreds of scratches that we believe to be made by fingernails . . .

Tess blinked through sudden bleariness; the pills were hitting fast.

Shame weighed heavy.

Not for the first time, she considered forcing herself to throw up, to get the pill back out of her body, but she knew it was too late.

She spotted one of Julia's hair barrettes on the end table, and a memory of Justin braiding her hair hit her like a tsunami, the time he spent getting it right when Tess would always hurry through it.

Focus, Tess.

Blurry-eyed now, she looked down at her father's notes.

Jeff Pritchard. Born Anthony Jeff Pritchard, on April 25, 1967, in Bowling Green, Kentucky. Raised Catholic. Altar boy at age ten. A loner . . .

The next paper she grabbed from the briefcase was her father's interview with a Bowling Green veterinarian from nearly two decades ago. She read about Pritchard holding his first dog as the vet put him down, and then his subsequent involvement with euthanizing so many other suffering animals. These wounded wanderers, he called them.

How did that compassion turn into something so much worse?

Is this how it all started?

No, it started earlier than that. She rooted through the briefcase. Where was her father's interview with the nun from the orphanage?

She picked up an old article from the *Bowling Green Daily News*, with the headline—*Mother and Father Killed in House Fire*. She already knew that Pritchard's parents were both killed in a fire, and that it had made him an orphan in his early teens. And that although it was never proven, many suspected Jeff's involvement in starting the fire that destroyed his childhood home.

Are we born evil or made that way?

A question she'd once asked her father, to which he'd gone off on a tangent on nature and nurture and how'd he'd seen enough of both over his years on the job to never truly know.

But what made Father Silence tick?

Tess rested back on the couch, closed her eyes as her head began to swim.

She knew how it ended. Four children were found dead in his basement, minutes after their deaths by poisoning—hydrocyanic acid mixed with wine. Initially, they'd thought it was some kind of morbid rendition of the Last Supper, possibly to match the painting on the wall of that hidden room. Another theory was that Pritchard had poisoned them in a panic, knowing the authorities were on the way. The cyanide had killed them quickly, with Noah Nichols the only one to survive. They'd found him hiding in a dark corner of the basement. All the kids had been branded at some point with an upside-down cross on the underside of their right forearms, apparently early in their captivity, because the burns had already begun to heal. Many books had been written on how it ended, but much of the in-between had been speculation by too many writers and wannabes hoping to scratch out a few months of fame. The *real* in-between, Tess realized, was inside this briefcase, because there was much more than she knew inside it. Much more than she'd remembered, because it seemed Daddy hadn't stopped searching for the *why*, even after Jeff Pritchard was caught and arrested and sentenced to death. Her father had kept his foot on the gas because he simply had to know. There was plenty here for Detective Leland Patterson to have written numerous bestsellers on the subject—and publishers had come after him in swarms, for a time—but he'd always refused. He'd always been so adamant that those tragedies *not* be made commercial, at least not by him, which Tess thought ironic, seeing how many true crime books her father read.

He was just hell-bent on never writing his own. And the same went for his partner, Detective Burt Lobell.

But for lack of a better place to store such valuable details, the contents of this briefcase *were* his laptop. This was his hard drive, and now, any other memories he might have had and hadn't written down had died with him.

Tess closed her eyes, welcomed the warmth blooming across her chest. The hydrocodone had entered her bloodstream. Her head was heavy, yet somehow weightless and full of clarity. Tears pooled in her eyes as thoughts of her father and mother hit her. She'd been so preoccupied with finding Julia that she'd never grieved her parents.

Yet all she could hear now was her father's voice telling her to focus on the one who was still alive. Focus on his granddaughter and grieve for them later, because that's exactly what he would have said.

"Jeff Pritchard was an outcast, too, like those kids he kidnapped," she said aloud.

"Who?"

Tess opened her eyes.

Standing next to her now, Eliza swam in and out of focus. "Father Silence." Tess sat up straight, rubbed her eyes, did her best to appear lucid. "He believed he was helping those children." She blinked hard, but blurry light still encircled her vision. Shrinking and expanding. She felt content but had no reason to be. "He put them down like dogs."

Eliza sat beside her. "Tess, you okay? You don't look good."

She leaned back, closed her eyes, nodded. "I feel good." Eliza put an arm around her. Tess leaned her head on Eliza's shoulder, and tried not to think of where Julia might be heading, to some place called the Playhouse. "Stay with me tonight."

Eliza said, "I'm not going anywhere."

Minutes later, thinking about the fire that burned down Jeff Pritchard's childhood home, Tess drifted off.

Before

FROM DETECTIVE LELAND Patterson's interview with Roger Pin-ichi, retired Fire and Rescue Chief, Bowling Green, Kentucky.

>   **Detective Patterson:** *So you didn't immediately suspect foul play when you got the call that the Pritchard's house was burning?*
>   **Pinichi:** *No, I usually liked to go into a thing thinking the best of people, you know? Like something electrical. Or maybe a grease fire. Something accidental.*
>   **Detective Patterson:** *And that changed when?*
>   **Pinichi:** *When we finally put the fire out and got inside the place.*
>   **Detective Patterson:** *And discovered it was arson?*
>   **Pinichi:** *Bedrooms were on the second floor. The fire started inside the parents' bedroom. They were burnt to a crisp, so you tell me. Mom and dad Pritchard. Their wrists and ankles, all blackened and charred, handcuffed to the bedposts.*
>   **Detective Patterson:** *And Jeff? He was, what, thirteen at the time? Where was he?*
>   **Pinichi:** *Found him out there in his weird little pet cemetery, watching the house burn.*
>   **Detective Patterson:** *He didn't phone it in?*
>   **Pinichi:** *No, a neighbor did, when they saw the smoke.*

Detective Patterson: And Jeff? What kind of shape was he in?

Pinichi (shaking his head): Weirdly calm. Face blackened from smoke, though, like he'd maybe gone back in there. I don't know. Entire night was strange. He didn't say much, but a couple of times he did say that he couldn't find the keys.

Detective Patterson: To the handcuffs?

Pinichi: I can only assume. Which was what saved him, in my opinion, from being charged with double murder. That, and the only prints found on what was left of the cuffs, belonged to the parents. Of course, the boy could have been wearing gloves, but who really knows. But all that, coupled with the tapes they found inside the chest at the foot of the bed . . ."

Detective Patterson: What tapes we talking about?

Pinichi: Ones that showed their true colors. Ones that got a little hinky, and word of that spread quicker around town than the fire did. I'll cut to the chase, Detective. Mom and dad Pritchard had at least three dozen sex tapes they'd made inside that bedroom, and most of them involved some kind of bondage. Handcuffs were commonly used. Same handcuffs we found on their corpses. Room full of candles. They'd light them ceremonially, each time, before they'd, you know, start into it . . .

Detective Patterson: And you think Jeff was aware of all this?

Pinichi: I would assume, especially at his age. No telling what the boy had seen and heard by that point.

Detective Patterson: And he was smart enough to know his defense was locked away in that porn chest.

Pinichi: And he was never charged. I'm sure he did it, though, Detective. Might not have said much that night and in the days that followed. And by that time, he'd been taken in by the Sisters of Mercy, down the street here. I'd go knock on their door next. Heard things maybe got a little weird there too before he left town. But that night, when we found him watching from the pet cemetery, if you would have seen the proud look in his eyes . . .

Detective Patterson: Oh, I've seen plenty of his eyes.

Pinichi: Then you know what I'm getting at.

Detective Patterson: They're hollow. Nothing in them.

Pinichi: Unless by nothing you mean the lack of something.

Detective Patterson: Like remorse?

Pinichi: Bingo.

17

M<small>OMMY . . .</small>

Tess opened her eyes to a dark living room. Her head felt muddled and thick. The wall clock above the television showed three thirty in the morning. Eliza snored beside her, both of them covered by a blanket she didn't remember grabbing from the closet. She sat up quickly, too quickly—a headache rolled in like an ocean tide. Car headlights flashed across the wall. Something crunched outside, screeched, and garbage cans rolled across the driveway.

Tess leaned over the couch, parted the drapes. "Shit." She nudged Eliza, hard. "It's Justin. Get up."

Eliza sat up, groggy. She looked out.

Justin's Ford Explorer had stopped with the front wheels in the neighbor's grass. His door flew open. Justin stumbled out, called Tess's name, and then fell in the mud. Cameras flashed. More vehicles than she had initially seen lined the street, vans and news crews from all the local stations and newspapers, waiting in the dark.

Tess tossed aside the blanket and hurried from the living room, nearly running into Danny, who'd appeared from the kitchen. They were each startled to see the other. "When did you get here?" she asked her partner.

"Couple hours ago," he said, yawning. "I've been working in the kitchen."

He must have seen them sleeping on the couch and covered them with the blanket.

Danny beat her to the front door, opening it just as Justin stumbled up the steps to the porch. Cameras flashed. Reporters closed in.

Tess slammed the door on their questions. "Justin, you're drunk."

"Yup." His eyes were red, his hair disheveled. Eliza appeared in the hallway with them. Justin eyed the three of them with suspicion. "What's going on?"

Tess said, "Nothing's going on."

Justin's eyes were wet, he'd been crying. She'd seen him tipsy too many times to count, drunk every so often, but never this spooked and irrational and wide-eyed.

He screamed, "What is this? Some kind of intervent—"

Danny's fist came out of nowhere, colliding with the side of Justin's right cheek, spinning his best friend into the wall.

Tess screamed.

Eliza shouted, "Danny!"

Danny flexed his fingers like it had hurt him too, a bit panicked himself now, like he didn't know where that sudden burst of violence had come from.

Justin moaned on the floor, covering his nose with fingers now running with blood.

Danny left them in the hallway.

Eliza watched him go, then returned her gaze to Justin and Tess.

Justin blinked, "He broke my nose."

At least he sounded less drunk now, Tess thought, like Danny had somehow punched the alcohol right out of his bloodstream. Or at least, some sense into him.

Tess knelt before her husband and tried not to judge how pathetic he looked. "Where have you been?"

"At the bar?"

"And that's it?"

"Yeah . . . where else—" He stopped there, shook his head. "Tess, come on. I told you . . ."

Yes, you did, she thought, helping him straighten against the wall, wishing she'd never brought it up. "Never mind," she said, and by the smell of his clothes, she believed him.

Eliza hurried back into the hallway with a wet towel from the bathroom.

Tess used it to soak up and dab at the blood on Justin's face.

"I'm sorry," Justin mumbled.

"It's okay," she told him.

"I'm serious, Tess. I'm so sorry."

"Justin, can you shut up for a minute."

"Yeah, I'll shut up."

"And how about answer your damn phone from now on?" She gently wiped his face, ran a hand through his hair, whispered that it was all going to be okay, even though she felt helpless herself, still calm, only because of the hydrocodone in her own bloodstream.

Maybe that's why she wasn't judging him.

He nodded, closed his eyes, opened them when Danny came back into the hallway. He flinched when Danny hunkered down, like he thought he might get another punch, but Danny held a bag of ice instead.

"Put it on there," Danny said, staring at his friend with what looked like a mixture of pity and sorrow and love. "Caught you pretty good."

"What was that for?" Justin asked, holding the bag of ice.

Danny pointed at the ice. "Put it on your face." He stood from his crouch. "I don't know. I've been wanting to punch you for weeks. You fucked up our Friday night get-togethers, Justin. There, I got it out of my system." His phone rang. When he pulled it out of his pocket, he mouthed that it was Chief Givens, and then took it in the other room.

Eliza stood shell-shocked—she had an accurate radar for bad news, and Tess felt it too. She helped Justin from the floor, and the three of them followed Danny into the kitchen, where he mostly nodded, listened, asked a few questions Tess couldn't make out, and then ended the call.

Tess said, "What happened?"

"Your hunch with Twisted Tree was correct . . . Burt Lobell was murdered four hours ago."

Tess's knees buckled, but she straightened before all the blood could run from her face. "Dad's old partner. They arrested Pritchard together."

Justin seemed to sober another notch. "The MO?"

"Similar, but not the same." Danny pointed at Justin. "Keep the ice on there. Knife wound across the neck this time, fatal. No hammer. Like here, the eyes were closed and painted black. And he was strapped to a chair facing an old article on Silence's arrest."

"Pinned to the wall?"

Danny nodded. "By the murder weapon. Carving knife."

"Two different states," Justin said. "Two sides of the country."

"We checked the airport," Danny said. "A flight left here yesterday around two. Landed at Louisville International in plenty of time."

Tess asked, "Did you check the passenger logs? We had police at the airport. How did he get past them?"

"We're on it, Tess. And I don't know. So far no one at the airport has seen anyone resembling that sketch. Or the kids."

"Two killers," Justin said.

"We don't know that." Danny wiped his face, looking as exhausted as Tess felt. "Although this one was bloodier. Lobell's blood was used to decorate the walls. Don't know all the details, but Givens said it was some sacrilegious shit."

A thought struck Tess in an instant.

Danny saw it: "Tess, what is it?"

"When he called in his crime from the cabin," she said. "He stammered. He said I did the bad thing, but before he said *I* he said *we*. Like he corrected himself."

"Different MOs," Justin said. "Two killers."

Danny patted Justin's shoulder. "I won't rule it out."

Tess said, "Danny, get us the first flight out in the morning."

Justin watched her. "Tess, we can't do that."

"If he's not there already," she said, "I'd bet my life that's where he's going."

"Givens said no."

"Fuck Givens."

"And Julia?"

"I'll be here," Eliza said. "I'll be here."

Danny exhaled, wiped his face. "He's got me a flight already. What you do with your free time I guess is up to you."

"He can't stop me from going home," Tess pointed out.

"No. I suppose he can't."

18

T HEY WERE RUNNING on fumes and occasional bursts of adrenaline.

Danny, after assuring them he'd sneaked in thirty minutes of sleep at the kitchen table before Justin made his memorable arrival in the middle of the night, took off for the police station in hopes of solidifying jurisdiction logistics and his travel plans to Louisville in the morning. He promised to say nothing to Chief Givens of Tess and Justin's plans to accompany him. Now that it appeared the murders had crossed state lines, the FBI would be moving in. Danny would have as long a leash as they allowed him, but since the authorities in Kentucky had requested a representative from the crime scene here, it appeared he would at least have a leash with which to work.

As soon as Danny left for the police station, Eliza fixed a pot of coffee and insisted Tess and Justin drink up. First task would be getting Justin sober, and Tess needed the caffeine as well.

She'd secured seats for herself and Justin on the flight to Louisville that Danny had booked. From there it would be a thirty-minute drive east to Twisted Tree. Tess was confident that they were chasing the correct angle, and knew that just because a second murder was committed across the country didn't mean Julia had been taken across state lines. But the feeling in her gut, perhaps linked to blocked memories from her past at Twisted Tree, was strong. She'd contact whoever they needed back home to pave her way—but she was coming with or without clearance.

The FBI had arrived in Missoula and agreed that there was more than likely a second killer. What had the FBI puzzled, like everyone involved, was that the boy kidnapped from the children's home in Boise, and now missing with Julia, had no connection, as far as they could tell, to anyone linked to Jeff Pritchard, Leland Patterson, Burt Lobell, or anyone involved with Father Silence.

So far, Tess thought.

At least the boy, Danny had said—unlike Julia—fit the bill for what Jeff Pritchard would have considered an outcast of society.

But Julia did not, and Tess couldn't get past that.

Her daughter was loved. She was wanted.

But this Outcast, she thought. There's no way he could have made it through the airports, and with the timing of the stolen Jetta found in the ravine near the college, no way he could have stolen another vehicle and driven to Twisted Tree to kill Burt Lobell.

Tess sat at the kitchen table with her hands wrapped around a hot cup of coffee Eliza had just poured her. Across the table, Justin had already downed two cups, and she could tell he was beginning to get his head straight.

Tess still felt the lingering effects of the hydrocodone she'd taken. She chuckled without thinking, and both Justin and Eliza gave her looks that said *What?* It was just that her father had always been so damn stubborn. Refusing to take those pills after his surgery simply because he'd been told to. She wished she'd had his strength. But for now, his stubbornness was her gain. She looked at it as his way of helping her from the grave.

Enabling her one last time.

Treating her like that soft pillow when she'd always pretended to be bedrock.

Like him.

After all these years, she now wondered if he'd known. Known something even she couldn't remember from her childhood. What Justin too often said she'd intentionally locked away.

Things had gotten so weird before they'd left Twisted Tree.

They'd fled after the bodies of those two high school boys had been discovered in the woods, Grisham Graham and Jeremy Shakes, stars from her school's football team. Both murdered. Blows to the head. Less than a mile from what the papers had for weeks been calling Father Silence's "House of Horrors."

Was it all connected?

What did it have to do with her? Could she have been involved somehow, seen or heard something? She'd been inside that house, but why?

She remembered homicide detectives—not her father or Burt Lobell—knocking on their door, speaking to her father, speaking to her. She didn't know what they were talking about. She'd barely known those boys, other than seeing them in the hallways at school. Fingerprints? What fingerprints? Words were exchanged upon their departure and things got heated.

We fled.

What did I do?

Nothing, sugar. You did nothing.

The counselor they'd made her see upon their arrival in Montana had smelled like mint. She chewed gum to mask the smell of her cigarettes. Tess had pretended to make progress, and eventually those meetings ended.

She'd continued to steal sips of Daddy's bourbon. She'd continued to look for ways to cope. To bury that deep splinter even deeper.

Tess started crying again.

Eliza grabbed her hand, squeezed it; she'd been quicker on the draw than Justin across the table. Sometime soon they'd have to bury both of her parents, but she couldn't think of that now. Not while Julia was missing. Stress from splitting up now seemed infinitely small in comparison. *Stupid even.* Tess squeezed Eliza's hand back, her way of telling her she was better now, and her friend took the hint and let go. Truthfully, she just didn't want to be touched. By anyone. She felt dirty. She was glad Eliza had come over, and was still here after Danny left, because she wasn't yet ready to be left alone with Justin, who suddenly looked pale and stood quickly. He hurried down the hallway to the bathroom and slammed the door. A toilet seat clanked and a second later she heard him throwing up, violently ridding himself of what was left of the alcohol he'd consumed earlier.

Eliza closed her eyes as if she was about to get sick as well, but opened them with what Tess thought looked like a new resolve, that next-level strength she'd seen her friend pull from whenever her kids began to overwhelm her. Or when her mentally taxing job as a social worker hinted at grinding her down. Eliza nodded toward the hallway, where they could both hear Justin being sick behind the closed bathroom door. "Should I go check on him?"

"No. Let him get it out." Tess sipped her coffee, watched her friend stare blankly across the kitchen, her mind probably running while Tess wrangled with thoughts of her own. "I shut him out, Eliza."

"Shut who out?"

Tess nodded down the hallway. "Justin. You know him. Needs to know everything about everyone."

"I call it nosy."

"Which is also why he's good at what he does."

"True."

Tess drank more coffee, stared down the hallway. "Eventually it got to the point where I gave him nothing. None of what he wanted anyway."

"Like?"

"My thoughts."

"None of his business."

"Some of his business, I guess. It is a marriage. And too often, silence speaks louder than any words. The unsaid breeds contempt."

"Tess, where's this coming from?"

"We had a miscarriage," she said. "Two years after Julia."

Eliza's eyes were full of emotion, and if Tess read it correctly, she saw sorrow and hurt and empathy—she and Danny had had one of their own, in between kids three and four. The hurt may have stemmed from the fact that she and Justin had never told them. Their closest friends, to whom they typically told everything.

And then Eliza asked it: "Why didn't you tell us?"

"I don't know," she said. "Justin wanted to. I just couldn't get past the fact that maybe I'd done something to cause it."

"That's not how it works, Tess," Eliza said. "Unless . . . you did . . . something?"

Tess shook her head. "No, of course not."

"Had you all been trying?"

"Yeah, it wasn't an accident, if that's what you're getting at. But I wasn't as gung-ho as Justin was. He wanted another one so badly."

"And you didn't?"

"Not really, no. I know that sounds selfish, but . . ."

"Not selfish," Eliza said. "Just being true to yourself."

"I always felt like I let him down. Justin. It's just nothing we ever discussed. Not like most couples do. Newlyweds. Kids, you know? How many and what not. And all of a sudden, early on, he says he wanted four. I thought he was joking, but he wasn't. And when he noticed how horrifying that thought was to me, I could tell he was wounded. Like I'd just shot down one of his lifelong dreams. I didn't want to become a baby factory."

Eliza said, "No offense taken."

"No, I mean . . . I'm sorry. I didn't mean that."

"I'm joking," Eliza said. "I'm Catholic. *Too* Catholic, you might say. Stupid birth control dilemma. Yadayadayada . . . Tess, *all* our kids were accidents." Tess smiled, finished her coffee. Eliza leaned forward. "And all that shit we talked in the past, getting on the two of you about having another one, about catching up to us like it was all some stupid contest, I'm sorry. Jesus, I'm sorry."

"Eliza, you don't need to apologize. It was all good-hearted, we know that," Tess said. "But he kept on me. He was sweet. He gave me time after the miscarriage. It hit us both hard. Although I could never get past the notion that we'd lost it because deep down I wasn't ready for a second one."

"Again, not how it works."

"I know that, but our brains . . ."

"Yeah, they go to crazy places."

"For a while we tried again," Tess said. "But I was secretly on the pill."

"He didn't know?"

"Hence the word secret, Eliza."

"Damn."

"I know, I'm going to hell."

"You're not going to hell, Tess. At least not for that."

That got another smile out of Tess, however brief. "Guilt got to me. I went back off it. Playing with fire, you might say, at least in my mind. And then over time he started giving up hope. It became too much of a chore. We stopped talking about it. Eventually, I'd . . ."

"You what?"

"Before his . . ."

"Affair," Eliza said. "Say it. He had an affair."

"We hadn't . . . had sex, for months. Six months, maybe."

"*Don't make excuses for him,*" Eliza said. "Stop. I still love Justin, but I'm glad Danny punched him. So stop."

"But it's never just one person's fault, right?"

"Did you screw what's-her-name?"

"No," Tess said with a chuckle. "Of course not."

"Then stop. He messed up, big time. What happens next might still be up in the air, but stop blaming yourself, Tess." Eliza stood, moved around the table to give Tess a hug. "You want my advice?"

"Yeah."

"Give it some time."

Tess nodded, welcomed her friend's embrace, Eliza's tears on her cheeks. "Eliza, thank you for being here, but go home to your kids.

Tuck them in. Hold them. Wake them all up if you have to, but hold them."

"Fine," she said. "But I'm coming back in the morning. You and Justin go do what you need to do. I'll be here in case anything breaks. In case somebody makes contact." She kissed Tess's cheek and let go. "Now can I tell you a secret?"

Tess looked up at her. "Yeah."

"I had my tubes tied," she said. "But don't tell Danny. And don't tell any of my friends at church either. If you're going to hell, I'll be right there with you. It's all bullshit anyway, right? Our bodies, we do what we want with them. After my last four kids came out C-section, my doc encouraged us to be done, and after Danny one day said we might as well put a zipper where the scar was, I laughed out loud but inside I said okay, I'm done. Not *we're* done, Tess, but *I* was done. Sometimes it's okay for us to have our own thoughts. Thoughts we keep to ourselves. They might think they need to know everything, but they don't."

"Thank you."

Eliza's eyes locked on hers. "You're a good mother, Tess."

Tess nodded but didn't feel it.

Eliza lifted her chin with a bent finger. "You hear me? You're a good mother."

They embraced again, and seconds later they heard Justin retching again down the hallway.

Eliza said, "Good luck with that."

Tess watched Eliza hurry across the lawn to her car, ignoring a reporter who'd gotten out of his car to approach her with questions. Tess closed the door, walked back to the kitchen, where Justin had returned to the table, pale but more put together than he'd been a few minutes ago.

"Better?" Tess asked.

"A little," Justin said. "Eliza leave?"

"Yeah, she'll be back in the morning."

"We really gonna do this?"

"Do what?"

"Fly off."

"Yeah." She sat next to him, gripped his trembling hand. "I think we need to."

"Tess, is this really happening?"

She nodded, bit her lip, squeezed his hand. Her cell phone rang. It was Danny. "Yes?"

"Tess, are you sitting down?"

"What is it, Danny?" She placed her cell on the table and put it on speaker so Justin could hear.

Danny said, "Four more kids have been reported missing back east. All in the past month. One from the Louisville area. One from southern Indiana, right across the Ohio River."

"That's two, Danny."

"And another two from Twisted Tree."

Tess exhaled, forced toughness when all she wanted was to melt. "What do we know about them?"

"All neglected," he said. "The kind of situation where the parents, if you could call them that, weren't even aware they were missing until it had been brought to their attention."

"It doesn't fit."

"What doesn't fit?"

"Julia," said Tess. "She's not like the others."

"I know," Danny said, "I know . . . I'm sorry, Tess."

"Yeah, me too." She ended the call and picked up the phone from the table.

Justin stepped closer, gently gripped her arm, rubbed his thumb against her flesh, not in any kind of sexual way, she could tell, but just the need to touch her. To connect. "We'll find her, Tess. Danny will find her."

She disengaged, not forcefully, but enough to give him pause and not follow her right away as she moved down the hallway toward their bedroom. But when she did hear his footsteps behind her, she quickened her pace, reaching their bedroom before he could enter with her. She slammed the door in his face. Maybe she didn't mean to, maybe she did. She locked it behind her, stood with her back to the door. Justin on the other side pleading for her to let him in. She unbuttoned her blouse and cried. Felt the door vibrating against her shoulder blades every time he knocked against it. She walked away from the door. Her bottle of Old Sam rested on the corner of the dresser from last night. She uncapped it and drank straight from it. A couple of swallows sent fire both down and up. Heat with the aftertaste of butterscotch and oaky spices. She cursed herself, her selfishness.

You need a clear head. Stop.

But she couldn't.

Old Sam bourbon, distilled in her hometown. Tall whiskey trees, fresh water, and limestone creek beds. The smell of the angels' share permeated every nook, cranny, and storefront, it seeped from the woods and aging houses and covered the small distilling town like a warm blanket. The silent rush of the Ohio River. Horse farms and grass so fresh it looked blue.

My Old Kentucky Home.

It wasn't how she planned on returning.

She hadn't planned on returning at all.

She took another swig from the bottle and then placed it back down on the dresser.

Justin knocked on the door again, but with less fight now. He'd always been afraid to push her.

She put the top back on the bottle and wiped her mouth, chest heaving.

She stepped out of her clothes, stood naked for a minute beside the bed, before deciding to take another white pill from the bottle of hydrocodone. She crunched it like candy on her way into the bathroom, wincing from the bitterness as she turned the shower water to near scalding.

The bathroom steamed and she stepped into the spray of water without testing it. Let it burn. Let it be penance for allowing Julia out of her sight, for everything she'd just admitted to Eliza moments ago, for everything she'd done as a teenage girl, all made worse by the fact that she remembered so little of it. She withstood the pain of the scalding water and closed her eyes until her hair was drenched and she couldn't distinguish her tears from all the hot soapy water. She willed the pill into her bloodstream, faster, so that it could mix with the alcohol and really take her mind away.

She grabbed the washrag and scrubbed, hard, washing away dirt she couldn't see because most of it was internal. After twenty minutes the water lost heat. The steam in the room dissipated, cloudy wisps of it slithering out the bathroom door. The water went from warm to cold with little warning, so she turned it off, leaned against the tiled wall, and rested her head against her forearm.

Dizzy.

Tiles bright.

The opiate was working.

The pills were supposed to mask pain, but didn't, not really. They just gave her the needed numbness. She toweled off. Tomorrow she'd be strong. She'd have no more tears left. She slid on a warm bathrobe from the closet in which she and Julia had dripped candle wax onto paper less than twenty-four hours ago. She wobbled toward the bed, using the bedpost for balance as she heard Justin still breathing on the other side of that goddamn door.

As bad as she wanted him to hold her, she kept that door closed and felt her way around the bed for another slug from the bourbon bottle.

Her father. Now Burt Lobell. Both murdered. Revenge killings, plain and simple. No, it was more than that. But she had to warn the others back home.

Through blurred vision she called Danny and waited for him to pick up.

When he did, she closed her eyes to steady herself and reeled off the names that had come to her in the shower. "Jack Findley, Morice Blake . . ."

"Tess, wait, what is this?"

"Just write them down, Danny."

"Tess, you're slurring."

"Jack Findley, Morice Blake . . . M-O-R-I-C-E."

"Slow down."

"Jack Findley."

"Morice Blake," he said. "I got that, go on."

"Steve Stouffer. O-U-F-F-E-R. Richard Masterson." She paused, listening over the phone to his pen scrawl. "Repeat them back to me."

He did.

"They're all in the Twisted Tree area."

"Tess, who are they?"

"They all had a hand in Father Silence's arrest." The room swirled. She closed her eyes, sat on the bed. Had to concentrate to even hold the phone. "All had a hand . . ."

"Tess?"

I was in that kitchen . . . why? "Send word. Protect them." Her eyes popped as another name came through. "Foster Bergman, with one n. Former priest."

"Twisted Tree?"

"Yes . . . have them protected . . ." She ended the call, and her fingers went slack.

The phone dropped to the floor.

She passed out atop the covers.

19

GORDON PUCKETT LIVED for the night. Always had, even as an infant and toddler. *Liked to drive us to the looney bin, Gordo.* His dad said that often when he was alive. *Cry all night, you would.* They made the mistake of getting him out of his crib and letting him play one night, so that became the norm. Easier than listening to him cry. Up until school age, he'd sleep during the day and play at night.

Got us a future gravedigger, his dad would say.

By the time Gordo hit fourth grade his dad had died of a heart attack and his mother had constant bags under her eyes. Two years later Gordo had gone goth—every article of clothing in his closet was black and his skin was about as pale as egg white. Suited him fine, though, unlike high school, which he quit halfway through his junior year. The hours weren't working out and the teachers frowned on him falling asleep in class. One day the principal, having already exhausted his one-on-one meetings with Gordo's mother, called him to the office and suggested he just go. So he did. He took that GED just like he promised and passed with flying colors—he wasn't stupid.

Just that high school didn't have the right hours.

When he saw that advertisement in the *Twisted Tree Gazette* for a nighttime security guard position at the local Crestwood Cemetery, he thought he'd won a lottery. And now, three years later, he told Snakes that he felt like he'd won the lottery all over again. There weren't that many famous people in Twisted Tree, other than the McFees who ran the town's Old Sam Bourbon Distillery, but when Gordo heard that Jeff Pritchard had requested he be buried back in Twisted Tree instead of where he was born, in Bowling Green, Gordo knew that he'd be the one to see him into the ground. He and Snakes. Snakes was a year into the job and kind of a shit-show. He never combed his hair and his breath smelled like a mixture of Hot Chili Fritos and pot. Snakes, who had a wicked collection of poison ones back home in cages, liked to go through the motions, while Gordo took pride in what he did, policing the grounds every night, all those hills and trees and dewy grass lit by moonlight. And never had he been more focused than on this night. They had Father Silence on the winch. The casket looked like any other as it lowered into the gigantic hole they'd dug. Snakes had taken six smoke breaks while Gordon had taken none. Burials like this only came once a lifetime, so he didn't want to cheat it by being apathetic.

One of those silent *burials*, Gordo thought, grinning as the casket hit bottom. He knew this wouldn't be one of those day burials where people gathered to mourn. All that would have showed would have been haters and reporters anyway.

And some of the Lost Children, of course.

That cult he'd just joined, unbeknownst to Momma. He had a brand-new mask at home to prove it—a rubber camel mask that looked real but smelled toxic—and he couldn't wait to get going on things. It all made what he was about to do even more special.

A handful of reporters were out there even now, in the middle of the night, just far enough outside the wrought-iron fence to make Gordo think they were respecting the moment.

"Hurry up and swallow that cigarette, Snakes, and grab a shovel. We don't have all night."

Gordon tossed soil atop the casket and watched it mist down. He loved the sound those first few shovelfuls made atop the wood. Like his dad drumming the tabletop with his fingers whenever he was pondering something. The hole seemed deeper than what they'd usually dig. Maybe he'd done it subconsciously.

"No hole deep enough for this guy," said Snakes.

Bite your tongue, Gordo wanted to say. *Dude was a hero, and he'll be vindicated.*

Snakes started shoveling, and he was quick about it. Like he was nervous the corpse might come jumping out.

"You okay there, Snakes?"

"Fine. Let's just get this over with."

Gordon watched him as they shoveled. "You hear that, Snakes?"

Snakes looked around. "Hear what?"

"Shhh . . . you hear the *silence*?" asked Gordo, stressing that last word, smiling as he plunged the blade into the dirt mound.

"Funny, Gordo. Real funny." Snakes shoveled faster, then looked up. "Some are taking bets he's gonna rise from the dead."

Gordo paused. "Dumbest damn thing I've ever heard, Snakes. You know that, don't you? Dude is deader than a doornail."

"I know," said Snakes. "Rumor has it it took three charges of voltage to end his life on that chair. Like he broke some kind of electric chair record."

Gordo had heard the same, and suddenly didn't feel so talkative anymore. His pace picked up too. They went for ten minutes not talking. Just shoveling and tossing, and as the dirt layers grew atop that casket, the sound it made changed, to the point where now it was just a hollow thud.

20

T ESS DREAMED OF Twisted Tree.
　　Specifically of the two massive trees for which the town had been named back in the 1890s. Two trees that had grown side by side, bark touching up until roughly the four-foot mark, at which point the two trees started to twist into one another, intermingling like braided hair, skyward into a canopy of branches and boughs that seemed to shade the forest for a mile all around it. The branches of the twisted trees dwarfed the old Crawley Mansion beside it, a two-story home built by the town founders—once burned to the ground only to be rebuilt even grander, with wild parties in the Roaring Twenties—that now had stood vacant for decades, with broken windows, a sagging porch, and boards that wept with the winter winds, destroyed for the second time in 1937 when the Ohio overflowed its banks and nearly swallowed the town.

It then became a home of haunts and teenage dares.

Tess, in the days before they'd moved out west, had gone on a dare with a boy into that house. Together they'd run down the dry-rotted porch steps toward those two twisted trees, where so many teens in town had had their first kiss. Even the trees themselves looked to be in a loving embrace, and that night Tess figured the boy would try to plant one on her.

And she let him.

His name was Matt. Or Mike?

She couldn't remember, only that she didn't really like him. She just wanted to see. There was something about those trees that frightened her, something she'd once encountered but buried deep, and she'd had some silly notion that her first kiss would magically unlock it all.

But his overly eager lips had only left her feeling flat and afraid and anxious, and soon after she'd insisted they return home. She felt sorry for the boy; perhaps she'd only used him. Several boys asked her out since their family had become somewhat famous. Father Silence's House of Horrors still stood on the wooded bluff overlooking the river just less than a mile away.

After that first kiss, she remembered the wind gusting, tugging on the low-hanging branches. The moon winking as purple clouds moved across the dark sky. She swore she could feel it watching, that house, that white colonial with the door red as blood, the wraparound porch enclosing it all like an evil grin.

The boy had asked what was wrong after she'd pulled away from that kiss, and she'd told him nothing, but a couple of weeks later her parents moved them out west and tried to convince her it was for the betterment of things. She was relieved even though she pretended not to be, often brooding to show her toughness, and acting as if she regretted being forced to leave her Twisted Tree friends behind, when deep down she'd craved a new start.

Tess, you'll find new friends in Montana, her father told her. *I promise.*

But that was all a smokescreen, because, she thought unbeknownst to her parents, she'd had very few friends left in Twisted Tree.

After what happened—something *must* have happened—she'd slowly pushed her friends away, preferring isolation instead of parties and group trips to the movie theaters.

Maybe that had been the real reason she'd agreed to come back out to the twisted trees next to the Crawley Mansion, in the hopes her memory might come back to her.

But no dice.

And truth be told she was glad to get away.

Start anew.

Tess didn't understand a lot of things—as Justin, nowadays, sometimes said, her memory had holes—but she understood enough to know back then that she'd never want to return to that town.

Or to those twisted trees.

To those memories she'd buried so long ago.

*   *   *

Tess awoke with a gasp.

Her heart hammered as a vision floated away, but not fast enough.

Two endless trees coiled into one another.

Lightning flashed, revealing a pair of eyes that couldn't be real.

A hammer gripped tightly.

A name on the tip of her tongue. *Amy Dupree. Don't tell, Amy. Don't tell.*

And then it was gone.

Tess was alone again in her bedroom, with morning only a few ticks away.

Ready to face it now—the day and what it held—she dressed quickly and opened the bedroom door.

Justin was on the hallway floor, curled up like a kid and sleeping with his head on a balled-up jacket.

She nudged him gently with her foot. His eyes opened.

"Come on," she said. "Jump in the shower. We've got a plane to catch."

"Tess, don't get on that plane."

"Sorry, Chief."

"Let Louisville handle it," Givens said, the phone connection giving way to static. "Let Danny handle it. We need you here."

"The FBI is here. I'd only get in the way *here*. I'm going home."

"For *vacation* . . ." His voice was loaded with skepticism about the excuse she'd given him as she and Justin moved across the tarmac.

"Yes, a little R and R."

She hung up, promised nothing. She'd already been in touch with the authorities back home and, although reluctant, they were willing to work with her as long as her emotional attachment didn't muddy the waters. They'd warned her she'd be on the periphery, and, as Danny had warned her last night, on a leash even shorter than his.

By the time their plane knifed upward through the clouds and settled into a steady flow above the billows, Tess's head had mostly cleared from the damage she'd done to it the night before. The two cups of coffee she'd had on the way to the airport effectively killed her hangover. She'd tucked the hydrocodone pills into the bottom of her purse, and security, after checking her badge, never searched for anything else.

Justin's nose was swollen and beginning to bruise from Danny's punch, but after a morning shower and a change of clothes, he appeared focused and ready to tackle the day. Right before takeoff, he'd palmed three ibuprofen into his mouth, chugging an entire bottle of water as a chaser. Justin didn't like to fly. In their ten years of marriage, they'd only flown together a handful of times, and he'd been a nervous pain in the ass on each one of them. Whenever he traveled to conferences and seminars, he'd drive, even if it was halfway across the country. She'd kid him about it, and he'd claim to like the open road with U2 and Pearl Jam and REM blaring on the radio, but she knew his fears were real. He had his and she had hers and rationality made no difference in dealing with them.

Their early morning flight was only half booked, and they had the last third of the plane to themselves. Tess and Justin had a seat open between them, with Danny across the aisle, so they had room to spread out papers from Tess's father's briefcase, which she'd divided between the three of them. She refamiliarized herself with a case and investigation she'd become too familiar with as a young girl. Although her father would never let her read much of what he'd put together, he often let her sit beside him as he worked at the dining room table, connecting dots and creating profiles alongside his partner, Burt Lobell, now dead too.

Murdered like her father for the very work they now held in their hands.

Tess had made a list of the names she'd given Danny last night over the phone. She went over it, combing her memory for anyone she may have left off. But she felt confident now the list was complete, and Danny had sent it to the authorities as soon as she'd hung up on him last night. There would be cars waiting for them at Louisville International as soon as they landed.

"Barrett Stevens," Justin said.

Tess looked over. "What about him?"

"Pritchard's old lawyer. Do you think he should be on the list?"

"They were on the same side, Justin. For seventeen years."

Danny added, "He was a defense lawyer just doing his job. Someone had to defend him."

Justin said, "But he failed to win any appeals."

Tess chewed on her pen.

Danny, across the aisle, said, "I agree with Justin, Tess. Barrett Stevens may be gray when the rest are black and white, but we can't afford to take chances."

Tess clicked her pen, added Pritchard's lawyer to the list of people who could be in danger, and made a note to forward it as soon as they landed. The look Justin and Danny shared before nodding in each other's direction spoke volumes. It was more than just the two of them agreeing on something—up until a few weeks ago, they mostly agreed on everything. But it was obvious some hatchet had just been buried, probably with last night's fist to Justin's face.

Tess wished it were that simple, and maybe between men it was. Rough it out and shake hands after.

Maybe if she were to punch him too, her anger would abate, but she didn't think so.

A minute later Justin leaned across the empty seat between them. "Here's an interview your father did with Sarah Nichols, Noah's mother."

Tess took the sheet from Justin, and noticed he had several more like it. "She died three years ago of colon cancer. Dad did this interview over the phone with her, months before she passed."

"Why so long after?" Danny asked.

"Sarah was as crazy as her son," Tess said. "That became clear after the couple of times Dad talked to her after Pritchard's arrest, and after Noah was returned home to his parents. A few years ago, she called Dad out of the blue, told him she was dying and was finally willing to talk. Mom wasn't happy about the call. Dad had gone more than a decade without dealing with anything to do with that case. It shook him for weeks."

Danny leaned closer, pointed to the page in her hand. "Your dad taped it, and then wrote the entire call down freehand?"

"He never liked to type. Refused, rather."

"Why does that not surprise me?" Justin said, reading on. "Sarah and Samson, Noah's father, never wanted a child. Noah was an accident."

"An outcast from the start," said Tess.

"She literally says right here that she never even liked him." Justin pointed to the words. "Or his demons."

"What demons?" Danny asked.

Tess heard him but didn't answer. She was too focused on the notes. "Noah was born during a flooding of the Ohio River. They lived in a trailer along the banks and had to take a ladder to the rooftop to avoid the water." She read aloud from what her father had written. "This is Sarah talking. *'I'll be honest with you. I never wanted that baby. I felt guilty bringing a child into a world so evil. But that morning during the flood I looked upon that child with loving eyes and named him Noah. God sent that baby to protect us from the flood waters.*

Noah's wailing saved us that day. A neighbor down river had a boat and followed the sound of it.'"

Tess looked back to the interview, skimming, paraphrasing out loud. "Samson, the father, never wanted anything to do with the boy. He drank a lot. Physically and maybe even sexually abused Noah for years. Sarah homeschooled him. She said he was just feeling the wrath of planting that wicked seed in her belly."

"She sounds like a lunatic."

"That your professional opinion, Danny?" asked Tess, without looking up from the paper.

Justin unbuckled, scooted to the seat next to Tess, buckled again, and then pointed at the page Tess held. "She says that she and Sampson were so much in love, and then Noah came and dirtied everything up."

Tess turned to the next page, the next few lines. "She thought Noah was possessed by the devil, even *before* he was taken by Pritchard. He had two imaginary friends."

"Called Oskar and Ruth," Justin said, eyeing the page.

"Mean anything to you?"

"Unfortunately, no."

Tess read from the interview again. From Sarah Nichols's own words. "'*Up in his room, he would talk to them. Both of those imaginary friends, and he'd change his voice too. Noah liked to pretend. To make believe. But after he returned from Father Silence, we didn't hear much from Oskar and Ruth.'*" Tess paused for a moment, then went on. "According to Sarah, Oskar was a troublemaker. And Ruth was a real booger too—her words here. My father: '*You speak of these two imaginary friends as if they were real, Mrs. Nichols.'*"

The plane rocked through a wave of turbulence. Justin closed his eyes. Tess touched his arm fleetingly, and then read through her father's interview with Noah Nichols's mother, reading quickly.

> **Mrs. Nichols:** *They were real. They were part of him. All of them.*
> **Detective Patterson:** *All of them?*
> **Mrs. Nichols:** *After he returned from that man, there were more of these imaginary friends.*
> **Detective Patterson:** *More than just Oskar and Ruth.*
> **Mrs. Nichols:** *Oh, my lands, yes. But Oskar was the worst.* **(Here she eerily switches into a British accent.)** *A rude sort of fellow.* **(Back to normal.)** *He always took up for Noah, especially when Noah was a baddy boy.*

Detective Patterson: *And the others you mentioned, after Noah's return from Jeff Pritchard?* **(Long pause. Sixty seconds, at least, prompting me to call her name three times. On the third one she finally responds.)**

Mrs. Nichols: *Where did my mind just go?*

Detective Patterson: **(I slightly changed course here to avoid that same lull.)** *Did Noah ever tell you what happened while he was in Father Silence's house?*

Mrs. Nichols: *I don't like that name.*

Detective Patterson: *Father Silence?*

Mrs. Nichols: *Yes. I don't like priests. I don't like Catholics.*

Detective Patterson: *Jeff Pritchard wasn't a priest.*

Mrs. Nichols: *Might as well have been. He was a Catholic. I hate them more than the Jews. They're all Christ killers. All Christ-killing baddy boys.*

Detective Patterson: *Mrs. Nichols?*

Mrs. Nichols: *Noah claims he remembers nothing from his time with that Father Silence man. But I think Oskar and Ruth remember.*

Detective Patterson: *About Father Silence?*

Mrs. Nichols: *I told you I don't like that name. Say it one more time and I'll hang up and burn the phone to the ground and make you eat the ashes.*

Detective Patterson: **(Here I pause.)** *Jeff Pritchard. You think Noah's two imaginary friends, Oskar and Ruth, remember what happened in that house?*

Mrs. Nichols: *Yes. Those two baddies always came to Noah's rescue.*

Detective Patterson: *Oskar and Ruth?*

Mrs. Nichols: *Yes, Oskar and Ruth. But we never heard from them again after he returned from that man. And then Noah went along and killed my Sammy.* **(Before I can get in another word here, she screams.)** *The flood waters came and took Noah away. Even the ark couldn't save him this time.*

Detective Patterson: *The ark?*

Mrs. Nichols: *That place where the baddy boys go. I don't want to talk about the ark. That's where the baddy boys go and Noah was a baddy boy. He killed my Sammy and the flood waters took him away.*

Detective Patterson: **(I pause here to let that sink in.)** *Mrs. Nichols, can we go back to Noah when he returned from*

Father . . . from Jeff Pritchard. Was he different than before? Did the time spent with Jeff Pritchard change your son?

Mrs. Nichols: *What kind of a question is that? Of course it changed him. He came back a monster. He came back with demons. I think those demons ganged up together and took the place of Oskar and Ruth. After his return, Noah drew pictures. So many pictures.*

Detective Patterson: (I prompt her here because she pauses again, twenty seconds this time.) *Mrs. Nichols? What would he draw?*

Mrs. Nichols: *Eyes.*

Detective Patterson: *What kind of eyes?*

Mrs. Nichols: *In the darkness. Eyes surrounded by darkness. Every picture. He'd hang them all over his room. He colored so hard the black crayons would snap in half. Evil baddy boy eyes that look like a cat but they're not. All of his new demons drew them. He had one demon who was a real booger.*

Detective Patterson: *Did this demon have a name?*

Mrs. Nichols (Quickly, almost frightened): *I don't know.*

Detective Patterson: *The Outcast?*

Mrs. Nichols (Quickly): *Maybe. How do you know?*

Detective Patterson: *Noah, after he killed his father, your husband, Noah carved—*

Mrs. Nichols: *I know what he did, Detective. Now go away.*

Detective Patterson: *Mrs. Nichols?*

Mrs. Nichols: *Go away. I put Noah in the ark until the police came. Locked him in. The flood waters took him away. Washed that baddy boy right back into the Bible.*

Detective Patterson: *Where is Noah now? Is he still at Berringer Hills?* **(Silence)** *Mrs. Nichols? Mrs. Nichols?*

Mrs. Nichols: *Cunt.*

Detective Patterson: *Excuse me.*

Mrs. Nichols: *Cunt bitch little baddy boy. I'll put you in the ark until you drown.*

Detective Patterson: *Is Noah still at the mental hospital? He's still at Berringer Hills in Twisted Tree?*

Mrs. Nichols: *Yes.*

Detective Patterson: *Do you visit him?*

Mrs. Nichols: *No.* **(Ten-second pause, and when she speaks again her voice seems drained, defeated.)** *He came back a monster.*

Tess handed the pages to the others to read, and when they finished she looked up. "She hung up at the end. Ended the interview. My father says here that he tried ten more times to get hold of her but couldn't. She died two months later."

The plane bucked through clouds and Justin closed his eyes again. Tess touched his hand this time, kept it there longer, but couldn't stop thinking of the eyes. *What did they have to do with it all? The eyes Noah would draw. The eyes painted on the window back at Mom and Dad's cabin. The black paint over their dead eyes.*

Eyes in the darkness.

"He came back a monster," she whispered.

The plane dipped hard, then leveled.

Justin gripped her hand.

She looked up. "She's alive, Justin. I can feel it."

He nodded, said nothing, probably thinking the same thing she was trying not to.

Julia might be alive, but they both knew that sometimes for victims, it was better off if they weren't.

22

Lisa Buchanon stood from her seat on the sofa, grabbed the remote from the coffee table, and turned off the television.

Turned off the pretty news anchor in mid-sentence.

Burt Lobell, one of the former detectives who arrested Jeff Pritchard, had been murdered inside his Twisted Tree home, only ten miles away from her house.

Brutally murdered, according to the news, with insinuations that a local satanic cult could be involved. Not too much unlike what had happened, according to the national news, to the other detective, Leland Patterson, the evening before, across the country in Montana.

The same night Jeff Pritchard was executed.

The same night the eggs had been hurled onto the façade of her house.

The same night the hoodlums had strung toilet paper all over her trees.

The same night she'd called the cops, who'd done very little, hardly offering to clean what the hoodlums had done. One of the cops had flirted with her, which was not uncommon, just untimely and unprofessional.

On her way from the living room, a bout of dizziness struck her. She leaned against the wide entrance to the foyer to right herself. *Damn it, not now.* She closed her eyes. Closing her eyes always seemed to help. They rarely lasted long, these dizzy spells, and often brought about feelings of nausea, and occasionally a headache. She hoped the headache would stay away with this one. She had work to do. More dried egg residue to clean from the façade of her house.

Her house.

Not *his* anymore.

Not Jeff Pritchard.

Not Father Silence.

The dizzy spells were nothing new. They'd been occurring for years, perhaps decades—she'd couldn't pinpoint the origin, but knew they'd been going on long enough to have become commonplace. She no longer feared them, but instead treated them like any other kind of annoyance.

She had a notion of what had triggered it. Seeing the picture of Burt Lobell on the news had reminded her that that detective had once been inside her house, arresting Jeff Pritchard.

And she'd told them! She'd warned those officers the other night. The threats out there were real. Now that Pritchard had been executed, she'd had a feeling bad things would start happening. Eggs she could clean off—and she still had hours of scrubbing to do; she'd taken a break from it, in fact, to come inside and see what the news had to offer, and *boom*, there it was, another brutal murder—but she'd feared worse could be in store for others. The real players in all this, and it turned out she was right, but those officers had just nodded with their sarcastic, twisted smiles. Because they hadn't believed her. They never believed her. Said they'd investigate it. Said they predicted anyone who might think they're in danger would probably be diligent about the matter, ma'am. And *Father Silence was dead*, the one officer said, the one with the wedding ring on his finger.

Finally, the other officer had added, the one who'd attempted to flirt with her, the one, after she'd ignored his pass at her, who then appeared overly eager to move on.

Well, she thought, as the dizziness waned at the doorway, Detective Burt Lobell hadn't been diligent enough, had he?

And I'm too young to be called *ma'am*.

She opened the front door, stepped back out onto the veranda, where her bucket of soapy water and washrags rested, and then resumed scrubbing at the stains of hardened egg residue on her house's siding.

Thinking back at how snarky the officers had been—*after* they realized the apparent single one had no chance at getting inside her pants—in asking how come these notions kept coming to her.

Ma'am. Them probably knowing her answer and just wanting to hear it, already snickering inside their heads, because she'd for years been telling the police things she was seeing, over and over, these notions, as they called them—she called them visions—were all happening, she was convinced, because of the house.

Because, she'd made the mistake of saying during one of her too-frequent calls, *the house is talking to her.*

23

Two cars awaited them at Louisville International.

One, officially, was for Danny, and paid for by the job; the other Tess had rented.

She drove the red Camry with Justin, while Danny followed in the gray Ford Edge. She'd been eager to get behind the wheel, eager to have control over something, even if only a car and the rapid pace with which she took to the roads. She didn't need the woman's computer voice coming from Justin's iPhone. She knew how to get to Twisted Tree, which was why Danny had allowed her to lead. But the directions gave Justin something to do, something to focus on, and the phone voice helped gap the silence between them.

She was speeding, twenty miles over the limit at least, thirty on the straights, northeast toward Twisted Tree, the wooded distilling town ten miles outside of Louisville Metro, hugging the meandering Ohio River like a blood-sucking tick, desperate for the streams and creek beds that fed into and out of it like branches from a massive tree trunk. A town that had been cut by Father Silence's tragedies years ago and was now facing it head-on again. She sped toward Burt Lobell's house as if there were still time to save him.

But Burt was dead.

What she sped to was a crime scene.

Hills and grass soon gave way to trees, and she took the exit ramp onto a road that dipped and curved under a thick canopy of overreaching tree limbs. Except for the flashes of sunlight through the breaks in the boughs, the blue sky was no longer visible through the windshield. She knew the sky wouldn't be blue for long. She'd checked the local weather forecast, something she always did when she traveled, and storms were expected for the next several days. She slowed only because she had to. The road twisted and bent, and she clung to every curve until Justin pointed—right here—in unison with the iPhone's command and Tess's memory, and they found themselves coasting down a long gravel driveway that opened up to the grassy patch around Burt Lobell's wooded property.

Yellow crime scene tape surrounded Lobell's home, and two cars were parked outside the boundary. One an unmarked sedan, the other a tan four-door with flashing roof lights that more than likely belonged to the Twisted Tree sheriff.

Danny pulled in and parked behind where Tess had skidded to a halt.

Two men met them at the yellow tape as they ducked under. One, the sheriff, in a brown uniform a size too small for his thick waist.

The other wore jeans and red button-down with sleeves rolled to the elbows, a black man with a chiseled face and closely trimmed hair. "Detective Andy Evans," he said. Tess shook his hand. He was barely taller than her, but his grip showed a hidden strength that made her feel both welcome and safe. "Sorry to meet under these circumstances."

She introduced herself and Justin.

Danny stepped up next. "Detective Danny Gomes. We spoke on the phone."

Evans shook his hand, suddenly looking leery of the out-of-town arrivals.

"Sheriff Kingsley, Detective." The other man nodded politely. His grip was soft like a pillow. His face was familiar. She tried to imagine him younger, thinner, and with more hair, because the name Kingsley rang a bell. And then he said, "I was a year behind you at school. Your father was a hero around these parts. I'm sorry to hear about what happened."

"Thank you," she said, following Detective Evans toward Lobell's house, already feeling bites of trepidation as she neared the porch. Steps she'd sat on as a kid, blowing soapy bubbles from little plastic rings while her parents and Burt and his wife sipped beer and grilled burgers and brats on a charcoal grill.

The letters *666* had been painted on the bricks beside the front door, on both sides and with so much hate and vitriol it sent shivers down her spine.

Sheriff Kingsley said, "Ever since Father Silence was caught, cults started popping up all over Twisted Tree."

Tess nodded. "I remember." Jeff Pritchard had been put behind bars, but the bruises he'd left behind would not be quick to heal. His story bred influence of the wrong kind, the nasty dark sort that lured followers seeking attention of their own. She noticed the small upside-down cross painted above the front door.

Detective Evans pointed to it. "Satanic cults. There's a new one sprung up that calls itself the Lost Children of Silence. They worshipped him. Now they worship the memory of him."

"Lately we've been finding dead animals in the woods," said Sheriff Kingsley. "Sacrificed during their secret rituals." The sheriff looked paler than he had a moment ago, like this was all too much. They were in over their heads, thought Tess. That's why they'd asked for help from the city in the first place, according to Danny. "We've been getting bouts of this vandalism for months now, leading up to that electrocution," Sheriff Kingsley continued. "Teens and college age mostly. Upticks in LSD and heroin use. Deaths by overdose. Séances in the woods. Music so dark it'd like to make you sick. We're making arrests every night. Breaking up parties that scare even me and my men. Kids dead behind the eyes they're so deep into it."

Evans said, "Same in the city, just not to the extent to what he's seen here."

The sheriff said, "Mostly, aside from fist fights and some weird parties where there was some cutting going on, it hasn't been violent."

"Cutting?" asked Tess.

"They cut themselves and drink each other's blood."

Are they vampires? Tess was unable to take her eyes off the vandalized—no, *degraded* house.

"They wear masks too," said the sheriff.

"What kind of masks?"

"Animals," Evans answered. "Any kind of rubber animal mask you can think of."

A memory smell hit Tess like a hammer blow, and she doubled over with hands on her knees. *Damn it, not now.* She smelled rubber, but knew, despite how suddenly intense it was, that it wasn't real. It was a phantom smell, just like she'd researched years ago—when she'd been so determined to solve her memory issues on her own—like when amputees feel phantom pain in previously lost limbs, even years after the fact. That's what this was, but it had been years since it had struck her like this, not since the day inside the Halloween store when she'd had a brief episode while Julia was picking out wings for the fairy outfit she'd worn that year. All it had taken was a glance down the wrong aisle, all those masks hanging on hooks, all that flimsy rubber. Rubber that wasn't so flimsy when there was a face inside it to fill up those eyeholes.

Justin touched her back. She blinked the disorientation away, a little terrified now at how the mere mention of the word *masks* had triggered it. Thunder and lighting, yes, had been constant fears since she was an early teen—and even more precisely, since Jeff Pritchard's arrest—but the memory of that dog mask, the smell of the rubber, the face behind it, those eyes peering through the eyeholes. She stood straight, willed strength from where she feared there was little left.

Evans watched her with obvious concern. "You okay, Detective?"

She nodded, because she had to be, and then refocused on what had started it all seconds ago. "They found masks inside the house." She felt them watching her. *Make sense*, she told herself. *Start making sense, Tess.* "Jeff Pritchard's house. In the basement. My father and Burt Lobell found dozens of animal masks hanging on wall hooks."

"Yeah, we see the obvious connection." Evans paused atop Burt Lobell's porch steps. "Look, I wouldn't be doing my job if I didn't say I had reservations about you being here."

Tess said, "You got kids, Detective?"

"I do," he said. "Which is why I'm allowing it. I'd be turning over mountains if I were in your shoes. But if this gets too personal, to the point where there's interference, I'll pull the plug."

Tess nodded in agreement, and so did Justin.

Evans said, "I've got pictures of your girl all over Louisville and southern Indiana, along with the composite your guy drew up."

"And here in Twisted Tree," said Sheriff Kingsley.

"Along with the other kids recently missing," added Evans. "The FBI is involved. I got your list. We've hunted down everybody on it and put them in safe houses. Except for Barrett Stevens, Pritchard's lawyer. We can't find him anywhere, but we're still trying."

"And Foster Bergman?" To Justin and Danny, Tess explained: "The former priest. Key witness at the trial. One of the first to grow suspicious of Pritchard at the school."

"We're currently arguing with him," said Evans. "He insisted on staying put."

Sheriff Kingsley added, "We've got men rotating in twos, twenty-four hours a day, watching him."

Detective Evans nodded toward the door, motioned them onward. "Come on, let's get on with it."

It had been months since Tess had prayed and even longer since she'd stepped into a church, but as she walked through the door Evans held open and passed beneath that upside-down cross, she instinctively marked herself with the sign of the cross, touching her forehead and chest, then left and right shoulder.

Unlike Danny and Eliza, she and Justin had strayed from the church for many reasons, and now she felt like a hypocrite. Her first prayer in a long time was that she hadn't strayed too far.

Inside, the air was thick and slow moving, even though some of the windows had been opened to vent. They entered a living room where she used to play board games with Burt's son, Brian.

"His son?" she asked Evans.

"We've got his family put up in a safe house."

Tess knew that Burt's wife had passed away from a stroke six years ago. She forced herself to look at the walls as they walked behind the couch. In what looked like blood, the words *Lost Children* were scrawled across the wall above the mantel where Burt and his family used to hang their Christmas stockings.

"Forced entry. We've yet to find any fingerprints that would cause alarm. No trace evidence either."

Justin shook his head. "The cabin in Lolo was full of prints."

"So I've heard."

Danny said, "So careful here and so careless in Lolo."

"Maybe two different UNSUBS," said Evans.

Justin eyed the walls and the graffiti, more satanic symbols written in blood. "Or he's changing his MO to throw us off."

"Maybe he's *from* here," said Tess. "More recognizable and easier to find, where in Montana, he's an unknown. Noah Nichols is from here."

"Noah is not our man," said Evans. "I'm sorry. He's locked inside Berringer Hills and there's no way he got out."

Tess knew as much; Danny had told her, but hearing it now from Detective Evans brought with it a finality that sank her heart. She noticed that the sheriff had not come inside with them. He'd probably seen enough.

Evans focused on Justin. "But you should still go see him. Noah Nichols. The warden there is expecting you both within the hour." He grew quiet, pointed. "Body was found in here." He led them down five steps of the tri-level house into Burt's study, where the sofa, desk, and bookshelves looked as Tess remembered. Tidy, while her father had been more scattered. Stricter and patterned, while her father often flew by the seat of his pants.

Perfect complements to each other. Like her and Danny.

She bet Burt kept all his investigation details on a computer and not on papers thrown inside a briefcase.

Evans stopped, pointed again. Like with her father in the cabin, there was a wooden chair facing the wall and blood stains on the floor below it. "Neck wound. Straight across. Stood behind, lifted the chin." Evans pointed to the wall, where evidence tags took the place of the real things. "Newspaper article was right there. Eyes were closed, the lids and sockets painted black. More circular, though, like they took their time painting inside the sockets instead of what I saw from the pictures you sent from the cabin."

"*They see the darkness,*" Tess said. "My father interviewed Noah's mother. Just something Noah said. And did. Noah often drew eyes surrounded by darkness."

"Noah—"

"I know," she said, holding up her hand. "I know. But I think this all has something to do with him. The note my father wrote. Pritchard's last words."

"*Beware the one that got away,*" said Evans. "Right . . . Which is why I still want the two of you to go see him. I want that briefcase of your father's, by the way."

"It's in the car," she said. "I'll give it to you to make copies."

"Fair enough."

The phone rang. They jumped. On instinct, each one of them reached for their cells before realizing they weren't the source.

Tess looked up the steps toward the living room, as the ringing echoed. "Landline." She ran, jumped up the steps, and entered the living room just as Sheriff Kingsley rounded the couch and lifted the cordless phone from a small table in the corner of the room.

"Hello." He panted from his sprint inside, and then held the phone out toward Tess.

She approached as slowly as the air moved. Sweat beaded across her brow. "Yes?"

The voice urged her heart into a gallop. "I'm sorry. I've done it again."

Tess steadied herself. "Where is she?"

Justin stepped closer, but she held him off with a stiff arm.

"She's fine," the Outcast said over the phone, so casual. "But at the Playhouse we l-l-like to play games."

"Games? What games? What Playhouse?"

"F-f-f-f." It sounded like he'd slammed the phone down, or into something, but then his voice returned, calmer now. "Find the eyes, Tess. Where oh where are Burt Lobell's eyes?"

"What? What are you talking about?"

"Find the eyes and your girl stays alive," he said. "I'm sorry. But you've got two minutes."

"Two minutes? For what?"

The line went dead.

Tess looked at Detective Evans, who'd overheard the call.

Evans said, "He didn't take Lobell's eyes. He painted over them."

Danny said, "Tess, like at the cabin. He painted eyes on the window. That's what led you to the briefcase in the closet. To Pritchard's last words." He turned on Evans. "Did you find eyes? Painted eyes? Anywhere?"

"No."

They scattered. Didn't need to be told to take separate rooms. Two minutes. One hundred and twenty seconds. Every tick was palpable.

Tess took the kitchen. Opened cabinets, drawers, the microwave door. She hurled the toaster from the counter. Sent dirty dishes crashing to the floor. Looked high. Looked low. She checked her watch. *Sixty seconds.* The others searched frantically in the other rooms as couches and dressers and bookcases were moved from walls.

Thirty seconds.

The phone rang.

Too early.

She answered. "You said two minutes."

"Did you find the eyes?"

Justin shouted from the bedroom. "In here."

Tess ran, sliding briefly on shards of glass she'd just broken, and hurried down the hallway toward the bedroom, where Justin had moved a dresser from the wall to reveal a set of eyes, painted black and staring across the room toward a vanity table and mirror, dust-covered since Mrs. Lobell no longer used it.

"Where do the eyes hide, Tess?"

"In the bedroom."

"More specific."

"On the wall. Behind the dresser."

"Facing . . . ?"

Tess approached the vanity, eyeing everything on it, junk, dusty junk, and then she spotted a medal, a round medallion with a red ribbon necklace. "Facing the medal. A medallion." It dawned on her. "Medal of honor. The one he got for . . . for arresting Father Silence." There was a lull that nearly made her sick. "Hello? Is that it? The medal of honor?"

"Okay."

"Okay?" *Not yes?* He'd said it as if that's not what he'd expected them to find and he was now disappointed. "I played your game. Now where is my daughter?"

Silence.

And then.

"Mommy?"

"Julia? Oh my God, baby. Where are you? We're coming for you."

She heard the Outcast's muffled voice. Rippling wind. He was coaching her what to say. And then Julia spoke. "We're going to the Playhouse, Mommy."

"The Playhouse? What Playhouse?"

"Where there are games." She sounded nervous, unsure, on the verge of breaking down. "Where's Daddy?"

Justin must have heard his name. He hurried over and Tess handed him the phone, cautioning him with her eyes to keep his shit together, and he did. "Julia. Daddy loves you. Mommy loves you. We're coming for you, honey. Do you hear me? The man you're with promised us he'd keep you safe. He'd never hurt you . . ." Justin's hands went slack, and he dropped the phone to the floor. "He hung up."

Danny put a hand on Justin's shoulder, patted it.

Detective Evans's eyes grew large as he homed in on Sheriff Kingsley. "Get as many units as possible combing these woods."

Sheriff Kingsley must have understood immediately. "That phone hasn't rung in two days. We checked the records." He hurried toward the door, down the porch steps toward his car.

Evans said, "We need to check every house up and down the street."

Danny followed, said over his shoulder to Tess. "He's close enough to know that you entered this house."

Tess turned toward the door, toward Justin. "He's watching."

24

"J ULIA!"

Tess leaped down the porch steps and pulled her gun as soon as her feet touched grass. While Evans and the sheriff hurried to prepare an organized hunt through the woods and neighboring homes, Tess entered the trees running with no plan.

It felt good to move, to get out of that house, to get away from that phone and that voice that still felt implanted in her ear. "Julia!" Her voice echoed across the great expanse of trees, river birches, ash and oak, bushes with sprigs of spring color.

A creek trickled, magnified water curling and spinning over mud-embedded rocks.

Deadfall crunched underfoot.

Birds scattered from trees every time she screamed her daughter's name.

Justin and Danny were visible between the hundreds of trunks, thirty yards apart from one another on the far side of Burt Lobell's house. They'd taken different angles into the woods and were shouting much like Tess was, but hearing it from them hammered home that their efforts were futile. The Outcast wouldn't have Julia that close.

And where were the other kids?

"Julia," she called again, defeated, turning in a slow circle, her gun so heavy in her hand she wanted to drop it. She wanted to pull the trigger and fire every bullet until the empty click echoed louder than her pathetic, desperate voice. And then quietly, one more time, "Julia."

The sky rumbled, distant, then close, loud enough to shake boughs.

Thunder.

She hunkered down and then panicked into a sprint with no direction.

Saw herself as a teenage girl sitting at a kitchen table inside a farmhouse, with him . . .

Jeff Pritchard.

And then weeds clipped her ankles. Branches brushed her arms, stung her cheeks. She pushed at them, kept going, deeper, chasing, chasing . . .

. . . rain pelted wet leaves. Thunder shook boughs, shook the ground, shook her very bones as she sprinted under canopies of limbs that looked like crooked fingers and claws . . . and lightning lit the sky in flashes of electricity, and he was there, running in and out of the shadows, she was chasing him, not the other way around, through the field, into the woods, into the woods . . . that mask . . .

. . . She opened her eyes, panting, smelled rubber. "I was chasing him."

Danny and Justin stood before her.

Why am I sitting on the ground, my back against a tree? Where is my gun? There. On the leaves.

She looked at Justin. "The thunder."

Justin squatted, eye level. "It was an airplane. A low airplane, Tess. No thunder."

Danny paced, scratched his head. "You said you were chasing. Who were you chasing?"

She shook her head. "I don't know."

"Another hole in your memory, Tess," Justin said.

Danny asked. "Like back at the cabin?"

"Yes." Justin helped her from the ground.

Danny said, "Tess, you okay?" And then to Justin. "Does she need to see a doctor?"

Justin said, "I am a doctor."

"A *medical* doctor."

"Not the kind she needs." Justin glanced at Danny.

"I'm fine," Tess insisted.

"Psychogenic amnesia," Justin said to Danny.

"Christ," said Tess, making it to her feet. She brushed leaves from her pants. "Drop it," she warned.

"Second time in two days, Tess."

"I can't have you picking me apart right now, Justin."

"Something traumatic happened in your childhood."

Danny watched them both. "What the fuck?" He stood, open-mouthed, looked hurt, like this was just one more thing the two of them had kept from him and Eliza.

Tess said, "Danny, go on. Do what you came here to do."

Danny hesitated, with a look that said *We'll talk later*, and then took off around the side of the house toward where more officers arrived, scattering to comb the woods and neighboring homes.

Justin gripped both her hands. "What just happened?"

"I need my gun." She bent down to grab it and came up lightheaded. She moved away when he tried to touch her shoulder. "I'm fine."

"Just because you can walk doesn't mean you're fine, Tess."

"How did he do it?" she asked. "How did he make it through the airport?"

"The plane probably landed before we got the sketch out."

"But even so, Justin." She nodded in the direction of Detective Evans out front. "His men showed that sketch everywhere, all over the airport, and we did the same in Montana. No one saw him. No one saw our daughter. What if he drove?"

"He couldn't have made it here in time to—" He pointed toward Lobell's house. "To do this."

"What if there's more than just him? The cults he mentioned. Lost Children of Silence?" She turned in a slow circle, scanning the trees, listening. "I heard wind, Justin. On the phone with him. Earlier. I heard wind in the background. Strong wind." She watched the leaves on the tall boughs, and they didn't move. "There's no wind here. He's not here. He's not close."

Justin reached out his hand. She took it, willingly, just long enough for him to help her over a wide thicket of weeds and deadfall, and then she took her hand back.

They walked side by side, their feet crunching over leaves.

She could feel another question coming.

"When did the blackouts start?" he asked.

She walked about ten paces, not wanting to give him fuel, but deep down she needed to at least start the conversation. "Soon after Pritchard was arrested. Several times in high school. Less often in college."

"Did anything prompt them?"

She knew he knew the answer but humored him anyway. "Stress."

"In particular?"

"Rain. Heavy rain. Storms."

"Lightning and thunder."

"Yes." *You know this, Justin.*

"Do you remember anything from the blackouts?"

"I smell rubber."

"Is that what happened earlier, when we talked about the masks?"

She nodded, could tell he was mentally taking notes. "I remember a dog mask. Someone wearing a dog mask."

"That's good," he said as they neared the back of Burt Lobell's property. "This is good, Tess. You've experienced a dissociation because of some unknown stress. Or shock."

"Justin . . . please . . ."

He stopped her, gently touched her elbow. "Tess, hear me out. Some people can't escape the trauma of certain events. The horror remains in their waking thoughts. But with you, I think you escaped the trauma completely by erasing it from memory."

"Doesn't sound possible," she said, walking again. "I'm not crazy, Justin."

He followed. "You erased it from your memory because you *aren't* crazy, Tess."

She laughed.

"That's why your mind couldn't handle it," he said, catching up to her again as they rounded the house toward the front yard clearing. "You endured something your mind couldn't handle. You've created a hole in your long-term memory."

"You sound like a book."

"You sound like a patient in denial." But he said it gently, and she let the truth of it linger. Justin went on: "You're forgetting only the things that are threatening. It's obvious it stems from this."

"What this?"

"Twisted Tree. Jeff Pritchard. All of it."

"But why now? Why is it starting to come back now?"

"Because you're home."

"That's not it."

He stopped her. "And because of Julia. Tess, you aren't the only one threatened by it now."

25

THE OUTCAST CLOSED his phone, scratched his head, and walked across to the Polaroid pictures he'd strewn across the floor.

Taking the pictures had calmed him; calmed him just before he felt the snap coming on. He knew the snap sometimes pushed him to grab the hammer and do the bad thing, and he didn't like doing the bad thing, but sometimes the hammer was the only way to get out the rage.

Instead, he'd grabbed the camera and just started taking pictures, one after the other, dropping them to the floor even as they developed and became real, and luckily that had worked. Not so much the pictures themselves, but the sound of the snap and hmmm as the pictures oozed out of the camera like magic.

He was glad they'd found the eyes he'd painted on Burt Lobell's bedroom wall. He wasn't sure why he'd given them two minutes to do so—that much had been spontaneous, like a game they played at the Playhouse—and truthfully, it had stressed him more than it had them. Those seconds ticking down. Because what was he to do if the time had run out on them?

Either way, it had excited the children, so he'd given them small doses of what calmed them. A little dust from some of the crushed white pills dissolved in water.

"Drink."

Soon they'd no longer want for food or shelter. There was schooling and learning at the Playhouse. Fruit and vegetables twice daily.

Good for growing bodies. He'd give them milk too, tall endless glasses of it. Calcium was good for growing bones and for strong teeth.

He tapped his forehead as if trying to remember something, or maybe he was trying to tap back the anger that had suddenly come up. *Don't be afraid of the eyes.* He thought positive, good thoughts. "Board games. Games with balls and bats. Games with dice. Plenty of games at the Playhouse."

The perfect house.

The kids were already dozing off.

Good night, sleep tight. Don't let the bedbugs bite.

He said a quick prayer and crossed himself.

"Just don't break the rules," he said aloud.

Julia was a smart girl. She surprised him by opening her eyes. Heavy lids, groggy. "Why not, Father Friday?"

Father Friday. He smiled. *Shouldn't have told her that lie. But it was the only way to get her into the car the day before. The easiest way.* And then he said, "Because, Julia, rule breakers get put in the Bad Room."

"What's the bad room?"

He squatted down, adjusted his sunglasses, gently smoothed her hair with his hand, and smiled. "Don't break the rules."

She stared at him until her eyes closed, and then she too drifted off.

The Outcast watched the children sleep.

He'd been following the news. Revenge killings, they called it, these murders, which, indeed, they were—all part of a bigger plan.

Not my plan. Not my revenge.

He'd been a coward back at the cabin.

At least that's what he'd been called for not going through with it. But the truth was, the retired detective and his wife weren't bad people who did bad things. They were good. So he'd been unable to do the bad thing, as had been requested of him. The snap had not happened, so someone else had done it for him.

I am not a coward.

And the news about the missing children . . .

How did the missing children fit in with the murders?

They don't.

That was *his* doing.

All except for Julia.

She wasn't like the others, he knew, and another part of their plan.

Make your lists, Tess.

There was no stutter in his thoughts. He shook his head because Tess just didn't get it.

He'd taken the time to paint those eyes exactly where he had inside Burt Lobell's bedroom—sneaking in there with his paint and a brush months ago while the retired police officer was deep in the Twisted Tree woods hunting deer. He'd taken his time, forming each eye, making sure they looked toward the vanity mirror across the room. But Tess didn't get it. Burt Lobell's medal of honor was *not* the intended piece to the puzzle.

Did I need to spell it out for you?

Did you even look in the mirror?

Before

PORTION OF THE *interview between Detective Leland Patterson and Mrs. Erin Randell (neighbor to the Nichols family) the day after Samson Nichols was murdered by his son Noah. (Mrs. Randell was the first on the scene, and later phoned in the crime.)*

> **Detective Patterson:** *And how were you alerted that the murder had occurred?*
>
> **Mrs. Randell:** *I was out in the backyard pruning when I heard Sarah Nichols screaming. Their house is a couple hundred yards through the woods.*
>
> **Detective Patterson:** *Did you know it was her right away?*
>
> **Mrs. Randell:** *When you're neighboring with that family as long as we have, you grow accustomed to their noises.*
>
> **Detective Patterson:** *What kind of noises?*
>
> **Mrs. Randell:** *Sarah Nichols was a screamer. Whether it be in anger toward the boy, Noah. Or in fear of her husband, who we know beat her. He beat the boy, too, although we fear that wasn't all that took place inside that house.*
>
> **Detective Patterson:** *Are you alluding to another kind of abuse? Mrs. Randell?*
>
> **Mrs. Randell (with tears in her eyes, nodding):** *Sometimes that boy's crying carried louder than the screams. That day wasn't the only time we called the cops on that family. Or social services.*

Detective Patterson: Yet Noah remained inside that house.

Mrs. Randell (nodding): He ran away here a couple of times. We'd take him in, of course. Give him something to eat. Clean him up. I'm not sure how often he bathed. Mostly, we'd just allow him a bit of peace and quiet, and eventually they'd come get him. Usually Samson, the father. He was a brute of a man. Never saw him without dirt under his fingernails.

Detective Patterson: How was Noah Nichols when he was around you? When you'd take him in?

Mrs. Randell: Quiet, mostly. Fidgety. He'd startle at the slightest sound.

Detective Patterson: His mother, she told the newspapers . . .

Mrs. Randell: I saw the article, Detective. The woman is crazy. She should be locked up.

Detective Patterson: In the article, she said her son had demons inside him. Did you ever get any hint of this?

Mrs. Randell (after careful thought): No, not really. Like I said, around us, he was quiet. Very reserved. Shy. (Wiping her tears again.) Not like what I saw in the driveway yesterday morning.

Detective Patterson: We'll get to that, Mrs. Randell. And I'm sorry to bring this back up, but in the weeks after Noah's return from Jeff Pritchard, did you see him at all?

Mrs. Randell: One time, he ran away, and arrived here, yes.

Detective Patterson: Did you notice anything different with him? Perhaps anything that had changed with his personality from when you knew him before his abduction? What I'm getting at, Mrs. Randell, is trying to understand the violence that occurred yesterday with Noah and his father. With what you witnessed . . . Did you ever see any signs of violence with him?

Mrs. Randell: No, Detective. Never. But I suppose there's only so much abuse a person can take. Even a child has a breaking point. But the one time, after his return, from . . . from that man, Father Silence, perhaps he was a bit colder. Quiet, yes, and still shy, but much more guarded. (Here she pauses, holds up a finger.) I have something to show you. Something you might need to see. I'll be right back. (She leaves the kitchen and returns thirty seconds later with two sheets of paper, upon which are two drawings, both made with crayons. One of what must be the house of Jeff Pritchard, what the newspapers are calling his House of Horrors. The other is of a pair of eyes surrounded by heavily colored black.) I have three grandchildren. I watched them a few days ago, and

I'd left the crayons out on the table, along with some paper, where Noah sat. He was especially quiet that day, and just seeing him at my door sent panic through me, with him being missing for so long, and on the news for having been saved from that house. I was on edge. I asked if he was hungry. He nodded that he was, so I made him a sandwich. While I had my back turned, he started coloring these two drawings. I watched him. It was like he was in a world of his own. Once he started coloring there was no stopping him. I said his name, but he never looked up at me. Not until he'd colored both of those pictures. What do you think they mean, Detective? His father came knocking soon after he colored them. He didn't even have time to eat the sandwich I'd fixed him. But take a look.

Detective Patterson (Here I turn both pictures toward me): *Well, one seems to be the house of Jeff Pritchard.* **(The carport is unmistakable. The river down off the bluff. The woods in the background. The field of grass. The red door almost looks like a nose, the covered porch an evil grin. The windows, however, have eight windows instead of four, and are asymmetrical, scattered haphazardly about the house's upper half instead of linear or even balanced. Almost shaped like a pyramid, with one at the top, slightly higher than the others. And standing at each window was a lone stick figure, some male, some female by the length of the hair.)** *This other picture, though, these eyes, I'm not so sure, Mrs. Randell. You mind if I take these with me?*

Mrs. Randell: *Please do. But what do you make of those windows? Right there in that picture of the house. The people in the windows.*

Detective Patterson (Here I take another look): *I don't know. I'd have to analyze it further. But right off I do know there are only four windows on the real façade.*

Mrs. Randell: *Yet this picture shows eight.*

Detective Patterson: *Indeed it does.*

Mrs. Randell: *And the stick person in each one of them? You reckon those could be some of the victims?*

Detective Patterson: *Could be. There's no telling what that poor boy saw inside that house.*

Mrs. Randell: *Turn them over. The pictures. Have a look at how he signed them.*

Detective Patterson (after flipping the two papers over, I see the name AMELIA on both): *Amelia?*

Mrs. Randell: *That's how he signed them. Not Noah. What do you think that means?*

Detective Patterson: *I don't yet know.* **(*I pause a moment to collect my thoughts.*)** *But if we can get back to yesterday. You heard Sarah Nichols screaming and you immediately went over there?*

Mrs. Randell: *Hurried as fast as this old body would allow. Still had pruning shears in my hand. I was accustomed to noises coming from their property. Screams and such. But this one was unlike any I'd heard. So ear-piercing birds scattered from trees.*

Detective Patterson: *And you found the family in the driveway? Samson Nichols already dead?*

Mrs. Randell: *Yes. I'd like to never seen so much blood. You know, of course, what was done with . . .*

Detective Patterson: *Yes, I do. But where exactly was Noah?*

Mrs. Randell: *You don't think he really did it?*

Detective Patterson: *I do. I believe that is indisputable, but what I'm trying to do is understand the situation better, and you were the first to arrive.*

Mrs. Randell: *Okay. Okay.*

Detective Patterson: *Take your time.*

Mrs. Randell: *Noah, he was still sitting on top of his father. Straddling him at the waist. His father was on his back. Noah . . . he'd already done what he'd done to the eyes. And what he'd . . . carved into his father's chest. When I arrived, Sarah Nichols was standing about ten yards away, like she feared him. She was screaming, YOU GET OFF OF HIM. NOAH NICHOLS, YOU GET OFF OF HIM RIGHT NOW. Over and over and over. GET OFF OF HIM, NOAH!*

Detective Patterson: *And what did Noah do?*

Mrs. Randell: *He looked at her and yelled right back. I AM MOTHER. I AM MOTHER. I AM MOTHER . . .*

Detective Patterson: *I am mother . . . ? Yet he didn't? He didn't get off of him.*

Mrs. Randell: *No, he didn't budge. Not until I shouted at him.*

Detective Patterson: *And he listened to you?*

Mrs. Randell: *Not at first, but yes. It was like he was in a trance, and it took a minute for my voice to register. But he got off of him. And . . . he looked at me. And then back to what he'd done to his father. Or what is claimed he'd done. But, Detective Patterson, I'd never seen someone so lost and confused. It wasn't just disbelief I saw in Noah's eyes, but more like . . . he didn't remember how he'd gotten there, sitting atop his father like he was.*

26

BERRINGER HILLS HOSPITAL for the Criminally Insane sat high upon a hill on the northern reaches of Twisted Tree, surrounded by tall, canopied oaks and meandering creek beds and coils of lazy barbed wire.

The asylum was an eyesore. Three stories of limestone stained by the weather, pocked by dry-rotted windows and doors that almost seemed to weep for the poor unfortunates within.

The wind picked up as Tess and Justin got out of the car. Dark slated clouds encroached from the west, spurring Tess's pace toward the main entrance, where a heavy wrought-iron gate covered in green-leaf and vine conjured thoughts of haunting instead of healing.

Once inside, the stench was noticeable. The heavy smell of disinfectant couldn't mask that of the forgotten. The hallways were a maze, the lighting poor, the floors and walls cold, and the warden's nasally voice echoed like an out-of-tune horn.

"The new mayor called this place a virus," said Warden Hofmann as he clutched the lapels of his suit. His hair was dark and slicked, his smile eager to please. "A virus in the blood of an otherwise prospering town." The warden scoffed as his footfalls echoed off undecorated walls. "Vows to have it demolished within the year. Of course, that's what they always campaign on. But the big elephant in the room." He held up a finger.

"What to do with the patients," said Justin.

"Exactly. What . . . to do . . . with the patients. What to do with the unwanted? What . . . to do . . . with the *outcasts* of society."

Justin responded, and whatever he'd said sparked a conversation about state funding, but Tess wasn't listening. She was too focused on staying in the center of the hallway as they'd begun to pass numbered cells. More of a prison than a mental hospital. Where were the nurses? The doctors? All she saw were armed guards, one on each end of the hallway. She forced tunnel vision, not wanting to look, but they didn't seem to be patients—they were prisoners, animals in cages.

They watched her from barred windows set inside doors that seemed infinitely thick. They hissed at her. One man spat. A man on the right had a head three times too big for his body, and it leaned against the bars like a deadweight while his eyes followed her, burrowing. She walked faster—she'd fallen behind.

Warden Hofmann moved onward as if oblivious, never breaking stride from a monologue on how understaffed he was. Finally he stopped talking, and they passed the next several cells in silence, which Tess now found worse because she could hear all the patients rustling, and it reminded her of mice and garbage.

The warden looked over his shoulder, found Tess's eyes. "We've got a mixture of everything in here. Depressed, suicidal, psychotic, bipolar, anxiety disorders, antisocial personalities, and the list goes on. All violent at some point, and convicted, which is why they send them here."

Tess asked, "Do they ever get visitors?"

"Rarely. We have a priest who comes the last Friday of every month for confessions, but other than that, it's few and far between. Occasionally we'll have college kids doing term papers."

Tess watched the back of his head as they walked. Her dislike of the place intensified. So did the stink of urine. She'd been inside similar facilities countless times but had never seen anything like this. How was it still running? How had this place not been shut down?

They turned down a hallway that dead-ended about ten cells down, where a beefy guard with a shaved head and thick beard stood from a folding chair as they approached. "Boss," he said.

"Ray," said the warden. "This is Tess and Justin Claiborne."

He shook their hands, nodded politely.

The warden motioned toward the last cell on the block, which was unlike any of the other cells they'd passed. This one had no door, but resembled a jail cell with floor-to-ceiling bars all the way across the threshold. "And this is Noah Nichols."

Don't be in there, Tess thought, looking to her left, finding a long-haired, bearded man in a sky-blue asylum uniform, sitting on the side of his bed, staring down at the concrete floor between his bare feet. Somewhere amid all that hair growth his mouth moved, as if nibbling on something. He was smaller than she'd imagined, forever equating Noah Nichols to the boy who'd murdered his father. But strength and determination and rage, she knew, didn't always imply size, and what she now saw before her reminded her more of a man who'd be more likely to mind-fuck you than overpower.

The warden's voice brought her back to the moment, to reality: "I'm sorry," he said. "But there's no way he could've escaped from these bars."

Ray said, "Not on my watch. Ain't that right, Noah?"

Noah acted as if he hadn't heard. His left ankle was chained to the bedpost, which was in turn attached to floor and ceiling with bolts the size of fists. A lone, rounded window cut the wall about seven feet from the floor, just tall enough to *not* allow a view of the trees out there.

The warden removed a heavy set of keys from his belt. "The rumors about inmates escaping from this place are false. What we lack in funds is made up for by diligence. Ray here keeps a special eye on Noah."

"You'll let us in?"

"An armed detective and a psychologist? Yes. I'll make an exception." *That eager-to-please smile again.* He opened the cell and Ray stepped in first, hanging a portable light from a hook in the ceiling.

"He doesn't like a lot of light," said Ray.

Rain forest noises sounded from a mounted speaker in the corner of the room.

The warden said, "The sounds keep him calm. Specifically trickling water. Rainwater."

Tess eyed the chain around Noah's ankle. Ray placed two folding chairs against the far wall, presumably far enough away so that if Noah were to get up and come for them, they'd be out of his reach.

Ray said, "Noah. You have visitors. Is that okay? They just want to ask you a few questions." He snapped and Noah flinched—or it could have been an affirmative nod, Tess thought. "Noah, look up."

Slowly, Noah lifted his chin and his red-rimmed eyes settled on them. Beneath the deep crow's feet his facial bones were prominent, his cheeks sunken. For his smaller size, his knuckles were big and knotted. He looked nothing like the sketch of their suspect in Montana.

The warden said, "Just a few questions, Noah."

Noah's beard moved, what could have been a grin. "Got nowhere else to go." His voice grumbled, as if rust needed to be knocked off.

Tess felt targeted by his stare, dark brown eyes like mirrors in a carny house. She saw the burn scar on the underside of his right arm and used it as a starting point. "Noah, my name is Tess Claiborne. I'm a detective." She swallowed hard. "I see the cross on your arm. Do you remember how it happened?"

He stared, blinked; shadowed eyelids like window shades that wouldn't stay down. "One of my many mysteries." He looked at Justin. "Who are you?"

"Justin Claiborne. I'm a psychologist."

Noah scoffed, looked down. "You two married?" When he looked back up, he appeared to be grinning, like he knew they'd both have trouble answering that very simple question.

Tess surprised herself. "Yes."

Noah brought both cuffed hands to his beard to scratch his chin. "Father Silence done it to me. But I don't remember. That why you come here? To talk about Jeff Pritchard?"

"In part," said Tess.

"Wasted trip." He shifted on the bed with a grunt. "Sorry. But I don't remember anything."

Tess shifted on her own chair.

Noah said, "You scared?"

"Should I be?"

He shrugged.

She leaned forward. "When Pritchard was executed, his last words were 'Beware the one that got away.' My father was one of the men who rescued you from that house, Noah. You were the only one to escape him."

"Didn't escape," he croaked. "Cops took me out. Like you said."

"I know," she said. "And right after his electrocution, my parents were murdered. My daughter was taken." She glanced at Justin. "*Our* daughter. And others. My father's partner, the one who carried you from that house. Burt Lobell. He was murdered yesterday."

"I'm sorry."

Tess paused, tried to disguise the surprise she felt. "Why are you sorry?"

"Seems like what needed to be said, Detective."

She leaned forward, elbows on her knees, fingers interlocked. "The man who killed them. The man who took our daughter. He calls himself the Outcast. Does that ring a bell?" He looked like he didn't understand, so she explained. "Does that make sense? Does it register?"

"I know what ringing a bell means, Mrs. Claiborne."

"So does it?" she countered.

"Should it?"

"You tell me," she said. "You killed your father a month after you returned home from that house. Carved the word *outcast* across his chest. Used glass from a broken bottle of bourbon. You cut out his eyes."

"So I was told," he said. "I don't remember any of it."

Justin looked restless in the neighboring chair, as if begging to jump in. She fleetingly touched his knee; he'd have his turn in a minute.

"This Outcast," she said. "He's painting the victims' eyes black. Like he's making them see some darkness. Does that mean anything to you?"

"You mean does it ring a bell?" His voice was so flat and haunting that chill bumps spread up and down her arms.

Justin leaned forward, but kept calm, his clinical voice. "Is this a joke to you?"

"Like my life, Doctor." He ruffled his beard. "These looks, they can be deceiving. I'm harmless. I could never dream of doing these things you say."

Tess moved from candor to confrontation. "Did your father think you were harmless?"

Noah shifted on the bed. Both the warden and Ray watched him closely. "I've been locked in here for so long the days bleed together and clot. I've never stepped outside these walls without supervision and armed guards. My father was murdered, just as you say. I hated him. And I wanted him dead." He sat more upright on the bed. "But what if I said I didn't do it? That I didn't kill my father like they said?"

Tess met his gaze head on. "I wouldn't believe you."

Noah glanced at the warden, and then toward Tess and Justin, pausing briefly on each one of them. "I'm sure the warden here has told you about my . . . condition? He hasn't, has he? Oh, I see. He wants the doctor and the detective to figure it out on their own." He looked at Tess. "Like some kind of game."

She flinched at the word *game*, and then straightened against the seat.

The warden looked at Justin. "Yes, Noah. Very astute of you. I would like an unbiased opinion from Dr. Claiborne."

"Do I get a ribbon?" asked Noah.

"I'm afraid not."

Noah's head sagged, but not so far that Tess couldn't still see his eyes, and for the first time she saw genuine emotion in them—sadness and fear and confusion all bundled up into one. He looked back up, and when he spoke, his voice had lost some of its edge. "I get asked the same questions. I doubt it'll differ with you. I'm a good man when I'm in control."

She leaned forward again. "In control of what?"

"My mind." He glanced at Justin, who'd just scooted his chair closer. "Sometimes it ain't my own."

"That's what your mother said."

"You talked to my mother?"

"My father did."

"She's dead."

"I know."

"Never came to see me. I'm glad, though. I wanted her dead too."

Justin said, "She mentioned something about an ark? And flood waters?"

"You know why she named me Noah?"

"Yes."

"Well, she made Noah his own ark," he said. "It was a closet inside my bedroom. Even painted the words above the door. She'd put me in there whenever I was bad."

He looked down, solemnly.

Justin leaned forward. "Tell us about Oskar and Ruth."

"What of them?"

"She said they were imaginary friends," said Justin. "But I'm not so sure they weren't more than that. Noah?"

Noah scooted back on the bed until his back hit the wall. He reeled his feet in, propped his elbows on his raised knees, and buried his face so that all Tess could see was the top of his head.

Something had just happened.

Warden Hofmann's eyes flicked to Justin as if wondering if he'd noticed.

Ray stepped closer to the bed but stopped.

Justin scooted his chair closer. Too close. Ray cautioned him.
Justin didn't seem afraid, but appeared suddenly rejuvenated. "Noah,
what happened to your imaginary friends? Oskar and Ruth. What
happened to them?"

Noah's head lifted, slowly. His eyes looked different; his face less
tense, which could have made him look younger under the ceiling
glow. "Noah's gone." What emerged from that beard was no longer
Noah's voice. Instead, it was the voice of a little boy who sniffled and
rubbed his nose. Not only had the voice changed, but also his
demeanor, which was now sheepish and small.

Justin, undeterred—or if he was fazed didn't show it—asked, "If
you're not Noah, who are you?"

"Dean." The young voice sent chills down Tess's spine. "Noah
was getting confused. Scared of the questions."

The shift in Noah seemed to fuel Justin even more. "Dean, do
you have a cold?"

"Yes."

"Does Noah?"

"No."

"How old are you, Dean?"

"Ten."

"Do you have a last name?"

"Can't remember."

"Try."

"We're all brothers under the same God."

"Is that what Noah says?"

He shrugged.

Justin said, "Who else is in there with you, Dean?"

Dean swallowed, then closed his eyes for ten seconds as if he'd
suddenly fallen asleep. "Noah's in here. Somewhere. Lost. He needs
help. We all do."

"Who is all?"

"Me, Stephen, Tom." He paused. "And Amelia."

Tess's pulse raced at the mention of the name Amelia. On the
plane, she'd come across a coloring done by Noah as a boy that he'd
signed *Amelia*.

"What about Oskar?" Justin continued. "And Ruth? Are they in
there?"

"Not supposed to talk about them."

"Who says?"

"She does."

"Who is *she*?"

"Mother."

"Your mother is dead, Noah," Tess said. "She can't hurt you anymore."

Noah began to rock slightly, hugging his knees, and, still in Dean's voice, said, "He's taking them to the Playhouse."

Tess bolted upright. "What? What did you just say?"

"The Playhouse."

"What is this Playhouse?"

Fear struck Noah's eyes. "I don't know. Sometimes the wires get crossed. All of our wires. He'll hurt us if we tell."

Tess couldn't fathom this voice coming from that man, like he was possessed.

Justin, who seemed in his element, stayed on point. "Do you know someone who calls himself the Outcast?"

"Don't know."

Tess jumped in. "Dean? Do you see the darkness?"

Dean paused. "We all do."

"Even Noah?" she asked.

"He does, but he doesn't remember."

"Do Oskar and Ruth see it?"

Dean nodded, but said, "Not supposed to talk about Oskar and Ruth."

Tess stiffened in her seat. *There's someone in there he fears, who can hear his voice but not see his actions.*

"Tell us about the eyes." Justin scooted his chair closer yet again, prompting the warden to caution him with a lifted arm. His eyes said, *No closer.* Justin asked, "What are the eyes, Dean?"

Noah trembled as if palsied. "They're always watching, staring, waiting . . ."

"Waiting? For what?"

"To come out and get us."

"Who do they belong to?"

"Don't know." Noah shielded his face. His handcuffs rattled. Suddenly he knelt on the bed, raised his arms toward the ceiling.

Ray grabbed his arms to calm him. "Easy now, Dean. They aren't going to hurt you."

"Words hurt."

"Yes," said Ray. "Words hurt." He glanced at the warden with eyes that said *Put a stop to this*, and Tess reassessed her opinion of this burly guard—but the warden didn't react.

Tess scooted closer to Justin. Noah's eyes had changed again, not in color, but in emotion, in personality, in confidence.

He's not Dean anymore. But he's not Noah either.

Noah blinked. The eyes changed again, became harder. Even kneeling, he seemed larger atop that bed.

"Justin," whispered Tess.

He took her hand.

Noah had removed a pair of sunglasses from his shirt pocket and put them on.

Ray turned toward the warden. "Get them out. *Now.*"

Moving more quickly than Tess would have thought possible, Noah lunged for the warden's throat, clutched it, and pushed him against the bars of the cell, showing a strength that seemed uncanny.

Ray was on him in an instant.

Their chairs toppled as Justin pulled Tess back against the far wall. Noah came at them, but the ankle chain cut his approach short, as did Ray, who, despite Noah's sudden uptick in strength, was bigger and stronger. But the voice was new, deep and familiar, much like the one she'd heard over the phone inside Lobell's house an hour ago. "I p-p-paint their eyes so they can see the d-d-darkness."

Ray forced Noah back toward the bed, pinned him under his weight, although Tess could tell the guard was being as gentle as possible. There was a connection there, a level of respect Tess couldn't help noticing as arms flailed and spittle flew from Noah's mouth.

But Tess couldn't get past the fact that Noah was somehow now the Outcast, or at least doing an incredible job of impersonating him.

Noah's eyes, amid the struggle, settled on Tess across the cell. "You remember, don't you? Under the t-t-twisted trees . . ." Noah grunted as Ray wrestled him still. He seemed to give in but wasn't done with his message, which along with being hurried, was clearly for both Tess and Justin. "These murders, they're only s-s-stepping stones," he said, gasping. "They're momentum. They're only setting the sta—" He stopped abruptly, as if something had suddenly pained him—not Ray atop him, but rather something internal. Like he was in a fight with himself.

But it was clear to Tess what he was about to say. *The murders are only setting the stage.* But for what?

Secured now under Ray's weight, Noah, who was still somehow the Outcast, fixed his eyes, hidden behind the sunglasses, back on Tess alone. "I'll t-t-take care of her, Mrs. Claiborne." He panted, deep and heavy. She stood, but Justin held her back. "We play fun games at the Playhouse." He smiled; it was still him but drifting. "We paint. We s-sing. We dance . . ."

Noah rested his head on a pillow. Ray gently ran a hand over Noah's hair, calming him further. Noah removed the sunglasses, dropped them to the bed. His eyes stayed open, focused on Tess, but they were softer now. His beard moved with a new voice, a younger voice again, that of a little girl Tess assumed was the one he had called Amelia. "My God, my God, save me from the thing I can't see," she said. "Save me from the eyes in the darkness. Take them away from me. My God, my God, save me . . ."

Tess went dizzy and stumbled back into the wall before Justin could grab her.

She closed her eyes.

Smelled the mask rubber.

Her mind opened.

She was a teenager.

Her father was talking to his partner, Burt Lobell, as she . . .

. . . pulled the wool blanket up to conceal her face in the back seat of her father's car. She was trapped. So stupid of her. But there was no turning back now. They were getting close. Her father and Burt had stopped talking. Nervous silence permeated the car, which came to a skidding halt atop gravel she could feel pinging against the car's undercarriage.

She hunkered down behind the seat. More cars pulled in behind them. Hushed voices. Shoes on gravel. Car doors opened, but not hers. She flinched as a clap of thunder shook the ground and then the clouds opened. Heavy isolated drops followed by the tumult. Lightning lit the dark sky, silhouetting the surrounding trees. And then her father, the driver, just on the other side of that leather seat, opened his door and stepped out.

Burt exited next. Their doors closed.

She was alone again.

Their footsteps moved away from the car.

She gave them time, counting to thirty, and then lifted her head out from beneath the blanket for air. She peeked over the lip of the window as the men closed in on that house. That big white colonial with the upright façade. The windows, like eyes. The bright red door. The wraparound porch stretched like an evil grin.

Her father had his gun out.

He closed in on the front porch with three other men while Burt Lobell went around to the side door. Her father knocked. Waited. Rain fell hard, drenching the officers like oil slicks.

And then the door opened . . .

"Tess."

Her eyes popped open.

Justin hovered, gently took her hand.

"I saw it," she said, the back of her head resting against the cold hallway floor where they must have dragged her.

"Saw what?"

"I was there," she said. "I was in my father's car when they arrested him."

Justin's eyes grew large. "Pritchard?" Yet he remained calm.

"Yes. I was hiding. In the car. So determined to be a part. So stupid."

"Tess, slow down."

"You were right, Justin." She gripped his hand, squeezed it. "The hidden memories. They're from my childhood. I was there the night they arrested him. No one knew. No one knew."

Before

*D*ETECTIVE *LELAND PATTERSON aimed his flashlight into the basement's dark corner shadows, revealing another room they'd yet to discover.*

The arched wooden door was open, lock busted, little slivers of the dry-rotted wooden threshold littering the concrete floor like toothpicks. He inched closer to the room, smelled evidence of human excrement and urine and sweat. Air that hadn't moved for a while.

He had a notion to call out to his partner, Burt, but knew he was busy with the boy back in the main portion of this evil lair, the only one found alive, the one who seemed too stunned to even recall his name, but had at least nodded when they'd asked if he was Noah Nichols. They'd run down the list of kids they'd been searching for now for weeks and this boy had matched one of them.

Detective Patterson inched his way into the dark room, flashlight beam unsteady due to the subtle shaking of his arm. Leland was typically unfazed by most things, but after that weird smile on Jeff Pritchard's face when they'd cuffed him—like the joke somehow was still on them— and seeing those dead kids in the other room, how could he not be on edge? And something told him the surprises weren't yet over.

But he didn't expect to see this.

He stopped in the center of the small room, ceiling low enough that he had to slightly duck. He turned in a circle, panning that flashlight, revealing dozens of candles burned to nubs, so many colors of melted wax, hardened on the floorboards, because there was no other source of light down here.

And then he saw the walls, each of them.

And then hunkered down to get a good look at the ceiling.

And he said, "Burt, I think you're gonna need to see this."

At which point Jeff Pritchard, in the other room, started laughing.

27

TESS SIPPED COLD water from a glass inside the warden's cluttered office, nursing a headache that was finally waning, her mind stuck on an image that had come to her while she'd been out, the secret room her father had discovered in the basement of Jeff Pritchard's old house.

What had been all over the walls and that ceiling?

And then suddenly, it left her, and the voices in the room warped in with no warning.

She sat pensively, listening to the two men converse, one in the chair beside her, the other across the desk in a wooden chair too big for his body, one she now felt closer to than she had in months, the other distrusted more by the minute.

Her husband and the warden.

Neither one of them had noticed the pill she'd grabbed from the bottom of her purse when they'd entered the office. Nor had they seen her palm it into her mouth before she took a drink of water and settled into the chair and told Justin for the fifth time she was better now. She could tell he didn't believe her.

In fact, by the look in his eyes, she'd bet he sensed what she'd just done.

But she'd needed to calm her nerves, and the pain pill had already begun to work. She sat quietly, as content as one could be in her situation, while Justin was irate, throwing around words like *lawyer* and *lawsuit* and Tess was doing her best to figure out how those things fit in.

She reached over and pulled him back down to his chair. "Justin, stop. I'm fine."

"He could have killed us."

The flustered warden folded his hands on his lap. "I'm sorry. Noah hasn't acted violently in years. That was *not* normal. Those rapid switches . . ."

Tess gripped Justin's arm this time to keep him down. "It's okay."

Justin took a deep breath, exhaled. In his eyes, she could still see the question he'd asked repeatedly when they'd pulled her from Noah's cell: *What was he talking about back there? What night under the twisted trees?* She'd told him she didn't know, and it was true, but what frightened her most was that Noah shouldn't have known. He couldn't have known.

The warden moved papers on his desk, pulled a file from a stack and opened it. "Look, Dr. Claiborne. Am I to assume you've diagnosed Noah Nichols with dissociative identity disorder?"

"I'm leaning that way, yes, but I'll need more time with him."

"You can have all the time you need. He's all yours. I only hope you can get out of him what you want. But what you saw back there, it wasn't normal. It was like he was showing off, switching like that . . ."

Tess's eyelids felt heavier every time she blinked. She was confused, yes, but worried even more, as that revelation of her hiding inside her father's car as a girl when they'd arrested Father Silence was not the only memory coming back to her. She'd been inside that house days before—she remembered sitting at Jeff Pritchard's kitchen table—but why? That memory had never left her from childhood. It had been pushed so deep she'd often thought it had been a dream, or a nightmare, but it had always been in her periphery. But her being inside the car the night of the arrest . . . that was fresh. So fresh and new it sickened her. She felt discombobulated, still, as the warden's voice warped back into focus.

"But he's so convoluted his personalities don't even know where they are," he said.

Tess closed her eyes, hated herself, demanded focus. "How often does the Outcast personality come out?"

"About four years ago he attacked a guard. He went for the eyes, but we got him settled before he could do damage. He's come out other times, but without attacking anyone."

Tess asked, "Then how could you tell it was him?"

"Same way you can tell with any distinct personality," said the warden. "The voice. His stutter. The actions. The aggressiveness is just a facet of his personality. But he doesn't have a name like the others."

"The Outcast," said Justin. "That much was obvious."

"The Outcast is not a name. Not a real name." The warden pushed the file he'd opened across the desk. "Noah's file. One of them, at least. It's thicker because he's more complicated. He's got at least five people in that mind of his. Perhaps as many as seven. I've tried, but I get nowhere with them individually. Maybe I'm asking the wrong questions, and he's not my only patient."

Tess said, "Prisoner."

"Prisoner, fine. Calling them patients helps make my day just a little less gloomy, so humor me."

Justin grabbed the folder, leafed through it. "Noah remembers bits of his past, but nothing from his weeks with Jeff Pritchard?"

The warden opened another file and pointed to a newspaper article. "He doesn't even remember killing his own father."

"Because one of his other selves killed him," said Justin. "Presumably the Outcast."

"Precisely." The warden's smile returned. "Noah understands his disorder. As a kid he would black out. Lose time. Draw pictures he'd never remember drawing. Get in trouble for things he didn't remember doing. He'd forget days, weeks at a time. It seems that during his time in that house, he lost an entire month."

Tess leaned forward in her seat. "Then at least one of his personalities should remember the time spent in that house."

"Or all of them," said Justin.

"I just haven't been able to discover it yet," said the warden. "And like I said, if he was my only prisoner perhaps I'd understand more. But, admittedly, he's not my problem. I've got some men in here who make Noah Nichols look like Charlie Brown."

Justin flipped through the file, looked up. "Noah's mother mentioned two others. A boy and a girl. Imaginary friends from *before* his abduction."

"Oskar and Ruth." Warden Hofmann clasped his hands. "I've never been able to figure out if they are, indeed, personalities. Not like what you saw with the others in there."

"Noah's mom seemed to think they were," Tess added. "She called them possessions."

"Indeed, I do recall her more than once using the word demons in regard to what we now know to be distinct personalities." The warden removed his suit coat and draped it over the back of his chair, revealing sweat stains at the pits. "Especially the two you just mentioned. The two I've never heard from in all my years here."

"Oskar and Ruth?"

"Yes." He loosened his tie, folded his arms, and sighed like he didn't know where to go from here.

Justin asked, "What do you know of the Lost Children of Silence?"

"Very little. Other than what was said in the newspapers."

"And what he said in there about these murders," Justin said. "Stepping stones to something bigger?"

Warden Hofmann shook his head. "I don't know. Unfortunately, cults have formed around these parts in response to all of this. This Lost Children cult just seems to be the newest, and most heard from. Hoodlums seeking attention. Vandals."

"But nothing that could link Noah to them?"

He pursed his lips, shook his head.

Justin pointed to Noah's thick file. "I noticed a pack of cigarettes in Noah's shirt pocket."

"Very observant."

Tess hadn't noticed it. She looked at both men. "You allow him to smoke?"

"No. I allow him to keep an unopened pack in his shirt pocket. A minor request I decided not to deny him." He held up a finger. "Although if he asked, at this point, I believe I'd let him."

Tess asked, "He's never smoked the first one?"

"No."

"Then why does he need them?"

"For some kind of security? I don't know. Probably the same reason Steinbeck had Lennie keep a dead mouse in his pocket to pet."

Tess hadn't expected a reference to *Of Mice and Men* from the warden, but for whatever reason it helped her trust him.

Justin continued: "Does one of his personalities smoke?"

"Not that I've seen. He just likes to have them just in case."

"In case of what?"

"That's what I've been waiting to find out."

Justin leaned back, raked a hand through his hair. "Who all have you heard from?"

"Well, there's Dean, who you've met. There's Amelia, the girl, she's the one you heard reciting that prayer. There's Stephen. He's eleven. And Tom, age eight."

"Where did they come from?" asked Tess.

"Where all dissociations and alternates and multiples come from."

Justin answered in quick professional mode. "From the host. They create them, and they can have quite elaborate histories and memories."

"Except in this case," said the warden. "Noah's alternates do not. They know only their names and ages, with very little to nothing of their past. Fictions created that aren't all that interesting. Nothing like other cases such as Billy Milligan, or . . . or Karen Overhill or Louis Vivet, one of the first diagnosed with something such as this."

Tess said, "Or maybe someone inside of Noah is keeping a lock on them. A lock on their memories."

The warden fanned out the top few pages from a stack of artwork, colored drawings and sketches piled two feet high atop the desk, and Tess instantly recalled seeing a specific coloring inside her father's briefcase. "There's more behind me here," the warden said, gesturing toward the cluttered shelves on the wall. "They draw them all the time, specifically these eyes. They dream about them. They have nightmares about them."

"They're afraid," said Justin. "They're literally drawing out their fears."

"Not all of them." The warden held up a finger, as if to say *Wait for it*. From the wall behind him, he grabbed another stack of drawings and placed them on the desk.

Justin immediately started looking through them, and it was only after seeing his shocked reaction that Tess looked too—these drawings were remarkable, showing the talent of an experienced artist rather than the childlike renderings of the others.

Pencil sketches, oil paints, watercolors, and charcoal sketches. Landscapes of the woods, she assumed, surrounding the asylum. Renditions of popular paintings she'd seen before, from art history classes in college, but couldn't remember their exact names. Portraits of men and women she assumed might be workers from the asylum, leading the warden to add, "We sometimes let this one paint the staff."

Justin flipped these over. "These aren't signed."

Tess said, "Who painted these?"

"The same man you saw come out in there."

"The Outcast?"

The warden nodded toward the stack of artwork. "Yes. At least, we assume it's him. He always puts the sunglasses on before . . ." He gestured toward the stack before them. "Before the talent comes forth."

Tess looked through the stack, one masterpiece after another. "This is unbelievable."

"Another interesting thing to note." The warden leaned forward, his elbows on the desk. "Noah gets older, every year."

"As do we all," said Justin.

"But not Noah's alternates." This was a new grin from the warden, one of genuine support for their cause. "They haven't aged at all. Not even enough to create new memories. They're just . . . in there." He sighed, exhaustedly. "Look, I want you to find him. I want Noah to be able to help find your daughter. But he's mentally unstable. Untrustworthy."

"Could it be possible that he's faking it?" asked Tess, suddenly hopeful. "Kenneth Bianchi, the Hillside Strangler—I read he faked multiple personalities and fooled several psychologists."

"He did," agreed Justin. "But I don't think Noah's faking. That was too eerie to *not* be real."

"Bianchi's plan was foiled in the end." The warden leaned back in his chair. "He couldn't keep it up. But Noah, I'm afraid, is the real deal. There's something terribly explosive inside him, Doc."

Tess rubbed her eyes, felt the hydrocodone fully coursing through her bloodstream. "How can those voices be so different? And these . . . drawings?"

Justin said, "It's rare. A very rare psychological phenomenon. But multiples exist. Usually with children, stemming from sexual abuse. The host, or original personality, subconsciously creates a pretend world for himself. Sort of a rescue from within."

"Like a rescue from life," she said.

"The ultimate protective device," Justin said. "The personalities might exist all in the same body but were not necessarily created at the same time."

The warden added, "And inside, the personalities are aware of each other, and aware of the host, but many times the host is not aware of them. Children often mistake them for—"

Tess finished, "Imaginary friends."

"Yes," said Justin, "Except we don't know where Oskar and Ruth went."

"No," said the warden. "And Noah can switch personalities very swiftly. Without even being aware of it. Sometimes the transition is so slight it is practically unnoticeable."

Tess said, "For the host, time is always running?"

"Whether he remembers it or not," Justin said. "And his alternates can exist even when he's in control."

The warden said, "When we were in that cell with him, they were listening, mentally taking notes, all ready to come out if needed. But unlike many with this disorder, Noah is at least aware of it."

"Which is the first step to putting him back whole," said Justin. "Have any attempts been made for integration therapy?"

The warden laughed softly. "I'm sorry. No. There have been no integration attempts with Noah. Unfortunately, I don't have the time, the resources, or even the proper help for any necessary treatment these prisoners might need."

Tess took a deep breath and stood. "Warden, I understand that Noah is too mentally unstable to have committed any of these crimes, but that alternate personality back there claims responsibility. How is that possible? How can the Outcast be out there doing what he's doing and also inside the head of a man locked in a cell right down that God damn hallway?"

Justin stood next to her. "That's my job to find out."

28

Officer Dewy Evanston checked his watch, and then his phone.

One more hour watching Foster Bergman's house and his shift would be over. As soon as he got home, he'd pop open a cold one and get the charcoal grill going.

Linda had been texting him all day. Mostly about the kids and how they didn't listen to her. *Don't listen to anybody*, he'd responded. And then she asked him to pick up some meat for burgers on his way home. Fine by him, he was starving. Might even eat two tonight, with cheese, and maybe some bacon if they had some left over from breakfast.

When they'd first told him he'd be one of the crew watching Bergman's house he was excited. After three years of working for the sheriff's department, he finally felt like a big shot, or at least part of something big. But now, as he neared the end of his first shift, the boredom was killing him. Not even a peep from those surrounding woods, where the punk kids had begun to cause problems all over town. Mostly at night, ever since Father Silence got sizzled. Stirring up some dark shit Dewy wanted nothing to do with. Satanic cults that had reached all the way into the city.

He checked his watch again.

Fifty-five minutes and he would be home free.

Fifty-five minutes and he no longer had to work side by side with this twitchy young buck from the Louisville PD. What kind of a name was *Jeter Janks* anyway? Officer Jeter Janks, who, in Dewy's opinion, looked too frail to ever make it in this profession.

Other than a quick introduction, they hadn't said much to each other since their shift began. Jeter had mostly kept to himself on the far side of the house, leaning against his patrol car, never standing in one spot for more than a minute or two. Always fidgeting with something—his belt, his watch, his badge, his goddamn phone while on duty, the cuffs of his long-sleeve shirt when it was plenty warm enough to wear short.

If he didn't know better, Dewy would have thought the young buck was on drugs.

Maybe he was.

Dewy at least understood the logic of this unique situation. Once these murders got too big for Twisted Tree, Detective Evans had come in from Louisville flashing big city tin, which was fine. But then he'd suggested the shifts watching Bergman's house include one officer from Twisted Tree and one from Louisville. Thought it would be better if the two men on shift didn't know each other well. That way they wouldn't be as tempted to talk or lose focus.

Dewy didn't think it was a bad idea at all, until he'd been given a rookie with the social skills of an empty bucket.

Jeter Janks.

Dewy checked his watch again, and he could already taste that burger. When he looked up, he nearly pissed his pants.

Officer Janks stood three feet away with a damn animal mask over his head. A sheep mask by the looks of it, the rubber hanging down so low it covered part of his uniform collar.

"Quit goofing off," he told Janks. "This ain't the time for it."

But Janks just stood there staring, brown eyes visible through the eyeholes. He bleated like a sheep would, a short burst, and then went quiet again.

Rookie for sure had some screws loose.

Dewy's phone pinged with another text from home. Linda wanted him to pick up milk too. He huffed. "You married, Janks?"

Janks didn't answer, aside from bleating like a sheep again.

And then out came a knife.

CHAPTER

29

WHILE JUSTIN TOOK another go at talking with Noah Nichols, Tess stepped outside the asylum in search of fresh air.

She watched the surrounding woods. Something moved in the trees at the bottom of the hill, crunching over deadfall, but nothing showed. Footsteps drew her attention west of the asylum, down the hill to her left near where she'd heard the sound moments ago. The head of a goat stared up the hill toward her, the body concealed behind a tree trunk.

Too tall off the ground to be a real goat.

She moved cautiously down the grassy slope, still wet from recent rains. The goat head moved. She stopped, saw black jutting from the other side of the trunk, black boots and pants, the elbow of a black shirt. Some psycho in a goat mask. Maybe one of the Lost Children. They'd said they wore animal masks. She pulled her 9 mm and balanced herself into a shooting stance, thirty yards away from the masked visitor.

"Come out now with your hands up."

Goat Mask didn't move. But something else did about twenty feet north, another figure in black. This one hunkered down on all fours like the animal it portrayed—a sheep instead of a goat.

Goat Mask took a step out into the open, showing more height than had been evident behind that tree. His frame was thin, shoulders not fully filled out.

Late teens, early twenties.

Tess took another step down the hill. "Show me your hands." Goat Mask lifted his arms. "Remove the mask. Now. Slowly."

Instead of removing the mask, he reached behind him.

She fired a shot into the leaves by his feet.

Goat Mask flinched. He held a knife that looked marine style.

"Put it down. *Now.* The next shot goes into your knee."

Sheep Mask had crawled ten feet up the hill while she'd been focused on Goat Mask. Sheep Mask then started bleating, an eerie rubber-muted cry that wavered too close to the real thing for Tess's comfort. Reminded her too much of the weird shit she'd just seen inside the asylum. And then Goat Mask started bleating, the sounds of both mingling as if in some kind of satanic competition.

Warden Hofmann hurried from the asylum, froze ten paces away. "I heard a gunshot."

"Stay where you are, Warden," Tess cautioned.

Sheep Mask had dropped lower to the ground, half-concealed by the grass.

"Lost Children," said the warden. She heard him inching closer. "They wear animal masks to represent those sacrificed in the Bible."

Justin came out next. "Tess? What the fuck?"

Goat Mask lifted his chin and bleated.

Sheep Mask dropped down on all fours.

Goat Mask lifted the knife.

"Drop it!"

Sheep Mask rose to his knees and bleated loudly toward the sky.

Goat Mask started up the hill, slowly at first, and then a charge.

Tess fired, plugged him right where she said she would, blowing out the right knee in a mist of red. Goat Mask dropped to the ground, screaming—the pained, human kind of scream.

Sheep Mask took off into the woods and Justin went after him.

"Justin, no!"

Justin had been a sprinter in college. He'd lost very little athleticism into his thirties, and quickly gained on the man in the sheep mask.

Once Tess lost sight of Justin in the woods, she moved with caution down the hill toward the man she'd just felled. Goat Mask writhed on the ground, but was laughing now instead of screaming, and the mask had ridden halfway up his face to reveal a chin and mouth. The teeth that weren't missing were meth stained. Piercings all over his lips, tattoos down both sides of his neck. She removed the mask fully, revealing a young man with deadpan brown eyes and black hair and more piercings in his eyebrows, gold stud and loops and inked tears etched into the skin below each eye. He smiled as life drained from him.

A child of the night.

But her shot shouldn't have been fatal.

She looked down, found the knife inches from his right hand. He'd somehow slashed both wrists while she'd had her eyes on Justin. An upside-down cross tattoo marked the underside of his right forearm. The young man's eyes were red-rimmed, drugged so deep he had little left. And he died, grinning, as if he'd accomplished something.

Like a martyr.

A sacrificed animal.

She'd read the Bible as a teenager, and one passage referring to animal sacrifice had stuck with her. "Without the shedding of blood there is no forgiveness."

The animal dies for the sinner. The animal is a substitute for the sinner.

In this case, the animal *was* the sinner.

Goat Mask, this Lost Child of Silence. He'd sacrificed himself to conceal some warped truth. *Coward.* She stepped over the young man and surveyed the woods. Justin had gone in unarmed.

Her phone rang.

"Danny."

"Tess, Foster Bergman is missing."

"I thought they had two men guarding his house."

"One of them is dead. One officer turned on the other and then must have taken Bergman from the house. FBI is on the way. Evans is losing his mind—one of his own. A rookie cop named Jeter Janks just knifed his own damn shift partner. While on watch. I'm with Sheriff Kingsley. We're heading to Jeter Janks's house right now. Feeling is he's part of that cult."

She gazed out toward the woods.

"Tess, you okay?"

"Danny, have them send reinforcements to Berringer Hills."

"Berringer? Tess, what happened?"

"I just shot one of them."

"One of who?"

"The Lost Children. He came at me with a knife. From the woods. He was wearing a goat mask. He's dead—he slit his wrists. Justin took off after another one." There was a pause where she heard Danny breathing. "Danny?"

"Tess, what's going on here?"

"How do you know Jeter Janks killed that other officer?"

"Because he wasn't dead when we arrived at the scene. He said it was Jeter. Wearing a sheep mask."

"Christ. Send men now!"

"Tess?"

"The guy Justin chased into the woods was wearing a sheep mask. It might be him."

Still holding the phone, she sprinted down the hillside and entered the woods about the same spot Sheep Mask had gone in, Justin on his heels.

She hadn't ended the call with Danny. His voice crackled as he repeatedly called her name.

"I've got to go."

"Wait! We overlooked someone on that list. The revenge list. The most obvious one."

She stopped cold. "Who?"

"You, Tess. What if Julia was bait?" Danny asked. "What if it all comes back to you?"

CHAPTER

30

Danny could feel his back-seat position in the investigation coming, especially now that the FBI was taking over.

He'd already been relegated to Sheriff Kingsley's command, and Kingsley, admittedly, had all but bailed from the lead role once Jeff Pritchard was electrocuted, perhaps sensing the coming storm—the build-up of cult activity in the weeks preceding Father Silence's execution had been strong.

He understood; he'd been warned back home it would happen, but now that he felt his grip on things slipping, and with the fact that it was happening so soon after they'd arrived, he was driven too much now by emotion. Every second wasted was another second Julia was in the hands of that lunatic.

All he could think of was his own kids, Danny Junior, Bethany, Sam, Clare, and little Tommy. He'd move mountains. He'd harm. He'd maim. He'd kill if that's what it came down to—and truthfully, Julia was family too—so waiting for a warrant, as Kingsley was warning him about as they drove, was something Danny wasn't about to consider for long.

And deep down, Kingsley probably felt the same, otherwise he wouldn't have been driving so quickly toward the home of Jeter Janks. The sheriff gripped the wheel tight, misty-eyed as he navigated the back roads—the slain officer at Foster Bergman's house had been a friend, and as each minute ticked by, Danny felt like he and the sheriff were more on the same page. Not necessarily reckless abandon, but close. If they wanted things done the right way, when so far it seemed everything was going wrong, that judge Kingsley spoke of better hurry up and issue the warrant, because Danny was going in regardless. Not only had Janks murdered another officer but was now apparently at Berringer Hills endangering his friends.

Sheriff Kingsley pulled his cruiser to a skidding stop at the curb outside the one-story brick residence of Jeter Janks, their murderer at large. Danny opened his car door and was on his way through the front yard before Kingsley had cut off the car engine. Beer bottles and discarded trash littered the yard, which was mostly dirt, with wild roots snaking outward from a tall, leafless tree. No car in the drive-way. Probably nobody home. Yet hard-driving, satanic music blared from inside the house, loud enough to shake the windows, windows concealed by what looked like unevenly festooned black bed sheets. Strobes of light flashed at the creases, and Danny's heart sped.

He hadn't liked the way Tess had responded to his thoughts before she'd ended the call moments ago, the fact that she'd hardly responded at all troubled him.

Just . . . *Danny, I gotta go.*

But it made sense.

Maybe it *was* Tess this Outcast was ultimately after. And it was clear he wasn't acting alone. The theory of multiple murderers was no longer a hunch but now more likely their reality.

Danny knocked hard, knowing Janks wasn't here if he was at Berringer, but where one rat lived there lived more. He knocked again and waited to the count of ten, which, as fueled as he was, was probably more like five—Eliza said he always went double-time when he was pissed, which wasn't often. But when he was, she said, he sure got his money's worth.

Hell hath no fury like Danny Gomes scorned, Eliza once said over drinks with Tess and Justin, and they'd all laughed, even Danny, because it was true.

Kingsley approached through the yard, hefting his belt over his belly, saying something about a warrant that Danny mostly blocked out. In this case he'd rather ask for forgiveness than permission, so he raised his boot and kicked at the knob, once, twice, before backing away to regroup.

Next thing he knew, Kingsley had lowered his shoulder, and with a sudden burst of rage, plowed into the door, splintering it at the frame, sending a chained bolt flying, the door now wide open and the strobes of light hitting them like they were entering a rave.

They went in together, guns poised. The satanic music played from a stereo system across the room, blaring from two large floor speakers. A strobe light pulsed from an otherwise empty mantel above the brick fireplace.

Danny stood as if in a stupor.

Kingsley touched his arm, asked if he was good.

Danny nodded that he was—but what had they just done? He didn't know what he'd expected, but an irrational part of him hoped that Julia was in there waiting for him to save her. That she'd come running and jumping into Uncle Danny's arms, clinging to him like she would with Justin when they did the Panda Tree. Instead, he saw filth and decay and degradation. He smelled old food and pot. Whiskey bottles, some empty, some half full, littered the hardwood floor. A used condom sat on the rug before the hearth, where remnants of trash and fast-food wrappers had been burned in a half-assed log fire. Drug paraphernalia was scattered out across a corner-chipped wooden coffee table, remnants of white powder, ghost lines of it next to rolled dollar bills and needles and spoons, and Danny just wanted to hit somebody.

Kingsley turned off the music. Walked over and turned off the strobe. Said to Danny, "That better?"

Danny nodded, but maybe the silence now was worse.

Kingsley held up his phone. "Warrant just came through."

"Knock, knock," said Danny, tongue-in-cheek. "We'll pretend that came in a few minutes ago."

"Just so we're on the same page."

"Same page."

Kingsley exited into the kitchen, Danny assumed, to start checking the rest of the house. By eyeballing the exterior on his way in, it couldn't have been more than twelve hundred square feet, no basement. It wouldn't take long.

Danny heard Kingsley as he navigated throughout the rooms.

Kitchen, clear. Bedroom clear . . .

But a suitcase next to the couch caught Danny's eye, and as he walked toward it, he tuned everything else out. Danny unzipped the old suitcase and opened it to find nothing inside it except for two boarding passes, round-trip tickets from Louisville to Montana and back, dated within the past two days.

He recalled what Tess had said about the initial phone call from the Outcast, when he'd first called about the crime at the cabin, claiming responsibility.

He was a stutterer, yes, but . . .

On the phone that day, he'd clearly misspoken. He hadn't stuttered.

We . . . I did the bad thing . . .

Son of a bitch, Danny thought, suddenly craving the fresh air outside and heading toward it. The Outcast hadn't been alone that night in the cabin.

Out in the yard, Danny inhaled the good, clean, fresh air faster than he could exhale the bad. Who could live like that? Who could be that dark? That mean? He'd seen plenty of filth in his day, and maybe this wasn't the worst—it wasn't even close to some of the hoarders they'd seen, some of the brutal, barbaric murders they'd investigated, some of the neglect they'd witnessed—but something about this hit him hard and fast, and he knew it had everything to do with the personal inner workings of it all.

He'd eaten dinner at the Pattersons' cabin.

He'd sipped bourbon on Leland Patterson's front porch.

He'd been there when Julia was born. He'd been to every one of Julia's birthday parties. They'd witnessed her baptism. Her first communion. He'd taught her how to tie her shoes. How to shoot the wrapping off her drink straw. How to fake-take-off her thumb and burp into the Parcheesi cup and bellyflop into the pool and God damn being at this house right now, the house of one of the fuckers behind it all, made him want to come out of his skin with helplessness.

He knew what he needed to do next—be a pro and call his superiors, Detective Evans here and Chief Givens, back home and let them know to check Jeter Janks on all those flight records, and he'd get to doing both in a second, but the first call before any of them was the only one he *could* make right now.

He dialed, paced across the shitty-ass yard, and waited until he heard Eliza's voice answer on the other end, from across the country, heard his kids in the background asking if that was Daddy and when's Daddy coming home and . . .

"Danny . . . what's wrong?"

"Eliza, baby." Tears swarmed his eyes.

"Yeah, talk to me, Danny. Tell me something good. Did you find her? Please tell me you—"

"No, we haven't found her."

After a pause of brief defeat—Eliza was never down for long—she said, "You will. You hear me, Danny. You stay strong. Danny . . . What's wrong?"

"Everything . . ." He swallowed, closed his eyes, felt strength and resolve already returning to him. "Just needed to hear your voice."

She sniffled, said, "You got your Kevlar?"

He wiped his face. "Yeah, babe. I got it."

"Then you keep going."

CHAPTER

31

TESS HURTLED THROUGH the woods, dodging trees, jumping over brambles and thickets of deadfall, following, looking, desperately trying to find signs to where Justin had gone, unarmed, chasing after an officer of the law now *wanted* by the law.

Maybe Danny was right, and this did come back to her. But why? She'd been a teenage girl when Jeff Pritchard was arrested.

You know why, Tess.

Deep down she did, yes. She'd told Justin she'd been inside her father's car when they'd arrested Father Silence, but she hadn't told him she'd been inside that house . . . but it was too fuzzy, why and how she'd gotten in.

A shot fired, echoed close.

Birds scattered from wide, gnarled boughs.

"Justin," she screamed.

Another shot.

She crept onward, her finger on the trigger of her 9 mm. Sirens approached from the east, louder as they sped toward the asylum.

She heard footsteps.

She ducked behind a tree, glanced toward the source. Twenty yards away, Justin stumbled, limping toward her, using the trees for balance.

Thank God.

She ran to him. He draped his arm over her shoulder, using her like a crutch. She took his weight as he favored his bent right leg.

"Are you hit?"

"Not with a bullet," he said, wincing as he limped. "I was gaining, and then out of nowhere, another one jumped out from behind a tree and hit me with a pipe. He was wearing a bull mask." Justin leaned on her for support. "Sheep Mask stopped running after I was down. He fired at me but missed. Twice. They took off running when they heard the sirens."

Justin's limp eased, like he was walking off a sports injury, and by the time they navigated the wooded hillside toward the clearing, he was walking on his own power.

"Foster Bergman is missing," she said. "Janks took him."

Four Twisted Tree police cars skidded to a halt atop the hill, lights flashing. Doors flew open and the warden pointed down the hillside toward Tess and the woods. Half of the men hurried toward Goat Mask lying dead in the grass, the rest toward Tess and Justin.

But Tess had already ducked back into the tree line, following a hunch. Near where Janks had been hiding behind the tree earlier, she saw a bucket with a long-handled brush propped on top. She ran to it. Dark red paint stained the bristles. She followed splotches of it from the leaves on the ground to the nearest tree trunk, and there they were, about five feet up from the ground, painted right onto the bark—a pair of red eyes.

As the Twisted Tree officers navigated the grassy downslope toward them, Tess turned away, followed where those eyes could have been staring.

"Detective Claiborne," one of the officers shouted.

She ignored the voice.

She walked deeper into the woods and Justin followed.

"Tess, that wasn't paint," Justin shouted after her.

"I know."

Twenty yards ahead she found another set of eyes, this pair on the bark of a tree facing north toward the river.

Stepping stones for something bigger . . .

She followed where those eyes were looking, and thirty yards away was another tree with bark recently painted with blood, and these eyes took her west another fifteen paces, and when she saw Foster Bergman's lifeless body propped up in a sitting position against another tree she began to sprint.

CHAPTER

32

Tess was numb.

She stood halfway up the hill, in between the woods and the asylum, avoiding the action.

The trees surrounding Berringer Hills were full of officers and detectives, technicians and forensics, men and women entering and exiting the woods with little emotion—professionals, all of them. Ordinary men and women willingly taking a close look at the ugliest dish of life one could serve and trying to make sense of it. The FBI had arrived ten minutes ago with its regional Child Abduction Rapid Deployment team, unsure if Julia Claiborne and Richard Moore had even been taken across Montana's state line—they weren't convinced the Outcast's call to Lobell's house hadn't been prompted by a second source—but they were taking no chances and were in constant contact with their CARD team out west.

A three-acre section of trees, from the point where Tess had shot Goat Mask to where Justin had been confronted by the Sheep and Bull, had been marked off by crime-scene tape. Goat Mask now had a name—Kyle Penters, age twenty-one—former A student and track star at Twisted Tree High School before drug use derailed him and two stints in juvie downed any hope.

Her shot earlier hadn't been fatal. The kid slit his own wrists like some martyr. Yet Tess couldn't shake the guilt from having put a bullet in him.

You didn't kill him, Tess, Justin had said minutes ago. *Life killed him. The drugs killed him. You understand me?*

She'd nodded.

She did understand. She'd done what she'd had to do.

He'd said it with so much confidence that she knew it was true, although true didn't make it easier to swallow. Here she was desperately searching for her daughter, and she'd just shot somebody's son. She was fine until Justin had reached out and wiped that tear from her left cheek, a tear she hadn't even been aware was there.

He rubbed her shoulder and went back into the asylum for one more chance with Noah—he'd had little success with him earlier, during their initial visit—and she knew right then, the moment he'd wiped away that tear, without her even glancing up the hill as he went, that she still loved him.

Despite all.

She closed her eyes against a newly arrived wind and smelled rain in the air, felt a chill against her cheek from where the tear had been. If only she could close her eyes to the memory of finding Foster Bergman leaning against that tree trunk with his eyes painted black.

And what Noah had said earlier in the cell, the word *momentum*. Stepping stones. If it was momentum they were trying to build, she believed it, as the time between murders had grown shorter.

As a kid, when Bergman was a priest, she'd visited him with her father numerous times, and he'd given her cookies and milk and interesting facts on Church history. His smile was genuine and kind. He'd been the first to start getting weird feelings about the parish's school janitor at St. Michael, a quiet man everyone in the community respected for so thoroughly minding his own business, shuffling through life with a mop and a bucket, with tools attached to his belt, never failing to leave a place cleaner than he'd found it.

But Jeff Pritchard had a kind smile as well, one he used to disguise and deceive. Roaming the alleys and back roads dressed in priest's clothing to lure in unsuspecting victims. Until one day Father Foster recognized that some of his clothes were missing from his bedroom inside the parish house. One of the hangers that typically held his pairs of black pants and black button-down shirts. He questioned the sacristan at the time, and she let out a short laugh before stifling her amusement with a hand, and then explaining that the clothes bandit was at it again. Father Foster didn't get it, so she, as the sacristan for the past fifteen years, told him that the same had happened to Father Gary, the pastor before him, and also to Father

Timothy, the pastor before that. In jest, those around the parish house, including the priests, had referred to the culprit as the clothes bandit, although they figured the clothes had just somehow been misplaced. Or lost. Or, perhaps, accidentally tossed in with the laundered hand-me-downs donated by parishioners before being given away to those in need. Father Foster had laughed right along with her, but, as he later told Tess's father at the beginning of the investigation, he soon realized it might not be so funny.

One priest's missing clothes was not a matter of concern. Two, maybe an interesting coincidence. But three? There was someone out there wearing clothes they shouldn't be wearing—clothes, in fact, possibly being used for all the *wrong* reasons. And then things started to click. Who at the parish had been there long enough to work for the past three priests? That list was long, but when narrowed down to those who'd had access inside the parish house, and had access to the bedrooms, it came down to one man. The one man who smiled often, but in Foster's opinion never for real—the janitor, Jeff Pritchard.

From that day on Father Foster had begun to watch him more closely. How he could never seem to make direct eye contact, even in passing. How painstakingly attentive to detail he was when he cleaned. A good quality for a janitor, probably, but to Father, as he told the detectives early on, a bit on the obsessive side. How he attended mass regularly but never went to communion or confession. And when asked, Jeff would schedule one the next day, as if eager to bury any concerns the pastor might have, to only then say, *Bless me father for I have sinned* when in confession. When Father Foster asked what those sins might be, Jeff grinned and said nothing.

Except maybe to Father Foster that grin said a whole lot because Jeff, at least with Father for the next several months, went silent from then on out. Like it was some trial run for the seventeen years of silence to come during his time on death row. A week later, a bedside rosary went missing from Father Foster's room. The next week, two chalices from the sacristy. And just as they'd made calls to have cameras installed, an alb and three cinctures went missing, along with other vestments Father typically wore during the Easter season.

Who had keys to everything?

Jeff Pritchard.

But Jeff had volunteered more than once to stand guard all night to see who might be sneaking in, and his offer, to everyone else at least, had seemed genuine.

Regardless, cameras were installed in places the pastor typically wouldn't want them, those deemed in the past too holy or private, but desperate times called for desperate measures, he'd told the detectives. Father Foster, to the chagrin of some of his parish council and coworkers, seemed to grow more paranoid by the day, and as soon as the cameras were installed, things stopped being stolen. It wasn't until a few weeks later that he'd seen Jeff Pritchard in the living room of the parish house, having paused in his vacuuming to watch what had just come across the news channel. Reports of yet another child gone missing, this one a boy named Noah Nichols, who had been missing for nearly forty-eight hours. Instead of turning off the vacuum, Jeff had left it running and turned up the television to an uncomfortable level, which had gotten Father Foster's attention. He'd been in the kitchen pouring himself tea from a jug when the volume went sky high, and then he'd found Jeff, one hand on the vacuum's handle and the other holding the remote, continuing to *up* the volume, higher and higher, completely unaware that his pastor was watching. Observing how Jeff seemed to find not only solace in the horrible news on the television but a macabre kind of excitement, because when the news showed the picture of Noah Nichols alongside the four other children who'd recently gone missing in and around the area, a wicked smile had oozed onto Jeff's face with such ease it made Foster's skin crawl.

Jeff had shaken his head in apparent disagreement when the news anchor suggested those children were at risk of harm—when, in fact, they'd later learn, the children were locked inside the basement of his riverside home—and had slammed the remote to the floor, popping the batteries loose. Foster had eased himself out of the room. The news went to a commercial for toothpaste, and Jeff resumed vacuuming, that toothpaste jingle chasing Father down the hall, his heart thumping so rapidly he thought it might burst like his father's had done at roughly the same age.

He called the police.

Detective Leland Patterson had said they'd look into it.

His hunch turned out to be true, but that call he'd made, in and of itself, hadn't been the death knell for Jeff Pritchard, and Tess, deep down, had always known that.

It had somehow been her.

But regardless, Foster Bergman's bravery had helped save lives. It had opened a door that had previously been shut or unknown to them.

But it also eventually got him killed.

Footsteps lured Tess's eyes back from her reverie.

Dusk had set in.

Danny approached from the glow of lights they'd set up atop the hill. He looked as tired as she felt. "How you holding up?"

She hugged her arms. "I don't know."

He watched the action in the woods. "I heard from Givens back home. No sign of our guy on any of the school cameras."

"Because he knew where they were."

"Possibly," said Danny. "But Chief got hold of nearly every parent at the school, showed them the pic of our guy. Three parents said they saw someone with sunglasses who looked like him walking in front of the school yesterday morning."

"And no one thought that strange? The sunglasses?"

"He was dressed as a priest, Tess."

"A priest?" Here we go again, she thought. "Of course."

"But he's not."

"How do you know?"

"They got that little girl to talk more. Julia's friend."

"Freckles?"

"She said the man seemed nice. That's why she agreed to take Julia's book bag inside. Said he was a priest. A friend of Father Beacon. Told her he'd talked to Father Beacon just last night and he said it was okay for Julia to go with him."

"Lying son of a bitch."

"Called himself Father Friday."

"Father Friday? What the hell is that?"

"Yesterday was Friday."

"Simple as that?"

Danny shrugged. "We checked the records across the country, every diocese and archdiocese, you name it, and there's no priest named Father Friday."

"Lured her in. Just like Pritchard. Perfect disguise."

"Not just any disguise," said Danny. "Once Freckles got talking, she really opened up. Said his clothes looked old, and didn't fit. Like they were too small. Pants too short. High waters."

"*No . . .*"

"My guess is yes. He didn't just dress like a priest. We think the son of a bitch wore Pritchard's clothes."

Clothes he'd stolen from others, decades ago.

Tess wiped her face as rage and sorrow bubbled in equal measure. Surely Julia was too smart for that. Too smart to go willingly with a man she didn't know.

Never talk to strangers. Never take candy from strangers.

They'd gone through it all, but had they hammered it in hard enough? Could they have done more to prevent it? If the Outcast, this so-called Father Friday, knew Tess, or knew about Tess's past, he could have used the information to lure Julia. For all she knew, he could have shown her the picture he'd stolen from her father's wallet, proving a link to Julia's grandfather as well.

I'm friends with your grandfather, Julia. I just visited them at their cabin in Lolo.

It could have played out in so many ways. You never know how a child might react, God forbid, until it happens.

Tess exhaled tension, conjured strength, until her emotions jumbled and out came a laugh, a memory of a joke Julia had told her a week ago. She said to Danny, "Why was six scared of seven?"

He looked at her blankly.

"Why was six scared of seven, Danny? Why was six scared of seven?"

"Why?"

"Because seven eight nine."

Wind moved the grass around her feet. She sniffled, wiped her eyes. *He thinks I've lost it. Maybe I have.* "One of Julia's jokes."

They stood silent for a several beats. "It's funny."

"No," she said. "It's cute. There's a difference." He watched her; she didn't like being watched, so she asked, "What did you find on Janks?"

"Has a ranch house the size of a shoebox halfway between here and Louisville."

"How deep was he in?"

"Cult?"

She nodded.

"Deep," he said. "Bomb shelter deep. His bedroom could have come from one of Dante's nine circles. Crazy tributes to the devil. To Father Silence. To Manson. Newspapers. Memorabilia. Enough to keep a truckload of detectives going for weeks."

"Flight records?"

"Janks was in Montana. No doubt. We have him on camera at the airport."

"Which one?"

"Both."

"Do you think he killed my parents? And not . . ."

"Yeah, I do," Danny said. "But if you're asking me to explain it, what exactly went on inside that cabin, and why this Outcast made the actual call, I'm not there yet. Not even close."

"Noah Nichols mentioned something earlier," she said. "About these . . . murders. The kidnappings, even, all setting the stage for something bigger."

"What could be bigger than this, Tess?"

She shook her head. "I don't know."

"And how does Noah know anything from this place?"

"Justin's trying to find that out."

Danny watched her with concern. He checked his phone, pocketed it. "Eliza wants to help."

"She already is."

"But she's doing what she can back home," said Danny. "When it comes to unwanted kids, she knows her way around the system. Has good contacts." He touched her arm. "I meant what I said on the phone. You gotta be careful."

"I'm a cop, Danny." She tapped her gun. "I'm my own protection."

He nodded toward the asylum. "You ready to explain what happened in there today?"

"No."

"Okay." He took a deep breath and nodded toward where Detective Evans was talking animatedly with an FBI technician. "I think I'm growing on him."

"You'd make a cute couple."

"You think Eliza would be jealous?"

"Doubt it."

He smirked, looked away, started down the hill.

"Danny."

He stopped, turned. "Yeah?"

"Thanks."

He tipped an imaginary hat and his pace picked up just as two Twisted Tree officers the size of NFL linebackers were heading up the hill.

She caught a whiff of their conversation. Something about that house on the bluff being vandalized the day of Pritchard's execution. They passed her and she sidled up beside them, stride by stride up toward the building—more like a haunted castle now under the moon glow.

"What house are we talking about?" she asked.

Both men stopped. The taller one said, "Jeff Pritchard's old house. It was vandalized a few days ago."

"Cult? Like what we saw at Burt Lobell's house?"

"No," said the shorter, stocky one. "Like good old-fashioned eggs and toilet paper. These Lost Children, they worship that house. They wouldn't vandalize it. Sometimes they gather in the woods around it, and we have to chase them off. Owner calls us about once a month on account of them gathering too close."

"Wait, someone *lives* in that house? I was under the impression it was going to be torn down."

"Never happened," said the taller officer. "Some lady from down south swooped in and saved it."

"Who is she?"

"Lisa Buchanon. Nice enough lady."

"Why?"

"Why is she nice?"

Tess shook her head, trying not to show exasperation. "No, why did she want the house?"

Short cop shrugged. "Location?"

33

"YOU SURE YOU want to do this?"

Tess nodded, watched out the window as Justin drove. She didn't *want* to do this—she *had* to. But fearing she'd have one of her episodes once they got close to that house, she'd thrown him the keys and directed him, which turned out to be the right move.

Three miles away, as trees stretched tall and roads narrowed, she'd started to feel uneasy. Dizzy and sick to her stomach, started getting that rubber mask smell. She massaged her forehead.

Justin asked if she wanted to go back, and she said no.

"I just want to ask her a few questions. We won't stay long." Talking seemed to help her nerves, so she kept at it. "No luck with Noah earlier?"

"No. He shut down the last two times I tried. Stared at me like he had no one in that head instead of an army."

She pointed. "Turn here. Maybe he's a morning person."

"Hope so." His hands were taut on the steering wheel, still internally raging from earlier, she could tell, when, before they'd gotten in the car, she'd told him about their Outcast posing as a priest, just as Jeff Pritchard had. "Why didn't he call?"

"Who?"

"The Outcast? After you found Foster Bergman in the woods, he didn't call like he did the other times."

"I don't know, Justin. Maybe this was just a rogue hit by these Lost Children. Maybe the Outcast has his own plan."

"Bergman was on the list, though."

"Our list," she said. "Maybe not his." Tess watched out the window as trees zipped by. The crescent moon blinked overhead as boughs had turned the road into a tunnel leading up the bluff toward the river. Her heartrate sped as he accelerated up the winding tree-lined road. When tires hit gravel her stomach churned, and suddenly she was a young teen again and hiding on the floor of her father's cruiser. The land beside the driveway opened into a clearing dotted by trees on the right and a field of tall grass to the left, beyond which rested dense woods that hugged the Ohio River for miles into the city.

Justin stopped the car. "So, you were here?"

"Long time ago." She watched out the windshield, heard heavy splatting raindrops but didn't see them. Just memory drops in her head. "It's changed. The barn is new. It was a carport back then. The house looks repainted. The front door used to be red. Reminded me of a clown's nose." She got out of the car and Justin followed. Wind swooped across the driveway, ushering in the smell of river water from just below the bluff, a nice thirty-foot drop-off of rock no more than sixty yards from where they now stood. "The pillars on the front porch are new."

It still had that southern appeal. Like an old plantation house.

"How could a janitor afford this land?"

"No kids," she said, like she knew. "Plus, this land has some dark history of its own. Probably kept the price down."

They started for the sidewalk that curved to the front porch—the walkway was bordered by meticulous landscaping and spring bloom—but then the side door opened, and a light came on over a small porch covered by an awning. In the glow stood an attractive middle-aged woman with blond hair gathered up by a clip on both sides.

Tess broke away from Justin and met her first. "I'm Detective Tess Claiborne. This is Justin Claiborne." They shook hands. Up close Lisa Buchanon appeared alluring, distinguished yet approachable in her yellow summer dress. Lisa's eyes lingered on Justin, a reaction from women Tess had grown used to over the years. Her eyes were baby blue, her smile broad, fingernails manicured. This wasn't what Tess had expected.

Tess entered the house with trepidation but tried not to show it. Justin knew she'd been outside the house years ago, the night of Jeff Pritchard's arrest, but she'd never told him she'd been *inside* it as well, *before* the arrest. And that visit, unlike the storm-filled events on the night of his arrest, she was starting to remember more clearly. She hoped this visit would clear it all the way. The interior of the house had changed drastically. The kitchen décor could have been pulled straight from *Southern Living*, with apples as the overwhelming theme. Lisa offered them seats at an oval wooden table and poured them sweet tea over ice, tea so bold and swimming with sugar and lemon that Tess downed half the glass in one tilt, just enough of what could have been considered home to make her briefly feel like she was there and her daughter was back in the bedroom playing, and her parents hadn't recently been killed by a psychopath who may or may not be intertwined with the history of this house. Ice clinked in her glass and the sound brought her back in a snap. In the kitchen light, Lisa's hair had more of a reddish hue, strawberry blond with no hints of gray at the roots. The officers had said she was fifty, but she didn't look it.

She poured herself a glass of tea and joined them at the table. "I'm sorry to hear what's going on. I'm not sure how much I can help, but I'll try."

"Why are you living here?" asked Tess. "I'm sorry to be blunt, but you do know the history of this house?"

Justin appeared embarrassed by Tess's question, so he smiled.

Lisa rotated the glass in her hands. "I'm originally from Russellville, a small town in southern Kentucky. But my grandparents lived here."

"In Twisted Tree?"

"Yes, but more specifically, in this house. This was my grandparents' house before . . . before *he* bought it."

"Jeff Pritchard?"

"Yes," she said, looking away, fiddling with her glass. "Jeff Pritchard. Father Silence." She scoffed. "This house has been in my family for three generations."

Justin said, "Minus the time Jeff Pritchard owned it."

"Yes, minus that time."

"How did he get it to begin with?" Tess asked.

"It went up for sale. He bought it. Very simple."

"But how did it end up outside the family?"

"A falling out between my parents and grandparents," she said. "My father was an only child. They assumed he'd stay in Twisted Tree forever. But he met my mother, fell in love, and ended up moving to Russellville, where she was from, and got married there. My grandparents were not happy about this, their only child abandoning them, as they put it. They refused to come to the wedding. To make a long story short, fences were never mended. Harsh things were said over the years. They cut my father, and this house, completely out of the will."

"And in comes Jeff Pritchard," said Tess. "Fresh from fleeing Bowling Green, after what we now know happened at his orphanage there, at the Sisters of Mercy."

Lisa gestured with her hands, as if to say *and the rest as we know is history.*

"And when you heard it was for sale again . . . ," Justin said.

"I thought long and hard about it," she said. "I drove up from Russellville and told myself, if it's still for sale, it's a sign that I should make an offer. If not, then it was never meant to be."

"Had you been here before?" asked Tess. "As a kid?"

Lisa's welcoming smile gave way to a look of solemnity. "Despite their differences, we did visit. My parents understood I was the only grandchild, so they made sure I knew my grandparents."

"And?" asked Tess.

"And what, dear?"

"What did you think of them?"

Justin squirmed. "Tess, I'm not sure what that has to—"

"It's okay," Lisa said, assuring him with an upright hand. "They had a full farm here for a time, when I was a little girl. It was like a zoo, almost, with cows and horses. Chickens and pigs and goats and sheep. I was fond of it all."

Tess closed her eyes, as the smell of rubber mask hit her. But the truth was she could now vividly remember sitting inside this kitchen as a girl as Jeff Pritchard poured her a glass of water from the sink.

She felt Justin's hand on her forearm and opened her eyes to find Lisa watching her with concern.

"Are you okay?"

Tess nodded. "The local cult, the Lost Children, they wear masks of animals."

Lisa said, "They know the history of this house. They do their homework. It's no secret what happened to the livestock here."

Justin asked, "What happened to the livestock?"

"They all died one summer," said Lisa.

"That's one way to put it," Tess said.

Justin watched them both. "What am I missing?"

"Hearsay," Lisa responded.

"According to—"

"Vicious rumors," Lisa said, interrupting her, and then, "I'm sorry. It's just that . . . even estranged, it's still family. And words hurt, especially where there are already bruises." She turned toward Justin, as if starting over. "There are some who say my grandfather, who we now know to have been mentally ill and battling depression for decades, shot all of his farm animals before turning the gun on himself."

"He committed suicide?"

"Yes. By the water well, right out there on the bluff overlooking the river."

"And the animals?" Justin asked, looking at Lisa and then Tess, waiting for one of them to offer up the story.

Lisa gestured toward Tess, as if to say *go ahead*.

"He shot them all," Tess said, in too much of a hurry to get it out. It was one of the stories that had drawn her to this house as a girl. The macabre. The dark. The unsettling. And then, out of respect, she added, "According to the rumors, of course."

"Before he turned the gun on himself," Lisa added bluntly. "But they were diseased. All the animals. They were losing weight. Not eating. Some of them were losing fur in splotches. Some had seemingly gone crazy, running into the fences, the side of the grain silo, some even escaping their confines to run right over the bluff here and into the river. So my grandfather, he . . . he put them out of their misery."

"He ended their suffering," Justin added softly, like a thought that verbally escaped. He glanced toward Tess, as if he was wondering if she'd also noticed the connection.

Young Jeff Pritchard helping all the animals from his childhood, all the ones buried in his own little pet cemetery.

Tess voiced her thought: "Do you think this is what drew Jeff Pritchard to this house. Its violent past? With what was done to the animals?"

"They were diseased," Lisa said again. "Don't confuse what my grandfather did with violence. Please. It only feeds the myth."

Justin asked, "But what kind of a disease would—?"

Lisa cut Justin off. "I don't know. They never knew, although my grandfather was convinced it was a lightning strike that caused it. One that split a tree right in the middle of the farm, leaving it charred and black. Perhaps it was some kind of odd version of mad cow, but nothing ever advanced past theories, guesses."

Justin asked, "What happened to the animals after—"

"He burned them," she said. "In fear of . . . of whatever they had spreading."

"And it never did?"

"No. No cases of . . . whatever it was, were ever reported. It was an isolated event."

"I'm sorry," Justin said. "About rehashing any of this. It wasn't our intent." Justin glanced at Tess, but he went on: "All we wanted was . . ."

"It's okay," Lisa said. "I understand why you're here. You're desperate to find your girl. I would be too. You wanted to know how I ended up in this house."

Tess said, "And now we know."

"And now you know," Lisa said.

Tess watched her, eyed her left hand, saw no ring on her finger.

Lisa caught her looking and offered a smile. "Is something on your mind, Mrs. Claiborne? I'm happy to be of any help I can, so ask away."

"Have you never been married?"

Lisa laughed. "No, I've never been married."

"It's just that . . ." Tess couldn't let it go. "You're an attractive woman . . . never mind. I don't know what I'm saying."

"That perhaps marriage isn't for everyone?" Lisa offered. "Would you believe at one point I flirted with becoming a nun?"

Tess smiled. "No, I don't think I'd believe it. You certainly don't seem like the convent type. What kept you out?"

"Just decided it wasn't for me."

"You've never wanted a family?"

"Tess, come on," said Justin.

Tess leaned back in her chair, agreed with what Justin was probably thinking. *Why was she questioning this woman?* "I'm sorry. I'm . . ."

"You have family on the mind," Lisa said. "I understand. I'm not offended. I was close to marrying a couple of times, before deciding it wasn't for me." She laughed again. "I had memories of this house, most of them fond, and so I moved from a small town that I felt had nothing to offer me any longer. When I heard this house sat vacant, I decided to save it from being demolished. I threw my heart and soul into renovating it. It's been a labor of love ever since."

"Doesn't it bother you, though," Tess said. "To know that a serial killer . . . ?"

"Of course it did, at first." Lisa sipped her tea and offered them more, which Justin took her up on. "The newspaper came out and did a big feature article on me and the house. It replaced those horrible pictures of old with this." She gestured to the décor. "I had everything gutted. Turned the basement into one big room for storage. Floors replaced. Restructured the rooms on every floor. Bright and lively. That was always my goal when I was decorating. My grandmother, when she was alive, always wanted things bright and lively." She settled her eyes on Tess. "It's beautiful here. I like it."

"We hear it was recently vandalized," Justin said.

"Oh, that was innocent enough," she said. "Although the egg was a hassle to remove. I took it as an attack on what this house once was, and not on me personally."

"But what about the others?" Tess asked. "The ones who gather in the woods as if paying homage to this house. The ones that perhaps aren't so innocent."

"I assume we're referring to the Lost Children?"

"Yes, ma'am."

"Oh, they gather once a month. I can hear them in the woods, but so far they don't get closer than a hundred yards. Cops have done a good job running them off."

"But not keeping them away?" asked Justin.

"My house has a nice security system," she said. "And this southern woman knows how to handle a gun." She lowered her head, rotated the glass atop the table, and looked up. "I read about that execution. Went horribly wrong, I hear. But it was closure for me, which is why I didn't even bat an eye when those eggs hit my house. Eggs wash off. Jeff Pritchard is gone now, and this house is back in the family."

Justin looked at Tess, raised his eyebrows.

Tess stood from the table, shook Lisa Buchanon's hand. "Can I ask one more question?"

"Shoot."

"Your last name?" Tess said, with a tilt to her voice. "This was once known as the Buckner Farm. Before it was owned by Jeff Pritchard."

"Hence the reason you asked if I'd never been married?"

"Well, yeah, that's what I was getting at."

"Two years before my grandfather committed suicide," she said. "My father did the same back in Russellville." She swallowed hard and looked away. "He hung himself from a beam in our barn. I found him hanging there. I was ten."

Tess stood stunned. "I'm sorry."

Lisa shook her head. "I screamed for Mother. Ran into the house. Found my mom in their bed, shot in the head."

"Jesus," Justin said under his breath, the guilty look on his face telling Tess they'd more than overstayed their welcome. "Look, we're sorry . . . thank you for . . ."

Lisa said, "It's no bother. Really." And then to Tess. "You see now why I was in no hurry to marry. To have kids and continue this gene pool I'd inherited. I was in and out of homes for a few years before a family adopted me. That's when I took the name Buchanon."

Another outcast, Tess couldn't help but think, shaking Lisa's hand and thanking her for her time and apologizing for bringing up her past. And thinking how important it was that she'd confronted this house without incident, but now how suddenly she felt the urge to leave it.

Outside on the gravel driveway, Justin again thanked Lisa, while Tess hurried to the car.

"My pleasure," Tess heard her say in the background.

When Tess opened the passenger door, she turned back toward the house, just in time to see Lisa's face moving away from Justin's cheek. At first, she thought she'd kissed him, but then realized she'd told him something.

As if for his ears only, and she'd intentionally waited until Tess was out of earshot.

Justin got in the car and closed the door. She stared at him as he backed out and headed down the driveway as if preparing to ignore what had just happened. But she saw how tightly he was clutching the steering wheel.

"That was weird, right?" he asked without looking at her. "I mean that past? Did you know anything about it?"

"Not all of it, no."

They drove in silence for a minute, before Justin said, "What? Tess?"

"What did she say to you back there?"

He got that wide-eyed look he sometimes got when he was not necessarily lying but concealing something. "Said she might not look it, but she's scared."

"Of what?"

"Everything that's going on."

"That's it?"

"Yeah." He wouldn't look at her. "Just scared."

She turned toward her window.

Neither of them talked all the way to the hotel.

34

J USTIN DIDN'T DRINK caffeine.

He didn't like how it made his heart race and his body fidgety, but ever since he'd left Lisa Buchanon's house and she'd whispered what she'd said in his ear, he felt as if he'd downed ten shots of espresso, and no matter how many times he paced the worn hotel carpet, he couldn't walk it off.

Call me tonight. After midnight.

It was the next thing she'd said that sent daggers into his heart.

I think I can help find your daughter.

But the suddenness of it had bottled him up. His hand tingled when she'd slid the piece of paper into his palm, and it was numb by the time he'd pocketed it, looking at it for the first time minutes ago, after Tess had gone without a word to her room and he to his, both adjoining, separated only by the flimsy white door between the television stand and the desk.

She was fixing a drink on the other side of that door. Ice clinked, and for Justin that sound was like drawing a desert nomad toward water. He moved to the door that joined the rooms and rested with his forehead against it, contemplating.

Lisa Buchanon's phone number was burning a hole in his pocket and midnight was still two hours away. Tess knew he was keeping something from her. He could tell. But if it meant finding Julia, he'd deal with her wrath later. While everything in him wanted to tell Tess, with Lisa's whisper still in his ear, he held back. If she'd wanted

Tess to know, she wouldn't have singled him out. She would have told them both.

While he was wrangling, Tess spoke from the other side of the door. "It's not locked."

It startled him.

He opened the door and entered her room.

A table lamp illuminated her seat on the closest bed.

"I saw your shoes under the door." With a drink in hand, she appeared calmer now. She nodded toward the small table in between the two double beds. "I made you one."

"I don't—"

"Drink it, Justin," she said. "You don't need to stop drinking."

He sat on the side of the second bed, facing her like a mirror divided them while they drank Old Sam on ice. She didn't ask about Lisa Buchanon. Her eyes looked glazed, a *high* look—too soon to be blamed on the drink she'd just fixed. A plastic baggie rested on the table between the beds, and in it were roughly a dozen white oval pills she didn't try to hide.

He caught her gaze, and she didn't shy away from the immediate disappointment in his.

"I took them from Dad's medicine cabinet. Help take the edge off. I'm sorry."

He looked away, clenched the anger wanting to erupt, remembering how hard it had been to get her to stop the pills years ago. The days of detox. The sickness coming out both ends while he held cold compresses to her sweaty forehead. But the situation now didn't call for an argument. There weren't too many practical ways to cope with this, and for now he'd give her hers. "Just be careful," he said, unable to look at her.

She nodded in his periphery.

"You promise me."

She nodded again.

"Let me hear you say it, Tess."

"I promise." She sipped her drink. "Till death do us part."

He gulped his drink, watching her now, still trying to figure her out after all their years together.

She took another drink. "I was hoping that house would trigger something."

"You sure it didn't? It looked like you had a moment in there."

"I don't know . . ."

He didn't push her on it.

I think I can help find your daughter.

He checked his watch, took a heavy swallow of bourbon.

With glazed eyes and slowed speech, Tess said, "According to a babysitter, Pritchard used to play a game he called *Now You See Me, Now You Don't*. He'd turn all the lights off and the babysitter was to find him. From different spots he'd shine a flashlight under his chin, highlighting his face. He'd say 'Now you see me' when the light was on. And then he'd turn it off and say, 'Now you don't.' And then he'd go hide elsewhere."

Justin reached over and removed the bourbon from her grip. She didn't resist.

She also wasn't finished. "He sounded so weird . . . Pritchard . . ."

"Tess, stop. Jeff Pritchard is dead," he said. "He does not have Julia."

"But his *people* do."

Justin couldn't deny that. Which was why he now needed her to fall asleep herself, so that he could do what he needed to do and get *that* over with.

As if on cue, Tess kicked off her shoes, and she did it in a way that, in another time and place, could have been seductive. But it was the drugs, he knew; at night they'd made her movements more feline. She lifted her legs on the bed, lay on her side with her head on the pillow, and watched him under heavy lids.

"Justin."

"Yes."

"Hold me like you used to."

He finished his drink and crawled on the bed with her, fully clothed, positioning himself behind her like two spoons in a drawer. He draped his left arm around her, and she held it for dear life. Her chest rose and fell against his forearm.

"How many did you take?"

"Just one."

One too many. He told her to try and rest.

She closed her eyes.

He thought she'd drifted off to sleep when she spoke. "The eyes you found painted on Burt Lobell's bedroom wall . . ."

"Pointing toward the vanity," he said, seeing it all over again. "Lobell's medal of honor."

"The eyes took *me* to the *mirror*, Justin. Not the medal of honor. I saw a reflection of myself, even stared at it for a second. He was warning *me*."

"About?"

"That I was also in danger."

"Why you?" He leaned over to get a better view of her face, but she wouldn't look at him. "Tess?"

She paused, and then, "Because I was the one who tipped them off."

"What? Tipped who off?"

"The police. My dad."

Justin settled back behind her on the bed, his face behind her head, his nose in her hair. This revelation should have surprised him more, but it didn't. "How old were you?"

"Thirteen," Tess said. "I was so eager to walk in my father's shoes. I'd overheard Foster Bergman talking to Dad about some of Pritchard's weird behavior at the school. Dad went out there, sat and talked with him, but in the end saw nothing of significance. But by that point in his life, Pritchard had learned how to master it."

"Master what?"

"Not getting caught," she said. "I'd been investigating this case right along with Dad and Burt. Not in depth, because they'd only show me snippets, mostly if they'd had a few drinks, but I'd done plenty of snooping in their files on my own. They had to sleep at some point, right? But I wasn't convinced, and I didn't need a warrant. I got on my bike. I'd seen Pritchard around school, pushing that mop bucket, keys always jangling from his belt. I was intrigued by how quiet he was. Just off enough to make you wonder about him. He was a good-looking man, smart, seemingly educated. I wanted to see what made him tick, so I rode the few miles there. Did my own stakeout in one of the neighboring trees," she said. "For six hours."

"And?"

"Didn't see much," she said. "So I decided to go knock on the front door."

"You *didn't.*"

He could tell the pills were hitting her. Her voice was slowing down. "I did. He answered the door. I told him I was lost. That seemed to interest him."

"Jesus, Tess. What were you thinking?"

"I wasn't. I told him I recognized him from school. He said he recognized me too. From the hallways. I was an eighth grader. He asked if I was thirsty. I said yes, real thirsty. He started to get me a glass, but I asked for a throwaway cup, if he didn't mind. It was getting late, and I needed to get along. So he got me a plastic cup. Filled it with water and ice."

"Weren't you scared?"

"I was terrified, now that it's come back to me, but I knew if I showed it, he'd sense something. I breathed the biggest sigh of relief when I made it back out to my bike. Once I was out of view, I poured out the water and ice and slipped the cup into a baggie I'd brought, with his fingerprints on it."

"Son of a bitch."

"Yeah," she said. And when he thought she'd drifted off, she said, "Stupid, right? But those prints matched those lifted from where one of his victims was last seen. Tom Dobbins, I think. One of the four found dead in the basement. Dad didn't know whether to kiss me or ground me, and truthfully, I think he did both."

"This all came back to you after entering the house?"

"Some of it," she said softly. "The rest . . ."

"The rest?"

"I'd always thought was . . . a nightmare."

She went silent for a minute, and he hugged her, held her as she drifted to sleep. Ten minutes later she was making that subtle snoring sound he'd missed now for weeks.

His eyes were heavy; the day had hit him hard. He wondered if she'd told him that now in hopes that he'd reveal what Lisa had told him earlier. Now that he'd given in to the comfort of the bed and the familiar contour of Tess's body, he wanted only to fall asleep with her. His muscles were sore, and his joints ached. Tension had squeezed him like a vise grip and was finally letting go. He'd missed the flowery scent of her hair. He hated himself for ever cheating on her. Making excuses why he'd strayed—she was too engrossed in her work, away from home too much, too often neglecting their bedroom for the couch, falling asleep with work files strewn across her chest and the floor, too this, too that—when the only blame came down to him, front and center.

I'm an asshole.

Or at least he had been that one time.

Now he hugged his wife. She dreamily pressed her body into his and moaned in her sleep. He kissed her head and whispered to forgive him, for what he'd done and what he was about to do, because his watch now showed five minutes past midnight.

He slid off the bed and covered her up with a blanket.

Before leaving the hotel room, he took a handful of pain pills and flushed them down the toilet, leaving just enough to get what he thought she might need but not enough to overdose. He quietly closed the door and pulled Lisa Buchanon's number from his pocket.

35

ATOP HER CAREFULLY made bed, Lisa Buchanon lay on her side, fully clothed, fearing she was about to have a moment.

Justin and Tess Claibourne were gone, but their questions had left a trail of unease that wouldn't be so easily sated. She reeled her legs into a fetal position and closed her eyes, because when it happened—not too unlike her dizzy spells—it helped to make herself small.

So that's what she did. She made herself as small as she could atop the bed.

Eyed her vast collection of childhood dolls across the room and told them it would be okay.

She ran her hand over the tucked confines of her pillow, because it helped to feel things, comfortable things, fighting the memories of that night as a girl when she'd cowered in the corner of this very room, covering her ears from the sounds of the animals outside.

The gunshots.

One echoed after another.

And the cries of the animals.

The bleating and the baaing and the braying from inside the barn.

They're diseased, Lisa. All of them. I'm putting them out of their misery. You understand that, don't you? I'm ending their suffering . . .

Her grandfather's voice, when he'd taken a break at the kitchen table, grandmother fixing a pot of coffee as the sun began to rise, a sliver of orange glow amid the trees out there, like the horizon was on fire.

Grandmother not saying a word.

Why isn't she speaking? Why isn't she stopping him? Why can't she look him in the eyes?

Why can't you?

He's sweating. He's shirtless and sweating, his overall straps hanging down like dead snakes from his waistline as he finishes his coffee and tells her about a time when he was a little boy, when *his* grandparents had taken him to Rose Island, right there across the river, that old abandoned amusement park, and he'd gone on roller-coaster rides there and swims in the pool and how he'd fallen in love with the animals in their petting zoo and she didn't care about any of it because it made even less sense now how he could shoot all the animals out there and claim they were diseased and he stands and stretches his back and grunts and grabs his gun and goes out for more because . . .

. . . *they're suffering . . . you get that, don't you?*

She'd nodded. Oh, how she'd nodded, and grandmother said nothing, and she walked out of the kitchen and locked herself in her own bedroom because maybe deep down . . .

. . . *go on now, get in your room and close the door and know that it's all for the good . . . we can't let the disease spread now, can we?*

Lisa trembled on the bed now just as she'd trembled then as a little girl, hunkered in the corner beneath the window, the rising sun painting smears of color through the dust motes and across the floorboards and onto the wall, as she shook her head and cried and recalled how gently grandfather had wiped tears from her cheeks moments ago in the kitchen, his thumb dirty with mud or blood and the smell of the dead animals and she feared he'd left the residue on her skin and she hoped the disease wasn't on his fingers because he didn't wash them and there were stains now on the coffee mug and on the chair back and across his bare chest and all over her heart and her mind because the animals won't stop crying, and the disease came from him, started with him, the disease of men and all the animals out there somehow know they're next.

And finally, the gunshots outside grow quiet.

As did Grandmother's tears from down the hall.

And the animals are no longer making noises because they're all dead just like everything at Rose Island was dead when he'd taken her and Grandma just to show them what it once was and Grandma knew and zippered her mouth shut and there's a fly beating against the window and the sun is almost all the way bright and she can hear Grandfather out there now, out by the water well, water sloshing as he cleaned his face and his chest and his arms as fog floats up from the river below the bluff and . . .

She found herself standing at the window, peering over the ledge, where there's a dead fly underneath the buzzing one, and Grandfather is nothing but a dark shadow out there, a black silhouette against the yellow sun, and then all of a sudden he puts the gun to his head and fires one more time and down he goes, his body falling in the same direction his brains just went in a mist toward the water well, toward where she'd left her bike in the grass last night, when he'd ushered her inside for a dinner of pork and beans, his strong fingers clutching her shoulder like they always did, letting her know how strong he was and that he was in control whenever he'd had that look in his eyes, that deep dark bottomless look that swallowed smiles whole and made her think he was diseased too and that maybe the disease had started with him or this house and here she was laughing now because he was dead out there and she was glad he'd done it to himself after he'd done it to all of them, it seemed only fair and . . .

She closed her eyes and called inside her mind for Mother, and only then did she feel safe and secure, and she wished she'd brought some of her dolls from home because Mother was here now to keep everyone safe and sound and snug as bugs in a rug . . .

Lisa's cell phone buzzed and grew bright with light.

She sat up in bed and answered it.

Said, "Oh good, I'd hoped you'd call."

CHAPTER

36

JUSTIN FOUND MCSHAUNESSEY'S Irish Pub easily enough, on the corner of Main and McFee. The streetlamps and wrought-iron benches looked old-timey. Bourbon barrels served as garbage cans outside the storefront, one on each side of the big, wooden door of the ornate black-iron façade.

Once inside, Justin felt oddly at home, surrounded by coeds and folksy guitar music and drunken laughter. Attractive young men and women, jockeying for position, flirting, and dancing with the Irish tunes. A young brunette holding a margarita eyed him as he walked by, but he ignored her. Smoke hovered below the ceiling. Beer mugs clanked and happiness reigned, and he realized he no longer craved this shit. He was a thirty-four-year-old man with a beautiful wife and daughter, and it had taken the potential loss of both to realize how much he had.

He spotted Lisa Buchanon in a back corner booth alone and nursing a bottle of Coors, now wearing jeans and a white V-necked T-shirt.

Justin, already not liking the vibes, slid onto the opposite bench and cut to the chase. "What do you know about my daughter?"

"I don't . . . I don't know anything for sure."

He stood to leave.

She grabbed his forearm. "Wait. Let me explain."

He sat back down. "I'll give you five minutes."

"It's the house," she said, with desperation Justin couldn't read. This wasn't the put-together woman with whom he and Tess had shared tea earlier. She seemed much more uptight, frazzled. She said, "I sometimes have visions."

Justin made another move to get up, but she straightened her leg and rested her heeled white shoe on the bench beside him, as if to block his exit.

"Sit. Please."

He eased back down.

"I'm not crazy," she said. "Although at times the notion has crossed my mind. And after the stories I told you earlier, I wouldn't blame you, as a psychologist, if you thought it."

He looked at his watch. "You're down to four minutes."

"Okay, look . . . I'm psychic." She looked around, spoke softer. "Clairvoyant, you might say. I can see things. Visions. I have these episodes, where I can hear a voice . . ."

"What voice?"

"A man . . . I don't know . . ." She leaned closer to him, elbows on the table. "I'm telling you, it's the house. It's because of that house. Why do you think the kids watch it from the woods? They come out for dares. The Lost Children, they . . . worship it."

"You had me come here because you think your house is haunted—"

"It's more than that. With everything that's happened in it, the history of it, I think all the death has left an imprint."

"An imprint? What are you talking about?"

"A fingerprint," she said hurriedly. "History that never leaves. An aura. Think Amityville. The Ax Murder House in Villisca, Iowa. Fox Hollow Farm in Indiana, the home of Herb Baumeister . . ."

"Herb . . . who?"

"The I-70 Strangler," she said. "Ed Gein's house in Wisconsin. The LaLaurie Mansion in New Orleans—"

"Stop, stop. I don't care. About any of it. Unless it has something to do with my daughter, I don't care. You have three minutes," he said, stone-faced.

She looked up, said calmly, "I saw a boat. I told you, I have spells. I see things, sometimes hear things . . ."

"What boat?"

"I don't know for sure," she said. "But the police, the FBI, whatever. They monitored the airports, they watched the roads. But . . . *what if your suspect is traveling the rivers?*"

37

MORNING SUNLIGHT LIT the hotel room, bringing with it a shred of confidence Tess had lacked when she'd fallen asleep last night. Or, more accurately, had passed out. She vaguely remembered telling Justin about her brief visit with Pritchard in his kitchen as a girl, and she was glad she'd told him, for many reasons, but she'd hoped for something in return. And maybe he would have given it if she hadn't fallen asleep.

Now, after her third cup of coffee, Tess's mind began to clear from last night's pills.

Julia was out there, alive, and she would find her.

She'd know otherwise; she'd be able to feel it.

Justin, on the other hand, paced like a caged animal in front of the window overlooking the hotel pool below, reviewing notes. He was preparing to leave for Berringer Hills in the next few minutes and was formulating new ways to approach Noah Nichols.

She checked her phone. Danny was on his way up. She'd gotten texts from him before the sun rose.

Still no sign of Jeff's lawyer, Barrett Stevens.

So far unable to locate Jeter Janks.

You decent? I'm coming up. I have news. Make sure Justin is there.

After that, she'd begun pacing like Justin, on the opposite side of the room. Falling asleep last night, in his arms, on that bed, had brought back feelings rubbed raw over time, and she'd awakened with thoughts of forgiveness on her mind—they would find Julia and start anew—but then she'd entered his room to find his clothes from yesterday bundled in a heap and reeking of cigarette smoke at the foot of the bed.

He'd gone out last night after she'd closed her eyes.

What little trust he'd begun to build with her began to bleed away, knowing those clothes had something to do with Lisa Buchanon and what she'd whispered in his ear yesterday before they pulled away. *Had they met up? He wouldn't. He'd promised.*

Someone knocked.

Tess let Danny in and closed the door behind him.

Danny immediately said to Justin, "You were right last night."

Justin stopped pacing.

Tess looked at Justin, then back to Danny. "Right about what?"

Danny nodded toward Justin, who was looking at the floor, avoiding eye contact. "The Outcast is traveling the rivers. Justin phoned Detective Evans last night. Had a hunch that our man might be traveling the rivers. Not the roads and air."

"And?"

"He was right."

Justin leaned against the wall with his arms folded, looking relieved.

Danny said, "They found his boat abandoned on the river near Lewis and Clark State Park, north of the Missouri River."

"When?" Tess asked.

"Thirty minutes ago. They had every state between here and Montana searching all through the night—and bingo."

Justin remained quiet.

Tess resumed pacing. "You said abandoned? How do they know it was them?"

"They found the priest uniform hanging up," Danny said. "And pictures of the kids all over the floor of the boat. Just random pictures. Polaroids. Mostly the kids weren't even looking at the camera. But there's . . . there's a third boy. A young black boy, identity currently unknown."

Tess said, "I want those pictures, Danny."

"They're sending duplicates." He scratched his thinning hair, stared out the window.

She watched him, knew he was holding back. "Danny, so help me God, if you're—"

"There was a picture of Julia."

"What did she look like?" Justin asked. "Smiling again?"

"No, but she wasn't terrified either. Just kind of a blank stare."

"He's drugging them," Tess added, looking back to Danny. "What about the picture?"

"Under her picture," Danny said, in obvious unease. "He'd written the name Judas."

Tess froze. "Judas?"

"Yes."

"As in Judas Iscariot? The disciple who betrayed Jesus?"

"I don't know, Tess. We can only guess."

She turned away, faced Justin. "How did you know about the boat? And don't say it was a hunch." She pointed to the clothes on the floor. "You left last night. Where did you go?"

"I went to meet Lisa Buchanon," he said, standing straighter. "She told me she thought she could help find Julia—I thought it was worth a try."

"Why you? Why just you?"

"She didn't think you'd believe her."

"What is it that I wouldn't believe?"

"That she has visions, that's she's clairvoyant," he said.

Tess and Danny both stared at him.

Justin exhaled, rubbed his face. "I know, I know. She can't conjure up an image. It just happens, like a flashback."

Danny said with a load of sarcasm, "Except what, it flashes forward?"

"Yes," said Justin. "She's convinced it's the house that triggers it. She thought they were nightmares, but after she saw the news, she figured it out. She was seeing visions *because* she lives in that house."

"How long has it been going on?" Tess asked.

Danny shook his head. "You gonna believe this shit too? Tess, really? You're a detective, not a ghost hunter."

"Danny, shut up. Give me a minute to think."

"Christ."

"So was she right? Huh? Danny? Was she right?" she asked her partner.

"Yeah," he said, shrugging. "Whatever." He got on his phone, thumb-tapped a message, looked up. "Fine. She wasn't wrong. How's that?" He exhaled, his shoulders relaxed. "Eliza's contacting some social workers in Bowling Green. Seeing if she can't get hold of somebody who used to work at the old Sisters of Mercy, where Pritchard stayed until he moved here. Something about leaving no stone unturned. With her everything leads back to somebody's childhood."

Tess turned back to Justin, repeating her question. "How long did Buchanon say this was going on?"

"Since she's been in the house," he said. "Mostly she ignores it. Assumed it was déjà vu, but with this she realized she was possibly seeing things before they happened. The police brushed her off." Justin was over by the bed now, searching through files he'd just pulled from Tess's father's open briefcase. "So she took a chance with me."

Danny said, "It was a Sea Ray SRV. The boat he left stranded. They're continuing to police the rivers in case he switched boats, like he did with the cars early on."

Tess shook her head. "He might not even be here yet."

"They're sending more men to the airports, just in case," Danny said. "They've got roadblocks set up from here to Missouri. If he's taken to the roads again, we'll find them."

"Unless he *is* already here," she said, defeated. "That boat could have been abandoned hours ago, enough time for him to coast right into Twisted Tree unseen."

"If this is where he's coming," Justin added.

"It is," Tess said. "He wants *me*. You might be right, Danny. He fooled us."

Danny checked his phone again. "He might not have killed Burt Lobell. Or Bergman."

"Or my parents, for that matter."

"He wasn't even here," Justin said, thinking aloud.

"They're coordinated," Tess said.

"It's a game to them," Danny said. "Which is good for us."

"How so?"

"He'll keep Julia alive because of it."

38

Tess drove, and for the first half of the trip to Berringer Hills, she and Justin sat in silence.

More of a contemplative quiet, rather than the awkwardness that had punctuated their time together since, and even in the weeks before, the affair, when they'd drifted into speaking only when necessary. The revelation of the Outcast's traveling the rivers had been huge, but also a deflating reminder that he was still a step ahead of them. After filling Danny in on yesterday's interactions with Noah and his diagnosed dissociative identity disorder, they'd left for Berringer Hills to talk to Noah again, while Danny planned another day accompanying the local authorities, taking whatever scraps they'd give him. Tess knew they were on the outskirts of the investigation—no one from local or the FBI considered Noah a viable lead, regardless of what Justin explained about Noah's personalities, specifically the one claiming to be the Outcast.

Claiming is the key word, Detective Evans had told Justin earlier. *You just said it yourself. I think he's acting, personally. He's yanking your chain, but be my guest, Doc, have at it if you think it won't lead to a dead end.*

Justin was convinced Noah was key—and as Tess drove, he kept looking at the crayon drawing of Jeff Pritchard's house that Noah had done as a boy in the weeks after his return from that house.

Justin turned the picture over for the third time since getting into the car and noted the name on the back—*Amelia*. Warden

Hofmann yesterday had confirmed that Amelia was one of Noah's personalities, the one they'd encountered briefly as she recited her *Eyes in the Darkness* prayer after the Outcast's emergence. But there was something more he wasn't yet getting, but he felt close. He flipped the colored picture back over, studied the windows.

As the car moved along, woods flashed past. The tip of an old silo protruded from the treetops, and dilapidated buildings stood amid the soaring evergreens.

Tess gave the structures a glance in the rearview.

"What was that?" he asked.

"The old Harlow Bourbon Distillery," she said, eyes back on the road. "What's left of it. For a time in the sixties and seventies, it was a competitor with the Old Sam Distillery. Back in the fall of seventy-nine, Skeech Harlow, the founder, blew his head off with a shotgun. It's sat vacant ever since. Whole family was nuts."

"So I assume that's not on any of the Twisted Tree walking tours?"

"Ha, no . . ." She trailed off. He watched her as she drove. Considered taking her right hand that now rested on the console in between the seats but didn't. He wondered if she'd taken it off the wheel, so that he *would* hold it. She looked over, caught him staring. "What?"

"Nothing," he said, eyeing the picture on his lap again, the house only the mind of a child could think was accurate. The bright red door. The porch with the columns that in the right light could have resembled teeth. The crooked walkway leading up to the porch. The brown patch of what he assumed was some kind of shrubbery centered at the very bottom of the page, with the sidewalk coming right from it.

"Seeing anything there?"

"I don't know."

"Something's churning in that head of yours."

"I'm close," he said. "It's like I'm seeing everything in here at once, but also nothing." He pointed to the brown patch at the bottom middle of the page. "That look like a bush to you?"

"Could be."

He focused back on the picture, the oddness of those eight windows, the stick figures standing at each one. How the windows themselves, if you looked at them cockeyed enough, almost resembled a pyramid.

He stole another look at her, then rested his left hand on her right.

"Justin?"

"Yeah?"

"What are you doing?"

"Holding your hand."

"Why?"

"Because I need to." She didn't pull away, so he interlocked his fingers with hers. As Berringer Hills came into view up the hill and through the towering evergreens and oaks, he said, "We're gonna get her back."

"I know." She squeezed his hand, but for the final curves to the asylum let go so she could use both hands on the wheel.

A thought struck him. He counted on his fingers, in his head, one, two, three, four, five, six, seven . . .

"What are you doing?"

"I need a pen."

"There's one in my purse." She nodded toward the floorboard next to his feet. He scrambled through her purse, found a pen, clicked it, and gestured toward the picture. "You mind if I write on this?"

"Why?"

"Because I might have figured it out. These windows."

She coasted into the parking lot, showed her badge to a guard at the gate, and entered the grounds. "Go ahead."

The notion had hit him so suddenly that he hadn't thought it completely through, but started writing names beneath each window.

Beneath the four windows spread out unevenly above the red front door, Justin wrote, from left to right, *Amelia*, *Tom*, *Stephen*, and finally *Dean*.

Tess parked, shifted in her seat to better face him.

Beneath the three windows on the next section up, he wrote *Oskar* beneath the one on the left, *The Outcast* beneath the middle window, and then *Ruth* beneath the window on the right. "Shit."

"What?" Tess asked.

"I thought it worked out," he said. "Seven personalities, not eight. Unless we're missing one."

Tess reached over, took the pen from him, and wrote beneath the single window at the top, *Noah Nichols*. She clicked the pen closed, smiled at him. "You forgot the host."

CHAPTER

39

THE SONG WAS joyous.

His heart swelled at the sound of their enthusiasm while singing the new ditty he'd made up.

The Playhouse had a way of doing that, opening his creativity, and they were so close now he could smell it.

He looked over his shoulder and urged them to sing one last time, which they did.

"Over the river and through the woods to that Playhouse we all like to go."

They grew quiet, suddenly, as the house loomed.

He'd warned them of a surprise when they got there. The girl Julia—who was sometimes too smart for her own britches—had thought that the surprise would be her parents and grandparents waiting there for a party. He didn't have the heart to tell her she was wrong. Way wrong. Her grandparents were dead. If it were possible to put the paint back in the tube he would. He watched in the rearview mirror as the children's eyes latched onto the surroundings. He gripped the steering wheel and took the last winding turn up the hillside, a road so choked with trees and foliage that the branches brushed the sides of the painted church van as he ascended and snaked for another hundred yards before leveling out again on the bumpy road of hard-packed dirt.

Thirty yards ahead, he approached what appeared to be a massive tree across the narrow road, a thick-barked white oak festooned with a patchwork of branches and limbs and deadfall all fastened carefully to the concealed fence-like gate behind it.

He put the van in park, told the kids to stay put, and hurried toward the horizontal tree blocking the road. After three heaves, the gate creaked, rumbled, and then coasted along the tracks embedded in the ground. Old rusty barrel runs from when the distillery once functioned.

He'd have to lubricate the wheels on the gate. For now, he hurried back to the van and drove on.

He took a sharp turn right, steered fifty yards down into the clearing. He parked and got out, inhaled the air, imagined it still thick with the angels' share, what had evaporated from the bourbon that had once aged here. He closed his driver's door and slid open the side one. One by one he ushered out the kids and they faced the Playhouse in awe.

Newly renovated and a labor of love.

"Gather around, kiddos." He knelt next to them and pointed over lush green grass toward the main house, where the veranda was freshly painted yellow on ceiling and floor, and the columns swirled with lines of red and white like candy canes. The windows were edged in blue while the main house was striped red and purple in alternating boards. A welcoming wooden-plank placard hung slightly cockeyed from two chains on the front side of the veranda's ceiling, just over the lime-green porch steps.

Welcome to the Playhouse! it said in a rainbow assortment of colored letters.

He couldn't tell if they were excited or nervous from all the color and life the playhouse contained, because none of them said a word. So, for the next surprise, he brought his fingers to his lips and whistled.

They waited.

He said, "Here they come."

And then the front door opened. Out stepped a boy roughly their age. And then another. Three seconds later two girls stepped out.

And they just kept coming.

CHAPTER

40

Tess knew Justin was onto something with what he'd just puzzled out inside the car, with Noah's old colored drawing and the eight windows, but the closer he got to the asylum entrance, where a guard already had a door open awaiting their arrival, his pace picked up, and he had another lightbulb moment look in his eyes.

She hurried to catch up. "Justin, what is it?"

He held up a finger, not rudely, but more of a *give me a second* gesture—as he was deep in thought mode when they entered the building and headed toward the warden's office to officially check in.

And he was still studying the drawing as he entered Warden Hofmann's office.

"Holy shit, Tess," he said over his shoulder, stopping at the warden's desk. "The names."

"What names?"

Warden Hofmann looked up from the paperwork he'd been doing, and then his eyes settled on the drawing Justin had just set down in front of him. Justin watched Tess and the warden and didn't start speaking until he had their full attention.

"The names under each window," he said. "We believe they coincide with the personalities inside Noah's mind."

This seemed to immediately steal the Warden Hofmann's attention, but Tess already knew this; they'd figured that out inside the car before their arrival.

Justin held up a finger, like he was about to hammer home an important point during a lecture. "Noah doesn't remember anything from his time with Father Silence."

Tess said, "We know this, Justin."

"Hear me out. Because, at the time, his two imaginary friends, Oskar and Ruth, endured the time for him. We now know they were more than likely alternate personalities from early on." Justin swelled with energy. "Oskar and Ruth were his defense mechanisms against any perceived threat. But now these new personalities, Dean, Stephen, Amelia, and Tom, they're keeping the original two personalities suppressed."

"Why?" asked Tess.

Justin pulled an old newspaper article from his shirt pocket, one she'd seen him studying earlier in the morning. "I don't think these new personalities were created by Noah's subconscious at all, not like the original two were when he was a child. But these newer ones, they were somehow taken, borrowed." He held up Noah's coloring from his youth. "Absorbed."

Tess shook her head, raised her eyebrows. "Absorbed? What are you talking about?"

He shook the newspaper in his hand. "This is an article from Pritchard's arrest. From the day you hid in your father's police car."

The warden stared at her, confused.

She said, "Later." And gestured for Justin to go on.

Justin showed them the names in the newspaper article. "Look. The names of the four kids found in that house with Noah. *Dean Roberts. Amelia Harris. Tom Dobbins. Stephen Kennedy.*"

Tess's jaw dropped.

Warden Hofmann said, "The four names of the personalities inside Noah."

Justin asked, "This has registered with you before?"

He shook his head. "Years ago, I might have known or remembered the dead children's names, but with all my other dealings here, I'd forgotten. And what you're insinuating, believe me . . . it's not possible."

Tess watched both men. "What isn't possible?" It couldn't be coincidence that Noah's other personalities shared names with the four children he'd been held captive with.

Justin pointed again at the article. "Look at their ages when they died. The same ages Noah's alternates claim to be *now*. They were . . . what did he call it, *put to sleep* by Father Silence, but somehow their personalities still live inside of Noah, the one who survived. He didn't *create* these alternates like he did with Oskar and Ruth as a child, he somehow took these on, *absorbed them . . .*"

The warden stood and rubbed his brow. "I've pondered it in the past, and . . . and there's just no other record of this type of thing ever happening. It's not possible. Is it?"

"The mind," Justin said, "I believe has untapped potential when it comes to trauma, and what it can do to avoid it, to escape it. What happened in that house was intense. It was an especially intense traumatic experience."

"Not too unlike me," Tess said softly.

"Except you blotted out your entire experience, Tess. And hopefully we'll get it back."

The warden watched Tess, as if he wanted to hear more, but she wasn't about to give it to him. She said, "So this goes beyond multiple personalities?"

"Dissociative identities," Justin said. "But yes. It might be even more complicated than I thought. This could be groundbreaking."

"But you can't just take on someone's personality," Tess protested.

"Think of it another way." Justin held up the drawing again. "People who have multiples create them to escape reality. To cope. Noah as a child created Oskar and Ruth for those reasons. He couldn't deal with the trauma of his childhood. But with whatever happened in that house, he felt the need to split even more. And fast. The trauma was there. It was intense. In a sense, he needed those other kids. He needed to split fast and create again, and they were there for the taking." He stopped pacing. "A quick fix. That's what they were. They don't age like Noah because they're officially dead. He took them on as they died right in front of him."

Tess felt her blood go cold. *It made sense, too much sense, but how could it be real? How could it be possible?* "Have you ever heard of such a thing? Read of a case like this? Either of you?"

"No, as I said, this is unprecedented."

The warden stared out the window, but his manner was one now of acceptance of a sort.

"I know it sounds ludicrous," Justin said. "But I'd be willing to bet that if—no—*when* I get to Oskar and Ruth, they've been aging all along, just like Noah."

"Son of a bitch," said Tess.

"What?" Justin and Warden Hofmann said simultaneously.

"The Outcast," she said. "He must have been absorbed by Noah too, borrowed like you say, along with the others. Soaked up like a sponge. He's still alive, though, and that's why the Outcast personality inside of Noah still ages. From boy to a man."

Justin said, "*There was another boy in that house*, Tess. One that nobody knew about. Probably the one who painted that basement room's ceiling like the Sistine Chapel. And *The Last Supper* on the wall." He nodded toward the warden's desk. "Painted that stack of artwork you showed us. Jeff Pritchard's last words: 'Beware the one that got away.' Pritchard wasn't talking about Noah Nichols."

As he said it, Tess realized the mistake they'd been making. "He was talking about the one that got away *from the cops*, not him," she said. "The one that slipped through everyone's fingers. The one hiding in the darkness, with the eyes the others could see and fear."

"Which is why he wears the sunglasses." No, she thought, the mask, briefly smelling the rubber of it . . .

"The Outcast, the one who doesn't even exist," Justin said. "Not then or now. And that's why we haven't matched any fingerprints from the cabin."

Pain surged through Tess's head. She hunkered over and both men moved toward her. She dropped to a knee, tried to fight it off, but it got through, the smell of the rubber mask intense.

. . . *she was sprinting through the field of tall wet grass, swaying in the wind, sprinting, not running from, but chasing, chasing, chasing . . .*

She opened her eyes, panting. *He was wearing a mask . . .*

Justin knelt on the floor with her, ready to help her up.

"Give me a second." She worked her way through a series of deep breaths and stood on her own. "I saw him. He's real."

"What's going on?" the warden asked.

"When I was a girl," she said. "The evening of the arrest. There *was* another boy. He was wearing a dog mask. I chased him into the woods."

Before

PORTION OF DETECTIVE *Leland Patterson's interview with now-retired Sister Lucinda Mast, Head Abbess (Mother Superior) of the Sisters of Mercy Orphanage (Abbey) in Bowling Green, Kentucky (now closed). Current residence: Convent neighboring the Parish at St. Gabriel, Bowling Green.*

> **Detective Patterson:** *And how many years was Jeff Pritchard in your charge at the orphanage?*
>
> **Sister Lucinda:** *He was thirteen when he arrived, shortly after the fire. And he moved on a few days before his eighteenth birthday. A few days before . . .* **(Here she closes her eyes, grips the rosary beads on her lap, and is noticeably more emotional when her eyes open.)** *A few days before what happened . . .*
>
> **Detective Patterson:** *And we'll get to that, Sister, but was this typical? Leaving at eighteen?*
>
> **Sister Lucinda:** *Yes, sir. Most would go out into the world at that age. With as much help and guidance as we could give them. Jeff Pritchard, however, left, as you know, a bit prematurely. Without our typical going-away festivities. A party with cake and some parting gifts from the staff.*
>
> **Detective Patterson:** *For those who never got adopted.*

Sister Lucinda: That's another way to put it. It's not easy to place teenagers. Most, by that point, age out, and they look forward to a life on their own.

Detective Patterson: And Pritchard? Was he looking forward to a life on his own?

Sister Lucinda: He was always a tough one to read. He mostly kept to himself. To his chores.

Detective Patterson: Which were?

Sister Lucinda: Cleaning. Maintenance. Keeping the grounds properly groomed. He took his job very seriously.

Detective Patterson: And you're aware of what his profession was when he was arrested?

Sister Lucinda: So, I've heard. **(She gives me a stern, accusatory look.)** He may have honed his cleaning skills here, Detective, but the rest . . . all the newspapers are saying he did, that evil he learned elsewhere.

Detective Patterson: I didn't mean to imply that, Sister. It's just that you seem to have a very clear recollection of him. He must have left an imprint. Even now, in hindsight, was there any clue to his behavior that may have gone unnoticed?

Sister Lucinda: Other than the rumors that followed him here. Of his pet cemetery. Of his parents being killed in the fire.

Detective Patterson: Did you, at the time, think he was guilty of starting that fire?

Sister Lucinda: He was not found guilty. He was no longer a suspect. He was kind and proper with us, and the boy needed a home.

Detective Patterson: Did he have any friends at the orphanage?

Sister Lucinda (after a long exhale): Oh, that was years ago. No one who stuck out, unfortunately. We'd see him conversing with others, of course, during recreation time, but no one we considered close. Jeff Pritchard was definitely one who we'd considered a loner.

Detective Patterson: Sisters of Mercy housed both boys and girls?

Sister Lucinda: Yes. All the way up until it closed.

Detective Patterson: Did Pritchard have any female friends at the orphanage?

Sister Lucinda (thoughtful pause): There was one girl he was close to, a few years younger, if I recall, although she was already living here when Jeff Pritchard arrived. I can't remember her name, maybe Diane something? It was over a decade ago, but *with how rarely we allowed the genders to comingle, it was never, to our knowledge, a relationship that raised any red flags.*

Detective Patterson: *As head abbess, would you say you got to know the kids very well, on a personal level?*

Sister Lucinda: *I knew all the children. Not as well as the sisters who were with them day to day, and in the classrooms, but I at least knew them all by name. I was more on the administrative side of things.* **(Here she looks at me.)** *But if this is your way of asking how things got so out of control that day, then let's go ahead and segue to it. I ran a tight ship, Detective. I did the best I could. The orphanage was a kind, gentle place, and the children were treated well. I did not see that coming. None of us did. And to this day I refuse to admit fault.*

Detective Patterson: *I'm a parent. I understand. You can do everything correctly, by the book, and kids are still going to do things that make you scratch your head.*

Sister Lucinda: *A young man was murdered in our courtyard, Detective. I may not admit fault, but as the Mother Superior I take full responsibility. But if you've come here for details, after all these years of me pondering the same things, I fear you'll leave here disappointed. And you'll find this a wasted trip. I still can't believe, for the life of me, that Jeff Pritchard did all that you say. To have murdered all those people. The kids in that basement . . .*

Detective Patterson: *Life often fools us, Sister. But . . . back to what happened . . . Had you seen the man before, the one found murdered?* **(I refer here to my notes.)** *Blake Sims?*

Sister Lucinda: *No, I'd never seen him before. Although a few of the sisters claim to have seen him around in the days prior. Not inside our grounds, but along the property lines.*

Detective Patterson: *A drifter?*

Sister Lucinda: *Perhaps.*

Detective Patterson: *And how did he end up inside the orphanage? The courtyard was surrounded on all four sides by buildings, was it not? Accessed only by buildings that surrounded it? Someone had to have let him in?*

Sister Lucinda: *Yes, someone let him in. My theory is that it was one of the older girls, and he was possibly a secret boyfriend.*

Detective Patterson: *And you were unable to check this with any of them?*

Sister Lucinda: *Any of who? Half the orphanage left that day. Most of the older ones, at least. They ran. Panicked. Like a mass* *exodus. The man was stabbed twenty-seven times in the face, chest, and groin. He was mutilated. We were able to keep the younger ones from seeing him, all the blood, but the older kids, you know how they are, they all heard, they all saw, and they all ran.*

Detective Patterson: *Including Jeff Pritchard?*

Sister Lucinda: *Yes. I never saw him again, but . . .*

Detective Patterson: *But what?*

Sister Lucinda: *He was the only one whose room was cleaned out. Not completely, but he'd certainly packed his belongings as if he'd planned on never returning. While the others, they . . . they just left. They ran away, at least a dozen of them. We couldn't escape the rumors. What the newspapers claimed happened. Rumors of one of our nuns having an affair with that man. Of one of our girls killing the man in a fit of rage and jealousy. All gossip. Horrible, horrible gossip. We were shut down immediately and the kids were sent elsewhere. They never found who was responsible.*

Detective Patterson: *Do you think Jeff Pritchard did it?*

Sister Lucinda: *Not at the time, no.*

Detective Patterson: *And now?*

Sister Lucinda: *If what they say about him is true, then perhaps it's very plausible he killed Blake Sims in that courtyard. Now the why, maybe we'll never know.*

Detective Patterson: *Was there any credence to the rumor about Sister Mary—?*

Sister Lucinda (she cuts me off): *No. None. She was a kind-hearted, pious, dedicated, and loyal nun. After what happened to that poor girl, and with her name and reputation being dragged through the mud . . . it's horrible. It's the devil at work.*

Detective Patterson: *She was the only other person injured that night?*

Sister Lucinda (clearly fighting her emotions): *Yes.*

Detective Patterson: *Do you know where she is? Is she still a nun?*

Sister Lucinda: *She became a Poor Clare nun in the weeks following that night. Completely cloistered and shut off. They have a monastery in the woods, a few hundred yards up the hill from the old Sisters of Mercy Orphanage.*

Detective Patterson: *Do you think she'd speak with me?*

Sister Lucinda: *No, I don't.*

Detective Patterson: *Can I ask why not?*

Sister Lucinda: *Besides the fact that she no longer has a tongue? And that someone cut it out that night? The authorities questioned her enough in the days after. She didn't speak then, and I don't think she'll speak now.* **(She turns to me again.)** *Can I ask why it matters? If it was Jeff Pritchard, and that was his first kill, what does it matter if he's already behind bars? Let it go, Detective. Please. Just let it go.*

CHAPTER

41

T<small>ESS AND</small> J<small>USTIN</small> occupied two chairs outside Noah's cell, while Ray, who seemed to be Noah's personal guard, watched from the hallway wall behind them.

Noah sat on the other side of the bars, hunched forward with his elbows on his knees, staring at a fixed point between Tess and Justin, his eyes flicking briefly to whoever asked the question, but so far, the answers had been lacking.

A conversation going nowhere.

A text came through from Danny on Tess's phone: ***On my way south to Bowling Green.***

She showed the text to Justin, who said, "Why?"

She sent ***??*** back to Danny and waited.

He texted back: ***Eliza found a nun who used to work at the Sisters of Mercy.***

Pritchard's orphanage? Tess responded, noticed how intently Noah was watching her.

Yes, closed now. She's in a monastery.

Somebody my dad missed?

Maybe. I'll let you know.

Tess placed the phone face down on her lap, found Noah sitting upright, not as bored as he'd been with them moments ago.

He watched them cockeyed, twisting strands of his hair, as if nervously, above his right ear. "Who ya texting?" he asked, in a voice that sounded young and female.

The sudden emergence of it jarred Tess. Justin leaned forward.

"My partner," Tess said, and then took a shot in the dark. "He's heading down to Bowling Green. Where Father Silence grew up."

"Smart," said Noah, offering no more, but obviously fidgety, looking around as if checking for spies.

Justin said, "Why is that smart?"

"The Lost Children worship him, right?"

"From what we can tell," said Tess, wanting to ask who exactly they were speaking to but afraid she'd break the sudden momentum. But she hoped it was Ruth, who hadn't surfaced yet.

Noah leaned forward, whispered, "Let's just say there's been some stones left unturned."

"What stones?" asked Tess. "Noah?"

Noah clamped a hand over his mouth. He'd changed back to the confused, unengaged man they'd been trying for ten minutes to pry information from.

Tess and Justin shared a look. She mouthed the word *Amelia* to him, and he nodded.

If it had been her, she was gone now.

Noah clasped his hands together and exhaled like he was bored, like he had no recollection of that voice, that personality.

Justin said, "Noah, I believe we just talked to Amelia."

"And?"

"And she mentioned some stones being left unturned," Tess said. "In Bowling Green?"

Noah raised his hands, dropped them to his lap, as if saying *Your guess is as good as mine.*

She texted Danny: ***Definitely go to BG. Might be something there.*** She looked back up to Noah. The unopened cigarette pack protruded from Noah's shirt pocket like a baby chick rooting for food.

"Cigarettes can take years off your life, Noah," Tess commented, just for something to say.

"Which one?" He smiled for the first time since they'd arrived twenty minutes ago.

Justin grinned. "Who are the cigarettes for?"

He shrugged.

"Why don't you ever smoke them?"

"Because I don't smoke."

Tess noticed a pair of sunglasses in the well of his shirt's other pocket and changed course. "Why does the Outcast wear sunglasses? What's wrong with his eyes?"

"I don't know."

"Is it something frightening, visually?" she asked. "Why are your alternates afraid of them?"

Noah sniffed like he had a cold. He brushed his curled index finger against his nose. *Had he just changed?* Tess looked for a sign but saw nothing. "Has the Outcast ever referred to himself as Father Friday?"

Noah didn't answer, but noticeably flinched, and then chewed on a fingernail. Finally, he shook his head.

Justin looked at Tess before his next question to Noah. "What did you mean yesterday, when you asked Tess here about the twisted trees?"

Tess looked away; she hadn't expected Justin to bring it up. She was still confused over how Noah, even as the Outcast, could know about the twisted trees.

Noah shook his head like he didn't know what Justin was referring to, but Tess also couldn't help but notice the hint of a grin.

Justin, however, must not have noticed it, as he moved on. "Is it the Outcast keeping them from talking?" he asked. "Maybe intimidating them, threatening them? I think Oskar and Ruth know who the Outcast is, and he's somehow keeping them suppressed. They're threats to him." Justin leaned forward, mirroring Noah's posture on the other side of the bars. "Noah, do you know your alternates?"

"Only by what the warden has told me. They're in there now. Listening."

"Where do you go when they're in control?"

"I don't know. I lose time. I go somewhere else and lose time."

"Do you go into the ark, Noah? A mental version of what your mother made you go into as a child when you were bad?"

"A baddy boy," Noah said, softly.

"Yes, Noah. You've been creating alternates since you were a child in order to cope."

"I've heard this before. How do you know?" His eyes fixed on Justin. "Have you studied me?"

"I'm trying to." Justin scooted his chair closer, gripped the bars. "Tom. Dean. Stephen." He shouted, which startled Tess—but she realized this sudden feigned rage was planned, to try to access the other personalities. He shouted again, "Are any of you in there?"

Noah closed his eyes, then opened them with a look that said *You stupid man.* "That won't work, Justin. They only come out when they want to. When they *need* to."

"Bring them to his defense," Tess whispered to Justin. "Try *threatening* him."

Justin looked over his shoulder at Ray, who gave a half-shrug and said, "Whatever helps you find your girl."

Justin turned to Noah. "You know some of the personalities inside you were once real people? They were found inside Jeff Pritchard's house with you. Noah, you *stole* them."

"I didn't steal anything."

"You have them in your head. Their pasts are inside you. Allow me to open them up."

"I don't know them."

"But they know you."

Noah shifted in the chair. His ankle chain rattled across the floor from the bedpost.

Tess moved beside Justin. "What is it like to have a killer inside you, Noah?"

"I'm not the killer."

"Then who is?"

"I don't know."

Tess said, "You and the Outcast are one and the same."

Noah shook his head in defiance, and then covered his face with his hands before he spoke. "He's not as bad as they say."

"Who?"

"The pressure builds and he snaps. He only does the bad thing on bad people."

"Where is he?"

Noah looked around the cell, craned forward to glance down the hall, then began bobbing in his chair. "I don't know."

"You don't know, or you won't tell?"

"*No longer suffer the children.*"

"What?" Justin asked.

"He takes care of the children. He has an orphanage, and he takes care of the children."

"How do you know this?" Tess asked.

"I just know." Noah looked Tess in the eyes, and she saw that his words were genuine. *He knows but doesn't know how he knows.* "Sometimes our memories get muddled. They cross lines and we don't know who they belong to."

"You share memory?" Justin asked.

"Crumbs. Sometimes the alternate leaves crumbs, but I don't understand them." He went silent again, closed his eyes, nibbled on his fingernails.

She'd noticed it before. Was it a subtle shift? But again, he opened his eyes, and nothing had changed. They didn't have time—they had to find Julia, had to learn where the Playhouse was. She put her face up to the bars and hissed, "You wicked boy. You wicked little boy."

Noah shook his head.

"Stop lying to me," Tess said in an angry voice she hoped would trigger something. And when it appeared by the suddenly boyish look on his face that it had, she went deeper, despite the qualms she felt at hurting him, at pushing him into horrible memories from his childhood. "I'll put you into the ark, Noah. Into all that darkness."

"No." He shook his head. "Please don't."

Into the ark, you bad little boy.

Noah folded his arms as if cold, and then doubled over like a sudden pain had hit him.

Tess flinched, but kept on. She stood, making herself bigger, kept her voice harsh. If tormenting the child within Noah was the only way to get to her own, she'd do it. "Wicked boy. *Wicked little baddy boy.* Where is Oskar? Where is he? That wicked child. And Ruth? Where are they?"

"I don't know. Go away. Please. Don't hit me. Oskar is gone. Mother took him."

Tess shared a glance with Justin, as if for confirmation, then asked, "Where did he go?"

"He's locked away."

Tess eased back down to her seat, softened her tone, sure now that a switch had occurred. "Was there another child in that house with you? One no one knew about?"

The voice that came out of Noah was soft and youthful, but not the one that had emerged last night. "Noah remembers nothing." He chewed on his fingernails, then reached into his right shirt pocket and removed two pairs of glasses—the sunglasses they'd seen last night on the Outcast personality and a regular pair of glasses. Her heart galloped as he looked back and forth between the two, before settling on the regular pair of glasses. He slid them on, adjusted them on his nose, and blinked. "Better," the small voice said.

"You wear glasses?" Justin took notes.

"Always have. I'm blind like a bat without them." He reached his hand between the bars for a shake. "I'm Tom."

Justin looked at Ray and the guard nodded approval. Justin shook the extended hand and Tess did as well. The grip was weak like a child's, not that of a grown man.

"I'm Tess," she said.

"I know, we met last night."

"I thought we talked to Dean?" asked Justin.

"You did, but I was listening. We *always* listen." He leaned back in his chair, fingernails lost in the beard growth. "You scared Dean last night."

"We didn't mean to," asked Tess. "And we don't have a lot of time, Tom. Do you know where you came from?"

"From Noah. He gave birth to me."

Justin said, "No, he didn't. You were a real person, Tom Dobbins." He pulled out his cell phone, thumbed to where earlier he'd brought up old pictures from articles, and showed Noah/Tom one of Tom's parents, distraught after the death of their son, murdered inside the home of Father Silence. "These are your parents, Tom."

Noah froze. Tears pooled in his eyes.

Justin switched to a picture of two little boys. "Tom, are these your little brothers? Joe and Nick?"

Noah wiped his eyes. Spoke with Tom's mouse voice. "Never seen them before."

"You have," said Tess. "He's listening now, isn't he?"

Noah flinched, maybe a nod, but Tess couldn't tell for sure.

Justin asked, "Are you scared right now, Tom?"

"Yes."

"Of what?"

"Of you."

"Why?"

"I don't trust you. And he believes strongly in trust."

"Who?"

"I don't know."

"You're dead, Tom. Are you aware of that?"

Noah shook his head. "No, I'm not dead, you're dead."

"You died in that house. Did you see another boy with scary eyes?"

"Hiding in the darkness," he said, shyly. "They put him there."

"Who?"

"I don't know."

"Who is they?"

"I don't know . . ."

Tess said to Justin, "Show him the picture, the drawing."

Justin reached under his chair for the colored picture Noah had done as Amelia, but didn't show it yet. "The warden has pictures, Tom."

"What pictures?"

"Pictures that you've drawn, over time," Justin said. "Pictures of those eyes. Of that house. Do you remember drawing pictures for Noah?"

He nodded. "Pictures help the pain get out."

"Yes," said Justin. "Yes, they do. Pictures can display a thousand words." Now he showed him Amelia's picture of Father Silence's house. Noah/Tom glanced but looked away. "Noah . . ."

Noah shook his head no.

"Tom," said Justin. "Look. Please look."

Noah turned, eyed the picture. "That's not mine."

"I know. Amelia colored this one. Soon after you were rescued. But, like you, Amelia never made it out."

"She died."

"Yes, but she's still inside you," Justin said. "Somehow." He held the picture with both hands, moving it closer to the bars, closer to Noah/Tom. "Do you know this house?" He shook his head. Justin answered. "It's Jeff Pritchard's house. The house of Father Silence. You were held there for a month. Eventually you were poisoned with wine he made you drink. I think with this picture you were calling out for help. Through Amelia. For you. She'd become one of Noah's alternates by then. Do you think we can talk to her, Tom? Is she in there?"

Noah closed his eyes, opened them, and still in Tom's voice said, "Amelia doesn't want to talk right now."

Tess pointed toward the picture, the windows, and the stick figures at each one. "Can you ask her if these windows . . . if they represent all of your . . . selves?"

Noah as Tom leaned forward as if to study the picture in more detail. He sat back again, folded his arms, and shook his head. "It's wrong."

"How?" asked Justin.

"Mostly right is still wrong."

"What part, Noah?" asked Tess. "What's wrong about it?"

"The hair."

Justin looked at the picture and held it so that Tess could view it again as well, and each stick figure did have hair, some more crudely drawn than others, but all about the same length, making it difficult to distinguish male from female, boy from girl, and perhaps that's where they'd gone wrong. Not so much the personalities, but perhaps the wrong names under the wrong windows?

Justin tapped the paper. "Tell us which ones are wrong. Tom?"

Tess said, "I used to think they were eyes, Tom. When I was a girl, I visited that house. I imagined the red door was like the nose of a clown. The porch was a mouth, similar to this drawing."

"And the eyes?" asked Tom, interested.

"The windows," Tess said. "The windows were the eyes. Did you see the eyes? In the basement. The eyes in the darkness that you all seem to draw . . . Do you remember?"

"Yes," said Noah, who, as far as Tess could tell, was still Tom. "We all do. We all remember the eyes. Except Noah."

"Because someone saw them for him," Justin said. "Was it Oskar?"

Noah looked away, chewed his nails.

Tess leaned in. "Did Oskar live that month with Father Silence? Does *he* see the eyes?"

"Yes." The voice was tiny, still Tom but sliding. "But he sees more. He knows everything and sometimes he tells us through the door and it's scary."

"What door?" Justin asked.

"The closet . . ."

Tess and Justin shared a glance. She'd noticed a change in Noah's voice as he casually removed the glasses and pocketed them.

He sneezed and wiped his eyes. "Oh, these terrible allergies." *The voice of another boy, slightly older than the other.*

Tess sat up straight in her chair, eyed Justin beside her and then Ray over her shoulder, to see if they'd also noticed the switch. She asked Noah, "Who are we talking to now?"

"Stephen." He looked bored, put out, like a celebrity tired of the questions at a press junket gone long. "Tom's gone now."

"Where did he go?"

"Back home."

"Where's Noah?"

Noah/Stephen leaned forward. "You really wanna know?"

"Yes."

"He's in the ark." He sneezed again, coughed, then pulled a wad of tissues from his pocket to wipe his nose. "It's cold in there. And dark. And it smells like piss and shit."

Justin said, "Is Oskar in the ark right now, with Noah?"

Noah/Stephen stared, blinked, and then replied. "Yes. He and Ruth. Regular Bonnie and Clyde those two are." He spoke fast, as if trying to say as much as he could before someone stopped him.

"They know everything. They're not scared of him like we are. But they can't come out and play because the door's locked."

"What door?" Tess asked.

"The ark. Noah's Ark. The door is locked. Only Noah can let them out."

"How?" Tess gripped the bars, rattled them, frustrated.

Noah lowered his head, clutched it at the temples like a headache had just emerged. He rocked slightly, forward and back on the chair. "I gotta go."

Ray stepped closer, Tess assumed, in case he'd need to intervene quickly.

"Not yet," Tess said to Noah, but also Ray now beside her. "Please . . ."

Noah sat rigid against the seat back. He removed the sunglasses from his pocket and casually slid them on his face.

Tess and Justin moved away from the bars, realizing what had just happened—the Outcast was now here. Ray approached the cell.

Tess tested the waters. "Outcast?"

Noah grinned. "Not my real name, Tessa. Who would ever name a kid that?"

"Then what is your real name?"

"Wouldn't you like to know?"

"Where's my daughter?"

"She's s-s-safe. Playing with the others."

Playing? Tess leaned forward, gripped the bars. "Where?"

"At the P-p-playhouse."

"Where is the Playhouse?" Tess pleaded.

"Somewhere you'll never find." He pulled out the unopened cig-arette pack and tapped it against his palm.

Tess let go of the bars.

Justin asked, making his voice casual, "Do you smoke?"

"No. Can't stand the smell of it." He placed the pack back in his pocket. "Just that Noah sometimes gets them out and he p-p-puts them back the wrong way."

Tess felt heartsick. She'd hoped for a breakthrough but never expected an extended conversation. "What is the wrong way?"

"Upside down," he said. "Don't like things upside down."

Tess said, "What about that scar on your arm? The upside-down cross."

Noah/Outcast shook his head and chuckled.

"What's funny?" asked Tess.

"Nothing's funny when children suffer and go hungry and l-l-liv—" He stood suddenly, kicked the chair over, but then took a few deep calming breaths to compose himself. "Live like animals."

"And so you help them?" Justin prompted. "You take them to your place. This Playhouse. And you help them?"

"No more suffering."

Justin was starting to tear up. Tess put a hand on his arm, asked the Outcast, "Did you kill my parents?"

He shook his head no. "Couldn't do it. I only do the bad thing on bad people."

Tess nodded—this made sense. Following a sudden hunch, she asked, "Do you know a man named Jeter Janks?"

"The sheep."

"Yes," said Tess. "The sheep. Was he at the cabin with you? On the phone, you said, oops, we . . . and then you said *I did the bad thing*. Was Jeter Janks there at the cabin? Did he kill my parents?"

"Yes," he said.

Tess took a deep breath. "Because you wouldn't?" she asked gently.

"Because I couldn't." He sat back down. "I only do the bad thing to bad people."

Tess covered her mouth, hands trembling. "Are you part of their cult, the Lost Children?" Noah as the Outcast looked up, and she saw sorrow in the way his face seemed to melt.

"You got me all wrong," he said, almost plaintively.

"You dressed like a priest and stole my daughter," Tess pointed out. "You called yourself Father Friday?"

"I'm not like them." He pointed to the upside-down cross on his arm. "Scars aren't so easily removed last I heard, Tessa. You of all p-people should know that . . ."

Tess felt Justin watching her—trying, she knew, to follow all this—and veered to another question: "Why did you take our daughter?"

"She needed to feel loved."

"She *was* loved." Tess clenched her jaw, sensing thin ice. "She is loved." She knew that taking Julia hadn't made sense, didn't fit the pattern, and then something hit her. "Why are you helping *them*?"

"If I don't do like they say they'll t-t-take the children away."

"From the Playhouse?"

He paused, nodded, "Said too much. She's gonna know." This may have been Noah again; she couldn't tell. And then he said softly, "Mother is gonna know."

Justin spoke up. "Noah, your mother is dead. She can't hurt you anymore."

Noah as the Outcast removed his sunglasses and slid them back into his pocket. He replaced them with the regular pair of glasses—Tom was back. "Now you see me, now you don't."

Tess stared at him.

Noah/Tom said, "Just a game we used to play. In that house."

"A game Jeff Pritchard played as a boy," she said.

Noah/Tom shrugged, like *maybe*. "I'm tired. I think it's time for a nap."

Tess didn't know what to say, and Justin was equally stunned. *Who were they all afraid of?*

Just when she thought they'd lost him, Noah leaned forward, still as Tom, and gestured for Justin to hand over the picture.

Tess said, "Go ahead."

He did.

Noah/Tom grabbed it, turned it toward him, studied it, handed it back. "Noah's hair wasn't that dark of brown, but it's close enough, I guess."

Tess and Justin studied the picture. Tess pointed toward the brown bush at the bottom middle of the page, what they'd thought was a bush. "Are you saying that's hair?"

"What else would it be?" He pointed toward the top window of the picture, the window and stick figure below which Tess had so confidently written *Noah* when they were in the car. "And that's not Noah." He pointed toward the brown bush of hair at the bottom of the paper. "That's Noah."

Tess felt sick, like she wanted to throw up, and beside her, Justin had gone pale. It was Noah, from behind. That was the back of his head, not a bush, and he was staring at the house, staring at all his personalities up in the windows—Tom, Dean, Stephen, and Amelia; and then Oskar, Ruth, and the Outcast—because *they'd* endured that month-long captivity for him. And this was Amelia's way of showing it.

Tess's finger shook as she pointed back to the top window. "If that's not Noah, who is it?"

At the top of the pyramid, she thought.

Noah as Tom whispered, "*That's* who everyone is afraid of." He looked around, as if to make sure no one could overhear him. "Everyone but Oskar."

42

D IZZINESS HIT THE Outcast as he chased Julia around the Duck-Duck-Goose circle.

The words sounded in his head: *Now you see me, now you don't.* His words, but he didn't know where they'd come from.

And that game, he hated that game.

They'd played it inside that basement with the other kids, just to scare them. Flashlight on. Just so they could see his eyes. But oh how that light would hurt.

He could have reached Julia in the Duck-Duck-Goose game, very easily—he enjoyed winning, and this game he liked—but what he enjoyed more was listening to the kids laugh and cheer him on as he struggled to catch the runner. She'd been difficult to convince to play anyway, depressed that her parents and grandparents *hadn't* been the surprise waiting for her once they'd reached the Playhouse.

He faked disappointment at not catching Julia. She was only beginning to warm up again, coming out of her shell with the other kids. She'd just barely reached the open spot in the circle before his fingers found her shoulder, at which point—while he pretended to breathe heavily—he tapped Julia's head and said, "Duck." By the time he touched the top of Timothy's head, his vision wavered, and the second "Duck" came out slurred. There was no third "Duck" as he'd wobbled to his right and crashed into the wall of the Games Room, the wall upon which three dozen board games were stacked in six uneven piles, the collision sending the red, yellow, green, and blue pieces of the board game *Sorry!* across the hardwood like a quicksilver rainbow.

The wave of dizziness ended a couple of minutes later.

The headaches he'd had before, and the sudden bouts of dizziness, off and on since he was a child, since his escape from that house, from that windowless room, and hearing the voices was not uncommon, but hearing these voices—so recognizable—somehow hearing Tess and Justin communicating with . . . with his own voice, somewhere else, *that* he'd never experienced with so much clarity before.

How was it possible? And the fact that it was somehow possible sent panic through him. It was Noah. Somehow his voice was coming through Noah, not only his voice but his knowledge.

He knows. . . .

He knows where the Playhouse is, because I am in him—that he'd been aware of for years now, but was it possible for it to go both ways?

Was he reading my mind? Was he sharing my mind?

The Games Room warped back into focus.

His sunglasses had fallen off and the children were now staring at him like frozen statues, some of them crying, others shielding their eyes. Julia clung to the neighboring boy she'd only just met— the one he named Matthew—and she trembled.

He needed to put them at ease. He spotted his sunglasses on the floor and hurried to get them on. Fully recovered now, he faced them on one knee, smiled as if he'd just performed a clever circus act, and said, "Goose."

A couple of the children laughed, but most of them still looked shocked.

"I'm sorry," he said. "I was born this way. Just as you were born your way. S-s-sins of the mother and father." He stood, casually clapped his hands together. "Now go clean up for supper."

They exited the Games Room.

The new children followed the others into the hallway, at the end of which were two bathrooms, one for the boys and one for the girls, just like at the small Catholic church where he worked, and their nervous voices carried, whispering—he just knew they whispered about him. They'd never seen his eyes before, and now he'd lost parts of them, parts that would take months to get back. More games and fun would help. More learning and activities—music and painting. He'd show them the Leonardo Room, and maybe later, before bedtime, he'd put on the clown suit and show them his tricks with the rubber ball.

He would fix this.

While they washed their hands, he went into the kitchen, where the oven clicked and hissed—he'd get a new one soon, one large enough to fix enough food for the entire orphanage at once. The frozen chicken fingers and potato tots would soon be ready, and the children would gather around the table in the Nourishment Room and fill their hungry bellies.

He hoped they liked their surprise.

At each of the twelve seats he'd placed a simple cardboard name card, one for each of Christ's disciples. He'd let them pick their own seat, their own disciple—this was a painting project for the mural on the great wall of the Leonardo Room. Now that he had the perfect number, they could model the entire scene for him and give life to a room that had consumed him now for years.

His childhood punishment—so many hours alone in the small, dark, basement room, with candles burned to waxy nubs and that lone, horribly framed print hanging on the wall, the one he'd done his best to duplicate for years in the dark—would be his masterpiece to rival the master himself.

If only the world could see it. But they couldn't.

The Playhouse could not be exposed.

In the window above the kitchen sink he saw his reflection. The beard was coming in nicely. The children had been surprised by his shaved head when he'd emerged from his bedroom hours ago, looking vastly different, but after he'd explained that it was for a skit they would soon perform in the Theater Room, they understood.

Children need not always know the truth, which was that he had to avoid detection. He needed a new appearance. His trip to Montana had exposed him in ways he'd never been exposed before, and for this he blamed *them.*

They would not leave him alone to do God's work.

To take care of those who could not take care of themselves.

The kitchen window gave a glimpse of more than just his reflection. Out there, buried underground, those mounds covered by leaves and brambles and deadfall, rested the bodies—*of how many adults now?*—too many to count.

"Bad people," he whispered at the window.

Abusive mothers and fathers, all of them.

Victims from when he'd snap and do the bad thing.

Which was why he had to go to work and pray now.

Go to the church and pray for forgiveness.

43

Danny had arrived in Bowling Green from Twisted Tree in just under two hours, a straight shot down south on I-65.

He had the address Eliza had sent him for the Bowling Green Monastery of the Poor Clare Colettines, and after a quick stop at a gas station to empty his bladder and grab a Mountain Dew, Danny headed straight to the cloistered monastery, hidden deep into acres of woodlands seemingly born for solitude and silent prayer.

He'd slowed past the abandoned orphanage at the bottom of the hill, the old Sisters of Mercy, where Jeff Pritchard had spent five of his teenage years, and saw the grounds overgrown and many of the windows busted. He made a mental note to get a closer look on his way out, even if it meant letting himself in. The front entrance looked chained, but a building that neglected wouldn't be hard to break into.

He called Eliza on his way up through the trees. "I'm here," he said over the phone. "What's their deal again?"

"The Poor Clares is the name of their Franciscan order," she said, reading from whatever notes she'd taken. "St. Clare Offreduccio was the first Franciscan woman . . . follower of—"

"Of St. Francis, yeah I got that, babe."

"She founded the Poor Clares in the year 1212."

"Jesus."

"Danny, do me a favor and watch your mouth in there," she said. "One, they don't talk much. They're contemplative women. Two, they probably wouldn't appreciate you taking the Lord's name in vain. In the grand scheme of things, as far as Catholicism goes, they don't mess around. Their entire life revolves around prayer, solitude, and silence."

"Seems fitting."

"These particular Poor Clares are Colettines," Eliza added. "Reformed by St. Colette of Corbie in fifteenth-century France. Observance of papal enclosure."

"The hell is that?"

"Danny, come on, *language*," she said. "Papal enclosure means they're about as cloistered and shut off as you get. They maybe get out to vote. *Maybe*."

"Seriously?"

"You almost there?"

"Just about." He turned a sharp curve flanked by evergreens, and the road leveled out toward the grounds of the monastery, acres of lawns dotted by concrete benches and tall trees and flowered walkways, quaint ponds and gardens, old courtyards to match the stones of the main building and walls that cloistered, according to what Eliza had told him earlier, twenty-three Poor Clares plus their Mother Abbess, with whom Danny had been granted permission for a meeting upon his arrival. Although, Eliza was quick to point out, it might not be immediately, depending on what part of the day he arrived, as the sisters would not be interrupted from their daily prayers. "It is beautiful," he said.

"You considering the life, Danny Gomes?"

"Would be a simpler life."

"And they go barefoot, by the way. What time is it?"

He checked his phone. "Looks like they're an hour behind Twisted Tree. So one o'clock here."

"Okay," she said. "Morning Angelus followed by Lauds at five thirty, that's morning prayer, bear with me . . . *With praise I will awake the dawn*."

He coasted into a parking spot reserved for visitors. "What?"

"Nothing," she said. "Just something I'm reading here."

"How the kids?"

"They're good."

"They asking questions?"

"Not as many as you," she said, mumbling, skimming whatever she was reading. "Hour of meditation. Mass. Rosary. Simple breakfast at eight thirty. Although Great Silence has ended, a peaceful stillness continues . . . work until nine thirty. Exposition of the Blessed Sacrament and then Terce, or midmorning prayer. Manual work until eleven forty AM, at which point the bell rings for Sext, midday prayer. The Angelus is said at noon. The community then processes to the refectory while reciting the Veni Creator, whatever that is. They eat at noon. It looks like if you hurry, you got a little bit of time before midafternoon prayer. So beat feet."

"Love you."

"Love you back."

He hung up, approached the front entrance with simple stone-work surrounding an arched wooden door, and knocked. While he waited, Eliza shot him another text: *Just to warn, any conversation might be through a metal grille.*

He texted back: *Great.* And noticed over the stone wall to his left that some of the Poor Clares were working in the gardens, feeding geese that surrounded the pond. A few looked to be doing needlework in the shade of a large weeping willow. One, farther back by a cluster of magnolias, appeared to be painting at an easel.

When the front door opened, Danny jumped.

He didn't know what he'd expected, but what he saw in the open doorway was a nun, presumably the Mother Abbess, dressed in full habit and garb, yes, but middle-aged and with a smile that exuded enough kindness and warmth that Danny immediately felt right about coming. He felt the tension of the past two days starting to ease just enough for him to think that maybe with the peacefulness of places like this the world wasn't totally going to hell in a handcart.

"You must be Detective Gomes," she asked.

"Yes, Sister."

"Your wife called," she said. "She seems lovely."

"The loveliest."

"I'm the Mother Abbess here," she said, gesturing for him to step inside. "But please, call me Sister Jane. Or just Jane."

Danny nodded, because he didn't know what else to do. He was Catholic, but still felt inadequate for some reason.

"You've come to see Sister Mary Rose?"

"Mary, yes . . . I don't remember the Rose," said Danny, recalling the name of the Sisters of Mercy nun he'd seen written in Detective Patterson's interview notes with Sister Lucinda from years back. The nun who'd had her tongue cut out on the night Blake Sims was found murdered in the courtyard.

"It's the same person," said the Mother Abbess. "She changed her name to Mary Rose upon joining our order here. You are aware of her . . . difficulty talking?"

Danny nodded.

"When she does speak, she prefers to do it in writing."

"I understand."

"Follow me." After a few paces down a plain bricked corridor, she said over her shoulder, "I am surprised she agreed to meet with you."

"Yeah? Me too."

"It's just that for years, she's gone without any visitors. Declining most requests, especially in the years following what happened down the hill."

Danny didn't answer, and it didn't appear the Mother Abbess expected a reply, but he could tell they both knew.

Jeff Pritchard was finally dead.

And apparently, he wasn't the only one ready to break a long silence.

44

"No." WARDEN HOFMANN leaned with his fingers splayed across his desk, shaking his head emphatically. "No, it's not possible."

Justin stood on the opposite side of the desk, mirroring the warden's posture. "Make it possible."

"We cannot take Noah Nichols out of this facility," he said. "He's too unpredictable."

"He says you've done it before."

"On the grounds," said the warden. "*These grounds.* Under guard. So he can paint."

Justin pushed the desk, turned away.

Tess put a hand on Justin's arm and then faced the warden. "The Outcast has our daughter somewhere he calls the Playhouse. Oskar knows where this place is. He's not afraid like the others. But he's locked inside the ark."

"The ark, yes, of course, the ark . . ."

"The ark inside Noah's mind," Tess insisted.

Justin had gained his composure. "This is the only way, Warden. Four hours. We take him back to his childhood home and show him that closet. The *real* ark. See if it triggers something. It could work. I know it's a long shot, but—"

"It's a very long shot," said the warden. "And risky."

"But one worth taking," said Justin. "The home sits abandoned since his mother's death. You said so yourself. Keep him cuffed.

Chained. Multiple guards. Bring a SWAT team. I don't care. I want Oskar. I want my daughter."

"You have kids, and a brand-new grandbaby," Tess said. "I saw the pictures on your desk."

The warden sighed, looked from Justin to Tess and back to Justin again.

"Four hours."

CHAPTER

45

Noah Nichols's childhood home rested in the middle of an overgrown four-acre field, surrounded on three sides by Twisted Tree woods and the fourth by Highway 62—two lanes of potted gray with no crossroads for miles. The driveway—where Noah had killed his father seventeen years before—was now mostly weed-covered. The two-story house was clapboard, painted white but flaking, and the steeply pitched roof was missing half the shingles. Aside from the large second floor window, all the rest were boarded up and the black shutters that remained barely clung to their fastenings.

Tess stood outside the house with Justin, waiting as the caravan parked in the weeds behind them—two security cars from the asylum holding four officers and a white Berringer Hills transportation van carrying Noah, the warden, and Ray.

Wind pushed the tall grass like ocean waves, and Tess smelled rain. Dark clouds had gathered suddenly from the west. The news had forecast storms, and they'd arrived. As if on cue, distant thunder rumbled. The approaching clouds looked ominous.

Noah shuffled between two armed prison guards; he was shorter than either of them. His hair blew in the wind. He raised his cuffed hands to scratch a beard that seemed fuller in the daylight.

The house had been sitting unused since Sarah Nichols's death—she'd stated in her will that she wanted it waiting for Noah when he was released from prison. But by the way Noah watched the house, it seemed clear that he would never willingly return.

Thunder cracked like a whip, and this time they all flinched.

Justin placed a hand on Tess's back and coaxed her inside.

The front door's threshold was warped, and the wood sagged. The air was stagnant, with hints of mildew and decay. The orange carpet was wet from recent rains. Flies buzzed behind a recliner that had been stuffing-plucked by some animal.

Noah shuffled in and they followed.

He'd yet to say a word until he stopped five feet from a steep set of narrow steps leading upward against the far wall. "My bedroom was up there."

Justin sidled next to him. "You ready?"

Noah didn't budge; in fact, he took a step back, as if to turn away.

Justin grabbed Noah's arm, not forcefully, but enough to halt him, enough hopefully to convey his desperation. "You remember why we're here? We agreed to this. We think Oskar and Ruth are trapped inside the ark in your head, Noah. Seeing the real ark, we think will—"

"I'm not dense, Justin. I remember why we're here."

Hearing Noah call him by his first name gave him pause. "Then we need to do this. Now."

Noah nodded, scratched his beard again. His wrist chains rattled.

"He's not leaving my sight," said the warden. "Ray goes with us. The rest of the guards will wait on the stairs, two at the top and two more at the bottom."

Tess was the first up the stairs, with Noah's unsteady footfalls directly behind. The old boards groaned under their weight. Noah's bedroom door was off the hinges and slanted against the wall at the top of the stairs. The heat was thick. Mouse and bird droppings littered the floorboards as they crossed the threshold into the bedroom. One pane from the window across the room was missing. A sparrow sat on the window ledge, watched them enter, and then flew out.

Raindrops gently tapped against the rooftop.

The ceiling resembled that of an attic, steeply pitched on both sides, yet they were all able to stand without ducking in the middle of the room.

He pointed with his cuffed hands. "My bed was against that wall."

It was vacant now, the wall with hundreds of tiny holes from what Tess assumed had been pushpins holding up all the drawings.

Wind hugged the house. The window shivered across the room.

Noah had already glanced toward that window twice. It was the only source of light in the room that was quickly darkening as storm clouds moved in.

Noah pointed to a series of scratches in the hardwood floor. "My desk was there." He nodded toward the closet across the room, opposite the window. The lock was rusted. The door was warped, and above it, the outlines of the words were still visible—***Noah's Ark***—although now most of the paint had flaked away to where only parts of the ***h*** and the ***k*** remained.

Noah took three cautious steps before stopping.

"Noah, what is it?" asked Justin.

Noah dropped to his knees on the floorboards. "Mother. She's here."

Justin knelt beside Noah. "Your mother is dead, Noah. Remember . . ."

Noah shook his head like he disagreed, like no one understood but him, but stayed focused on the closet, the ark he'd been banished to for punishment.

The warden and Ray watched from the room's entrance.

Tess hugged her arms as another burst of thunder shook the house and lightning lit the sky, briefly illuminating the room, casting shadows. Justin's focus was on Noah, but he glanced her way, probably unsure what to expect from both her and Noah as the storm threatened.

"Mother knows I'm here. She knows what I'm doing."

The sky opened and rain pounded the roof, the sound deafening.

Justin raised his voice. "Ignore it, Noah." He'd said it loud enough for Tess too.

Noah pointed toward the ark. "They're in there. Oskar and Ruth."

Tess hunkered against the wall; her throat tightened; her breaths turned to hurried gasps.

The warden and Ray watched her with concern. Ray said something muted.

She held her hand up when Ray stepped to help her.

She closed her eyes, heard Noah's voice.

"They want out," said Noah, eyes large, his tone more determined. "I can hear them."

Lighting flashed. Thunder boomed.

Tess's hearing warped in and out of focus as she watched the ark's door.

It rattled.

Just a wind gust, she thought.

But then the wind got heavier, harder.

Noah scooted closer to the door. "They want out," he cried. "I need to let them out."

* * *

The Outcast's paintbrush was inches from the mural when his hand started to shake, inches from ruining his masterpiece. He paused, closed his eyes, whispered, "Don't let them out." Although he didn't know why he'd said it.

"Mr. Benjamin," one of the kids said behind him. Thirty minutes ago, he'd officially given the new arrivals a name to call him, a name he'd given himself years ago, a real name of his choosing, not the Outcast, not Father Friday—those weren't real—but the name of Benjamin Knowles. A name that had allowed him a bit of peace and normalcy in a world gone mad. The same child behind him said, "You look sick."

Another of the children said, "Don't let who out, Mr. Benjamin?"

I don't know. Yes, you do. Oskar and Ruth. He's letting them out and they know too much. Oskar isn't afraid . . .

"He knows where we are," he said aloud. *But how?* He dropped the paintbrush to the floor of the Leonardo Room and clutched his head. The brush streaked red paint across the floor like blood splatter.

He pinched his eyes closed.

. . . Saw Father Silence standing on a basement stage, facing the children. The children they'd stolen for him. Now they were dying. Don't drink the wine . . . But there's one still breathing, still alive. He didn't drink the wine. I can save him. What is your name? Noah . . . Noah Nichols . . . the boy had asked him, What is your name? I don't have a name . . . Everyone has a name . . .

He remembered snatching a rubber mask from a hook, one of so many hanging in that basement, this one a mask of a dog. He pulled it down over his head. *There's a window, and moonlight, go . . . take your freedom, you're out of the room, go . . .*

And he went . . .

The Outcast's eyes popped open, found his sunglasses askew on his nose, and straightened them quickly.

The children were frightened.

Don't let them see your eyes again. Don't frighten the children.

Even in their moment of unease, the children had somewhat held their pose—so trusting, all of them—modeling as each one of the twelve disciples as he painted his perfect replica mural.

Who is Oskar? I don't know. Yes, you do. He's the only one not scared of Mother.

He pulled the hammer from the tool belt at his waistline.

And he snapped.

*　　*　　*

Wind whistled.

Rain hit like pellets against the roof.

Tess pushed backward into the corner as Noah knee-walked closer to the ark's door. "They're in there," he whispered.

Justin glanced toward Tess, and with her eyes she told him to stay with Noah. She would be fine. Justin turned back toward the prisoner, his patient. "Open it up and let them out, Noah."

Noah crept forward, shuffling across the wood floor on his knees, a grown man suddenly young and afraid.

Lightning lit the sky, lit the room. Shadows flashed, and in them Tess saw strange eyes, large white sclera and tiny black pupils, and she screamed. *Not there. They're not there.* Thunder boomed. Tess closed her eyes, pushed back against the corner, pushed and pushed as if trying to become part of the wall.

It can't hurt you, she said to herself, just as glass cracked and rainwater sifted in through the broken window across the room.

"The water," Noah screamed. "It's coming."

"Open the door, Noah," Justin said calmly.

Rainwater trickled in across the room, forming rivulets that meandered along the uneven floorboard cracks.

Noah looked straight at Tess. Maybe it was Noah, maybe it was someone else, she couldn't tell. He mouthed the words, *I know what you did . . .*

And then he crashed his right boot into the door. The old wood split down the center.

Tess rolled to her side, clutched her stomach.

. . . under the twisted trees . . .

Lightning flashed, three quick bursts.

. . . what we did . . .

She was a teenager again.

In her father's police cruiser.

It was storming . . .

. . . She shouldn't have come. She was too young to play detective. And now she wanted to run, but where? Her father had entered the house. Rain beat down on the car in torrents. She saw movement at the side of the house, near the foundation, where a small rectangular window rested behind weeds. A basement window. The glass moved. Hands pushed against it, and then a head emerged. A head unlike any she'd ever seen, before realizing it was a mask. A shirtless boy in a dog mask. A boy, perhaps close to her age, trying to escape. The window lifted, angled from top hinges, and the boy crawled out into the grass and mud wearing only blue jeans. He shielded his eyes from the rain and waited beside a tall oak.

She contemplated calling him over toward the dry car, but sensed fear, from herself and the boy, who suddenly took off across the driveway, passing quickly between the hood of her car and the tail end of another. Lightning flashed. He entered the field to the left, sprinting across the knee-high grass. Why was he running? My father came here to save him. He was heading for the woods. Why? Without giving thought to reason, she opened the car door and stood in the downpour.

A spiderweb of lightning etched the dark sky, and it spurred her onward, into the field, running, chasing after that boy . . .

Tess opened her eyes, panting.

Noah's heavy boot laid waste to that ark door and the wood crumbled. Darkness emerged from the closet as if it had form, like smoke and mist and soot, and suddenly shadows had depth and the wind held whispers and the storm rumbled on, over the house, rapidly to the east as the rain died down and lightning stopped. She wasn't the only one panting. The warden rested with his back against the wall, pale as a sheet. Ray's eyes were fixed on Noah, who had made it to one knee, then stood in the middle of the room. He seemed taller now, or was it an illusion from her position on the floor? The room grew lighter as the storm moved on.

Drizzle touched the roof, replacing the deluge.

Tess's breathing fell in rhythm with her settling heartrate.

Justin nodded and she nodded back. She'd survived. She looked up at Noah, as did everyone else in the room, and suddenly feared him more than ever. Because this wasn't Noah.

His posture had changed from sheepish to confident, his eyes dark and cold. An unlit cigarette dangled from his lips, and he held the recently opened pack in his hand.

Justin's voice shook. "Oskar?"

Noah/Oskar winked, his voice cocky and raw. "Got a light?"

*   *   *

Julia didn't huddle together with the other children when Mr. Benjamin started hammering the wall.

At first, she'd been certain he was going to use the hammer on them—he'd taken two steps toward where they'd been posing for his mural before stopping and turning toward the side wall, which was dominated by sketches instead of paint—and then clobbered that wall until chunks flew and hidden wooden boards splintered, and white dust floated in the air. The children pushed closer together every time that hammer connected with the wall.

But Julia didn't hunker with them.

It was storming outside and all she could think about now was her mother. Her mother and how they'd make art out of melted wax inside their walk-in closet back home, how they'd drip candle wax on paper and form pictures and eventually the storm would go away. Julia pretended to be scared, although she wasn't. She knew of her mother's fears and pretended to share them—that was their bond.

Was it storming where her mother was? Did she have candles and paper? Word games with pictures?

Suddenly she didn't feel right being in this house, the Playhouse, with all the bright colors and games and toys and art and music. She'd never seen anyone paint like him before. And the hour they'd spent inside the Music Room had been magical—Mr. Benjamin's strong voice and piano playing had filled the room with enough joy to make her heart warm—but now it felt wrong.

Her mother loved her.

Julia's bones rattled every time Mr. Benjamin crashed that hammer into the wall. Didn't matter that one of the older kids was now whispering in her ear—as if he could read Julia's mind—*Don't run, he'll catch you. He'll put you in the Bad Room.*

He's a nice man, said another voice behind her, the girl he'd given the name James, son of Alphaeus, moments ago. *He has his fits, but he takes care of us. Don't run.*

Julia ran.

She darted from the Leonardo Room, down a hallway where more rooms jutted off catty-cornered—the Music Room with all those instruments, the Movie Room with the television, the Relaxation Room with the beanbag chairs, the Clown Room with the funny suit and wig hanging from the hook on the wall—before making a right turn into another hallway and more rooms on either side.

She paused in the kitchen, took a right into another hallway—it was a maze—and heard footsteps behind her, heavy footfalls that made her want to cry.

My parents love me, and this is not my home.

She turned again, another hallway, more rooms, and there was the front door.

She ran toward it, but before she could reach for the knob, he grabbed her. She squealed but couldn't speak because his large hand covered her mouth. His prickly beard scratched her cheek and suddenly, even though his words were nice, his voice struck fear like twenty splinters pulled at once.

"I'm sorry, Julia." He'd calmed drastically from his episode of hammering the wall. "I'm so sorry." He walked her quickly down a hallway, and another, turning, turning again. "But I just had this feeling you'd be my traitor." He turned, walked quickly down another hall of rooms, and at the end of this hallway was another door marked above by a wooden board that read, *Bad Room.* He opened it. It was dark inside. He walked her in, placed her gently, lovingly almost, on the floor as if tucking her in at bedtime right after a story. There was a pillow and blanket. He patted her on the head. "Be a good girl. I won't be gone long. But I couldn't leave my Judas running out and about with thoughts of f-f-fleeing." He made as if to close the door, but then stuck his head back in the opening and smiled. "Two hours tops, Julia. And I'll be back and let you out, lesson learned. Can you say that for me? Lesson learned?"

"Lesson learned," she said, fighting tears.

"Don't cry," he said. "Don't make my heart bleed." He closed the door. A lock snapped. His voice from the other side. "Two hours. I'll be back and we'll have milk and cookies."

His footsteps trailed away.

She considered screaming, but somehow knew it would do no good.

The others wouldn't dare unlock it.

*　*　*

"No light?"

Noah/Oskar let the cigarette dangle, unlit, resting amid all that beard growth. "Too bad for you then, Doc."

They'd conjured Oskar from the deep, without fully considering the threatening consequences—there was no putting this genie back in the bottle, this spirit back into the Ouija board. Justin reached out a hand, not for a shake—this personality didn't seem in the shaking mood, not with those dark brown eyes squinted like tunnels and the neck, suddenly corded with muscle and tension, reddening by the second—but a *hear me out before you strike* gesture.

It didn't work. Oskar grabbed Justin by the throat, lifted him from the floor, and spun him toward Ray, who had his gun out, but Justin was now a human shield.

Tess pulled her gun, aimed from the floor, but couldn't take the chance of hitting Justin. Neither did she want to seriously wound the one man who might possibly know how to find the Playhouse and Julia. Justin kicked and tried to pry Oskar's hands from his throat but couldn't. Finally Oskar let go, ramming Justin's body into the warden and knocking them both back against the wall—Justin rolling to the floor gasping for air and the warden's head hitting the wooden floor with a concussion-like thud. Almost in one swift motion, Oskar had Ray in his grasp and they were struggling with his gun. It fired into the ceiling and dust sifted down. Oskar struck Ray with the back of his hand and the blow spun the security guard into the open entrance of the doorway as two more guards were running in, guns pulled.

Noah/Oskar ran across the bedroom, lowered his shoulder, and burst through the window, shattering glass and splintering wood, free-falling to the ground below.

Tess hurried to the broken window.

He landed hard enough to imprint the muddy grass below, but made it to his feet, limped for twenty yards, and then settled into an all-out sprint for the woods as shots were fired from two more guards who'd just exited the front of the house in pursuit.

The guard now standing at the window beside Tess aimed his gun out the opening. She pulled his arm down. "Don't shoot."

We still need him.

By then the man had disappeared into the woods.

Panic surged through Tess as she stared out the broken window of Noah's old bedroom. They'd convinced the warden to bring a prisoner outside the walls of his prison, and now, because of them, he was gone.

Any information he might hold about their daughter, gone with him.

A phone sounded.

She turned back toward the room, found Justin fumbling inside his pocket. He pulled out his cell and stared at it while it chimed.

"Who is it?"

"Local number," he said, voice strained, neck reddened from having recently been choked.

Tess snatched the phone from Justin. "Hello?"

A woman's hurried voice said, "It's Lisa. Lisa Buchanon."

"What do you want?"

After a pause, she said, "I was right about the boat, wasn't I?"

"What do you want?"

"I had another vision. St. Michael Church. Pritchard's old parish. The priest there might be in trouble." Then Lisa hung up.

Justin had regrouped and was now on his feet.

The warden and Ray had hurried down the steps and out of the house and sirens sounded in the distance.

Tess handed Justin his phone, and together they ran down the stairs and outside to the car. She called Detective Evans, who picked up immediately. "Go to St. Michael," she said. "The parish where Jeff Pritchard used to work as a janitor. The priest there—"

"Detective . . . ?" Evans sounded confused. "We're already there. There was an attempt on Father Leonard's life ten minutes ago. But it was thwarted."

"By who?"

"The music director," Danny said. "Of all people. But Father Leonard is safe. I was getting ready to call you."

"I'll be there in ten minutes."

"Detective Claiborne . . . how did you know?"

"Just a hunch."

And she hung up.

46

WHEN DANNY SAT down in the chair that Sister Jane, the Mother Abbess, had offered him inside a waiting room adorned with framed pictures he assumed represented the twelve stations of the cross, he thought, *Eliza, you weren't kidding*, because the metal grille separating himself from the nun he was about to meet was real, and although the bars were thin and easily seen around, he couldn't help but think of a prison.

Yet he knew that's not what this place was.

Not even close. They were all here voluntarily. They'd chosen this life.

And when Sister Mary Rose—formerly just Mary—sat down and smiled at him, rosary beads intertwined in her fingers like white vines, he felt comforted all over again. He noticed how carefully she smiled without opening her mouth, without showing her teeth, without, of course, revealing any part of her missing tongue. But the first word to come to mind when he spied her through the bars of the grille was *lovely*.

She was lovely, and she exuded so much peace and tranquility just in the way she sat that he wished Eliza were here to witness it.

He thanked her for her time and she nodded, still with a hint of that welcoming smile, but then pulled a paper and pen from the folds of her habit and rested them on the ledge before her like she was ready to get this going—which she probably was, as the clock was literally ticking toward their next hour of prayer and the Mother

Abbess had already warned him she must be in attendance. The sisters were twenty-three hearts beating as one.

Of all the people he'd ever interviewed or interrogated, this one, Danny thought, needed no small talk, but he didn't know how to start talking to someone who couldn't, and was relieved when she started writing.

She wrote in cursive. Her penmanship was flawless. She finished writing and turned the paper toward him.

Jeff Pritchard wrote to me the day before his execution, asking for my forgiveness, and to pray for his soul.

"And did you?" Danny said, almost writing his response, before remembering she could hear fine. "And do you?"

She nodded, he assumed, a yes to both his questions.

"Had he tried to reach out to you before? In the decades since he fled the orphanage?"

She shook her head no.

"For what exactly did you forgive him?"

He waited as she wrote her response.

For what happened at the end. I always knew Jeffrey was troubled. He had a darkness in him that was only heightened by his quiet nature.

"I know a little about what happened that day," Danny said, leaning his elbows on the ledge in front of him, trying his best not to be intimidating, but feeling the need to get as close to her as possible. "The man who was killed in the courtyard at the Sisters of Mercy. Blake Sims. Do you think Jeff Pritchard killed him?"

Sister Mary Rose stared him directly in the eye and shook her head, emphatically, *no.*

"Then who did?"

She paused, fingered the rosary beads in her lap, and when she looked back at him, he could tell she was wrangling with her thoughts, and for the first time looked scared.

Danny did his best to help her out. "I've looked through some past interviews, done by the grandfather of one of the kids who is missing. You know about the kids, right?"

She shook her head no.

Of course she didn't. It wasn't like she watched the news.

So Danny told her about the murders, the kidnappings, the cult now running around in animal masks, and with every detail—as hard as it was for him to speak of it to this innocent little nun it seemed like it was harder for her to hear it—Sister Mary Rose grew more emotional. She fingered the rosary beads with just a little more desperation, or perhaps faith, and suddenly it felt like the grille between them had drifted away. The room had grown smaller. And the more distraught she looked the more he felt helpless to comfort her, even though she was right there, clearly needing it.

"You wouldn't talk to Detective Leland Patterson so many years ago," Danny said. "After that tragic night. But we need to know what happened. It could maybe help us now, somehow . . . In his interview with Sister Lucinda, there was a girl mentioned. An acquaintance of Jeff Pritchard, at the orphanage . . . Her name was Diane, I believe?"

Upon hearing the girl's name, Sister Mary Rose's eyes grew larger, and then somehow drifted inward. She turned the paper, started writing, and as she did, Danny did his best to get a sneak preview reading upside down, but it was tough to decipher all the loops and swirls he'd so egregiously butchered through all his years of Catholic school cursive writing. When she finished, she turned the paper back toward him.

Diane Cherry. She was younger than Jeffrey by three years, but he'd taken to her instantly upon his arrival. Or he'd taken to her, I should say, as she'd been in the orphanage since she was ten. She was an emotional girl. A lightning rod inside the orphanage. She could be sweet and calm at times, but mostly she was the storm. I don't know all the details of her childhood before her arrival at the Sisters of Mercy, but we'd all feared it was cruel. Deeply harmful. She was no doubt abused in many ways.

"What was her relationship with Jeff Pritchard like?"

As she wrote her response, he texted Eliza: **Check out a girl named Diane Cherry. A few years younger than Pritchard at the orphanage.**

Sister Mary Rose finished writing and turned the paper to Danny.

He followed her around like a lost dog. Despite him being older, he tended to follow her lead. We in theory tried to keep the boys and girls separated, but those two found ways to see each other.

"Pardon me, but I know no other way to put it," Danny said. "Was it sexual in nature?"

She shook her head no, and then wrote: *There was one point where we caught them in the woods, experimenting with some touching, and they were reprimanded, but we never got the sense that they were that way. When I questioned Diane, she laughed, as if she'd never. As if Jeffrey was her pawn to be maneuvered around her chessboard, but never taken seriously enough for that level. She used him. There was no doubt of that.*

"Did she kill Blake Sims?"

She bit her lip, nodded yes, and then wrote *I believe in my heart she did. I didn't see it. But I heard her screaming from the courtyard. I heard . . .* Here, Danny noticed the pause in her writing, and a tear dropped to the page before she resumed. *And the closer I got to the courtyard, the more clearly I heard the sound of that knife blade going in and out of that man's body. When I reached the courtyard, I saw Jeffrey fleeing down a pathway that led to their living quarters. The man was bleeding out. Already dead. I took off after Jeffrey, and someone grabbed me in the shadows. I know it was her. I didn't see her, but I knew. Her voice has never left these ears. She told me, "Mother has you now." She shushed me, her breath right in my ear. She said, "You saw nothing. You'll never speak of this." And even though I'd nodded yes, that I would not speak of what I had not seen firsthand, she pried my mouth open anyway. She said, "Mother says you need a reminder." She grabbed my tongue. And she cut it out. I never saw her again. I never saw him again. I never spoke again.*

Danny sat straight in his chair, exhaled the anger bubbling up. "And you don't know what happened to her?"

Sister Mary Rose shook her head no.

"Why?" Danny asked. "Assuming it was her who killed that young man so violently, why?"

She sniffled, wiped her eyes, and then wrote: *She was with child.*

"Diane?"

She nodded, wrote: *Seven months along, but hiding it well.*

"But you knew?"

She nodded, then wrote: *Jeffrey told me in secrecy.*

"Was it his?"

She shook her head no, and then wrote: *Diane was prone to sneaking out at night. She found trouble as often as it seemed to find her. She was raped. By that man, Blake Sims. It was his baby in her. I don't know how she did it, but she lured him there that night.*

"Why do you think Pritchard told you what was told to him in secrecy?"

Because she'd told him one night she was thinking about killing the baby inside her. That she never wanted to see it. To look at it. He said she could feel it moving inside her like it was a monster wanting to get out. Jeffrey truly feared for her and the baby. That's why he told me.

"What did you do?"

I prayed. For hours, to give me strength. I was young. I was scared. I was only coming up with a plan that night when it all happened. And then it was too late. The authorities looked for her. They looked for him. They looked for all the kids who left that night.

"But they never found those two?"

She shook her head no.

"Do you think they stayed together?"

I don't know. And then: *Her room is still intact. Down at the orphanage. It was never touched.*

At his questioning look, she added, *It was believed to be unclean. Sacrilege. Tainted by demonic symbols on the walls.*

"Can I get in there?"

She grinned, wrote: *I won't tell.*

Across the grounds, a bell started ringing and Sister Mary Rose immediately stood, for what he assumed were midafternoon prayers. But before leaving, she wrote: *I used to paint at the Sisters of Mercy. Out on the grounds, at an easel. That was my hobby. I was a lover of art. Jeffrey would watch me. We weren't allowed many possessions, but my most prized was a book on Leonardo da Vinci and all his artwork. Jeffrey loved that book.* She paused, as if to think about how best to phrase what she wrote next, then continued. *I truly believe when he asked for my forgiveness in that letter, it was for that. For taking that book on the night he fled.*

47

S T. MICHAEL'S CLASSIC cathedral-like exterior soared with a bell tower, turrets, and stained-glass windows, a Gothic church her father always said never seemed to fit in the otherwise bland town of Twisted Tree, a church made famous for a time during the arrest and trial and now execution of their former janitor, Jeff Pritchard. But now a half dozen cop cars were parked along the street, lights flashing prisms against the church's stone façade, where Sheriff Kingsley paced the first of five low steps with his cell phone to his ear, and in the distance Detective Evans talked animatedly with two men Tess assumed were FBI.

Tess and Justin shot out of the car and hurried toward the church. She assumed the white-haired gentleman in the black clerical garb atop the church steps talking to another FBI agent was Father Leonard, the priest who'd been in harm's way.

Evans spotted them in the distance. He broke away from the FBI agents and hurried toward them. Tess didn't like the look on his face, or his tone. "What's going on here? First the boat and now this?"

"Lisa Buchanon," Tess said, feeling foolish even as the words emerged from her mouth. "The woman who lives in Pritchard's—"

"We know who Lisa Buchanon is," said Evans.

"She's unstable." Sheriff Kingsley, now finished with his phone call, had come down from the church steps. "She's called us before with these . . . visions she claims she gets from the house, and they never pan out."

"These last two have."

Evans glared. "So you lost Noah Nichols?" When neither of them answered, he said, "And now we've got a circus show."

Justin said, "Don't forget one of your own killed Foster Bergman, the very man he was supposed to be protecting." And then he added, "I'll find Noah."

"You must be Detective Claiborne?" Father Leonard said, approaching them from the church steps. "Tessa Claiborne?"

"Yes, Father?"

"I knew your father," said the white-haired priest. "He was a good man. I'm sorry for your loss." He gestured toward the church. "Please, come in." And then to all of them. "We'll have no more pointing fingers."

They followed him in.

The inside of the church was ornate and smelled of incense, with soaring columns and dark carved pews, windows of colorful glass and painted murals, the ones on the walls depicting the stations of the cross, with the art on the ceiling showing Mary's assumption into Heaven.

Father Leonard repeated what he'd told Detective Evans and the FBI before their arrival. He'd come early for afternoon confessions and was in the sacristy when he heard voices in the church and then what sounded like a hammer blow on stone. He hurried down the hall and entered the church behind the altar. He saw two men, dressed in black, wearing animal masks, a sheep and a bull. The bull had a sledgehammer and had taken a chunk from the limestone. Father Leonard pointed toward the flat steps leading up to the altar, where red, blue, and purple light shone through the Gothic stained-glass window behind it.

"They had paint and brushes. They were going to vandalize the church. These . . . these Lost Children. But they were grown men. They came at me. I prayed. I could see it in their eyes. Drugged eyes. They would have killed me. They said that . . . Father Silence was the only true savior."

Tess said, "Because every cult needs one."

Father blinked, nodded in agreement. "Just before they were ready to strike, I was saved. By the music director, of all people."

"Why 'of all people'?" asked Justin.

"Because Benjamin Knowles is blind," said Father Leonard, with a waver in his voice. "Not only is he a talented musician, but Benjamin actually painted these beautiful murals."

Tess eyed the intricate artwork all over the church, the walls, the ceiling—it was like something more suited to Florence, Italy, rather than a town like Twisted Tree. "I thought you said he was blind."

"He is now, I'm afraid, legally blind." Father gestured toward the ceiling. "But not when he completed these murals. He was going blind then. A degenerative disease. These murals were done six years ago. He would be inches away from the wall as he painted. And for the ceiling fresco, he painted from scaffolding. On his back just like Michelangelo and the Sistine Chapel. Took him two years in all, and by the end he'd lost virtually all of his sight. But he's been a godsend. And now, my savior."

Justin moved toward the altar. "How did a blind man run off two men with weapons?"

"He has a walking stick," said Father Leonard. "A heavy cane. He said the cops were on the way. Seconds later we heard sirens, and they hurried off." His face paled. He put a hand on the back of the nearest pew to steady himself. "I don't see why they wanted *me*. I was at a parish in Indianapolis when Jeff Pritchard was arrested."

They heard footsteps, a clicking sound, and all three looked toward the piano on the right side of the altar steps.

A bearded man with a shaved head and sunglasses had just entered and was fumbling for something atop the piano.

"Ah, Benjamin," said Father Leonard. "The man of the hour."

The man looked quickly up toward the voice, as if he hadn't expected anyone to be in the church. "Father."

Father Leonard motioned for Tess and Justin to follow him up the center aisle. "Benjamin, I've got two friends here you should meet." The man shuffled two steps with his cane. Father Leonard said, "Stay where you are, Benjamin. We'll come to you."

They stopped five feet away.

Father Leonard introduced Benjamin Knowles, who was tall, thick, and broad-shouldered. "An artist, musician, and now a hero."

Benjamin grinned, briefly faced Tess, but then looked away. "Nice to . . ." He paused as if to gather himself, sunglasses aimed toward the floor. ". . . to meet you." He turned away, tapping his heavy wooden cane on the floor as he exited toward the hallway and the sacristy.

Father said to Tess, "Not a man of many words. But you should hear him sing sometime. A basso voice that makes the walls tremble." He called out to the music director just before he'd exited into the hallway. "Benjamin, do you need a ride home?" He whispered to Tess, "I often take him."

"No," the man said, again taking his time, as if concentrating on every word. "Thank you."

After the music director had gone, Father Leonard walked them down the center aisle.

Tess trailed the two men—something had unsettled her, but she didn't know what. They hit the outdoor air, thick and humid after the rainstorm.

Only two police cars remained, and Detective Evans stood outside the nearest one parked against the street curb. In her head, she replayed the events inside the church, and something didn't feel right about Benjamin Knowles.

When Father Leonard had introduced them, he'd looked away from her as if repelled. And when he'd entered from the back of the church, he'd acted surprised, like one would when they'd walked into something they wished they hadn't. The slow way he'd talked. *That voice.* So concentrated, as if trying not to say too much.

Trying not to stutter.

Tess turned back toward the church. "He's not blind."

Father Leonard faced her. "Who?"

"Your music director."

Justin's phone rang. He pulled it from his pocket, listened, and his eyes grew large.

Tess asked, "What is it?"

Justin waved her on, then moved quickly toward the car.

Tess ran back into the church and Father Leonard followed.

"Detective Claiborne? I don't understand."

She hurried up the center aisle and rounded the front row pew toward the choir chairs and piano. There was sheet music on the stand. A pen and a marker. A pink pad of sticky notes with doodling. A to-do list resting atop a file beside the piano. *Milk. Eggs. Bread. Another board game?* "Have you not noticed any of this before?"

Father Leonard stammered. "No, I . . . I have no reason to come near his things."

"He's not blind." She said it more to herself than to him as she looked around the church and moved away from the piano. "Father, have you ever heard him stutter?"

"Yes. That's probably why he said so little earlier. He's embarrassed by it. But he doesn't stutter when he sings."

"Oh my God."

"I give him rides home," said Father Leonard, softly, as if only now realizing things he hadn't before. "Detective Claiborne . . . you're frightening me. What's going on?"

"He has my daughter."

48

Phone pressed to his ear, Justin hurried toward the car just as Tess and Father Leonard reentered the church.

"How did you get my number?" Justin asked. "Noah?"

"Try again, boss."

The voice had a distinct edge to it. "Oskar?"

"*Ding, ding, ding,* folks, we have ourselves a genius. Are you in the car yet?"

Justin closed the door, started the car, and sped past a confused Detective Evans. "I'm on my way. Where are you?"

"It's where I'm going that's important. If you want to know what I know, then do exactly what I say. Are you ready?"

"Yes."

"Are you on the way to my old house?"

"Yes. Jesus. What do you want?"

"I want the fat-ass cop sitting in his car to choke on his doughnut and die. But if you can't make that happen, get him gone somehow."

"How?"

"Use your brain, Doc. By the looks of him he's as gullible as you. Which is why they gave him the job of watching the house I'd be crazy to return to. But get him gone. We've got some business to do in that house. Nasty old baddy boy business, old boss."

"I'm five miles away."

"I've got some requests. Some necessities."

"What?"

"I need some matches. I'm jonesing for a smoke, but I've no way to light these suckers."

"Matches. Is that it?"

"Of course not. Bring gasoline. In a gas can."

"What? Why?"

"Don't ask questions. Just do as you're told."

He spotted a gas station on the right, fifty yards down the road. They should have everything requested. Someone beeped in—probably Tess—but he couldn't switch over.

"And, Justin."

"Yes."

"Get me some Twizzlers."

"Twizzlers? Are you kidding me?"

"The red kind. And hurry."

49

Tess burst through the church doors so fast Detective Evans, who was getting ready to get in his car, pulled his handgun.

She paced the sidewalk, searching the street for Justin and the car.

Evans holstered his weapon. "He took off two minutes ago."

"Where?"

"No telling. You look like you've seen a ghost." Father Leonard exited the church behind her, pale and in a hurry. Evans watched them both. "What's going on?"

"The music director might be the Outcast."

He looked at Father Leonard. "The blind man?"

"Apparently he may not be blind," responded the priest.

Evans ran around to the driver's side. "We have an address, Father?"

"Just drive. I know how to get there." Father Leonard jumped in the back seat and slammed the door. "Barbary Street."

"I'm not from here, Father."

Tess pointed. "Straight. Right at the light." The car picked up speed. The siren choked and blared, flashing through encroaching dusk. She looked over her shoulder toward Father Leonard in the back, mumbling, praying with his eyes closed. "Father, was Benjamin around the church the past few days?"

"No. He'd taken the week off." His face had gone from pale to red, his voice laced with anger and embarrassment. "How could I have been so stupid?"

"You're not the only one he fooled, Father."

"Perhaps not, but at least now some of his confessions are starting to make sense."

CHAPTER

50

Danny found his way into the old Sisters of Mercy orphanage easily enough.

While the front doors were still chained and locked, he had his pick of broken first floor windows to climb through and decided on one closest to the orphanage's small cemetery, which, unlike the rest of the grounds, had been kept up and even had fresh flowers at the foot of several headstones. Before Sister Mary Rose had hurried off for prayers, she scrawled Diane Cherry's old room number: *138, first floor looking out over the cemetery.*

The hallway floors were dusty, and the stagnant air smelled of mildew and damp, but other than mouse droppings and evidence of other animals having taken up dwelling inside the abandoned building, to his amazement no graffiti or signs of vandalism marred the walls. The numbers carved into the woodwork above the doors to each room were painted black and clearly visible, so Diane Cherry's old room was not hard to find.

The door was closed.

He felt his phone vibrate. He looked at it as he approached her room. A text from Eliza, about his inquiry on Diane Cherry: ***I'll call in a minute. Good stuff.*** He pocketed the phone, opened her door, and stepped inside the small, stuffy room, lit only by the sole window opposite the bed. As Sister Mary Rose had said, it gave a perfect view of the cemetery beside it. And the room had indeed been left as is—the bed unmade, sheets rumpled and hanging half-way off the mattress. A mouse scurried along a baseboard beneath the window. Atop a dusty desk rested schoolbooks and notebooks and pens, and beside it a vanity with a hairbrush and hair clips and a curler. Clothes had been left in piles across the floor. The dresser drawers had been left open, a few with clothes, but most empty. The ceiling fan in the middle of the room spun gently a few ticks and then stopped as a subtle breeze moved through the open door-way, as if the room was suddenly breathing, coming to life, which unnerved him only because of what he was seeing and at the same time refusing to look at on the wall adjacent to the one where her bed rested.

The dolls resting on the bench had sent chills down his spine the instant he saw them. Dozens and dozens of old dolls sitting in rows, the kind of dolls grandmas would keep from their childhoods and store in spare rooms they didn't use or in attics so no one would see them, dolls stacked one atop the other, all facing him. On the wall above the bench full of dolls was written, in what was maybe red lip-stick, the words MOTHER LOVES YOU SLEEP TIGHT. And all around the written words—each letter nearly a foot tall and seemingly scrawled with menace—were the satanic symbols Sister Mary Rose had spoken of.

Mother loves you . . .

Danny turned away from them. The woman who attacked Sister Mary Rose the night Blake Sims was killed, the one she was sure was Diane Cherry, had told her *Mother says you need a reminder.* He then realized there were another six dolls on the bed, ones, he guessed, she must have slept with at night. And on the floor, lined up against the baseboards rested more dolls.

Jesus . . .

Danny removed his phone, snapped pictures. Sent them off in a hurry to Eliza. To Justin. To Tess. He'd explain later. He moved slowly across the room toward the window, looked out toward the cemetery, toward five rows of headstones, the closest row no more than five feet from her window.

His phone rang. It was Eliza.

"Hey. You get the pics I just sent?"

"Yes, that's fucked up, Danny, but get this. Diane Cherry's mother's maiden name was Buckner. Dolores Buckner. And she was from Twisted Tree," Eliza said. "After she married David Cherry, they moved to where he was from in Russellville, Kentucky, not far at all from Bowling Green."

Danny listened intently, even as he stayed focused on the cemetery outside, particularly the closest tombstone.

"You hearing me?" she asked.

"Yes. I'm gonna put you on speaker."

"Why?"

"I need to take a picture." He opened the window, which was stubborn at first, before yawning wide for him, allowing in a swoosh of fresh air. "Keep talking."

"When she was a girl, her father murdered his wife, her mother, and then hung himself from the rafters of their barn. Diane found them both."

Jesus, thought Danny, to both what Eliza had just told him and to what he was seeing now engraved on the headstone just outside the window: *Lisa Buchanon. May She Rest in Peace. 1911–1926.*

"Danny, you there?"

"Yeah, babe, go on." He took a picture of the headstone, sent it. "Look at what I just sent you."

She did. "Lisa Buchanon?"

"It's the name of the woman living in Jeff Pritchard's old house. It must have been a girl who died here at the orphanage in the early nineteen hundreds. She died young. Eliza, Diane Cherry fled here over two decades ago, seven months pregnant. She wanted a new name and took this one. One she must have seen outside her window every day."

"Danny . . ."

"Yeah?"

"Diane Cherry, after the murder-suicide in Russellville, was sent to live with her grandparents in Twisted Tree. Inside that house. Pritchard's house. It was the Buckner Farm then. It's where all those animals were killed one summer. The grandfather went crazy and shot them all. And then the grandfather turned the gun on himself."

"Eliza, I gotta go," Danny said, hearing something in the hallway. "I gotta let Tess know."

"Diane's grandmother sent her away. She sent her to live at the Sisters of Mercy in Bowling Green. Why would she do that?"

Because the little girl was a monster.

Danny heard footsteps and turned toward the open doorway, where a man in a pig mask stood, holding a gun. Before Danny could react, the man fired, hitting him in the chest, sending Danny hurtling against the window frame.

His phone landed face up on the floorboards. Eliza screaming from it, screaming his name over and over until it faded, along with the pig's footsteps.

CHAPTER

51

As dusk burrowed deep into the marrow of the woods sur-rounding Jeff Pritchard's old riverside home, Sheriff Kingsley coasted to a stop behind two cars parked side by side in front of the barn.

A black Acura and forest green PT Cruiser.

He'd been out to the old Pritchard house before, on one of the many times Lisa Buchanon had called the sheriff's department on trespassers, and knew she drove the Acura. The other car he didn't know, and it made his radar blip only because he knew she typically kept to herself out here and wasn't one for company.

After the scare at St. Michael with Father Leonard and hearing that Detective Claiborne and her husband had been alerted to it by Lisa Buchanon, Sheriff Kingsley, tired of being a near bystander in his own town as the higher-ups and out-of-townies did their thing, decided he'd pay Ms. Buchanon a visit, if for no other reason than to warn her to stand down and stop interfering.

And maybe she'd sit with him for a spell and pour him some of her sweet tea.

The veranda was decorated with a wide porch swing, hanging flower baskets, and matching rocking chairs. On the front door hung a painted, wooden fleur-de-lis with red ribbons sprouting from the top, and two planters flanking the first step.

Just as he was about to knock, he noticed the front door was ajar, just an inch.

"Ms. Buchanon?" he called, ringing the doorbell, waiting, growing more impatient the longer he waited without hearing anything. No footsteps. No sound of movement. He knocked on the door's framing, waited, and then put his knuckles to the door itself, knowing good and well it would open it wider, and when it did, he saw clear into the foyer and a stairwell leading upward to the second floor.

"Ms. Buchanon," he said from the open threshold. "It's Sheriff Kingsley. Just need to ask you a few . . ." He trailed off when he noticed, down the hall, left of the stairwell, red-heeled shoes on the floor of what he assumed to be the kitchen. Shoes connected to a woman's feet and bare legs that weren't moving, lying there in a way that made his heart kick into high gear. The rest of her body wasn't visible to him. He radioed for backup and entered the house, hoping she'd just passed out but fearing worse. And then the red heels disappeared, as if she'd been suddenly pulled away or had reeled them in on her own.

He hustled down the hall, gun drawn.

"Help," shouted a woman's voice.

He entered the kitchen. She was gone. "Ms. Buchanon." The window above the sink had small curtains, and they, like every window in the house, he now noticed, were closed.

Something snapped outside, and the house went dark.

Appliances shut off.

The power cut.

He heard the front door slam shut, and knew it wasn't the wind. And he knew it wasn't her who'd closed it, as he could hear her laughter coming from the darkness to his left and the front door was well to his right.

Either way, he thought, *I'm fucked.*

He raised his gun, thinking he should fire but doubting himself at the same time. *What kind of game was she playing here?* Her laughter moved, he turned with it in the dark, following her sounds, eyes adjusting but not fast enough. He could see slivers of moonlight around the edges of the window above the sink, and just as he started that way to open it wide and allow in a bit of outside light, something slashed at the back of his ankle, slicing his Achilles tendon. He dropped toward the floor, caught himself on a kitchen chair that toppled under his weight, smashing his hand.

Male laughter sounded across the room.

Wincing in pain, Sheriff Kingsley fired blindly, missing.

And then the flashlight illuminated the darkness ten feet away, but instead of an upward glow beneath Lisa's face, the light beam revealed a bull mask, strange dolls watching from the counter behind her, and a male voice said, "Now you see me." It clicked off.

Laughter, both male and female.

"And now you don't," Lisa said.

A gun fired and Kingsley felt the bullet like fire through his sternum, blowing him back across the floor, sliding, the floor lubricated by his own blood.

He mustered enough strength to prop himself up on his elbows. He stared into the dark, saw two shadowed silhouettes moving closer.

And then the flashlight again.

Click.

Lisa wearing a wolf mask, and Bull Mask beside her.

Click.

Darkness again, and he knew it was final.

He felt her breath against his ear, the smell of cinnamon, of that rubber mask and her perfume against his nose as she said, "Sleep tight, Sheriff."

52

J ULIA STARTLED AWAKE when she heard the approaching voices and footsteps, and instinctively moved toward the locked door of the Bad Room to listen.

But when the other children started screaming—not fun screams but ones of pure terror—her heart began to pound against her ribcage. A friend at school had a grandfather who'd recently died of a heart attack. *Is that what I'm having?* She took deep breaths to slow it down, but all that did was make her want to cry.

More footsteps sounded out in the hallway.

Running, screaming.

She lowered her face against the floorboards, spied beneath the crack under the door, and saw black boots. She heard a sheep's bleating, although she saw no sheep, and then realized the sound had not been from a real animal. A dog barked, but it wasn't a real dog.

A man's voice. "Where?"

Another man's voice. "Rose Island."

The screaming died down. Or maybe the children were now outside, their voices muted by so many walls. The black boots made the floorboards creak.

Go away, go away.

The black boots did just that, but then stopped suddenly at the end of the hallway. A breath stuck in her throat. The black boots approached her door again, and then the knob jiggled. She couldn't bottle the yelp that came out, no doubt alerting whoever was on the other side of the door to her hiding spot—what had previously been her place of punishment. She turned to the side wall, spotted the marker on the small ledge connected to the hanging whiteboard, and wrote a message her parents would understand if they ever found this place.

The door rattled. She flinched, dropped the marker.

The doorknob clunked to the floor.

The door opened and a dog looked in, down on all fours, barking, not loud like claps but a rolling guttural sound. But then the dog stood. Because it wasn't a dog at all.

It was a man in a mask.

And then he grabbed her.

53

Benjamin Knowles clutched the steering wheel and focused on the winding roads.

He picked up speed on the straights, chewing up pavement with no regard for the speed limit, but now, as he neared the abandoned Harlow Distillery, the curves forced him slower. He couldn't get home fast enough, not the home on Barbary Lane where Father Leonard often drove him back after mass, but to the Playhouse. He'd been gone longer than he'd hoped.

Julia had been inside the Bad Room for far too long.

The girl that—unlike his other children—they'd forced him to kidnap back in Montana. The girl he knew wouldn't fit in like the others *because* she was so loved. And he knew that a loved child would be missed. A loved child would be hunted. But he'd had no choice. Take her or they'd take *all* of his.

Lesson learned, Julia. Lesson learned. I'll make it up to her with cookies and milk. And extra free time before Lights Out.

But things had gone wrong, and some things couldn't be predicted.

He felt certain that Tess had identified him inside the church. If not, his appearance had made her think. After his scheduled confession earlier with Father Leonard, and then the unexpected arrival of Sheep and Bull—a warning sent by Mother, no doubt, a threat should he deviate from the plan he wanted no part of—things were in flux.

And so *his* plans had to be altered.

He'd refused to let them harm Father Leonard.

So he'd attacked with the cane, swinging blindly although, of course, Sheep and Bull knew he was not blind behind those sunglasses. They'd had him in numbers, but his advantage had been the quick arrival of the sirens, and even more important was that both masked men feared him. Even if they did not know where the Playhouse was—only Mother knew, and somehow Noah—he felt sure they'd heard of it, specifically about all the bodies buried there, victims of when he'd snap and do the bad thing and one more abusive parent would be buried.

Two can play at this game, Mother.

But that was what had gotten him noticed.

His need for payback.

Going back in to paint those eyes on the hallway wall outside the sacristy, and then hurrying to the piano to grab the calendar he kept inside his bench seat. He hadn't planned on Tess being there, and then Father Leonard forcing those awkward introductions. On his way out, he'd frantically pinned the calendar to the corkboard directly across from those painted eyes, and now he questioned whether he'd displayed the calendar as he'd envisioned—he'd been in such a hurry. Had he opened it to the date he'd circled so heavily in black ink, the same date on every page? The third day of every month. If Mother was going to send cowardly messages and threats, then he was going to continue to parcel out his own little hints, for those who now worked hard to bring him down. Clues that he hoped could bring *her* down.

He accelerated up the serpentine hill, hugging the curves as overgrown branches tapped the van like gunfire. He climbed and skidded, accelerated and bounced, tunneling up and over to the straight shot that took him to the tree across the road, the hidden gate he'd so cleverly constructed, the ultimate deterrent for anyone who braved the hillside to sneak around the abandoned Harlow Distillery.

But the tree wasn't there. *Someone had opened the gate.*

"No."

He floored the gas, skidded on rocks and grass at the bend near the silo and tore down the drop toward the clearing where the Playhouse waited. He left the car running, the driver's side door open, and sprinted to the porch, slipping because it was wet from the rain.

The front door was open.

The screen door swayed.

Once inside, he called to the children, but no one answered.

The Music Room was empty. The Leonardo Room silent. He found no one in the Kitchen Room or the Nourishment Room or any of the other rooms as he stumbled down every hall, sucking in panicked breaths.

"No, no, no, no."

Tears welled his eyes.

He put a fist through a wall in one of the bedrooms. Vacant bedrooms, all of them. *Mother.* She'd been here. She was the only one who knew of this place. She and her followers. Her sick twisted followers too cowardly to go without masks.

He screamed and the windows shook.

He screamed again and birds scattered from trees.

He screamed until it felt like his heart split down the middle, thumping, lurching, beating to the same rhythm as the pulse now throbbing inside his head.

"She took them."

He wavered down a hallway, past the Clown Room, where the uniform hung lifeless from a wall hook. *She took the children. Years of work. Years of nourishment and safety. Where did they go? Had she done this in retaliation for him saving Father Leonard? For interfering with her stupid plans?* Plans of which she'd only told him part. "The only part you need concern yourself with," she'd hissed.

He froze, went rigid. Had she planned this all along? Had she been using him like she'd always used him? Like trash. Like throwaway trash. The son she'd never wanted to even look at. *You bitch! Where did you take them? You lying bitch.*

He turned a corner.

If only they'd caught her back then. If only they'd found her in the basement with Mr. Pritchard. But she'd escaped too, just like he had, but on the opposite side of the house, through the cellar, and she'd later found him deep in the woods. Deep in the woods. After what he and Tess had done under the twisted trees.

There you are, Benjamin . . .

Mother found you. Mother always knows where you are.

He turned into another hallway.

More rooms. Always more rooms. He'd get them all back and add even more rooms if that's what the kids wanted.

And there it was.

The Bad Room.

"Julia."

The door was open.

He hurried toward it, flipped on the hallway light so that he could see into the room with no bulb in the ceiling and one lone dormer high up in the far wall where moonlight entered, illuminating the board he'd installed for drawing. Because even his Bad Room should not be completely bad. He'd had no light in *his* bad room as a child, which was why he'd learned to draw and create in his mind, and what he'd ultimately put on the walls would come from memories of that book on Leonardo that Mr. Pritchard had allowed him to keep.

Replicas of the masterpieces he'd create from nothing, his mind the palette.

He shook a memory away, of Mother kneeling on Mr. Pritchard's neck before the police came in. The kids were dead, all except the boy named Noah. She was trying to pry Mr. Pritchard's mouth open, threatening to remove his tongue so he couldn't talk when they caught him. But he promised. He wouldn't talk. *Don't take my tongue,* he'd said. *I won't talk. I won't talk!*

The door to the Bad Room swayed.

They'd broken the lock to get in.

He entered the room.

Julia had left a message on the wall. Hastily drawn.

Smart girl.

It was a game he recognized. A game he'd played with some of the children before, although not with her.

A word was spelled wrong, but that was nothing that couldn't be explained later. When Mother had come, they probably wore the terrifying animal masks. They'd frightened her, and Julia had reached out to him.

CHAPTER

54

DETECTIVE EVANS PULLED to a slow stop outside the one-story shotgun brick house, narrow and deep like the rest up and down the street.

On the way, Father Leonard had made a quick call to the parish office and the Barbary Street address was confirmed—the only one they had on file for Benjamin Knowles.

If that was his real last name.

Evans took the front door and motioned for Tess to go around back. The neighborhood of shotgun homes had back doors that cozied up to courtyards and patios, but most of them looked overgrown and either fenced or bricked in. Benjamin's backyard had neither, and all he had for gathering was a small stoop that could have maybe fit a charcoal grill. Other than that, the yard was weeds. Unlived and uncared for, with no signs of children having lived here. No toys or balls in the yard. She lifted the top of the trash can and found it completely empty. Maybe the trash had recently been picked up, but by the looks of the over-full cans in the neighboring yards, she didn't think so. She knocked on the back door and peered through the small window into the kitchen. No table. Nothing on the counters. An empty gap where the refrigerator would go. Defeated, she made her way back to the front of the house.

"I don't think anyone lives here."

Evans knocked on the door anyway.

Father Leonard was on his way up the sidewalk, having abandoned the car in which they'd told him to wait. "There's a key under the front mat," said the priest. "I've seen him fumble around for it. Or pretend to fumble. No wonder he declined my offer to help him inside. I would have been able to see through the windows." Father did just that. "Looks like no one lives here."

Evans said, "Father, please back away."

Tess moved the mat and found the key. Before Evans could stop her, she'd opened the door and stepped inside. No alarm sounded. No electricity. With the light from her phone, she cased the front of the house while Evans took the back. A minute later they reconvened in the front room, and both came to the same conclusion.

"It's a decoy home." She turned in a slow circle. "Son of a bitch." Her phone pinged—a text from Justin.

On the way back to meet Oskar. Don't tell anyone. He's agreed to talk. But to me only and he doesn't want anyone to know.

Evans heard her phone and must have seen her reaction to the text. He stood with his eyebrows raised, waiting.

"It was Danny," she lied, but then noticed that Danny had, indeed, sent her a text she hadn't seen, one with pictures she now viewed, swiping until she'd seen them all. "He sent me pictures from Bowling Green. From the old Sisters of Mercy orphanage."

He must have seen the confused look on her face. "And?"

"I don't know," she said, going through the pictures again, stopping on the one of the wall where the words MOTHER LOVES YOU SLEEP TIGHT had been written above the bench of creepy dolls.

"Tess?"

"I . . . I don't know," she said, stepping away to call Danny. He didn't pick up. It went to voice mail. She saw that Eliza had called three times during the chaos at St. Michael, and had left a message.

Before even playing Eliza's message, Tess felt trepidation coiling inside her gut, squeezing her heart to double-time. She listened, and Eliza was hysterical and crying.

Tess, I think Danny has been shot . . . he's in Bowling Green . . . I heard a gunshot, and he won't answer his phone . . .

Tess screamed, "*Fuck! Fuck!*"

Evans hurried over, as did Father Leonard, to comfort her.

"What happened?" Evans asked with urgency.

"Danny was shot in Bowling Green," she said. "Get hold of someone down there, please, now. He's at—"

"I got it," Evans said, already on the phone, leaving Father Leonard there next to her.

"My child," the old priest said, opening his arms.

She settled into his embrace just long enough for her heart to settle a few ticks, and then moved away, thinking now of Justin and his message, of him hurrying off to meet Oskar at Noah's childhood home, and she feared Justin too was heading off to his doom.

Evans returned to them. "Bowling Green PD was already on the way to the orphanage."

Tess whispered, "Thank you," sure now that Eliza had called them. She opened a nearby closet, shined her light inside, finding it full of hangers on a cross-pipe, with clothes, uniforms—scrubs for a doctor, a shirt for what could have been a maintenance job, a sweat suit like a coach would wear, the dark pants and shirt for a priest.

"Disguises he uses to lure kids," she said to herself, watching Father Leonard move outside like he might get sick. She followed him out into the fresh air, scrolling through pictures on her phone, flicked left until she found the one she'd taken of the drawn composite of the Outcast in Montana, who they now knew to be Benjamin Knowles.

"Tess?" asked Evans, "What is it?"

She held up her hand. *Give me a minute.* She found Warden Hofmann's cell phone number and sent the pic to him, with the question: ***Does this look like anyone you know? Call me. Now.***

She waited outside, paced the sidewalk, needing to call Eliza back but not wanting to face that call yet. She at least texted her: ***I'm so sorry. Keep in touch.***

Her phone rang.

It was Warden Hofmann from Berringer Hills, responding quickly enough to make her think he'd been waiting. "He looks familiar. But, Detective, I've seen this picture before."

"I know you have. Look harder. He's changed his appearance. He's shaved his head. He has a beard now. Would he look familiar to you then?"

She paced the sidewalk. He paused. And then, "Dear God."

"What?"

"Father Knowles."

"Father Knowles?" Tess asked, suddenly remembering the warden's words the day he'd first introduced Noah. Mentioning that a priest came on the last Friday of every month to hear confessions from the prisoners. *Father Friday.* "You recognize him? Is he the priest who visits the last Friday of every month?"

"Yes." The warden's voice was weak. "Everyone calls him Father Friday."

"Does he see Noah when he visits?"

"Yes. He always saves him for last. Detective, what's going on?"

"Warden, Father Knowles is not a priest. He's a kidnapper of children. And he's evidently been visiting Noah once a month for God knows how long, right under your nose."

She hung up, hands trembling.

What next? What now?

Father Leonard's cell phone sounded. He fumbled at it with arthritic fingers and answered hurriedly. "Yes, yes . . . oh, dear God. A calendar? On every page? Yes. Take a deep breath. Thank you. Yes. I'll be there soon." He ended the call.

"What was that about?" Evans asked.

"That was our sacristan. In the hallway leading to the church, she found a pair of eyes painted on the wall."

"Looking at what?"

"A calendar."

"That's why he came back," Tess said. "When you introduced us. To paint the eyes. What was on the calendar?"

"The third was circled in black."

"The third? What does that mean? Today's the eleventh."

"He circled the third day on every page. The third day of every month."

Tess taxed her brain and found it running slow, sleep-deprived. *Think, Tess. Third. Third day. Three.* "Father Silence."

Father Leonard said softly, "Matthew 17:23. They will kill him, and on the third day he will be raised to life."

Tess felt weak in the knees, like on the verge of having one of her blackouts. "They believe Jeff Pritchard was some kind of messiah."

The murders were only setting the stage . . .

"I've prayed for them. For their souls. These Lost Children."

"Father, Jeff Pritchard was put to death three days ago tonight."

He crossed himself. "Then I shall pray for us all."

CHAPTER

55

Getting rid of the guard was easy.

Justin pulled through the weeds at Noah's old house and found him napping in his cruiser. He tapped the window hard with a knuckle.

The guard jumped, rolled down the window. "What can I do for you?"

Justin flashed his badge from the Missoula Police Department. "I just saw someone who looks like Noah Nichols entering the woods about a mile north from here." Justin slammed his open hand atop the car. "Go." He showed him the handgun tucked in his belt. "I'll watch the house."

The panicked guard turned on his siren and sped away.

Justin waited until the police car was a blip before removing the gas can and plastic bag from the trunk, and then hurried into the house. Noah's old bedroom was muggy after the storm. Glass and wood splinters littered the floorboards from where Noah had broken through the window. Puddles rested from when rainwater had come in. On the opposite side of the room, next to the ark, was a pile of hair, a pair of scissors, and a razor he could only assume had come from Noah. From Oskar.

At some point he'd gotten back into the house despite it being guarded.

Justin paced the room, waiting. He pulled out his phone but barely had service this far out in the boondocks. He pocketed it, paced, turned toward the door when he heard footsteps approaching up the stairs, and then Noah/Oskar showed himself in the doorway. His face was clean-shaven, his hair cut short—seemingly hacked— and an unlit cigarette dangled from his lips.

"Hello, Justin," Oskar said. "Got my shit?"

Justin tossed him the bag.

Oskar rummaged through it, found the matches and the Twizzlers. He lit the cigarette, inhaled so deeply Justin thought he might shrink it to a nub with one pull. He exhaled and smoke filled the room. He opened the bag of red Twizzlers, pulled out a handful and offered Justin one.

"No, thanks."

"Suit yourself." Oskar ate the Twizzlers like they were trees going into a woodchipper, eyeing Justin the entire time he chewed and smoked, chewed and smoked, squinty-eyed on the inhale and relaxed on the out. "Oh, the small pleasures of life."

"Where's my daughter?"

"Right to the point, huh?" He gnawed through another Twizzler. "Patience is a virtue, Doc. Ever heard that one?"

"Who hasn't?"

"You'd be dead if I wanted you dead. Remember that."

"Then kill me."

"I don't do that." Oskar inhaled, exhaled, let the smoke linger before blowing a tunnel through it. "No." He pointed with a Twizzler. "I like you." Oskar lit another cigarette, antsy, fidgety. "Once Noah returned from Father Silence . . . Don't you just love that name? Well, then I was able to blame all kinds of shit on the Outcast. He took the fall for me too many times to count. Still does. Stupid, stuttering idiot. Doesn't even know it's me he conjures." He did air quotes with his fingers. "When he snaps."

"So, he is somehow inside you?"

"No, Doc, he's somehow inside Noah. Just like me. But there's some weird shit that goes on between this mind and his. It's kind of a two-way street."

"What are you talking about?"

"Don't know for sure. But somehow . . . when the Outcast comes out in me . . ." He pointed to his head. "I think *he*, wherever he might be, can hear what we're saying. I think he can eavesdrop."

"Where's my daughter?"

"But not just him," Oskar said, laughing. "Her too."

"What are you talking about?"

"Oh, I'll get to that. As a head shrink, I think you're gonna like what you hear."

"Where's my daughter?" Justin repeated doggedly.

Oskar looked at the scissors and razor, and then made a quick move as if to grab both. Justin flinched. Oskar laughed, then lit another cigarette. Smoked them like they were nothing. "Making up for lost time, Doc."

"The Outcast locked you in the ark. The one inside Noah's mind."

Oskar exhaled. "I said he was stupid. But I didn't say he wasn't strong."

"You haven't killed me because I let you out?"

"Possibly," he said. "And also, just maybe, because I'm not the killing type."

"You killed Noah's father," Justin said, not so much as a question, but a sudden matter-of-fact notion that just struck him like a lightning bolt between the eyes. "Right out there on the driveway. It wasn't the Outcast at all. You blamed it on him . . ."

"No, I didn't do that."

"Didn't do what?'

"Kill his father," Oskar said.

"Then who did?"

Oskar grinned, evaded. "And his name is Benjamin, by the way. Benjamin Knowles. At least that's the name when he finally escaped that house." He pointed with his cigarette. "Noah doesn't get many visitors at the asylum, but Benjamin visited once a month. If you'd been listening, the warden mentioned a priest who visited the last Friday of every month."

"For confessions."

"Except he ain't no priest, Doc. All the inmates call him—"

"Father Friday."

Oskar pointed with his cigarette. "Bingo, bango, ding dang done. We're having fun now, aren't we, Justin? Can I call you Justin? I don't want you to think I signed up for some kind of therapy. The warden, of course, just referred to him as Father Knowles. You know why?"

"Why?"

"'Cause that's what he said his name was."

Justin wasn't amused.

Oskar laughed. "Dude isn't even blind. But have you seen his eyes? Jesus wept, that's some scary shit. Whether he was born that way or became that way because they always kept him down there in the dark, I don't know. But they were all afraid of those eyes. Those strange eyes lurking back in that dark corner." Oskar seemed to be gaining steam as he talked. "Of course, sometimes they'd put him in that room for days with no light." He exhaled smoke rings. "Hell of an artist, though. Sometimes we could hear the scratching of his pencil against those walls, like little mice scurrying. We make the best of things, don't we?"

"If you didn't kill Noah's father, who did?" Justin asked, pulling Amelia's picture from his back pocket and unfolding it for Noah to see. He pointed to the pyramid of windows, the stick figure in the top one. "Who is the eighth window, Oskar? We were told that you don't fear this one. Who is the eighth personality?"

"A sadist," Oskar said.

"Who is he?"

"Who is *she*, you mean?"

Justin blinked. "She?"

"Nature, nurture, with her maybe a solid combination of both, but damn . . ." Oskar looked to his wrists, both of which were scraped and scratched and bruised. "Would you like to know how I got the handcuffs off?"

"Who is in the eighth window?"

He ignored the question. "I found an axe on someone's farm. Rubbed the chain against the blade until it snapped." He gnawed through another Twizzler. "You know *she's* the one who branded us on the arm with that cross. Upside down. I took the pain for Noah. Ruth and I shared time in that house, but I took the pain. I've always taken the pain."

"Where is Ruth?"

He exhaled up toward the ceiling and grinned. "Now that's a hot piece, that Ruth." He winked. "And sometimes she lets me get on it." He pointed to his head, gently tapped the temple. "Oh, she's still in here. Stubborn woman, though." He made a clicking sound with his mouth. "But that's what I love about her."

"There's a satanic cult in Twisted Tree. They're killing in the name of Father Silence. They wear masks of animals."

"What about 'em?"

Justin raised his arms, flabbergasted. All he wanted was a straight answer.

Oskar finished another cigarette, smashed it into the floorboards, and pulled another Twizzler from the bag. "Father Silence put poison in the wine."

"We know—he made them drink like some morbid Last Supper."

"Not really . . . it was more of a hurry up and kill them type of thing. She wanted to get bloody. It was Pritchard who talked her into . . . spiking the wine instead. Something he'd been testing off and on for years," Oskar said, knowingly. "Altar boys can have easy access to communion wine if they have a mind to tinker."

"What are you talking about?"

"Back in Bowling Green. He started adding rat poison to the wine." Oskar held his right thumb and index finger an inch apart. "Just a smidge. Just a pinch. Just enough for people to start slowly getting sick. And Father Jim, back in those days, at St. Timothy, he took the brunt. Priests, of course, finish all the wine after communion, after it's been, what do you call it . . ."

"Consecrated."

"Bingo. And Father Jim got really sick. May have even eventually got cancer from all those teeny doses of rat poison Jeff Pritchard sneaked into the chalices. Of course, he never really cared for that Father Jim. It was her idea, though, all of it."

"Who?" And when he didn't answer, Justin asked, "How did Noah live when the others didn't?"

"Benjamin," he said without hesitation. "They'd let him out as soon as they heard the car tires on gravel outside."

"And he saved you? Saved Noah?"

"More or less." He blew a smoke ring. "You ever wonder . . . I'm sure those detectives did back then, why they'd switched to children?"

"What are you talking about?"

"All the bodies they found buried on that property," Oskar said. "Not only were they adults, but they were all men—"

"That no one cared about," Justin said. "Not enough to know they were missing . . ."

"Until those children . . . ," Oskar said, letting his words dangle like the smoking cigarette in his fingers.

"The same ones inside you right now."

Oskar shrugged. "Yeah, sure. Whatever you say, Doc."

"And it was the missing children who eventually got him caught. Because the missing children brought about the attention that led to him."

"And your dear wife."

"What about her?"

"We know what she did when she was a girl."

"Who's we?"

Oskar tapped his head again. "All of us, Doc. How she sneaked her way into the house and sat at Pritchard's kitchen table and asked for a drink of water. Only to get his fingerprints."

"She was brave," Justin said. "She's always been brave, and smart, and—"

"But that's exactly what'll end up getting her killed, Doc."

"What do they have planned?"

"You know we were all down there that day. Us kids. Heard your wife's little thirteen-year-old feet on the floorboards, creaking down on our ceiling. Mother down there threatening to slice our throats if we made a peep. We believed her because there was blood on the knife. She listened from the top of the steps. Heard every word Tess said. She blames her, you know. For undoing it all. But at the same time, maybe it was a blessing."

"Why?"

"Because on that day, after Tess rode off on her bike, Mother started covering her tracks. Got every remnant of a woman living in that house gone, so the police would never know. And they didn't."

"Who is she?"

"You're not that dumb are you, Doc?" Oskar ate another Twizzler. "Have you ever wondered why they snatched those children? *For Benjamin.* They did it for Benjamin. He'd been begging for years for someone to play with. For a friendly companion. Always stuck inside that room. So, Father Silence . . . I just hate saying that name . . . Jeff Pritchard went out and got him some. Oh, she was mad. She was steaming mad. She hated that boy. What he represented. What he reminded her of. Couldn't stand to even look at his face, that child of rape. I think Blake Sims was his name. Dude found butchered at that nun orphanage way back when. And here Pritchard had gone out, against her wishes, mind you, and brought back some companions for that boy. And it worked for a time. Until she got sick of them."

"Who was she, Oskar? Who is the eighth window?"

"Same bitch who lives there now," Oskar said, "And whoever told you I wasn't afraid of her is wrong. We all are. It's just that I don't care anymore. She can come and get me."

The shock of it nearly took Justin's breath away. "Lisa? Lisa Buchanon?"

"That's who she is sometimes," Oskar said. "She was Mother when it all went down in that basement. Depended on which side of the coin you got with her. Lisa, she wasn't so bad. Of course, she was born Diane Buckner. Also known as Diane Cherry. And don't even get me started on *that* childhood. Jesus wept. But she wasn't so different from Noah, except she just has the one other identity. The one who always came to her rescue during that screwed-up life of hers. And with the one as big and bad as Mother, that's all you need. You should see her collection of dolls . . ."

"And you," Justin said, pointing toward Noah/Oskar. "You absorbed that personality—Mother's—just like you did with the others. Dean, Tom, Stephen, and Amelia. The Outcast. *She's* somehow inside you too."

"It was intense." He pointed with the cigarette. "But right you are."

"Mother killed Noah's father," Justin said, putting it all together. "In the driveway. Holy fuck . . ."

"What's that?"

"The neighbor," he said, recalling the interview Leland did with the neighbor who'd come running through the woods when she'd heard Sarah Nichols screaming that morning. "The neighbor said Noah's mother was screaming for him to get off of his father. And Noah kept saying *I am, Mother.* But he wasn't answering her. He was telling her who he was at the time. *I am Mother.*"

The figure in the eighth window.

"Funny, right?" Oskar said with a wink.

Justin pulled out his phone, but before he could send a message to Tess, Oskar snatched the phone from him and slammed it to the floor, stomping on it for good measure.

"The fuck are you doing?" Justin screamed, picking it up, but the screen was smashed. "Are you crazy!"

"Yes and no," he said. "But I think Benjamin had had enough, and he wasn't about to let it all go down without a fight."

Justin was still in shock, and it took a minute to register what he was talking about—when those kids were killed in Pritchard's basement.

"He made eye contact with me," Oskar said. "Well, with Ruth, really, she was in control of Noah at the time, and then she tagged me in. I came out in a hurry, though, a little discombobulated, and didn't understand what he was getting at, and truthfully, Benjamin scared the shit out of me with those eyes, so I looked away. But he was within arm's reach of me, so when the other kids drank as they were told, he jumped and knocked mine to the floor. Pissed Mother off something fierce. She grabbed a Louisville Slugger that was leaning against the wall and hit him on the back so hard I thought she'd killed him. I gotta hand it to him because the boy got up for more. Stood strong like he was begging for another. And Pritchard takes the bat from her and was about to hit her with it before she coaxed it back from him. He'd do anything she said."

"Father Silence?"

"Don't get me wrong, he was a piece of work himself, but she was always what made him tick. You see what I'm getting at? All those dead men they found buried?"

"She's the one . . ."

"Who spun the web," Oskar said. "Now you're getting it. Or more precisely, she'd wait on the web like the plump spider she was, and Jeff Pritchard would do her bidding. He'd lure in men for her. Homeless men. Addicted men, vagrants nobody would miss, and she'd get her fill. She'd take out whatever rage would build up over time for whatever the previous men in her life had done to her and . . ." He paused. "One more life gone. Starting with the shooting of that grandfather of hers."

"She told us he shot himself, out by the well."

Oskar shrugged. "She lies a lot. That's how killers don't get caught, Doc. And what she did to her own parents in Russellville. Or *Mother* did, rather. Luring her own father up to the top of that barn and slipping the noose around that neck."

"She said he hung himself."

"More lies."

"After he'd shot his wife."

"After *she* shot her mother," Oskar said, putting a finger to his lips. "But shhhh, don't tell. Don't talk, Jeff Pritchard. Don't you spill the beans on me."

"He refused to talk . . . ," Justin said, thinking aloud. "From day one he refused to talk . . ."

"He became Father Silence."

"To protect her," said Justin.

"Bingo," Oskar said. "Now why do I feel I'm the one giving the therapy here? Maybe I should charge you a fee?" He leaned in and said with sarcasm, "The one that got away . . ."

Justin felt sick. He leaned against the wall.

"You okay, Doc?"

He ignored him. Closed his eyes to fight back nausea.

"He'd call them martyrs," Oskar said. "Can you believe that? Lured in the sick and the homeless, the destitute and deranged, promising salvation, but all he was doing was ridding the world of the unwanted. Bottom line is she liked to watch men die. She liked to watch them suffer."

Oskar lit another cigarette, inhaled, and exhaled a smoke ring, and then another. Watched them float across the room and disperse into the air. "You're not from here, are you?"

"I'm from out west," Justin said, quick to redirect. "When were you born, Oskar?"

He pushed out another smoke ring. "Is that even important, Justin? Can we not focus on the present instead of the past?"

"Where's my daughter?"

"Fine," Oskar said, and Justin perked up, but instead Oskar answered the question he'd asked previously. "I'd say I was born around . . . hell, Noah was probably seven, eight maybe. It was a long time ago." He laughed. "Truthfully, I know the exact moment. Noah's father, a true squash cow of a shithead if there ever was one, Justin, but he was pissed about something." Oskar pointed to the open doorway. "He was on his way up those stairs there with a belt, primed and ready to put some blisters on Noah's back. Noah knew it was coming. Couldn't for the life of him remember what he'd even done. He was playing with these little plastic green army men." He pointed to the center of the bedroom. "Right over there on the floor. He started shaking so badly he could hardly grip them. Starting to drool. It was messy. Embarrassing. He stared so hard into that cluster of army men, those little soldiers, and somehow, hell, I don't know . . ." Oskar snapped with the fingers that weren't holding a Twizzler. "He conjured me up. Just like that. I came to his aid. I took those belt lashes for him. Quite an entrance into his warped little world, but I took them no matter. Like a little army soldier doing his bidding. Sixteen slashes before he got tired of swinging." He finished the Twizzler. "Blood all over my back. On the floor. Damn."

For the first time since he'd let Oskar out, Justin noticed civility and hints of remorse, to the point where he questioned whether another personality had emerged. "Why won't Ruth come out?"

He laughed. "Trust me, you don't want Ruth to come out."

"Why not?"

"Cause she can be a little sultry. And she's a snake when she's hungry."

"Then feed her."

He pulled out another Twizzler. The pack was nearly gone. "What do you think I've been doing, Doc? I prefer the black kind.

No, the stage isn't big enough for Ruth. Kind of a diva. But you know what? That's why . . ."

"You love her. I got that."

He pointed with the Twizzler. "I could cut your balls off with those scissors. Watch your tone." He lit another cigarette.

"What does this cult have planned?"

Oskar shrugged as if bored, and then grinned, pointed at Justin with his cigarette. "You're probably wondering how a young boy like Noah could even conjure someone like Ruth?"

"I don't care."

"I think you do."

"I don't care right now."

"That same day." He paused for an inhale of the cigarette. "Same day I took the belt. Same day he created me from those little green army men, he found something on his daddy's bedside table." He snapped again. "That's it. That's why he was in trouble. The porn mag."

"What are you talking about?"

"Noah, he found his daddy's *Playboy* magazine," he said. "Or maybe it was *Penthouse*. He was flipping through it. Daddy caught him. So to answer your question—"

"I didn't ask."

"Tone, Justin. Watch your tone. But to answer your *curiosity*, because I know you have it, the boy had naked ladies on his mind that day, as well as army men. I brought Ruth right along with me into that bedroom. I took the pain, of course, but she sure did help ease those bloody wounds."

"The cult," Justin shouted. "What do they have planned?"

Oskar pointed to his right temple. "Use your noggin, Doc. They believe he's some kind of messiah. Of course, it was Mother who put that stupid idea in their heads. She's the goddamn Messiah if you want to know the truth." He stood from the floor, cigarette dangling, and lifted the gas can. He sniffed the nozzle. "It's gasoline all right." He started sloshing lines of it all over the floor and walls. He shot a good dose of it inside the ark and backed his way out of the bedroom.

Justin had an idea what Oskar was going to do with the gasoline, but now that he saw the nonchalant way he was going about it, he wished he'd had no part in it.

And he still hadn't helped his cause, other than knowing now exactly who Lisa Buchanon was and wasn't.

Justin bypassed the back-pedaling Oskar and screamed, *"Where is my daughter?"*

Oskar paused at the top of the steps. "Did you just scream at me?"

Softer. "Where is my daughter?"

"You act as if I took her."

"Where is she? Please."

Oskar removed the lit cigarette and dropped it to the landing atop the stairs.

A line of blue-orange fire shot across the floor, back into the bedroom, and then another line followed Oskar as he sloshed gasoline down the steps to the first floor, following the can in his hands as if he were coaxing a pet along.

"Please," Justin pleaded. "You know where she is? Tell me."

Oskar splashed gasoline across the living room floor. It splatted on the hardwood and then soaked into the carpet as he walked backwards across the house.

Something upstairs ignited in a whoosh of light and Justin jumped.

"Please."

Oskar finally turned toward him, paused, and then splashed gasoline in a line across Justin's chest, soaking his shirt.

"You're insane." Justin scrambled to unbutton his shirt, hurrying toward the front door.

Fire literally walked down the stairs and turned toward the carpet below.

Oskar laughed, yelled, "Let it burn. Let it burn. Justin, watch this." He sloshed gasoline toward the ceiling and at the same time— *when did he strike that match?*—tossed a flaming match into the liquid flow and a stream of fire hissed into the ceiling, spreading out and catching every bit of that liquid burst. Oskar whooped and hollered as it ignited. "Watch it burn, Justin. Watch it burn."

But Justin was already outside, shirtless, hands on his knees, panting.

Oskar backed out of the house.

By the sound of it, the gasoline can was finally close to empty. The roof was on fire. Wood snapped, crackled.

Heat enveloped him.

Justin ran away from the house, toward the car, wanted to drive away and never see this lunatic again, but he'd come here for a reason, and it came out as an atavistic roar that gave even Oskar pause.

"Where is my daughter?"

Oskar dropped the gasoline can just as part of the roof popped and shingles flew off like shrapnel. He approached the car, wiping his hands on his trousers. "Damn. I left the last two Twizzlers inside."

Justin backed away from him, tripped over a root, and landed in weeds.

Oskar held out his hand. "Give me the car keys, Justin."

He crab-walked backwards, away from him. "Where is she?"

"Give me the keys, Justin."

"Where is she?"

"Where she is, Justin. She is where she is, now give me those keys before I cut your eyes out. Give me the keys, Justin. Give me the keys." Faster. "Givemethekeys." Sing-song. "Give me the keys, Justin."

Finally, Justin dug into his pocket and hurled them at Oskar's chest.

Oskar caught them, jangled them in his cupped hand, and then patted Justin on the head. "She's at the Harlow Distillery. That old broken-down scab of a place. That's where Benjamin's orphanage is, old boss."

"The Playhouse?"

"The same." Oskar walked toward the car, got in, started it, then coasted right up next to Justin in the weeds.

"Thanks, Doc." He tipped an imaginary hat.

"Why did you need me here?" Justin asked. "You didn't need me to burn this place down. You could've done it all on your own."

"I didn't need *you*, Justin." He patted the outside of the door. "I needed a car."

Justin walked alongside it. "Don't leave me here."

The car rolled.

"Don't tell me where she is and leave me behind." Justin screamed. "You broke my phone."

"When you see your pretty little wife, ask her about the hammer."

"What hammer?"

"One she and Benjamin used on those boys that night. Under the twisted trees?"

"*What* are you talking about?"

Oskar pointed back toward the fire, thumbing it like a hitch-hiker. "I wouldn't leave you high and dry, buddy. The fire will communicate for you. Just like the olden days."

Justin stared, confused, saw a change in Oskar's eyes, and then a new voice emerged, more sultry and definitely female. "Smoke signals, Justin." And then a seductive wiggle-wave of the fingers. "Toodle-oo."

Ruth . . .

The car sped away.

CHAPTER

56

Tᴇꜱꜱ ꜱᴀᴛ ɴᴜᴍʙ in the passenger's seat as Detective Evans sped toward the Twisted Tree cemetery, where the FBI had already sent men in fear of Jeff Pritchard's body being stolen from his grave.

Backup from the FBI had arrived at Benjamin's Barbary Street address. Father Leonard was escorted back home, and the parish was heavily guarded in case Benjamin returned.

Tess stewed as Evans broke speeding laws, siren blaring, lightbar flashing into the encroaching darkness as they zipped past trees and hills and picket fence–enclosed properties toward the cemetery. Tess's mind returned to Danny, shot down south in Bowling Green. They should have heard something by now. And what were those cryptic pictures he'd sent from the orphanage? She'd tried Eliza but got no answer. She tried Justin for the third time since jumping in the car but had no luck there either.

Leads led to more leads, but nothing had gotten them closer to Julia. She needed the pills in her pocket. Deep breaths helped, so she took those for the next few miles, listening with her eyes closed. But the rumbling drone of rubber on blacktop was too hard to bear, so she spoke to override the silence.

"The crime scene at the cabin in Lolo was so different than the others," she said, thinking out loud. "But they seem to be fighting each other."

Evans chewed on it. "Go on."

"The Outcast—who we now know is Benjamin Knowles. We know he took Julie, and we thought he killed my parents. But he didn't commit the crimes here." She turned in the seat to face him. "The crimes here, although driven by revenge, like in Lolo, are dripping with cult. Aside from the upside-down cross on Benjamin's arm, which was burned there as a child, he's shown nothing of the sort. On the phone calls, he's shown remorse. He's mentioned praying for forgiveness. He painted those eyes on the cabin window, pointing toward the closet where Dad kept his briefcase."

"Which you would have found eventually."

"True, but those eyes painted at Burt Lobell's house were directed toward me. Not the medal of honor on the vanity. But my reflection in the mirror. He was warning me."

"Why?"

"Because I was the one who tipped the police off. When I was a girl."

She explained as he drove, and as she revealed what she'd done that day as a thirteen-year-old, he began to drive faster. Evans took a corner too quickly and the wheels skidded, but then he leveled out again on a straight road flanked by woods.

Tess said, "Follow this road for three miles. Cemetery will be on the right."

Evans brought them back to her original point. "And now Benjamin left painted eyes at the church."

"Warning us about the third day," Tess said. "Yes. The cult has something planned for the third day. Possibly the third night." She checked her phone, shot Justin another text: **Where r u?** "But Benjamin seems to be working with them. But also against them. Cryptically."

"They have something on him."

"He doesn't want to do their work, but he has to," she said, willing her phone to ring. "He's leaving little hints."

"In hopes that we'll catch *them* before—"

"Before we catch him."

"Jesus."

Her phone rang. "Justin. Where are you?"

"On a fire truck heading back into town. I'll explain later. Oskar proved useful after all."

"Where is he?"

"I don't know, he burned the house to the ground and took off in the car."

"Burned the house—"

"Tess, listen. It sounds like you're driving. Wherever you are, turn around. Julia is at the old Harlow Distillery."

"Harlow? On the mountain?"

"Yes, that's where the Playhouse is."

She said to Evans, "Turn around. Harlow Distillery."

She braced her hand against the dash as Evans did a move with his car that would have made the Dukes of Hazzard proud.

"He said something about you and a hammer," Justin said over the phone. "When you were a girl? You and Benjamin Knowles under the twisted trees? With those two boys that were killed? Tess?"

". . . I don't know . . ."

But hearing it had triggered her. She closed her eyes and mind to what was threatening to come up, and managed to keep it down. For now.

Justin must have sensed her unease, and told her what she needed most to hear: "We're going to find her, honey."

She nodded, as if he were able to see her.

"You hang in there."

She nodded again, managed to say, "You'll come?"

"I'll meet you there. As soon as I get access to another car," he said. "But Tess . . ."

"Yeah?"

"I know who's in the eighth window."

CHAPTER

57

Across the Ohio River in southern Indiana, Benjamin coasted the painted church van to a stop on the outskirts of Charlestown State Park, where all was silent, and trees swayed under moon glow.

He'd walk the rest of the way, on paths he knew well.

Mother rarely allowed him out of the basement as a child, let alone the house—as far as records go, he didn't officially exist—but on the occasions when they did, they would bring him here, under the security of night and to protect his sensitive eyes. In these woods, across the river from Twisted Tree, they would summon spirits of those long dead, those buried in the flood decades ago, now clinging to the trees and walkways as memories. Nowadays, in daylight, men and women and children walked under the old archways and strolled the sidewalks of the abandoned amusement park—the woods now home to ghosts, according to Mother—every so often stopping to turn the handle on the voice box to learn the tidbits of history that had made this place so popular in the Roaring Twenties, where music played, people danced, and roller-coasters shook under the weight of so much speed on the turns. There'd been a zoo, with a popular black bear named Teddy Roosevelt. A pit with alligators. Men in suits and women in fancy dresses. Tennis courts and summer cottages. Games aplenty. A pool so fine the water seemed majestic.

Benjamin entered the woods.

He imagined it all now as he imagined it as a child, when Mother spoke of ghosts and haunted grounds, of trees that could see and wind that whispered, and Prohibition gangster deals gone bloody. How *she'd* imagined it as a little girl when her grandparents had spoken so nostalgically of Rose Island. Her only good memories of staying with them, she'd often told Benjamin, when she wasn't Mother. Benjamin would have preferred to hear the laughter and the gaiety instead and imagined it now as he walked deeper into the dark. A waterfall poured over rocks nearby, a familiar sound that told him he was heading in the right direction. Otherwise, the woods surrounding the abandoned amusement park and peninsula upon which it once stood were quiet at night, as most normal folk dared not enter. The legends of ghosts, for sure, kept most away, but lately the rumors of Lost Children gatherings and séances held sway.

It made his heart race to think that Mother had brought his children here to witness her evil event. Or even worse, to be part of it. If they were to ever move from animal to human sacrifice, this would be the night. He'd kill them all, every one of the Lost Children, to get *his* children back.

In the distance, through the trees, over the water, and across the bridge he saw firelights on the peninsula. Tiny glowing orbs in the shadows.

Worse, though, were the sounds.

Sounds of the animals, like a kennel of demented beasts.

The Lost Children had begun to gather on the Devil's Backbone.

D ANNY HEARD SIRENS.
That's what woke him first.

Or maybe it was the pressure on his chest, the sense that it was caving in on itself, crushing his lungs and his heart into pulp.

No, that had only been a nightmare.

His eyelids fluttered, stayed open, and through blurred vision he saw orbs of light flashing through the window of the orphanage.

He heard voices outside.

Footsteps approaching in the hallway.

I'm alive.

I'm at the Sisters of Mercy.

He looked at the wall above the bench of creepy dolls.

MOTHER LOVES YOU

SLEEP TIGHT

He grunted, propped himself up to his elbows, thought, *Damn, where's my phone?*

A policeman entered, shined a light in his face. Danny raised an arm to shield his eyes. They announced themselves. He announced himself, "Danny Gomes, Detective . . . Missoula PD."

A medic hurried in to check him over.

Somebody said, "A gunshot was reported. Were you hit?"

He said, "Yeah, in the chest." Breathing heavily, really feeling the pain now from the impact, he unbuttoned part of his shirt, showed them the vest underneath. "Where's my phone?"

The officer looked around with the flashlight, found it a few feet away on the floor. He handed it to Danny.

Danny immediately called Eliza, who picked up on the second ring.

"Danny? Danny? Is that you? Please tell—"

"I had my Kevlar," he said in a pained whisper.

Eliza started sobbing, mumbling, *thank God, thank God*, and then she managed to say back to him, "You had your Kevlar."

CHAPTER

59

J ULIA SHUFFLED IN darkness of her own choosing.

Closing her eyes and moving blindly—roped together with the eleven other children—was better than seeing all those scary people in the woods wearing animal masks. Once they'd crossed the bridge, dozens became what seemed like hundreds, and they all held torches of light that rippled and hissed, casting shadows across so many wicked eyeholes.

She pinched her eyes closed and wished she could use her tied hands to cover her ears, to block out the sounds of the barking and the bleating, the mooing and meowing, the chattering and neighing—sounds once mundane and ordinary had now become horrifying.

As was the lady's voice.

The voice coming from the Wolf Mask, ordering them onward. *Follow the walkway of roses.*

But Julia saw no roses. Maybe they had once been there, but they weren't there now. Only concrete and trees and grass and weeds.

She only allowed herself to look down. She watched the heels of Richard's muddy shoes in front of her, focusing on the sound they made whisking against the concrete. *Move along, Bartholomew,* said the Wolf. The lady had been amused by the pretend names Benjamin had given them when they'd posed for that mural, so she'd kept them.

Perfect, she'd said. *My little apostles all marching toward their last supper.*

Julia heard an animal noise she didn't recognize, and instinctively looked toward the source. A man wearing a camel mask, lumbering along as a camel would, glared at her, so Julia, to keep from screaming, focused on the sidewalk again.

The walkway of roses that had no roses.

She only hoped someone would see what she'd written on the wall inside the Bad Room. Even if it was Benjamin.

She'd give anything now to return to the Playhouse.

CHAPTER

60

BEFORE THE MOVE out west, Tess, unlike the older teens, had never sneaked into the old Harlow Distillery.

She knew enough of the sordid Harlow history to be leery, and sneaking atop that wooded hill was much more dangerous than when she'd accepted the dare to run through the abandoned Crawley Mansion next to the twisted trees. If the twisted trees were where the teens went for their first kiss, they climbed the Harlow hillside with condoms in their pockets, booze in brown bags, and nothing but home runs on their minds.

And so now, after glimpsing the broken moonlit buildings and faded silo, she felt no regret for having never gone, only sadness for the imprint the place had left on the town, and sickness in her gut because, like the Barbary Street house moments ago, this one looked unoccupied too.

Detective Evans pulled to a stop but left the headlights on, highlighting a house so colorful and bizarre it could have been from a Candy Land board game.

No cars. No van.

Another dead end.

On the way up the oddly colored porch steps, Evans, having already reached out to his contact from the FBI, pulled his gun, and then knocked on the door with the butt of it.

Tess pulled her gun with one hand and checked her phone with the other. A text had just come in from Eliza: ***Danny's alive. He's on his way back to Twisted Tree.***

"Thank God," Tess said.

"What?"

"Danny's alive. He's on his way back."

"Good luck always starts somewhere, Tess."

While they waited, and sensing nobody home, she thumb-texted Justin. **Car yet? We're at the house. Creepy as hell.**

It stalled but went through as Evans knocked again, and then motioned for her to walk around the house.

He went the other way and moments later they met up again at the back side of the house, near an old wooden shed with no doors. Along with some gardening tools and a trio of shovels, a lawn mower rested inside the shed, recently used by the smell of clippings. Next to the shed was a seesaw, painted red with sky blue seats. And beside that was a horseshoe pit, cornhole boards, and a bright yellow swing set and sliding board. While seeing playground equipment typically brought about warm feelings of nostalgia, these macabre, colorful pieces so close to such an oddly colored house sent shivers of dread up and down her spine.

Kids live here, she thought, as they walked together back to the front of the house, what Benjamin called the Playhouse. At a side window, Tess tiptoed to spy through the glass, and unlike the Barbary Street house, this one was lived in. Dirty dishes were stacked against the sink and a bowl of soggy cereal rested on a table big enough for an army.

A field of tall grass bordered the side yard, with bumps in the terrain that immediately screamed buried bodies.

Evans must have sensed the same, as he nodded toward the grassy mounds and said, "I don't like the looks of that."

They closed back in on the Playhouse's front door.

Evans knocked hard enough for the door to unlatch and creak inward. Tess took that as an invitation and stepped inside.

Evans followed. "Like Willy Wonka lives here."

Garishly bright colors everywhere, but neatly done, from the yellow baseboards to the red walls and blue crown molding.

With no warning, thunder rumbled outside.

The first one always comes with no warning.

She kept her gun poised should someone suddenly show themselves around a corner as they entered the kitchen, where three hallways angled off like spokes on a wagon wheel. Or a maze, she thought. The closest one opened to an oval-shaped dining area with another large table. Benches instead of chairs. The walls had been put together with precision. Curved in places, angled in others, sturdy and strong.

The work of an architect. A woodworker. An artist.

"The original Harlow house couldn't have looked like this," she said, eyes roaming. "He gutted it to build his own funhouse."

"Quite the handyman."

She thought of the artwork on the church's ceiling and walls. The artwork inside that room in Pritchard's basement.

A second burst of thunder shook the windows. She closed her eyes, took a heavy breath, and moved on toward the nameplates on the dining room table—twelve folded pieces of cardboard with twelve names. *Thomas. Bartholomew. Simon the Zealot. Matthew. Andrew. James and John. Judas Iscariot.* She looked away—could too easily guess the rest of them—and left the room.

She flipped on every light she saw.

"Tess?" Evans said from another room.

This hallway led to what had been named *The Leonardo Room.* She entered with Evans on her heels. She flipped on the light. "Good God." Every wall was dominated by paintings and sketches and drawings, all replicas of works by Leonardo da Vinci. The work of an expert, just as she'd seen earlier inside St. Michael's Church. One entire wall was a perfect replica mural of *The Last Supper,* and it was nearly complete except for a few of the faces. On the wall opposite was a giant drawing of the *Vitruvian Man,* perfectly detailed and symmetrical. Beside it, the eyes and nose of the *Mona Lisa.* Mary's left hand hovering protectively over her son, from *Virgin of the Rocks.* More sketches, partial paintings, Christ on the cross. Sketches of wings, some flying devices.

A genius. A monster. He has my daughter.

On another wall—his practice wall—were sketches of the same disciples later drawn and painted on the final mural, but chunks of this wall were missing, recently damaged.

She backed out of the room into the hallway. More rooms, and every room had a name. *The Clown Room. The Play Room. The Music Room. The Art Room.*

Jesus.

Thunder again, and now rain tapped lazily on the roof. Another hallway. *The Study Room. The Exercise Room. The Sick Room.*

Claustrophobia closed in.

She screamed. "Julia!" Nothing. She was gone.

Always one step behind.

Her phone pinged. A text from Danny: **Lisa Buchanon is behind it all. Call me and I'll explain. Stay away from her.**

Thunder boomed, followed by lightning this time.

She closed her eyes to it all. She already knew. Justin had just told her on the phone.

I know who's in the eighth window . . .

The FBI was already heading toward her place.

"Tess!" Evans called from the other room. "You've got to see this."

Mother Loves You

Her vision blurred.

Her knees buckled.

She braced herself against the hallway wall, slid to the floor, closed her eyes . . . *the tall blades of wet grass clipped her bare legs. She squinted through the downpour. The boy stopped before the tree line. Thunder sounded as if it had ripped the land apart. She wobbled, steadied. Looked back toward the house, where her father was inside. A hero. She took off sprinting, toward the boy in the dog mask, toward the woods he'd just entered. Her rain-soaked ponytail clung to the nape of her neck.*

Lightning illuminated the sky, visible even through the broad boughs and leaves and gnarled limbs. He followed a dirt path, forty yards ahead. Veiny roots crossed the path, glistening slick with rainfall. The river was close, then far away. Where was he going? Running aimlessly or toward something? Who are you? Stop running. That came out as words, but the boy didn't listen. He kept running, turning, jumping over brambles and deadfall. The tree trunks were more widespread. A road overgrown with weeds meandered in a path in and out of the trees. After another thirty seconds of running, she saw the old Crawley Mansion.

And thirty yards over, the twisted trees, coiled together and soaring upward to a canopy of limbs large and full enough to block out the rain. The boy had stopped beside them, panting, shirtless and rain-slick. She approached slowly. He turned. She jumped back when she saw his eyes through the mask's holes.

"I'm sorry," he said, shielding them. "Don't look."

She stepped closer. "Who are you?"

Without looking at her, he said, "I'm no one."

She stepped closer. "Why did you run? My father is here to save you."

"Not me. No one knows about me. I'm the outcast." He made as if to look at her, but then turned away, shielding his eyes again as thunder boomed and lightning lit the sky above the twisted trees. "She's evil."

"Who?"

"Mother," he said. "She's the one who keeps me in the dark room." He shielded his eyes, but rain found ways through the canopy. "She calls me a monster. But she's the monster."

Laughter sounded from behind them, and then three teenagers emerged from the Crawley Mansion . . .

. . . Tess's eyes flashed open, and she screamed.

Detective Evans hovered directly over her; he jumped back. She made it to her elbows, trying to process. "Lisa Buchanon had a child no one knew about." She stood, weak-kneed, gathered herself with a flat palm against the hallway wall. *"Benjamin is her son.* I saw him. Something happened. It's not finished."

"What's not finished?"

"My memory," she said. "It's not done."

Evans's phone sounded with an incoming call. He answered it, turned away from her as he listened, and a minute later hung up.

"What?" Tess asked. "Who was that?"

Rain pelted the roof. Thunder rumbled.

"They took Pritchard's corpse," Evans said. "A dozen of them came riding into the cemetery with shovels and animal masks. Killed the guards. Four dead from the feds."

For the first time since she'd met him, he looked lost.

The front door burst open.

If not for the heavy rain they would have both heard the approaching tires on gravel outside. But the car had coasted in with the headlights off and its occupants had been silent up the porch steps. Bull Mask entered the living room, followed by Sheep Mask, both with twitchy LSD eyes and shotguns leveled.

They fired simultaneously and blew Detective Evans back against the wall.

Tess fired, clipped Bull Mask in the right shoulder, but he kept coming. She slipped on blood splatter, went down to the floor as Sheep Mask stepped into the kitchen, hunkered down and started bleating. She grabbed her gun, scrambled into the hallway, bouncing from one wall to the next, turning, turning again through the maze as their animal noises followed, bleating and calling her name.

She ran into a dead end. But she couldn't turn back. Their sounds grew louder.

At the end of the hallway was another room.

The Bad Room.

The only room with a door.

She headed for it, closed it behind her, but the damn door didn't close. The lock was busted.

"Tess." Jeter Janks turned the corner, now on all fours, bleating. *Freak.*

She kicked the door open, raised her gun, and fired twice, hitting dead center on both.

Jeter Janks lay writhing on the floor, blood pumping from the two holes she'd put in him. She screamed when a shotgun blast tore a chunk from the wall at the far end of the hallway, knocking the gun from her hand, and out stepped Bull Mask, bleeding from the shoulder but otherwise unfazed.

Afraid to put herself back into the range of the shotgun, she left her gun where it lay across the hallway and backed herself into the room behind her. It was futile, but she closed the door anyway, held it there by the hole where the knob had been before it was knocked off. The light switch didn't work, so she sat in near darkness, until lightning flashed and showed a glimpse of the side wall and the writing and pictures on it.

She let go of the door to allow a tunnel of light through the knob hole.

Julia had been here.

She'd left a message, knowing they would come. It was one of the games they'd play at home during storms, drawing pictures to form words. She could have easily written the words on the wall, but this message was for her and Justin personally. To let them know she was alive.

A rose. An eye. And a straight line she always used for the word "land."

"Rose. Eye. Land. Rose Island. The old amusement park," Tess whispered. "At the Devil's Backbone."

She turned on the flash on her phone and snapped a quick picture. She tried to send it to Justin but it stalled, and Bull Mask's shoes were on the other side of the door.

He won't kill me. He needs me alive. He'll take me to her.

"Come on out, Tess." He bent down and looked through the door hole. "Or I'll huff, and I'll puff, and I'll blow this door in."

If she had something to shove through the opening and pop his eye out, she would have. Instead, she nudged the door open and came out on her own. He backed away, watched her, and then removed his mask to reveal a satisfied smile.

She recognized him from pictures, and after a beat she recalled who he was, from the newspapers and newscasts, standing there gaunt-faced and drug-crazed, with a careful part down the center of his hard-combed hair, his sheep buddy dead in the background.

Jeff Pritchard's lawyer.

"Barrett Stevens," she said. "We've been trying to find you."

"I know. I've been following." He pushed her along with the barrel of his shotgun, back through the kitchen and out of the Playhouse.

Once outside, he popped the trunk of his car and told her to climb in.

She did.

Relieved that the fool had neglected to take her phone.

CHAPTER

61

INSIDE THE DARK trunk, as the car moved, Tess sent a series of texts
to Danny—Justin hadn't yet responded—afraid if she tried to get
it all into one that Stevens would stop and confiscate her cell phone
and nothing would get sent. Or they'd hit another patch of Twisted
Tree where the phone service was sketchy.

On her side in the pitch black, stomach clenched to help keep her
from rolling all over the trunk, she thumb-tapped the keys:

> *Bull Mask is Barrett Stevens, Jeff's lawyer.*
> Send.
> *I'm trapped in the trunk of his car.*
> Send.
> *Go to Rose Island, the peninsula known as the Devil's
> Backbone.*
> Send.
> *Julia left us a message.*
> Send.
> *She's alive.*
> Send.
> *Evans was shot at the Playhouse.*
> Send.
> *I killed Jeter Janks, Sheep Mask.*
> Send.

They're doing a ritual at Rose Island. That's where they're taking his exhumed body.
Send.
And me.
Send.
Next, she attached the photo of what Julia had drawn on the wall of that room.
From Julia.
Send.

For a long moment she thought the last text wasn't going to go through, but then it did. She breathed rapidly. The air in the trunk seemed to be getting thin. The car turned. Turned again. The road became bumpier. She assumed they were approaching the woods surrounding Rose Island, which had been a popular amusement park during the Roaring Twenties, surviving even through much of the Depression until the Great Flood of 1937 completely buried it, sweeping away all the buildings and structures, the zoo cages and rollercoasters. She'd heard stories of the haunted grounds. She could only guess what was about to happen—the cult, these Lost Children of Silence, probably begun by Benjamin's mother, was going to try and resurrect Father Silence. Or at least summon his spirit through some kind of séance, of which she would soon be a part.

Otherwise, they would have shot her back at the Playhouse.

They would have crossed her off the list days ago.

She'd assumed there would be an animal sacrifice tonight. But something this big could require more. That was why they needed her. *She* was the sacrifice.

The trade.

They'd used Julia to get her back home.

For what? For stealing Jeff Pritchard's fingerprints so many years ago?

You're getting too big for your britches, Tess.

Her mother's words upon learning what she'd done. And then how she'd yelled at her father, *And you do nothing but encourage it, Leland!*

One day it was going to come back to bite her.

It already had.

She just couldn't remember it all.

Not yet.

For the first time since being thrown into the trunk, she fought to get out. Searched for a safety latch but found none. It was an old car, or else the latch had been removed.

She kicked and pounded her fists against the trunk's ceiling. Futile moves, panicked moves, but she felt claustrophobic, just as she had inside the Playhouse before her episode. Part of her wanted another one, another vision. Wanted to see how things ended that night. Anything to take her away from the increasingly tight confines of the trunk.

The pain pills.

They were still in her pocket.

Six remained.

She needed something to calm her hands, her racing heart. She felt shame at the truth of it, and knew she'd be more clear-headed with them in her bloodstream, because over the past few days she'd taken enough of them to *need* them all over again. She'd understood it as a cop back then, what the pain pills did to the system. But that was with druggies, she'd thought, *not me*, unaware the drug had already gotten its claws into her. It had already begun to rewire her brain and mess with her pain receptors and settle in for the long haul, becoming almost human in its defiance, as if folding its arms and laughing—you *need* me now, Tess. Just to exist every day, you *need* me. And boy, had she ever, until Justin had taken her to task, until Justin had refused to lose this battle.

And here she was, locked in a trunk, two days in and *needing* all over again.

She pulled out two and crunched them, winced, and swallowed. She willed them to work. *Faster. Faster.* Just enough to take off the edge, but still be able to function.

It was how she'd moved through life for more than a year after the gunshot.

Getting to Julia was her only goal.

But then what?

The car stopped.

She checked her phone. Nothing from Justin or Danny.

The driver's side door closed.

Footsteps.

The trunk popped, raised slightly. As soon as she saw moonlight, she kicked. But Barrett Stevens caught her ankle, twisted it, and then, quick as a snake bite, snatched the phone from her hand.

"Bad girl."

He gripped her throat, squeezed until she choked, and then let go to pull her from the car. He kicked behind her knees and sent her to the ground, on concrete, a sidewalk leading into the woods. He pulled her arms back and tied her wrists behind her with rope.

She sat on her heels, pushed through shallow breaths, defeated. "When did he turn you?"

"Get up." Roughly, Barrett helped her stand.

"Was it during the trial?"

His eyes were crazed. "Stop talking."

"Or did it happen slowly over his seventeen years on death row?" He kicked her into a walk along the concrete path, into the woods where the dark night grew darker. "When did he put all of this into motion, counselor? Was she his first follower, or you?"

He'd put his bull mask back on, and the mouth of it brushed her ear. Rubber mixed with stale breath as he whispered. "Who said *he* put any of this into motion, Tess?"

Torchlight glowed in the distance and animal noises carried with the wind.

Bull Mask howled as he tugged her along, his sound mixing with the cacophony of others down below, across the bridge, and onto the Devil's Backbone.

Tess's eyelids grew heavy. For the first time she realized he was wearing Sheriff Kingsley's badge on his shirt, and it was stained with blood. She said, "Bulls don't howl, you stupid son of a bitch."

"Tonight they do. Mother is Great Wolf. And it's mating season."

62

BENJAMIN WATCHED FROM the shadows as they gathered atop what was once the Rose Island swimming pool—now filled with concrete and acting as the perfect stage for the night's event.

Lost Children had come by the dozens, over a hundred at least, all in animal masks and holding torches. Flames rippled and hissed as raindrops found ways through the thick canopy above. Masks of sheep and goats, horses and cows, dogs and lions, tigers and donkeys, giraffes and camels and zebras. Drugged eyes shone like beads through mask holes. Needles entered veins. Pills were passed.

Benjamin hated them all. Wished them gone.

Where are the children? Where is the Wolf?

The only animal not duplicated in the crowd.

There was a figure in the middle of the pool, a mound covered by a white sheet. He didn't believe Mother would do it, but Father Silence had been exhumed, and there he was as the Lost Children gathered around the circumference of the rectangular pool. None of them stepped atop the concrete, the arena, as if they'd been warned not to; but they tested the boundaries like jackals, hovering, all clearly tempted.

And then the Bull emerged from the shadows.

He dragged a woman along. She had a wool sack over her head.

Tess.

Just as Mother had promised, they were fixing to sacrifice her atop that concrete pool. Her blood would be consumed by the Lost Children.

He watched Tess.

There was movement in the shadows on the south side of the pool.

A line of children emerged, not Lost Children but *his* children, all in a line and connected by a rope. Benjamin's heart raced. He no longer held thoughts of saving Tess. The children now were his only concern. Mother expected him to be a part of the event—she'd warned him not to stray from the plan—and so a part he would be.

But not the part she expected. He would not do her bidding. Not one more day.

He felt his belt line.

They were there, one on each hip.

One hammer for each hand.

He approached the arena, felt anger coursing through his veins, faster with every step.

Mother must have heard him coming because she turned his way, the whites of her eyes gleaming through the holes of the wolf mask.

"There you are," she said.

"Here I am, Mother."

He gripped one hammer, and then the other.

63

B ULL MASK SLUNG Tess to the ground.
　　She'd expected dirt and grass but landed on concrete, and it felt like her bones had shattered. He pulled the hood from her head and the wool scratched her face. Above her were dozens and dozens of men and women dressed in black and wearing masks. Human-made animal sounds echoed through the trees, a cacophony of lost, haunted souls. She turned her head, saw the children, including her daughter, marching in a line, shuffling, as Wolf Mask escorted them to their spots on the hard surface of the concreted pool. The woman placed them in two rows of six, facing each other as if placed around an imaginary table.

"Julia." It first came out as a whisper, a pushed breath of desperation, and then the next one was louder. "Julia."

Julia looked up, red-eyed. "Mommy!"

Tess made it to her feet and started toward the children, but Bull grabbed her arms before she could get away. She flailed in Bull's grip, screaming her daughter's name while Julia shouted hers. And then Giraffe Mask stepped forward with a baseball bat and landed it across her back.

Lightning struck down her spine. She dropped to her knees, seeing stars, whispering, "Julia."

Giraffe hit her again with the bat, this time on the shoulder, and she toppled to her side. His weight fell on her. His knee forced her chest to the concrete floor.

Thunder boomed above the treetops.

Lightning illuminated the sky, flashed through leafy boughs.

Rain filtered in as mist.

Animal masks laughed, closed in, bleating and howling and barking as more rain entered the arena. Her eyes flicked from one to the next, and then she saw Benjamin Knowles, next to Wolf Mask, with a hammer in each hand.

He made eye contact with Tess, and nodded.

She didn't know what he meant by the gesture, until he raised both arms, both hammers, and, as Tess faded into dizziness, she saw him powerfully swing a hammer toward Wolf, his mother, connecting with the side of her head . . .

. . . and she was a teenager again, shivering as rain found ways through the canopy above the twisted trees. Benjamin stood shirtless, shielding his eyes, not from the rain but from her. So she wouldn't judge him like the sources of laughter echoing from the old Crawley Mansion, where two teenage boys and a girl had just emerged from the missing front door.

Seniors from Tess's high school, both boys wearing Twisted Tree Varsity Football shirts; and the girl, athletic in her own right, short blue shorts and a blouse that hugged curves. But she wasn't laughing like they were. Tears mixed with rainfall, and she made as if to run from the porch, but the dark-haired boy easily stopped her with an outstretched arm. This triggered more laughter but got Benjamin's attention.

The other boy was taller, more athletic looking, with light brown hair and icy blue eyes. He approached Tess and Benjamin as the other boy clutched the squirming girl's arm. "Well, well, what do we have here? Two young doves out for their first kiss. Dude's already got his shirt off. But what's with the mask?"

Dark Hair laughed, then puckered his lips and made kissing sounds. "Make sure you give her the tongue, dude."

Benjamin said, "Go away."

Brown Hair stopped. "Did he just give us an order?"

"Sounded like it," said Dark Hair.

The girl in his arms wrestled and punched his chest. "Let go of me, Grisham. Take me home. This isn't fun anymore."

He mocked her. "This isn't fun anymore."

"You're an asshole," she hissed.

Benjamin, still shielding his eyes with his hands, said, "Leave her alone."

"Another order," said Brown Hair. *"You hear that, Grisham?"*

"I heard it, Shakes."

Tess shivered violently. Every instinct told her to run, but she didn't.

The one called Shakes approached her. "You kiss him yet? You give him what he came for?" He grabbed her arm, forced her two steps toward Benjamin, who backed away, hiding his eyes beyond the dog mask. Shakes let go of her to imitate Benjamin, shielding his eyes just like he was. "What are you doing under there, pal? Huh? You hiding? You kiss her yet? Let me show you how it's done, bro." He turned toward the girl in Grisham's arms. Grisham held her tight while Shakes kissed the girl and then grabbed at one of her breasts. She tried to kick him, but he stepped away and both boys laughed again.

Thunder shook the ground and neither boy flinched.

Grisham nodded toward Tess and said, "Little young, Shakes, but we could have one for each of us."

"Always were good at math, Grisham." Shakes stepped toward Tess but pointed at Benjamin. "This douche doesn't know what he's doing anyway."

"Don't touch her," said Benjamin, voice muffled by the rainfall.

Shakes reached out and touched Tess's shoulder. "How's that? Huh?" He pulled Tess close and grabbed her rear end.

Grisham laughed. "Get rid of him, Shakes. She's all yours."

Benjamin stepped out of the shadows and moved his hands away from his face, revealing his eyes.

Shakes jumped back. "Jesus. Wow. Dude."

Grisham said, "What the fuck? Like some monster. I'd wear a mask too with eyes like that."

Tess looked away, but made herself look back. Her voice cracked. "He's not a monster."

"She speaks!" Shakes leaned in toward Benjamin. "You wearing contacts or something, bro? Huh? You freak." Before Benjamin could stop him, Shakes pulled the dog mask from his head and shook the flimsy rubber in his hand. "Get out of here. Go." He looked at Tess, smirked. "I've got a lesson to give." He ran a hand over her soaked hair, and she stayed frozen to the ground. His touch felt like ten kinds of disease. Then he shoved the rubber dog mask over Tess's head and held it down, laughing. "Bark for me, girl."

The girl in Grisham's arms vomited without warning and Grisham let go of her, stumbled away. "Son of a bitch. Oh my God. Bitch just puked on me."

Shakes laughed, released his hand from the mask, long enough for Tess to pull it off.

Grisham didn't think it was funny. He wiped his shirt off as if he'd just been sprayed with toxin. "You gave her too much bourbon."

"Gave her more than that, Grish."

Grisham grinned. "You put the dust in there already?"

The girl on the ground was slow to get up. She'd been drugged.

Benjamin took another step. "Don't call her that."

Shakes turned. "Call her what, freak?"

"Bitch. Don't c-c-call her that."

"Freak Show s-s-stutters too," said Grisham, standing over the girl. He nudged her onto her stomach and unbuckled his belt. "You watching this, Freak Show?"

Slowly, Tess lifted her foot. She willed herself forward.

Benjamin trembled, and then it happened. He held a hammer. The handle of it must have been hidden in the well of his jeans pocket. She hadn't noticed the head protruding under his hip line. Without sound, and in seconds, the claw on the other side of the hammer was deep in the left side of Shakes' skull, just above the ear, and the whites of his eyes showed as he dropped to the ground, first on his knees, and then his face and chest landed in the grass twenty paces from the twisted trees.

Grisham, stunned, backpedaled to get away, but tripped, his eyes on the blood leaking from his friend's head.

Benjamin mumbled. "I'm s-s-sorry."

They're the monsters, Benjamin. Not you. Tess thought of Shakes's hands on her, the smell of that rubber mask over her face, and snapped just as he had. She put her foot on Shakes's shoulder and yanked the hammer free. She brought it down hard on his back, his shoulder, then two shots to the back of his head. Benjamin wrestled the hammer from her. She backed away, realizing now what she'd just done. Out of body. Out of mind.

He was dead already. Already dead. You didn't kill him, Tess.

Benjamin was on Grisham fast, like a lion pouncing on fresh kill, striking a death blow to the forehead. Rain came down in sheets, mixing with the thunder and lighting. He pulled the hammer free, mumbling, "I'm sorry, I'm sorry."

Tess put a hand on his shoulder.

He stood, stepped away. "I d-did the bad thing."

The other girl had made it to her feet, wobbling, crying, eyes so distant she didn't even flinch when lightning hit a tree fifty yards away. She took the hammer from Benjamin's hand and swung it *repeatedly down on Grisham's chest, and then his groin. Benjamin wrestled the hammer from her, and she fell again.*

What had they done? Tess locked eyes with the girl. "Don't tell anyone."

The girl nodded, stood, unsteady, and then ran off into the trees, in the opposite direction from which they'd come, in the direction of the Old Sam Distillery.

Hammer in hand, Benjamin backed away toward the abandoned Crawley Mansion.

Lightning again lit the sky.

Current hummed across the grass. Her hair stood on end as rain pelted and slashed, wind-blown, a great gust swooping down under the canopy. Benjamin held the hammer in the air. Something sizzled and cracked. The sky opened, bright, hot, and crackling, as a bolt of lightning hit beside the Crawley Mansion. Right beside Benjamin and briefly blinding her.

The current found her—like she was burning but she wasn't. Smoke and rain and sizzle and light. Benjamin was on the ground. It was dark again. He moved, crawled, hammer still in hand. He faced her. "Go."

She stepped toward him. Could hardly feel her legs, they were so wobbly and numbed from the electricity and static in the air.

"Go."

She ran.

Away from Benjamin and that lightning strike—what the brilliant flash of light had been—away from the bodies of those two dead boys. She ran uphill, under the boughs, but rain still found her, clipping her face like shards of glass, and in the distance, toward where her father's car was parked, gunshots sounded. Still, she ran toward them, toward the bullets, toward the echoes, knowing that every step away from that nightmare under the twisted trees was another step buried in her mind.

Lightning flashed.

She ran.

. . . Tess opened her eyes. Her right cheek lay against the cold concrete floor of the old Rose Island swimming pool, and inches away was the Bull, the lawyer's dark eyes unblinking from the mask holes, dead, with blood pooled around his head. She scrambled to a sitting position, pushed away from Bull Mask's body, and bumped into the Wolf—Lisa Buchanon—who lay unmoving on the concrete pool with her legs twisted and the left side of her head caved in. Blood pooling around her mask, which rested cockeyed on her head. Feet away stood Benjamin, the Outcast, clutching two bloody hammers like a modern version of Thor, as thunder boomed, and lightning flashed, and now gunshots pierced the woods' leafy boughs.

The Louisville police had arrived with the FBI and local authorities from the sheriff's department. Justin was out there somewhere, amid all the panic. She could hear his voice, calling her name. The Lost Children scrambled and screamed. Some fought back. Some ran. As if testing an electric fence, some braved the boundaries of the concrete pool, eyeing the Great Mother, the Wolf, now dead, and beside her, Father Silence's corpse, covered by a white sheet, but fear ultimately kept them outside the arena. A giraffe stepped in, then right back out. A goat bleated, turned in a tight circle right outside the pool, panicked and drugged to the moon.

Julia and the other eleven children had gathered in a cluster through the panic, all of them distraught, no doubt having witnessed the brutal attacks from Benjamin's hammer. The man who had been their protector, was still trying to protect them.

Tess had missed it all.

One nightmare traded for another.

"Julia," she screamed, slowly making it to her feet. Disorientation sent her back to the ground. She felt sure she had a concussion, at the very least. The children swam in and out of focus.

She crawled toward them. "Julia."

"Mommy."

Benjamin was coaxing the children off the concrete floor into the woods, as masked Lost Children fled the authorities. Many of them had dropped their torches, but the ground and air were so saturated with rain that the flames, when they hit the ground, hissed instead of spread. One after another, authorities ordered Lost Children to the ground, on their knees, hands behind their heads. Most did, while others had to be wrestled to the ground. A few of the more drug-addled pulled guns of their own and were swiftly shot down.

Justin emerged from the shadows. He and Tess briefly locked eyes, and then he ran toward the cluster of walking children, stopping ten paces away, his gun leveled at Benjamin.

"Down on your knees," Justin said. Tess knew her husband had never fired a shot outside of a shooting range. But he looked unafraid.

Benjamin moved deeper into the cluster of children, no longer roped together, until they surrounded him, serving as human shields.

Justin would not, could not fire. Benjamin ushered them along. "Come along, children. I'll keep you safe."

Tess slowly gained her equilibrium. She made it to her feet and approached the children from an angle that mirrored Justin's.

But she was unarmed, exposed, and hobbling badly from her wounds.

An FBI agent shouted for Benjamin to halt, but he instead moved deeper into the woods.

"Daddy," Julia yelled.

Justin, reacting like a father now, ran toward the children and reached to grab Julia's outstretched hand. Benjamin, on what looked like instinct, lowered the hammer on Justin's shoulder, catching his ear. Blood flew and Justin staggered but didn't let go of Julia, and just as Benjamin appeared ready to strike another hammer blow, Tess saw realization dawn on his face—Benjamin had seen Justin's desperation to stay connected to his daughter and her desperation to stay with him—and he let her go. *She was the one who had someone who loved her, a family that loved her.*

Justin pulled Julia free from the group and she clung to him. Tess, struggling to get to her feet, cried out in relief.

A bullet whistled through the air, hitting Benjamin in the right shoulder, spinning him like a top. He squatted low, bleeding from the arm, urging the children onward. They parted, made way for his escape. He ran for the woods.

Orders of "Freeze" shouted from every direction.

Tess reached Justin, his right ear bleeding freely, kneeling on the ground, hugging their daughter, both of them crying. She joined them in an embrace, kissed Julia's head and squeezed her tight, and when she looked up at the sound of sudden commotion, she saw Benjamin Knowles disappearing into the trees toward the bridge connecting the mainland to the Devil's Backbone, where Fourteen Mile Creek emptied into the Ohio River right along the devil's curled spine.

And the rest of the children were following him.

He was, after all, she thought, the one who had saved them, first from their former lives and from whatever had awaited them here.

Tess spotted Justin's gun on the ground and grabbed it. She kissed Julia again and promised she'd be right back.

This nightmare had started for Tess forty-eight hours ago with that phone call from Benjamin Knowles. Her daughter was safe now. But she needed to see this out, needed to be there, whatever would happen to the boy who had saved her and that other girl so many years ago. Tess sprinted deeper into the woods alongside the sheriff's deputies and FBI agents, but with the angle she'd taken into the trees, she quickly passed them all. Eerie pangs of déjà vu fueled her as she tore down the dark narrow path that funneled toward the Devil's Backbone.

Benjamin was long-legged and fast, and desperate, but slowed once he'd noticed the children following and now had stopped in the middle of the path, forty yards ahead, to give them time to gather.

Authorities trailed behind Tess, radioing for help on the other side of the footbridge crossing Fourteen Mile Creek.

Wet branches from dripping ferns clipped her at every turn. She followed, contemplated whether or not to shoot every time a clearing opened up, but then another outcropping of trees would swallow the path.

Knowing what she now knew of Benjamin Knowles, she knew the children weren't in danger from him. They followed him because they trusted him. He'd kidnapped Julia because they'd made him, but he'd let her go at the end.

Lightning lit the woods.

Darkness swallowed it.

Her head grew dizzy, likely concussed from the injuries she'd sustained atop that concreted pool, but she also knew there were still crumbs left, memories, and she felt them coming on.

Grisham Graham and Jeremiah Shaker.

The two stars of the Twisted Tree football team for whom the town mourned for months. They were cowards, sexual predators. Four weeks after they were killed their bodies were found buried under the twisted trees, and that's when the speculation had begun, theories that their deaths had somehow been connected to the capture of Father Silence. Tess's parents had moved her out west, days after the bodies were found. The realization hit her as she burrowed down the muddy path.

He knew.

Her father hadn't moved because of the attention from Jeff Pritchard's arrest, but because he'd suspected her involvement in the disappearance of those two boys. After their bodies were found, the newspapers speculated that they could have been heroes rather than the predators they were, and theories came about that they'd stumbled upon the truth inside Pritchard's house and were killed trying to save the children.

Bullshit.

The river and creek, both swollen from the rains, were close; the sheer power of the water gushed like distant thunder. Ahead of her, Benjamin's pace slowed near the clearing at the Fourteen Mile Creek bridge. Officers awaited on the other side, guns poised.

He was blocked, unless he ran toward the river with all those children now circled, almost protectively, around him.

Tess slowed on the grassy slope, side-stepped down so she didn't fall.

The girl from that night flashed through her mind.

Amy Dupree.

She'd discovered her name in the days after. A senior soccer star at Twisted Tree High School, who'd suddenly stopped playing despite a handful of college scholarship offers. She and Amy spoke once after that night, meeting behind the bleachers of the football field, both already beginning to turn inward, losing bits and pieces of that night, but agreeing to never tell the truth.

They'd gone their separate ways.

Amy Dupree killed herself six weeks later, overdosing on anxiety pills her parents had insisted she begin taking. Tess remembered seeing the article on her suicide on her father's desk, an article he'd thrown away instead of keeping.

Focus, Tess.

Benjamin was trapped in the clearing, appearing increasingly panicked as he noticed not only the authorities surrounding him on all sides, but also a half dozen Lost Children in animal masks now emerging from the shadows.

64

BENJAMIN KNELT AMONG the frightened children who'd gathered around him, who'd come with him, and now felt the urgent need more than ever to protect them.

Aside from a stray bullet, he'd feared no harm coming to the children from the authorities now surrounding him, but now some of Mother's cult had shown themselves, approaching now from the woods in their masks, their crazed eyes visible, like part of their interrupted night, their evil ritual, was not yet complete; he had to protect them, whether they were coming for the children—perhaps to sacrifice—or for him, the one who killed Mother and Bull Mask.

He told the kids to get low, and his words came out without a stutter.

He eyed Tess on the periphery of the tree line, and then looked at the Lost Children slowly approaching, seemingly unaware or not caring that they too were surrounded, that guns were sighted on them from every direction.

Ssshhhh, he calmed the hunkering children. "Close your eyes. Hold your ears. Think of happy thoughts."

And then he began to reach to his belt for his hammer.

CHAPTER

65

TESS STOOD IN a shooting stance as rain poured down from the
sky, a tumult into the grassy opening between the trees and the
creek and river bend.

Her finger twitched on the trigger. She had him in her sights, but
the emergence of the masked cult members complicated things, and
now, she feared, removed all hope of them talking Benjamin Knowles
into peacefully surrendering.

FBI agents pinched closer, surrounding them.

But while Benjamin remained in place—and the kids around
him were all hunkering down now—the masked cult members continued their approach.

Authorities on the far side of the bridge, crossing Fourteen Mile
Creek, stood with handguns leveled.

Benjamin shouted to Tess. "I don't do the bad thing. The bad
thing does me."

Tess said calmly, "I know. Move away from the children, Benjamin." She eyed the authorities all around her, and too many of them
seemed overly eager now to shoot, to do something as the masked
Lost Children closed in on the kids around Benjamin Knowles.
"Don't shoot," she called out to them. "He won't harm them."

But you stood by while my parents were murdered.

You stole my daughter.

But he cared for these children, these abused and neglected children he had wanted to save.

In this situation, one bullet fired could turn into a bloodbath, and as Benjamin moved a hand, she sensed it coming.

"Freeze," an FBI agent shouted.

But Benjamin continuing reaching toward his belt, for his hammer, Tess knew, to protect the children from the approaching masked figures.

"It's not a gun," she shouted through the rain.

But too late.

Someone fired, and then an array of bullets pierced the night.

Benjamin's body, highlighted by another lightning flash, jerked and spasmed like a marionette supported by unseen strings, as bullets struck him from multiple directions.

He dropped to the wet grass, unmoving, the hammer still in his right hand.

CHAPTER

66

T ESS SCREAMED, "NO," as she saw Benjamin's body unmoving on the ground, and all around him the children were crying, panicked, and farther away, the masked members of the cult had been shot too, and were also lying on the ground, except for one, a man in a pig mask, who knelt with his hands up in surrender. "Keep your eyes closed!" she shouted to the children, eleven of them now that they had Julia.

Now that the chaos had died down, Tess heard Justin calling out to her.

And Julia: "Mommy!"

But Tess couldn't stay focused enough to find them. She felt the blackout coming, but stayed on the verge of lucidity, and recalled, as clear memory, the end of that night.

. . . *she sprinted through the woods, following the path that had taken her down toward the fleeing boy and the Crawley Mansion, like it had never happened . . . like that hammer was never in her hand. She exited the woods in the same place she'd entered what seemed like hours ago. Her father and Burt Lobell were still in that house. She was soaked to the bone and shivering, still tingling from the close lightning strike. She ran to the car and slipped into the back seat, just as she had hours ago, and closed the door. Her breath fogged the glass.*

The side door of the house opened. Out rushed her father's partner, Burt Lobell, carrying a sandy-haired boy to safety.

Her father emerged next, escorting a handcuffed Jeff Pritchard toward the car, toward her. The man had a mustache and short hair, trimmed and graying around the ears. Black pants and shirt and white clerical collar.

"Bless me, Father, for I have sinned," Tess whispered to herself, before ducking under the blanket that had helped conceal her on the way.

But then she made the mistake of peeking, and saw Jeff Pritchard staring at her, grinning, and then mouthing the words, *clever girl.* And then what could have been *Beware the one that got away . . .*

Two days later Tess remembered none of it.

Two weeks later the newspapers had given Jeff Pritchard the moniker of Father Silence.

CHAPTER

67

Rain fell, but it was cleansing now.

Julia hovered above where Tess lay in the wet grass. Her daughter smiled, physically unharmed. The rest, they'd have to wait and see.

Tess sat up, opened her arms, and Julia jumped into them.

They cried.

Twenty feet away, the officers surrounded where Benjamin lay dead in the grass. Tess shielded Julia's vision from it. FBI agents and local officials had gathered the other children into a group and were trying to protect them from seeing the carnage around them. Several members of the Lost Children lay dead in the grass, and those who still moved were being handcuffed or attended to by medical personnel now arriving at the clearing.

"Mind if I join you?"

Tess and Julia both looked up, saw Justin, his head wrapped in gauze and tape, approaching through the rain.

"Daddy!" Julia ran toward her father and jumped.

He caught her, held her tight, just like he would every day in the doorway.

The Panda Tree . . .

Tess smiled.

No, I don't mind at all.

After

F OUR WEEKS AFTER returning from Twisted Tree, their lives had settled down.

The new normal, as Tess had called it, after Justin's moving back into the home, back into their daily life. During the day, Julia showed no negative effects from her abduction by Benjamin Knowles and her time at the Playhouse, although at night she was sometimes stricken by nightmares of men in animal masks and would end up in Tess and Justin's bed.

Justin didn't fight it and neither did Tess, who in the days follow-ing the real-life nightmare in Twisted Tree, rarely let her daughter out of her sight. Over time, and at the insistence of Julia, she'd allowed her more space. More freedom. But as she'd already told three parents in the past week who'd called for play dates, she wasn't ready to let her go.

Maybe next time.

They'd begun to have family bike rides, usually in the mornings, and even then, they'd box her in between them. Whenever Julia steamed ahead, one of them, usually Justin, would speed right past to take the lead again. If Julia had caught on to their paranoia, she didn't show it. One day they'd loosen that leash, but Justin knew it would be later rather than sooner.

Even though Tess told him she'd stay away from it, he knew she was following the goings-on back in Twisted Tree.

Daily.

But that was okay. It was part of her own therapy he felt she needed for closure.

They all needed it, and Danny was the first one to seek it out upon his return from the nightmare, especially after being shot in Bowling Green, and then later that night, when everything was going down at Rose Island, him driving to Pritchard's old house to find it surrounded by cop cars and FBI. Finding Sheriff Kingsley being loaded into a body bag, finding what he had in the basement of that house. Maybe Lisa Buchanon, or Diane Buckner or Cherry, or whatever her name was, had renovated the basement from when Pritchard had lived there, but it was clear that what they'd found down in her basement had been just as horrifying, if not more so, than what Leland Patterson and Burt Lobell had found seventeen years prior. The murders had never stopped after Pritchard's arrest—of course they hadn't.

And it was also clear, if not for the five children they'd abducted back then—Noah, Tom, Stephen, Dean, and Amelia—that perhaps they never would have been caught in the first place . . . *And those dolls down there*, Danny had said, shaking his head, unable to conjure the words.

As for Benjamin Knowles, none of the children he'd abducted had been physically harmed. Aside from Julia, the other children—six girls and five boys—had been sent to foster homes, in small groups so none of them were alone, until more permanent homes could be found or suitable relatives who wanted them could be located. Beginning the day after Benjamin Knowles was gunned down on Rose Island, back at the Playhouse, the FBI had unearthed the remains of what they believed to be twenty-seven adult bodies, both male and female, in the clearing on the north side of the house, what was once the main house of the Harlow Distillery back in the 1950s—apparently the adults who had abused and neglected the children in their care.

Still sweating from the bike ride, Tess sat at the kitchen table, drinking cold tap water, and even now Justin could tell she was searching for more stories on her phone.

They'd yet to learn what had happened with Noah Nichols. The last anyone had seen him was Justin, seeing Noah/Ruth speeding away as Noah's childhood house burned, with Ruth then in control. They'd never found Justin's rental car.

"Anything new?" Justin asked once Julia had left and was out of earshot.

"Twenty-one of the twenty-seven victims of Benjamin Knowles have been identified," Tess said, reading from her phone. "Tests ongoing for the other six. The one common thread, Justin, was of that of those identified, all had done time for or had at one time been accused of abuse against children."

Justin walked up behind her and kissed the top of her head. "What time are Danny and Eliza coming over?"

She placed her phone face down—since reuniting they'd both gotten better at reading cues, of paying more attention to what the other might want or need or was thinking. "Seven o'clock," she said, leaning back to kiss him. "But they'll be on Gomes time, so probably seven thirty. Burgers and brats okay?"

"Divine."

"You stink," she said. "Is a shower in your future?"

He sniffed at the pits of his sweat-soaked T-shirt. "That an invitation?"

"Maybe later."

He watched her walk down the hallway toward their bedroom, and started leafing through the stack of mail he'd brought in earlier and dropped on the island. After opening a few bills and tossing some advertisements, he noticed a postcard with the Golden Gate Bridge on it and pulled it from the pile. He glanced at the postmark, from San Francisco, and then the message.

He felt his blood pressure spike immediately.

On the back, in sloppy handwriting was:

Just wanted to check in and let you know we've been thinking of you, and that Noah says hello. He's in good hands now. My mind sometimes fails me, but I don't think I ever thanked you for those Twizzlers, but even more, for letting us out. I've never seen Ruth so eager for life. Someone once called us a regular Bonnie and Clyde, but I don't think that's accurate. Bonnie and Clyde were eventually caught, and I'm afraid that's just not in our plans. Until next time, old boss.
Oskar

ACKNOWLEDGMENTS

HERE WE ARE at the end of another novel, and I'm still pinching myself to check if it's all real. Dreams come true and all that. Slowly but surely, I'm forging a career by making things up, but I learned long ago that I am nothing without those I lean on daily for balance. I usually save my wife Tracy for last—as goes the saying we all know so well—but now I feel I should thank her first. By the time this book is published we will have been married for twenty-five years, and I've cherished every one of them. Thank you. To my children, Ryan and Molly, keep making me proud. To my parents and siblings, you are my foundation. To my friends, you are my rock. Thank you to my cousin John for always reading my stuff; this one may seem familiar to you, it's only been on my mind for a few years. It's funny how books come to be, and just when you think you have a plan on which book will come out next, a curveball is thrown. *Sleep Tight* is a story that has been on my mind for a long time—being kidnapped was a real childhood fear of mine, and I've always wanted to portray this fear in fictional form—and I've been working on this story for years. I'd like to thank my wonderful agent, Alice Speilburg, for reading a draft of this, helping me finally bring it to fruition, and then selling it in world record time. Thank you, Sara J. Henry, my amazing editor at Crooked Lane, for really pushing me on this one for more; I believe I went down deep and found what I was looking for. Thank you to everyone at Crooked Lane: Matt Martz, Rebecca Nelson, Dulce Botello (possibly the coolest name ever), Madeline Rathle, Thai Fantauzzi Perez, Mikaela Bender, Melissa Rechter, Heather VenHuizen, and everyone who had a hand in the entire publication process—sorry if I haven't met you all! Thank you to all those loyal readers of much earlier versions of this story—it definitely takes a village, and in some cases a little more time. Thank you to Gill Holland for reading the screenplay I'd written for this book years ago, and to Jamie Buckner for your advice in the building of it. And finally, thank you, loyal readers. I'm humbled by the number of you who reach out with kind words and encouragement. I'm currently working on another stand-alone horror novel I'm calling *Dig*. I promise, for those who are asking, that I WILL return to continuations of both *The Nightmare Man* and *Mister Lullaby*, with the strong possibility of intermingling both storylines, combining both worlds, but until then, please, sleep tight.

Continuously onward and upward . . .

—James